"I second that."

Emmory shot Zin a look. "I trust you, Highness. Don't shoot anyone who's not trying to kill you, and for gods' sake, just kill them. Don't shoot pieces off them."

"Zheng Quen was fibbing, Emmy. I didn't shoot his toes off one at a time because he insulted me."

"True. I believe the reason for it was because he tried to kill you, ma'am."

I tucked my tongue into my cheek and dipped my head in acknowledgment. That actually wasn't the whole truth either. Quen had tried to kill Portis because I'd snaked a deal out from under him. We'd just left Po-Sin's employ, and I knew that without a reputation for violence, we'd be space junk before the year was out.

When I'd found out about the hit on Portis, I'd visited the man Quen had paid to kill him first, and then I paid Quen a visit.

Civilized people gasp and shake their heads at the story, but I don't regret it one bit. Gunrunning is as far from civilized as you can get—short of maybe the SpaceBoxing League. I could have killed Quen for what he'd tried to do, but live people spread your reputation around a hell of a lot faster. It bought us the space we needed to build our own business up without looking over our shoulders all the time.

After that incident, only the truly idiotic tried to cross us.

BEHIND THE THRONE

THE INDRANAN WAR: BOOK 1

K. B. WAGERS

www.orbitbooks.net

Copyright © 2016 by Katy B. Wagers
Excerpt from *After the Crown* copyright © 2016 by Katy B. Wagers

Cover design by Lauren Panepinto
Cover images © Arcangel and Shutterstock
Cover copyright © 2016 by Hachette Book Group, Inc.

Orbit
Hachette Book Group
1290 Avenue of the Americas
New York, NY 10104
orbitbooks.net

First Edition: August 2016

Orbit is an imprint of Hachette Book Group.
The Orbit name and logo are trademarks of Little, Brown Book Group Limited.

The publisher is not responsible for websites (or their content) that are not owned by the publisher.

The Hachette Speakers Bureau provides a wide range of authors for speaking events. To find out more, go to www.hachettespeakersbureau.com or call (866) 376-6591.

Library of Congress Cataloging-in-Publication Data

Names: Wagers, K. B. author.
Title: Behind the throne / K. B. Wagers.
Description: New York : Orbit, 2016.
Identifiers: LCCN 2016006484| ISBN 9780316308601 (paperback) | ISBN 9781478938477 (audio book downloadable) | ISBN 9780316308595 (ebook)
Subjects: LCSH: Space colonies—Fiction. | BISAC: FICTION / Science Fiction / Adventure. | FICTION / Action & Adventure. | FICTION / Science Fiction / Space Opera. | FICTION / Science Fiction / General. | GSAFD: Space operas | Adventure fiction
Classification: LCC PS3623.A35245 B44 2016 | DDC 813/.6—dc23 LC record available at https://lccn.loc.gov/2016006484

ISBNs: 978-0-316-30860-1 (trade paperback), 978-0-316-30859-5 (ebook)

Printed in the United States of America

RRD-C

10 9 8 7 6 5 4 3 2 1

To all the women who inspire me on the daily.
Past, present, and future generations.
I am here because I stood on the shoulders of Amazons.

1

Hail. Get up.

The voice cut through the nausea, sounding too much like my father. I suppose it made sense in some twisted way. If I were dead, it wasn't completely illogical to be hearing the voice of a man who'd been shot in front of me twenty-one years ago.

The bitter tang of blood filled my mouth and nose when I inhaled, rusted iron and the awful smell of death. The stale air of a carrion house screamed of the violence that had taken place in my cargo bay, violence I couldn't remember through the pounding of my head.

Hail, get up now.

Whoever's voice was in my head, it was enough to make me move, or at least try to. I scrambled to my feet, pain stealing what grace the gods had gifted me. My boots—gorgeous red-black Holycon IVs I'd borrowed from a dead raider six months prior—slipped on the blood-slick metal. I went down hard, cracking my already abused face on the deck, and the world grayed out for a moment.

More pain flared when I tried to flop over onto my back and failed. All right. So—not dead. Because even now at my most cynical, I didn't believe for an instant the gods let you still feel pain after you died. It just didn't seem proper.

"Look at this mess."

This voice was outside my head, which made it infinitely more dangerous. I froze facedown in what smelled like someone else's guts.

Judging by the events filtering back into my brain, I suspected the guts belonged to my navigator. A vague memory of trying to strangle her with her own intestines flashed before my eyes. Memz had been a tough bitch. She'd landed a few good punches before I'd given up and broken her neck.

"Weekly saints preserve us."

I heard several other curses from behind me, but the high, lilting call for the saints to my left was what caught my attention. It was edged with a Farian accent, and that was enough to keep me from moving.

Farians. An alien race who could kill or heal with a touch. The only thing that kept them from ruling the universe was some strange religious code enforced with a fanaticism privately envied by most governments. They had seven saints, one for each day of the week. It was the Thursday one, I think, who abhorred violence.

According to Farian scripture, he'd set an edict on their power. It was to be used for healing, not death. Killing people with their power drove Farians crazy. I'd never seen it firsthand, but the vids I'd seen had given me nightmares: grief-stricken, screaming Farians held down by their own comrades as an executioner put them out of their misery.

Not moving was a good idea. Anathema or not, there was always a chance this Farian was ghost-shit insane, and I didn't have a gun.

"You claimed to sense a life sign, Sergeant." A female voice several octaves lower than the Farian's didn't so much ask the question as pick up a previous conversation.

"Did, Cap. In this room. Only one," the lilting voice replied. "That's as close as I can pinpoint it."

"Fine. Fan out and check through this"—the owner of the voice paused, but I resisted the urge to lift my head and see if she was looking around the cargo hold—"rubble," she finished finally. "Sergeant Terass says one of these poor sods is alive. Figure out which one."

I kept my eyes closed, counting the footsteps as my unwelcome guests fanned out around me. There were five people total, all moving with military precision. They were probably fucking mercs come to claim my ship. I hadn't been able to figure out whom Portis—my bastard of a first officer—thought he was going to sell *Sophie* to when he started his little mutiny.

You mean when you killed him.

Grief dug razor claws into my throat, and I choked back a sob. *Gods damn you, Portis. Why did you betray me?*

Except I wasn't entirely sure he'd been trying to kill me, or that I'd been the one to kill him in the end. My memory of the fight was as fuzzy as a Pasicol sheep and had teeth just as sharp. Trying to dredge up anything resembling coherency made the pain in my head turn on me with snarling fury.

I snarled back at it and it dove away, whimpering, into the recesses of my brain. There were more important matters at hand—like getting these bastards off my ship and getting the hell out of here.

Sliding my hand through the gelling blood on the floor, I wiggled my fingers deep into the thick, squishy mess. A spark of triumph flared to life when I closed my hand around the hilt of my combat knife. I knew it was mine because I felt the nick in the handle even through all the gore.

The day was a fucking waste, but at least I was armed.

The intruders moved past me. By some grace I'd ended up partially beneath the stairs and out of sight. I eased myself sideways, rolling over Portis's torso and away from the abstract blood painting on the floor. I saw his profile, and all at once I wanted to kick him, curse his name, and drop to my knees and beg him not to leave.

There's no time for this, Hail. You have to move. The voice I now recognized as my own damn survival instinct shouted at me with the crisp precision of an Imperial Drill Sergeant. I got my feet under me and rose into a crouch. My left leg protested the movement, but held my weight.

The strangers had their backs to me. I almost thanked the gods for it and then reminded myself there was nothing the gods of my home world had done for me lately. Portis had been the believer, not me. The dim emergency lighting might be just enough for me to slide into the shadows and make it to the door.

The ship's AI wasn't responding to my *smati*'s requests for information. At this point I couldn't tell if I'd been hit by a disrupter that had shorted the hardware wired into my brain or if the problem was with *Sophie*. Either way it didn't matter. I had to get to the bridge and access the computer manually. If I could space these jokers, I would be long gone before they finished imploding.

If.

I backed straight into the sixth intruder before I had time to remind myself what *If* stood for.

He was hidden by the shadows I was trying to blend into, as still and silent as a ghost. He didn't make a sound when I spun and drove my right hand into his ribs. The blue shimmer of his personal shield flared and I swore under my breath. It would smother any strike I threw at him, making the damage laughable. But the kinetic technology didn't extend to his unprotected head, so I swung my left up toward his throat, blade first. He caught my wrist, twisting it back and away from his head.

I matched him in height, and judging by the surprised flaring of his dark eyes, we were nearly equal in strength. We stood locked for a stuttering heartbeat until he drove me back a step. *Sophie*'s emergency lighting made the silver tattoo on his left cheekbone glow red.

My heart stopped. The Imperial Star—an award of great prestige—was an intricate diamond pattern, the four spikes turned slightly widdershins. But what had my heart starting again and speeding up in panic was the twisted black emblem on his collar. He was an Imperial Tracker.

"Bugger me."

The curse slipped out before I could stop it—slipped out in the Old Tongue as my shock got the better of me. There was only one reason for a Tracker team to be here. The reason I'd spent the best part of twenty years avoiding anything to do with the Indranan Empire.

Oh, bugger me.

Trackers always worked in pairs, but I couldn't break eye contact with this one to check for his partner. Instead I eased back a step, my mind racing for a way out of this horrible nightmare.

My captor smiled—a white flash of teeth against his dark skin, just enough to bring a dimple in his right cheek fluttering to life. The fingers around my wrist tightened, stopping my movement and adding a high note of pain to the symphony already in progress.

"Your Imperial Highness, I have no wish to hurt you. Please let go of the knife."

Oh, bugger *me.*

"I don't know what you're talking about," I lied easily. "I'm just a gunrunner."

He tapped a finger next to his eye, just missing the tattoo, and now I could see the silver shadow of augmentation in their dark depths. "I see who you really are. Don't try to fool me."

A stream of filth that rivaled any space pirate poured out of my mouth and blistered the air. The modifications I'd paid a fortune for after leaving home had stood up to every scanner in known space for the last twenty Indranan years, but of course they wouldn't stand up to this one.

Trackers were fully augmented. Their *smatis* were top-of-the-line. The DNA scanner had probably activated the moment he grabbed my wrist, and that, coupled with the devices in his eyes, had sealed my fate.

Bluffing wasn't going to get me out of this. Which meant violence was my only option.

"Highness, please," he repeated, his voice a curl of smoke wafting through the air. "Your empress-mother requests your presence."

"Requests!" My voice cracked before I composed myself. "Are you kidding me? She fucking requests my presence?" I wrenched myself from his grasp and kicked him in the chest.

It was like kicking the dash when *Sophie's* engines wouldn't power up—painful and unproductive. Fucking shields. The Guard stepped back, his suit absorbing my blow with a faint blue shimmer as the field around him reacted to the impact.

Hard hands grabbed my upper arms.

There was the other Tracker.

I snapped my head back, hoping this one was as helmetless as his partner. The satisfying crunch of a broken nose mixed with startled cursing and told me I'd guessed correctly.

I spun and grabbed the man by the throat with one arm as I flipped the knife over in my hand and smiled a vicious smile at Tracker No. 1. "You come any closer and I'll cut his throat from ear to ear."

It was a good bluff as they went. I knew the Tracker wouldn't risk his partner—couldn't risk him. One of them died and it was likely the other would follow them into the Dark Mother's embrace. It was the price of the connection, the bond that had been set when they were just children.

"I don't know who you are or what you promised Memz to try and take my head, but it's not going to happen today."

"Highness, we weren't responsible for this." The Tracker took a step toward me.

"Back yourself off me and get the hell—"

The sound of phase rifles powering up cut off my snarl. Shit. I'd forgotten about the others.

"Hold." The Tracker held up a hand. I dared a glance to my left and wasn't surprised to see the others arrayed around us with their guns at the ready.

"Highness, your sisters are gone to temple," he said formally. The words drove into my gut like a hot knife, and my grip on the semiconscious Tracker loosened.

Cire. Pace. Oh gods, no.

An image flashed in my mind—Cire, two years my senior, her raven-black curls flying behind her as she sprinted over the hand-painted tiles of our quarters. Cire chasing a tiny blond Pace, whose laugh was like the bronzed waterfalls in the palace square.

"Princess Hailimi Mercedes Jaya Bristol, your empress-mother, and the whole of the empire need you to return home."

"No." I breathed the word, unsure if it was a denial of the formal command or of my sisters' deaths.

I thought I saw some sympathy in the Tracker's expression. He extended a hand toward me, unfurling his fingers in an impossibly graceful movement. Pale lavender smoke drifted across the space between us, slithering into my mouth and nose before I could jerk away.

"You fucking rat bast—"

I passed out before I could finish the curse, falling on top of the Tracker whose nose I'd just broken.

I awoke in the dark, my head still pounding, and muttered a vicious curse when I remembered the events that had put me here in the first place.

"Be at ease, Your Highness."

The voice and the sudden light sent me rolling from the bed. I landed on my bare feet, settling immediately into a fighting stance as I swept the room with a quick glance. Two men watched me carefully—the one by the door was the Tracker I'd faced off with, and I could only assume the one on the opposite side of the bed was his partner.

There was no evidence of my head strike, which meant the Farian had healed him. This Tracker was a little shorter than me with bronze skin and eyes like the sand on Granzier. The gray-green color even shifted like those sparkling sands.

"Your Highness, we mean you no harm." Tracker No. 2 had his hands up in a useless placating gesture; his polite tone and downcast head made my stomach turn.

Here you go, Hail, back to the pit. I answered his platitude with a snort and a cold glare at the Tracker by the door.

"I want my clothes, my boots, and my ship," I replied with a wave of my hand at the drab gray tank and pants someone had dressed me in while I was unconscious. "My name is Cressen Stone. I don't know who you think I am, but—"

"Liar." Tracker No. 1's voice was all smoke and heat, like the smoldering coals of a fire about to burst back into flame. It drifted lazily through the air, the taunt burning as it slammed into me.

I'd been away from home a long time, and I was well used to the way the rest of the universe operated—preferred it even—but to hear an insult delivered with such casualness from a man of the empire stunned me a little.

"Emmory." Tracker No. 2 had raised his head, but didn't look away from me as he issued the rebuke.

Not that it had much of an effect on his partner. Emmory kept his arms crossed over his chest, his eyes boring into mine. Finally, he gave me a small nod. The barest of required acknowledgments. "My apologies. You are a liar, *Highness*."

"*Dhatt*," Tracker No. 2 sighed at the ceiling, running his tongue over his teeth. Then he looked back at me with a surprisingly earnest smile. "Please forgive my partner, Your Highness. He's not a people person."

"Fine," I said, only because I knew we wouldn't get anywhere if I didn't forgive the man. Inappropriate behavior or not, he'd been right. I was a liar, and we all knew it.

As Trackers, they'd have a file of my whole life. They would have studied me, gotten as deep into my head as humanly possible—all for the express purpose of hunting me down. I wondered briefly if they really knew why I left home, or if they had the sanitized version about me running away. Judging by the attitude, I guessed it was the latter.

"Let's start at the beginning, shall we? We are here on a mission from your empress-mother. Do you promise to foreswear violence against me and my partner?"

I considered it, then shrugged. "I promise—for the moment," I added, careful to keep from swearing an open-ended vow.

"Who are you? You can't keep me here." I kept my voice as even and cool as I could, given the circumstances. "Bugger you, you bastards. My head hurts." I pressed a hand to my temple as the pounding increased.

"Tell me about it," Tracker No. 2 replied automatically. Then he winced. Apparently out of the two of them, he had some sense of propriety. "Sorry, Highness. The *sapne* was for your own safety."

"Foul lavender smoke," I muttered. I realized as he was apologizing that my head was the only thing that hurt. All my other aches and pains were gone and my mouth dropped open in shock. "You let that Farian touch me."

"Sergeant Terass is fully vetted, Highness," Emmory said. "There was no question of your safety in her care. Given the circumstances, we felt it was better to return you home in full health."

I glared at him a moment, then transferred my gaze to the other man. "Who are you?"

"Apologies for my rudeness. I am Starzin Hafin, Your Highness, Level Five Tracker. This is my partner, Emmorlien Tresk. We've been sent to retrieve you and bring you home. You are needed." Starzin was all palace formalities and proper folding of the hands. It was amazing how that immediately put my teeth on edge. I preferred Emmory's hostility to the obeisance.

"Fine." The chance of lying my way out of this had been nonexistent from the moment Emmory had touched me and gotten a verified reading. "What does Mother want with me? I'm having a hard time believing she just wants me back to have a chat about my sisters' deaths. We didn't exactly part on the best of terms."

That was a bit of an understatement. Officially, I'd run away from home to avoid an arranged marriage just after my eighteenth birthday. Less officially, but still not approved by my mother, I'd left home to hunt the mysterious third man responsible for my father's death.

My mystery man had vanished like coven smoke in a stiff breeze shortly after the first year away from home. And no matter how many feelers I'd put out over the years, I never got a good lead. I'd expected General Saito or Director Britlen to send Trackers after me when I told them I wasn't coming home. I'd seen how the rest of the universe lived. It was far from perfect, but I'd sworn to myself I'd never go back to Indrana and her antiquated ways. I wasn't willing to give up on my search for my father's killer and had kept hunting him long after the trail had gone cold.

Both Trackers winced at my sharp words. I was trampling over every social convention possible—asking questions, being callous about my sisters' deaths when all I really wanted was to scream out my agonized grief to the stars. I buried that desire as deep as it could go. Better that they thought I was a cold, heartless bitch rather than a grieving sister. Better for my chances of getting out of this mess with at least some of myself intact.

"Highness, your sisters have gone to temple." Starzin's voice was low and filled with pain. "You are the heir. It is vital you return home."

His words slammed into me, burning like the ten thousand volts of a Solarian Conglomerate police Taser.

"What?" I gasped for breath. "No. Cire had a daughter, I saw her on the news. Atmikha is heir, not me." My older sister's only daughter should inherit the throne.

"Princess Atmikha was killed in the same explosion as her mother."

The air rushed out of my lungs. Added grief for a niece I'd never known. One more log on the pyre set to burn my freedom to ashes. The hope I'd had of getting out of this mess was lost in that instant, and I couldn't do anything but stare at Emmory in abject shock.

"Damn it, Emmory!"

At his partner's sharp curse, Emmory looked away from me. I shoved my grief down with the rest of it and took the opportunity to glance around quickly for a weapon. There was a heavy metal bottle—probably water—on the bedside table. I inched toward it.

"She deserves to know, Zin," he replied.

Zin shook his head, his eyes a little wild. It was too blunt a discussion about the dead. Talking about them could drag their souls back to their bodies, trap them here. Only a priest was supposed to speak of how they died and their names shouldn't have been mentioned at all.

But Emmory had already started it, and I was twenty years absent from our social conventions and not in the mood to play the games required. I didn't believe saying their names would do anything to my sisters. They were dead and gone.

Just like Portis.

I swallowed back the tears and fixed my eyes on Emmory. My niece and both my sisters dead added up to something ugly going on at home. Whatever my feelings for my mother and homeland were, my sisters had meant the world to me. It had killed me to leave them. Killed me even more to cut off all contact when I'd decided to disappear. I'd known the minute I chose to go with Hao that if anyone had heard me talking to my sisters and discovered who I was, they'd have killed me, or worse, tried to ransom me back to my mother. "How did Pace die?" My question hung, ragged, on the recycled air.

"Highness, it's not for us to speak of how your sisters went to temple. You will need to speak with the priest." Zin tried again to gain some control over the situation.

I wasn't about to let it go so I ignored him and pinned Emmory with a fierce glare.

Portis had always told me I could kill a man with one look from my hazel eyes. According to him, they flared with green when I was angry, brighter than a dying star. He'd always had an overdramatic bent.

Emmory was as cool and calm as could be in the face of my determination, his face an expressionless mask.

"How did Pace die?" I repeated.

"Ebolenza, Highness."

This time it was as if someone had sucked all the air out of the room. I stumbled back against the wall, sliding down to the floor when my knees gave out and refused to support my weight. Images of my sweet little sister dying the kind of vicious, blood-soaked death ebolenza caused made bile burn my throat. At least Cire and Ami had gone quick, but Pace...

There were only three people in the whole universe I'd wish that kind of death on—and not even my mother was on the list.

Certainly not Pace.

Ebolenza wasn't a naturally occurring disease. It was biowarfare at its worst, and that my sister had died of it meant only one thing. Someone had killed her, too.

I snapped my eyes open just before Zin touched me and slapped his hand away. It felt even more stupid and petty when I spotted the confused hurt flickering in his eyes, but I stomped on those emotions as hard as I could. I couldn't afford to let these people see any weakness. As Po-Sin had always said: *Show no fear. Not to friends, nor enemies, and certainly not to strangers.*

The thought of my old gunrunner boss was enough to push me upright. I'd run guns for the most feared Cheng Gang Lord in the universe. I'd earned my keep, earned my own ship, and earned my reputation. All on my own. I wasn't going to be welcomed home with open arms, and that worked fine for me. I could think of a thousand places I'd rather go than back into that gilded cage.

Scrambling to my feet, I spread my hands wide and gave the Trackers my best gunrunner smile. "So someone murdered my sisters and my niece. Tried to kill me, too, from the looks of it, unless I'm to believe this little mutiny was coincidental. Now Mother wants me to come home like a dutiful daughter. For what? So they can get a second crack at me? I'm not sure I want to go home and put my life on the line. What has the empire ever done for me?"

My diatribe shocked both men into silence—at least on the surface. I was willing to lay ten credits down they were having a heated conversation over the communication lines provided by their *smati.*

I moved casually to the bedside table and grabbed the bottle. Emmory stiffened, so I shot him a grin over my shoulder.

"Easy, Tracker, just thirsty." Ignoring the cup, I drank straight from the bottle. Cool water, tinny with the familiar taste of onboard recycling, flowed over my tongue, erasing the lingering bitterness of the sleeping drug. I dropped my arm to my side, two fingers looped loosely around the neck of the bottle.

I didn't know how I was going to get out of here. As the Trackers talked, I spun several scenarios and dismissed them all. At this point I didn't particularly want to kill either of them, whatever I'd threatened back on *Sophie.* They were just doing their job.

I could go home, find out who killed my sisters. That thought appealed to the anger in my gut. Revenge would be exacted for this—one way or another. However, I didn't have to go to the palace for that. In fact, it would be easier if I weren't trapped by protocol and the endless cowshit of royal requirements. I didn't want to see my mother, and I really didn't want to be the heir to the gods-damned throne of the Indranan Empire.

Discarding the idea of a frontal attack, I took another drink from the bottle and set it back down on the table. Crossing my arms over my chest, I leaned back against the wall and favored Emmory with a smile I hoped hid my frantic indecision.

"Look, Emmy—" His mouth tightened fractionally at the nickname and I was glad to see I could do something to needle that stone exterior. "I'll give you my word. I'll go see Mother, have a little talk with her. But I need clothes, and I'd much rather travel on my own ship."

"We have clothes for you, Highness," he replied, and an uncomfortable look scuttled across his sharply planed face.

"I want *my* clothes, Tracker, and my ship."

"There are clothes in the wardrobe for you." He gestured behind me. "I'm afraid your ship has been removed from the equation."

"What?" An icy fist drove into my chest. "What did you do to *Sophie*?"

Emmory shot Zin a sidelong glance before looking at the ceiling. "Several charges on the reactor. I saw to it myself. Your ship is space dust."

"You blew up my ship?" Somehow I kept my voice even. I fisted my hands, blunt nails cutting into the skin. "The moment's over, Tracker."

The warning surprised me. I should have just taken my much-needed advantage and struck, damn my oath to blazes. Gods, how easily I slid back into the social bindings of the empire. My hatred of them couldn't overcome the conditioning. If we'd been anywhere else, I would have struck without warning.

Both men put their hands on their guns, nasty-looking Hessian 45s with a stun function worse than the SC models. For my part, I wished I hadn't put down my only weapon.

"Highness, it was necessary to remove proof of your crime," Zin explained.

Necessary. Not even back on planet locked in the confines of the palace yet and I was already sick to death of hearing that word. My things all gone. My *Sophie* gone. My—

"Wait, what? What crime? My gods-damned crew tried to kill me. I defended myself. What do you care if I killed a bunch of gunrunners?"

An inscrutable look I almost thought was pain flashed over Emmory's face. "Portis was ITS, Highness. He was there to protect you—sworn to do so with his life. He wouldn't have tried to kill you. He was trying to bring you home, nothing more."

My laughter shocked them. "Portis was ITS. Emphasis on the *was.* They kicked him out."

"Lies are easier to believe when they're based on truth," Zin replied softly. "Portis's records reflected a banishment from service, Highness, but it was all for show. He was undercover, recruited by your BodyGuards and Director Britlen. It was necessary. The easiest way to keep you safe."

For the third fucking time all the oxygen fled my lungs, faster than an open airlock in a vacuum. That's why General Saito hadn't argued with me, hadn't sent Trackers after me. They'd had someone watching me all along. My Primary BodyGuard had sent Portis after me?

My brain pulled up the introductions I'd let slide by earlier. "Tresk. You said Emmory *Tresk.*"

I whipped my gaze from Zin to Emmory and back again, my mouth hanging open. They were lying to me; they had to be. Otherwise—

Oh, bugger me. *My whole life had been a lie.*

"Portis was my brother, Your Highness. He accepted a request for assistance from your *Ekam* and sacrificed a promising career to babysit you. He died so a spoiled princess could run away from her duty." The derision and fury in Emmory's reply were improper, but I couldn't get past my whole foundation sliding out from underneath me like quicksand.

"Holy cowshit." I spat the curse at them, grasping at my anger for protection from the grief. "Whatever Portis was doing there, he certainly wasn't protecting me. Of course, we can't prove any of it, can we? I can't remember what happened and your Farian conveniently erased the evidence!"

There'd been a furrow cut into my hip from poorly aimed laser fire, and I was pretty sure Portis had broken a rib or two when he'd tackled me.

"If I didn't know better, I'd even say he was trying to kill me." Emmory crossed the room so swiftly, I didn't have time to react. He grabbed me by the throat and slammed me into the wall. I was so stunned by the assault that I didn't retaliate.

I could almost see the reflection of my own hazel eyes in the glossy darkness of his.

"You will not speak a word of it, Highness. I won't allow you to dishonor Portis's memory with lies." He was deadly serious, and full of fury, but his voice was as calm as if we were discussing the weather.

"Emmory!" Zin grabbed Emmory from behind, breaking his hold on me and spinning him around before I could come up with a reply. He pressed his forehead to Emmory's, speaking to him in a low voice. Emmory replied back, his voice a growl, but he didn't resist his partner's restraint.

As I got my breath back, I tilted my head to the side and watched them curiously. I couldn't quite tell if they were sleeping together or not, but it was fairly common practice among Trackers who weren't related. It was obvious these two had been together for a long time. They'd know each other's movements, each other's thoughts, and could anticipate their reactions. It was the kind of relationship Portis and I had—or close to it anyway.

Zin finished with whatever he'd had to say and turned on me. "Your Highness, please forgive Emmory."

I could only gape in shock at Zin when he folded his hands together and bowed low. His anxious, almost desperate apology tumbled into the air as if I were the Mother Destroyer Herself.

"Emmory's family has endured years of believing Portis a traitor. Now they have the chance to know he was a hero. If you claim Portis tried to kill you, it will ruin everything he worked for, desecrate everything he gave up." Zin dropped to a knee in front of me and held out his hands palms up. "Please do not take offense at his behavior."

When he moved, I caught sight of Emmory staring at me. The look on his face was a decent mix of fear and anger. The fear wasn't even for himself, though I could have him flayed alive for assaulting me, it was the fear that Portis's name would be stained and forever reviled.

A sick stab of pain speared me in the gut as I realized just what was going on. Zin meant every word and was terrified that Emmory had crossed the line with me.

He had crossed the line, but I wasn't some prissy noblewoman who saw a man punished for stepping out of line. The fact that he'd struck me, not once but several times, wasn't even an issue as far as I was concerned. Someone else could make an issue of it if they chose.

What intrigued me was Emmory's temper and his loyalty to his family. It was a failing I could possibly use later. Right now, I had to address Zin's concerns.

I had my pride, but it wasn't worth a man's life.

Walking around Zin, I stopped toe to toe with Emmory and studied him for a moment.

"The next time you grab me," I said, "be prepared. Because I will make you pay for it."

"Highness." There might have been a flicker of respect in his eyes, or I might have been deluding myself.

"Get out of here," I snarled. "Both of you get out of here before—" I chopped off the threat. If I gave voice to my fury, I'd have to follow through, and though I was angry, I didn't like my odds in a fight against these men. At least not right now.

Zin looked like he wanted to say something, but he dipped his head and turned for the door. Emmory gave a little half bow, never taking his eyes off me as he backed toward the door.

"We'll be floating into warp soon. It will take us about a day to return home, Highness," he said and the door slid shut behind him.

2

I dropped, shaking, onto the bed and stared at my hands as I fought to contain my grief and anger. The ship probably had surveillance and I didn't doubt my hosts were going to keep a close eye on me. *Don't show them anything, Hail. Don't give them anything to use against you.*

Portis—dead. Cire—dead. Pace—dead.

I couldn't stop the pain from running rampant through me. Or the gleeful little voice in the back of my head reminding me the worst thing of all.

You have to go home.

The mere thought of it made my throat close up. I'd stood up to pirate ships and police, walked unarmed into Zhou-owned houses and back out again without a scratch on me. I was feared on more planets than I could easily name.

I had been beaten up, bashed around, nearly killed more times than I could count; but the thought of seeing my gods-damned *mother* had me almost in tears.

You've got to get your shit together, Hail.

Opening my eyes, I stared down at the scarred surface of my left arm. A pale line marred the dark skin. I'd gotten a wire wrapped around my forearm during a bank job on Marrakesh, the last one we'd done for Po-Sin before he let us go our own way. The wire had almost snapped the bone before Portis cut me loose.

There'd been panic in his green eyes, the emotion lacing his voice as he'd gathered me against his chest and gotten us both out of the mess before the authorities showed. We'd managed to get to a body shop and most of the damage had been repaired, just leaving that single winding scar.

Shaking the memory loose and cursing Portis, I linked my fingers together and stretched my arms above my head.

Once upon a time my skin had been several shades lighter— more like the teakwood trees that grew on Pashati. It was darker now, but still not as dark as Pace's, whose rare golden hair had stood out against skin almost as black as Emmory's.

My baby sister. A second shard of heated metal sliced my heart. I'd grieved for her and Cire once when I left, but it had felt more like me dying than them. Now I grappled with the idea that my sisters were dead and it was impossible to wrap my head around.

And Portis—not a banished, thieving misfit. The thought was equally unbelievable. Except—

I swore viciously. Except for his unwillingness to talk about his past, for the sneaking suspicion I'd always had that there was something important he wasn't telling me when I'd catch him looking at me strangely.

You mean like the fact that he was *Imperial Tactical Squad?* The voice in my head was sharp with derision, and I flinched away from it straight into a shattered memory.

"Baby, stay down. Just stay down, okay?" Portis's voice was breathy with pain.

Gunfire cut off my reply, shredding our shelter. Portis dove to the side and I rolled after him into the questionable cover of a stack of priceless weavings we were supposed to be taking to the Solarian Conglomerate.

"What the fuck is going on?"

"There's no time to explain. Just keep your head down."

"You're not getting off this ship alive, Tresk. Neither of you."

Memz's voice echoed out of the darkness, and the sudden cold look on Portis's face froze my blood.

I rubbed my hands over my face. I couldn't figure out why my memory was in such tatters. Had I been drugged? These bits and pieces floating back were less than useful. There was little about it I could trust. Why would Portis try to kill me? To steal the ship? None of it made sense.

It had been *our* ship. He'd had half a stake in it, was entitled to as large a share of the profits as I was. He hadn't even cared half the time if he got paid—claimed he was doing it for the fun.

Now I knew why he didn't need the money. He'd been on the empire's payroll all along.

We'd fought. What pieces I could pull from my brain, glimmering like little glass splinters, told me that my scattered memory of gunfire and punches was real. His death rattle apology wasn't enough to make me think for a second that Emmory was right and Portis was trying to bring me home.

Home. There was no fucking way I was going home and I was wasting precious time weeping over the past instead of planning for the future. I had to be off this ship before we floated into warp or I was done for.

Pushing to my feet, I stalked to the far wall and slapped my hand against the faintly glowing panel. A door slid open in the wall, and I groaned.

"Oh, for fuck's sake."

The wardrobe was filled to bursting with the worst clothes imaginable. Never mind my intense hatred for the traditional royal colors of white and gold, but everything in the meter square opening looked like the toppings on a fairy cake. It was all pretty and otherwise useless.

If I was sneaking around on a starship, I didn't want to look like something worth eating. Which meant I was stuck with the military-issue pajamas they'd put me in.

Digging through the yards of fabric with muttered curses falling from my lips, I found little to nothing I could use as a weapon. There was a box of hair ornaments that might work in a pinch to put someone's eye out, but otherwise all I could hope was that someone would die of fright—or laughter.

I tossed a pair of white silken pants to the floor. They were embroidered around the cuffs with gold thread and little gold beads along the edge.

Useless.

I snorted in disgust, flicking my heavy green braid off my shoulder, and headed to the door, trying to make it look like I was pacing.

The panel by the door was palm activated, and as I suspected, my new friends had locked me out of the system.

It wasn't a problem.

I leaned against the wall and queued up my *smati*. I sighed in relief when it linked up easily with the shipboard computer. Whatever trouble I'd been having with *Sophie* had been with her computer, not my head.

It appeared I only had limited access. My Tracker friends didn't trust me at all, and really I couldn't blame them.

I was aboard the *Para Sahi*. The Royal Wing. What else would they send to retrieve a wayward princess? Rolling my eyes at the smooth white ceiling, I let loose another snort of disgust. I hated royal starships. They were so fucking sterile. I wanted back on *Sophie* with her brightly colored walls and random doodles that Pip had scribbled in unexpected places.

The thought of the little space orphan we'd rescued on Xi 5 jarred loose another flash of memory. He'd taken a shot at me and I'd returned fire, nailing him between the eyes. I felt a flush of shame and covered my face with my hands. He'd been sixteen.

I shook the feeling loose and focused again on my problem. Hacking the system wasn't an option. Emmory was probably watching for it. Giving me access to the *Para Sahi*'s computer made it easier to track me, but I knew enough to be able to mask my signal from him when I needed it. I spun on my heel and headed back to the wardrobe, queuing up the room's lay-out and the location of the digital cameras.

Initially I'd been pissed about the body mod screwup that had left me with this permanently green curly hair. The color had grown on me and the rest of it—from my darker skin and my tall, rangy build to my narrow face with a pointed chin—was more than suitable. Now the thought of the hysterics my hair would cause at home made it worthwhile. Maybe I'd go home, hang around just long enough to see the look on Mother's face.

You are crazy, Hail. I tightened a fist around the chain of my wild thoughts and jerked them short. I wasn't going home. I didn't want to go home.

I had to get out of here.

I dove into the wardrobe, flinging clothes out in the best imitation of a temper tantrum I could muster. Emmory believed I was a spoiled princess; I'd give him a performance worthy enough to distract him.

In the midst of it I grabbed a bottle of makeup out of the drawer and hurled it at the far corner. Blue powder splattered across the lens of the hidden camera, hopefully obscuring the surface. Two more bottles and matching spots of black and red covered my escape.

I grabbed the box of hair doodads and pulled out a long golden spike with a cascade of pink pearls attached to the end. Stripping the pearls free, I flung them away and they scattered across the floor looking like bunshinberries.

Sliding the thin piece of metal between the panel and the wall, I levered it off.

Several twisted wires later the door slid silently open. The two ITS troops turned in surprise. My well-placed strike put the first woman on her knees, choking and gasping for breath. It wouldn't kill her, but she wasn't getting up anytime soon.

The other woman had time for a startled squeak that ended when I slammed her head against the wall and she slid bonelessly to the floor.

I sprinted on bare feet down the deserted hallway, moving as quickly and quietly as possible, waiting for the sirens. They never came, and I felt a frisson of disappointment. "I figured you for better than that, Tresk," I muttered and continued toward the shuttle bay.

The rounded tunnel was as sterile and white as my quarters, with a strange humming silence only found on battleships. I was familiar enough with the layout to know I was probably deep within the ship—safe from any battle damage, and a long damn way from the shuttle bays.

Lucky for me, royal starships were all designed the same way. If I could get to a shuttle before the FTL bubble formed, I'd be long gone by the time they noticed.

If. I barely suppressed the sigh as Portis's dry voice filled my ears. *You know what that stands for, don't you?*

I'm fucked.

I hissed a curse when voices echoed down the rounded tunnel

of the hallway, and I jumped over a railing onto the walkway below. I bent my knees as I landed, tucking into a roll. I scurried across the walkway and ducked into an arched doorway, with only the whisper of air. A pair of blue-uniformed Imperial Navy officers passed above me as I held my breath and pressed as close to the wall as possible.

"Why do you suppose they sent us all the way out here? We're not normally a shuttle service for Trackers."

"Who knows? Everything about the empire is in chaos right now. All the empress's children and grandchildren of note either dead or vanished. They needed a lift, so we gave them one," the stouter of the pair said.

"You'd think they have better things to do right now than hunting up some random gunrunner. Even one as dangerous as her. I caught a peek at her file on the captain's computer; she's one of Po-Sin's."

"Maybe they think she had something to do with the princesses' deaths?"

"May their road to temple be filled with light," the first officer replied automatically. "If she did, I almost feel sorry for her. Sick or not, the empress will take her apart."

The pair moved out of earshot as I stood frozen. How sick was Mother and with what? My amusement over the gossip trickled away, and for an insane moment I contemplated following them to find out just what the news about my mother was.

The grating was cold under my bare feet; the rough edges that were meant to give running boots traction bit into my unprotected soles and shook me back to reality. I needed to get out of here, then I could worry about the rest of it.

I made it down three more levels with only one close call and slid through the doors of the shuttle bay. Staying low, I skirted around the shuttles near the door and made for the one closest to the force shield. The space beyond was a severe block of black against the white walls of the bay. Only the slight shimmering of the shield betrayed its presence.

The door of the shuttle was open, and I crept into the dark interior, feeling my way along the wall toward the pilot's seat. I was two steps into the shuttle when I froze.

Someone was already inside.

"It's good to know my instincts are right on track with you. Zin overestimated your sense of honor. You gave your word."

"I said I'd go home to see Mother. I didn't say I'd go with you."

"I'll remember that next time. He thought you'd come home like a good little princess and the show in your room was just you having a tantrum."

The lights came up. Emmory sat in the pilot's seat, one foot braced on the middle console and a smug smile playing at the corners of his generous mouth.

"Highness," he said and tilted his head to the side.

"Tracker," I replied. "So you thought different, huh? Even though you're the one who called me a spoiled princess?"

"I was angry."

"You still are angry." *Because I may have killed your brother.*

He shrugged. "You're not the type to pitch a fit like that. You didn't kill your guards."

I blinked at him. "What reason would I have to do that?"

He shrugged a shoulder. "Just an observation."

My options were racing through my head at the speed of light. Did I run? I could possibly get to another shuttle and get the door closed before he tagged me.

Unless he had people outside. In which case I was screwed because I still didn't have a damn weapon.

Which left me with fight, or bribery.

If he had people in the bay, they wouldn't come storming in here. Not only would it hamper Emmory's attempts to subdue me, but any shot fired in this cramped space had as much chance of hitting him as it did me. I tapped the door control as a precaution. It slid shut behind me and locked with a cheerful little chime.

I gave Emmory a smile and spread my arms as I crossed the space between us. "So where does this leave us, Tracker?" Without waiting for an answer, I kicked him in the face, seeing the flicker of surprise just before my bare foot connected and snapped his head back.

I moved in, intent on knocking him out while he was still reeling from my kick. But the Tracker was better than I'd given him credit for, and his booted foot landed in my solar plexus like a sledgehammer. I staggered back, gasping for air.

"Highness, this is unwise." Emmory wiped the back of his hand across his mouth and stood. He moved like a panther, all muscular grace and deadly intensity.

"I love how you kick me and then call me Highness like it matters. You don't follow the rules very well, do you?"

"I follow them when they're needed. Right now bringing you home is more important than treating you like a princess."

"I'm not going home. I left for a reason." I hated myself for saying it, hated that it sounded like I was betraying my sisters by running. There was nothing I could do for them locked up in the palace. "I'll have better luck finding answers here than at home. I don't want that life."

"You don't have a choice." Emmory's voice was quiet, but it lashed through the air like a whip. "This is your life, Highness. This is what you were born to do."

"Don't give me that destiny bullshit."

"Fine." He snarled the word at me, advancing with his hands

spread. "My brother gave his life to bring you home. I'm not letting his sacrifice be for nothing."

My laughter was brittle, shattering on the metal at my feet. "News flash, Tracker. That's what the empire does: uses you up and spits you out. My father gave his life for the empire, too. Do you know what he got out of it after some crazy woman shot him down? Ridiculed and forgotten. Blamed as the reason my mother gave in to the Saxons. You're a fool if you think the empire gives a fuck about your brother. He was just a man, useful as cannon fodder or for making daughters, that's it."

Emmory stared at me—through me—for so long I wasn't quite sure what to do next. "You don't believe that, Highness," he said finally.

"It doesn't matter what I believe. That's what Indrana does, Emmory. Chews us up and spits us out. I left for a reason. I'm not going back to give my life for an empire that couldn't care less about me." I decided to try my luck at bribery. "Look, the empire doesn't want me back any more than I want to go back. Trust me. I've got money stashed. Just let me go. I'll drop you and the shuttle off. You can tell them I overpowered you."

"You know I can't do that, Highness," he said, and flicked his left hand at me. But this time, when the *sapne* powder unfurled from the tips of his fingers, I was ready for it.

Swinging my leg up, I kicked his arm to the side and the lavender powder was sucked away into the air filter. I let the momentum spin me, planted my left foot, and brought my other foot out in a vicious side thrust that caught him in the ribs. For once my luck held and my Tracker had made the unfortunate mistake of turning his shields off while on the ship.

He staggered back with a whoosh of expelled air.

Neither of us was suited to fighting in close quarters; our height and reach actually worked against us in the confines of the shuttle. It didn't take me more than a few seconds to figure out that I'd misjudged Emmory. He was at least as skilled at hand-to-hand as I was and more than willing to fight dirty. Plus I was tired, and that first kick of his had really hurt.

It was going to cost me the fight.

I missed a block, my head slamming back into the bulkhead when he drove his palm into my cheekbone. Stars of pain exploded behind my right eye.

He caught my next punch, thrown half-blind, and locked up my right arm as he stepped into me. It was luck more than skill that allowed me to get a grip on his throat, but I stilled when I felt the edge of a blade under my chin.

"I think Sergeant Terass is just outside the shuttle, Highness, but I'd rather not test the theory. If you move, I can't guarantee your safety."

"The gods-damned irony of this is overwhelming," I muttered, staring into his dark eyes. "It's obvious you don't like me. Someone out there wants me dead, and Mother sure as the fires of Naraka didn't send you to bring me home. Not after all this time. Why don't you just kill me and get it over with?"

He blinked at me, clearly shocked by the suggestion, and I had to choke back the urge to laugh.

"Highness, we are here to retrieve you. You are not safe. Surely what happened on your ship proved that to you." His voice dropped to a whisper. "The empire needs you."

"The empire got along fine for twenty years without me," I replied, flicking my eyes downward. "Mother's probably got Ganda all ready to go. Trust me, no one will be happy about me coming home."

"Highness, the situation is delicate. There are things you need to know. I can't explain them to you here."

I frowned, confused by the earnest pleading in his eyes that crowded out his anger, and the urgency in his lowered voice. This was at odds with the cold man I'd seen earlier. "What things?"

"Watch this." He pressed a miniature file into my palm, and raised his voice for his next words. "Will you swear to me you will not try to escape again, Highness?"

I closed my eyes with a second curse. It didn't help me pretend I wasn't pinned to the chill wall of a shuttle bulkhead with Emmory's knee digging into my inner thigh and his thumb poised just above my racing pulse. It didn't do a thing to erase Portis's blood-filled plea for forgiveness, or my terror at returning home.

"Fine."

"Highness?"

I opened my eyes and gritted my teeth, choosing my words carefully. "I swear, Tracker. I swear I will not try to escape this ship."

The muscle in his jaw twitched at my words. "You swear no further harm to me or the crew? Do you swear to return home with me without further incident and do your duty?"

He was damn good. I had to give him that even though I wanted to spit on him for trapping me. I couldn't go back on my word; it was all I had left and he knew it.

"What if I don't swear?"

"I knock you out and drag you home like the criminal you are."

Returning home trussed up was an unappealing option. I'd only known Emmory for an hour, but I was pretty sure he'd drag my ass across the floor of the throne room. If I had to go home, it'd be on my own two feet. My duty, though, was to my sisters and my sisters only, and I didn't see a need to clarify that to him as I nodded my head. "All right, Tracker, I swear."

"Done," he said and released me. As he stepped away, the tiny blade disappeared back into the thumb of his glove. He turned to the wall and tapped the controls, gesturing at the now-open door with a bow. "Highness, if you would?"

I jerked my chin into the air, and didn't look at Zin or the seven remaining ITS troops clustered around the shuttle. They were busy not looking at me, either, dropping into formal bows when I passed.

Zin fell into step in front of me without a word. Emmory was a silent shadow hovering just out of the corner of my right eye as I stalked back to my room. I dropped onto the bed, my hands in my lap, and my eyes locked on the floor. I didn't want to give Emmory any reason to suspect he hadn't just won that round.

"There will be new guards outside, Highness. I wouldn't try that again," Emmory said, and the door slid shut, leaving me alone with the stinging taunt that I couldn't be trusted to keep my word.

The warning tone for warp echoed through the room and I braced myself. The *Para Sahi*'s Alcubierre/White Drive revved, and the familiar queasiness rolled through my stomach as the wall of the bubble expanded to encompass the whole ship. It dragged us out of normal space-time into a place where FTL was possible.

The Alcubierre/White Drive was as old as man's flight into the stars. In all the years that had passed, no human had found a better solution, and if the nonhuman races had a better one, they'd chosen not to share it with us.

An AWD created a bubble in space-time that belled out behind a ship and contracted in front, carrying the ship along outside of conventional space at a speed much faster than light traveled. Once inside the bubble, the ship was carried along in the wave, so the only power expenditures were getting into and out of the wave itself.

We passed through the wall and the warp engines cut out, leaving me in an abrupt silence. As soon as the nausea passed, I uncurled my fingers, staring down at the flat black square in my palm. I flopped backward onto the bed, pillowing my head in my hands, and slipped the card into the slot hidden under my green curls.

My *smati* recognized Cire's royal code stamped onto the files and responded in kind. It was a message from her and with that code I knew it hadn't been tampered with or delivered under duress. No one else even knew those codes existed; our father had given them to us when we'd been kids so we could pass messages in secret.

I shook away the encroaching memories as my computer uploaded the file. Something about Emmory's warning made it obvious that it wasn't safe for anyone else to see this. I played the video internally, closing my eyes to shut out distractions.

Cire appeared. The pretty sister I remembered had grown into a stunningly royal princess. Her blue-black curls were pinned up and away from her doll-like face. A face that was exhausted, the gunrunner part of me noted critically.

"Hail," she said, smiling sadly. Her perfect, soft voice washed over me. "Unfortunately, if you're watching this, it means I won't get to say anything to you in person. Emmory has orders to deliver this to you in the event of my death." A tear slid down her round cheek, and Cire brushed it away with impatient fingers.

"Damn it. I'm sorry for that. Sorry you'll get that news on top of everything else I'm about to tell you, and sorry I'll never get to see you again. I'd always hoped I would someday. I've missed you so much, you have no idea. Pace is dead—"

Cire straightened her shoulders, the grief sliding off her face like water off glass. She looked every bit the empress she would never be, and my heart writhed in pain.

"Someone killed her, Haili, and it wasn't the *Upja* rebels no matter what Mother might claim. Knowing you, you don't trust anyone. I need you to come home for Ami. If I'm gone, there's no one to protect her and Mother is sick.

"There are dark, dangerous things at work, Haili. People are trying to destroy the empire from within. I've attached what information I can, and you can get the rest of it from Emmory.

"I know you don't think it, but the empire needs you. I needed you, but I'm afraid I waited too long to admit it, and since you're listening to this, it's too late for me." Cire stopped, muttering a curse that had me raising my eyebrows. Then she fixed her eyes back on the camera with a forced smile. "It's damned hard to see into the future, Haili. I don't know what things will be like here by the time you get this message. I only know you need to trust in Portis—he's been watching after you since you left."

Those words sliced through me and stole my breath. Emmory's announcement I could dismiss as lies, but my sister would never have lied to me. The doubt coalesced around my heart, threatening to crush it to dust. Had I mistaken Portis's intentions? Had I killed him when he was really just trying to protect me? Why couldn't I remember what had happened?

Cire continued, "Also trust Zin and Emmory, Haili." She laughed softly. "Emmory is unconventional and extremely improper at times. You will probably butt heads quite a bit, but he has your best interests at heart. Keep him close to you even after you get into the palace. They'll be able to help you find out who is responsible for all this."

Cire glanced off-camera, frowning at whatever noise she

heard. "I'm sorry to drag you home, but I know you can help. You always sold yourself short where these things were concerned. Ami will need your wisdom and your strength, and hey, it's not like you'll have to be empress."

She looked directly at me, her dark eyes filled with ten thousand things left unsaid between us. "You are the only one left who can help my daughter save the empire. I love you, Hail. Please come home."

The message ended, and I lay on the bed with tears leaking from behind my closed lids. They tracked down the sides of my head to hide in my hair.

"Gods damn it," I muttered at the ceiling. "You deserved better." I wasn't entirely sure if I meant the words for Cire or for myself.

Ami had been alive when Cire made the message. Hell, Cire had been alive when she recorded the message. She'd been alive when she sent Emmory after me. Now they were all gone.

Trust Emmory, Haili.

I hadn't trusted anyone except for Portis for a long time. Even if he hadn't tried to kill me, he'd lied to me, and his betrayal had shattered that trust. I didn't know if I could recover enough from it to trust a total stranger, no matter what my sister said. But Cire had always had a knack for the truth, for knowing who to trust. If I couldn't take her word for it, where did that leave me?

Walking into the snake pit without so much as a sharp stick. I snorted on bitter laughter.

The fact that Emmory hadn't tried to kill me straight off was a step in the right direction, though. Only I wasn't sure if it was onto solid ground, or onto a burning transport ship.

My face hurt.

Getting up from the bed, I leaned against the sink and poked experimentally at the shiner swelling my right eye. Gone was the eighteen-year-old princess, erased by twenty years and a haywire body mod. The sharp-faced woman in the mirror flinched.

These injuries were child's play in comparison to the ones I'd gotten in the fight on *Sophie*. My shoulder had been—I paused and frowned at my reflection. I'd hit *Sophie*'s deck hard—first my shoulder and then my head snapping back against the metal floor. It had only added to my fucking addled brain.

Why was my memory in pieces?

Thanks to my BodyGuards, I'd had some training before I met Portis, but Portis had been the one to really teach me how to fight, and I couldn't see him falling for the kick I'd lashed out with after I fell, but I remembered the grunt of pain in the darkness. My shot had struck home.

I fisted my hands around the lip of the sink and rolled my shoulders. Things that seemed just coincidence at the time were starting to fall into place with alarming speed.

All the self-defense lessons Portis had forced on me. Teaching me how to shoot, teaching me how to fly. What had been the purpose of it all? I'd thought it was because that was the only way to survive as a gunrunner, and maybe that was true. But an ITS-trained guard standing in as my BodyGuard would have seen it as one more tool in a survival kit.

I'd run into Portis just weeks after I left home. I was an inexperienced eighteen-year-old hiding on the streets of Delhi, only four planets away from home and in way over my head as I tried to track the man I was certain was responsible for my father's death.

He'd saved my ass from a gang of street punks, and even after I'd nearly taken his head off with a two-by-four, he had still been calm enough to get me out of that alley and back to the boardinghouse before the cops showed up.

"We'll stick together. Watch each other's backs," he'd said

after I'd fed him a story about being an orphan trying to get off-planet to see the stars.

I'd taken him up on it, and somewhere along the way, I'd fallen in love with the bastard. Now I was faced with one of two choices—either he'd betrayed me from the very beginning, or at the very end.

He was dead, and I'd never know for sure. Hell and fire, I might have been the one to kill him.

Check your smati, *stupid.* The voice in my head now sounded a lot like Hao, my former mentor and the man who'd sponsored my way into Po-Sin's gang. He had the habit of taunting me with that when we argued—even though more often than not, my recording of our conversation proved him wrong.

Smatis had a recording feature. They only looped on a seventy-two-hour cycle to save data space. Mine was a little longer, by dint of my royal hardware, but even the standard was enough to show me what had happened on the ship.

Provided that whatever was keeping me from remembering in the first place hadn't also impacted my system. I tightened my hands on the lip of the sink again as I queued up the footage. Heart pounding and my breath clogging my throat, the image of all of us at dinner overlaid itself on my vision. We'd just done a hell of a deal. I'd hijacked a new shipment of handguns and a few heavier pieces destined for the Solarian Conglomerate's police force. Turned around and sold them to the Cheng for a profit that meant we could take a few years off if we wanted to. Not that I'd particularly wanted to do that.

We'd been headed to the outer territories to drop off some cargo that had been taking up space in the bay for a while, but Portis kept trying to get me to take a job in Hortsmith. I'd been so pissed at him for pushing it when he knew I wanted those damn rugs off my ship.

I sped through the recording until it went black as I passed out and for what seemed like an eternity nothing happened.

"Baby, wake up." Portis's voice filtered through the black, but my eyes didn't open immediately. *"Fuck,"* he muttered and rolled me over. *"Breathe in for me, baby, and wake up."*

"What's going on?" My voice was slurred and I reached a hand out but missed his face by several inches.

"Someone drugged you, we need to go."

It was a surreal experience to watch through my drugged-up eyes as Portis got me dressed, armed, and out the door in a matter of moments. Now I could see the things I'd missed in my haze. The fear tightening his mouth and making his hands shake. We stumbled down the hallway to the cargo bay.

"Help's coming. If we can just get to the shuttle." We were on the stairs. Portis swore and shoved me. I fell down the stairs into the cargo bay, crashed to the floor, jamming my leg on the way down. It was dark in the bay, but it lit up when someone fired in my direction. I fired back and heard a body fall.

"Get down!" Portis tackled me and we slid across the cargo bay floor.

"Captain, get away from him! He's trying to kill you!" Memz's sharp voice echoed through the darkness.

"Haili, baby, please stay down."

Awful terror lanced through me, as sharp as a tempered blade. "What did you call me?" I blinked at Portis as the emergency lighting flicked on, coating the cargo hold in a wash of red.

Guilt flooded his face and Portis held a hand out to me. "Baby, don't do this now. Please. You have to trust me. I'm trying to get you out of here."

"What. Did. You. Call. Me?"

"Hailimi Mercedes Jaya Bristol," Portis whispered. *"I know who you are. I've always known. You let me handle this, get to the shuttle."* Portis's voice was breathy with pain.

I caught him as he fell to his knees, blood smearing across the front of my white shirt and staining my arms where he grabbed me.

"Baby, I'm sorry. You've got to get out of here."

"I don't understand. How did you know?" I dragged him backward until we were reasonably safe from the gunfire peppering our position.

"I've always known. It doesn't matter." He pressed his gun into my hand. *"You get to the shuttle and get the hell off this ship. Emmory's coming for you, I sent coordinates. Trust him. He'll keep you safe."*

"Who's Emmory?"

Portis coughed, splattering me with blood. *"Just trust him, Haili. I'm sorry. I'm sorry for lying to you. I'm sorry it turned out like this and you have to go the rest of the way alone. But all that matters is you staying alive. You have to go. Now."*

He shoved me away from him, pulling another gun free as he staggered to his feet and rushed out into the center of the cargo bay.

I gasped, wanting to look away, but instead I watched the rest of the scene play itself out with painful clarity. Memz shot Portis again as he rushed her, but she missed me, barreling right after him, and I tackled her with the precision of an Austro footballer. Our fight was brutal and I finally tore myself away from the replay when the crack of her neck shot through my brain.

"Your Highness, are you all right?"

Blinking dry eyes back to the present, I realized I was on my knees a meter away from the sink. Both Trackers were in the room, but at a cautious distance. Zin was holding my boots. Emmory had his arms crossed. I'd thought his eyes were black, but in this light I could see the earthy brown layered over the silver of his augmentations. Portis's green eyes—bright sunlight through leaves—flashed into my vision and I felt another tear slip down my wet cheeks.

Rocking back on my heels, I rose in a smooth motion and held my hand out. "My *smati* remembered what I couldn't, Tracker. Would you like to see?"

"Highness, you swore an oath."

"I keep my oaths. This isn't an elaborate ruse to try and escape again. My recording shows what happened on *Sophie*." I wiggled my fingers. "Zin's welcome to take his gun out if it will make you feel better."

Emmory gave me a look and took my hand. Our *smatis* synced and I queued up the file once more. Emmory didn't get that glazed look people sometimes had when they viewed things on their *smatis*; instead he looked right at me the whole time. Like water washing away a sand castle, his anger melted. It was replaced with grief and I pulled my hand away, turning my head in respect.

"Why didn't you make it to the shuttle?" There wasn't any accusation in the question, but I flinched anyway. Now that I'd seen it, the memories rushed back in like a wave, shredding my composure in its path.

"I couldn't leave him." My confession echoed loudly in the silence. "I couldn't leave him to die alone like I'd left my father. After everything we'd been through, I didn't want—" I choked the words back down, not wanting to admit that to anyone.

I could remember it now, as clearly as the surface of a quiet pond. When the realization that I was going to lose Portis hit me, I hadn't wanted to survive either.

"Zin, are we clear?"

"Have been since we came in. They'll probably get suspicious, but I can keep the surveillance scrambled for as long as we want. Someone might come knocking, though."

"You don't trust these people?"

Emmory gave a short shake of his head. "There wasn't time to vet the whole ship. Gill's people are crewing the surveillance for your room, but others could be listening in..." He raised a hand and wiggled it. "At this point, it's best not to tip anyone off."

"That's why no one knows who I am." I tapped one hand against the boots before I tossed them on the bed. "My sister said to trust you. I was right. She's the one who sent you, not my mother."

"We are not the enemy here, Highness. I swear." Emmory held my gaze, his eyes filled with concern and frustration. There was no trace of his previous anger; I wondered if he was just hiding it or if it was gone for good.

Wiping my face with the heels of my hands, I exhaled, letting the ice settle around my heart and across my face. There wasn't time to grieve for everything I'd lost. I was headed into a situation more dangerous than anything I'd faced outside the empire. No friends, no weapons, and far too little intel. If I didn't keep it together, I was going to end up dead. "Who is?"

Emmory looked away, his jaw flexing, and I was pretty sure he was trying to think up a nonoffensive reply. Cire was probably right about us butting heads. Trackers were a different breed. With so much exposure to the outside worlds, they had trouble acting like proper Indranan men: no biting of their tongues as was expected in conventional society.

Of course, I wasn't much good at that either. There was a good chance Emmory and I would get along just fine.

3

W e don't know, Highness," he said finally.

"Memz was on my crew for years. Someone offered her something worth killing me for." I let a brief smile flicker through even though I'd never wanted a drink so badly as in that moment. "Or trying to kill me. Am I correct in assuming whoever it was, they're responsible for the deaths of my sisters?"

"It's likely, Highness."

"You can understand my hesitation, then, Tracker, to just throw myself at your mercy."

"I am loyal to Indrana, Highness. I swore an oath to Princess Cire to bring you home and keep you safe," Emmory whispered, and gods damn but he looked hurt. He took a step toward me, his gloved hands held out in supplication.

"Bugger me, I don't know you!" The furious reply slipped out, and I wasn't in the mood to lie to him so I went with it. I swallowed, glared at him, and continued, "Either of you. I'll trust you both as far as I can, but you drugged me, kidnapped me—"

"I retrieved you. As I was ordered to do." His voice dropped to a whisper. "As *your sister* ordered me to do."

"Ordered! Don't talk to me about orders. Portis was ordered to lie to me and *babysit* me. It's all sophistry," I snarled, advancing on him. I jabbed a finger into his chest and then pointed it at Zin.

I thought I'd been free. I'd thought that my life was my own. The one thing I really wanted, the thing I'd given up every piece of my life at home for, had turned out to be a lie. I choked on the sudden tears and spun away before they spilled free.

"Highness—"

"Fine, you were doing your job. Give me one reason I should trust you." I looked up at the ceiling, blinking the tears away before I faced him.

"You don't have anyone else," he said. Brutal honesty cut right to the heart of things. "And you need us."

He was right. I didn't want to set foot on Pashati without someone I could trust. I scrubbed my hands over my face and muttered a curse that had Emmory raising an eyebrow. "When did Cire die?"

"Yesterday afternoon. We were already off-planet. She'd wanted to make sure your empress-mother couldn't stop us."

"Why did she send you after me? What is going on?"

"She needed you, Highness. I don't know how much you've been paying attention, but things are bad."

I hadn't been paying attention at all lately and it was about to bite me in the ass. "Dump the title, Emmory. We don't have time for it."

A smile fluttered to life on his face, vanishing as quickly as a flame in space, and I got the feeling he was going to ignore my order.

"The empire is in chaos. Things are falling apart even more rapidly than your sister feared. Read the files she sent you, and I'll catch you up when I can. We've been off the grid for too long already."

"Who's responsible? Who blew up Cire? And Pace—"
I couldn't even finish the sentence. "What in the Mother
Destroyer's name is *my mother* doing about it?"

"Your Highness, we don't know." Emmory held a hand up
before I could say anything. "We've been off camera for too
long, we've got incoming. We need you to come home." His
voice was abruptly distant.

It was my turn for a sharp nod as I bit my tongue and swallowed back the hundred or so questions I desperately wanted
to ask. We were apparently back on camera. Besides that, now
wasn't the time, and I knew it, even though I hated it. Hated
falling right back into the politics and politeness.

I wasn't going to get stuck. I would go home, find the bastards responsible for murdering my sisters, and then figure it
out from there. I gave Emmory a second sharp nod. "I'll come
home with you."

"The empire is in your debt, Highness." Emmory's bow was
formal and I barely managed to keep from rolling my eyes.

The empire can kiss my ass. I'm only doing this for my sisters.

"It's a pleasure to do my duty," I said out loud.

"We'll be in warp for several hours yet," Emmory said, still
sounding stilted and formal. "I'd suggest some sleep. We could
all use it. Shall I send Sergeant Terass in?"

I locked eyes with him, recognizing the test for what it was,
and nodded. Emmory nodded back and the door slid open.
A slender young woman with burnished copper hair came
through. She was barely over a meter tall, a fragile-looking waif
of a girl.

I didn't have to see her pointed ears hiding among the curls
to know what she was. Her stature coupled with her wide,
round eyes and heart-shaped face was more than enough proof.

Farian.

Only my pride kept me from stepping back.

"Highness, Sergeant Fasé Terass."

"Your Imperial Highness. It is a great honor." She bowed, keeping her golden eyes on me. Her lilting voice was the same one I'd heard while lying on *Sophie*'s deck.

I answered the bow with a nod, palace manners so ingrained in my being that the years away couldn't wipe them out. Fighting down my instinct to bolt, I smiled at her instead.

Fasé offered up a tiny smile in return. She tugged the glove off her right hand and my heart pounded so hard it bruised itself against my ribs. "Death you deal and death you shall become," she whispered the edict, holding out her hand. "I am loyal to my gods and to you, Highness. I will not harm you."

I swallowed, and laid my hand over hers. I fucking hoped she was telling me the truth. Otherwise, I'd just committed suicide.

I'd been healed by a Farian a time or two before, most memorably when Cire had blacked my eye. I'd gone one taunt too far about her short legs and the resulting punch had been brilliant.

Being healed is similar to weightlessness. A strange floating, slightly out of control feeling. I often wondered what the Farians felt, but I've never had the guts to ask. These strange aliens were among the first to welcome humanity to the stars, but though they'd integrated themselves into our lives so seamlessly, there was very little we knew about them.

They spent time with humans as part of some pilgrimage. An offering to the Tuesday god who'd given them the gift of healing. It was a double-edge sword of a gift, packed with the ability to kill, and if they hoarded the gift instead of sharing it, they would die. Hao had explained it to me as if a battery was being charged with no fail-safe. The energy just kept building until it burst.

As the ache in my face subsided and all my other minute complaints vanished, I released the breath I'd been holding. A second smile, shy and tired, fluttered at the corner of Fasé's pale mouth.

"May you feel better, Highness," she whispered the benediction and pulled her hand from mine. With another quick bow, she left the room, leaving me alone with Emmory and Zin once more.

"I brought you your boots," Zin said as though nothing about this scene was out of the ordinary. "You won't have much of an occasion to wear them in the palace, but I figured good boots are hard to find."

"Thank you," I murmured, earning a smile.

Emmory bowed his head a fraction. "Sleep well, Highness."

I thought of a dozen pithy replies before I said, "You, too." And as they left the room, I was pretty sure I wouldn't be the only one staring at the ceiling all night.

I didn't actually stare at the ceiling the whole time. Most of it was spent reading through the files Cire had attached to her message and silently cursing myself for the last few years of near obsessive avoidance of Indranan politics.

The empire was crumbling, and as harsh as it sounded, my sister's death was simply one more awful thing in a string of events that were knocking the foundation of Indrana out from underneath her.

I paced as I listened to Cire. What had started with civil unrest and ended with mounting tensions with the Saxon Kingdom was a tangled mess of economic failures, political demonstrations, riots, and the assassinations of three members of the royal family.

None of it was as shocking as the medical report attached to another short message from Cire.

"Mother has Shakti dementia. She started presenting symptoms about six months ago."

Space madness.

A genetic mutation triggered by exposure to radiation in the early days of space travel had resulted in a new form of dementia that none of the known cures could touch. We said those who had it had been "touched by the Mother Destroyer" and were lost to her unforgiving hands. Once it manifested, it moved fast. Shakti dementia was what had killed my distant ancestor-grandfather when we first landed on Pashati. Men were more likely to suffer the effects, and the initial colonists struggled to overcome the onslaught. The balance of power shifted enough to allow my ancestor-grandmother to take command. Though the priests liked to say it was the will of the goddess that started the whole thing.

It started with wandering attention and an inability to focus. Then speech issues—forgetting words, garbled and unfinished sentences. As the disease progressed, there was memory loss and confusion of time where the victim started living in the past.

It was genetic and there was no way to test for the risk, no way to guard against it except to never leave the planet surface—something that was damn near impossible for members of the royal family. Still, since my ancestor-grandfather there had only been three other incidences of the dementia in my family.

"Ven noticed first and told me. I had Dr. Satir run some tests and she gave me the bad news. We haven't told her yet. I decided it was for the best when the doctor said it could make the disease progress faster." Cire looked haggard, but it was impossible to tell if she'd recorded this vid before or after the other. "You'll have to tread lightly, Haili, at least until Atmikha is crowned. She has her good days, but she's twitchy and the slightest thing can set her off. I remember how you and Mother were." A smile flickered to life on her face and it made my heart ache. "Try not to piss her off too much."

"I'm not making any promises," I whispered.

I kept reading files until I passed out, dropping into a fitful sleep in the middle of a memo about troublesome Saxon activity on some of our border worlds. My dreams were spotty, filled with images of Portis dying, Cire vanishing in flame, and Pace choking to death on her own blood.

The last was too much and had me waking with a gasping sob that I muffled in the bedsheets. I rolled out of bed and stumbled to the bath. My stomach didn't care about the fact that I hadn't eaten anything for a good thirty hours and tried to empty itself repeatedly.

"Water?" The appearance of a cup over my shoulder startled me as much as Zin's voice did, and my jerk almost resulted in the offered water being dumped over my head.

Zin swung it out of the way of my flailing arm and dropped into a crouch to offer it again.

"I hope your expectations of your new empress aren't set too high," I said after rinsing my mouth out and spitting into the toilet. "Because you're in for a shock, Zin. I was a disappointing princess, according to my mother. I doubt I'll be much better as empress."

Zin smiled and offered me a hand up. "I try not to put expectations on people, Highness. It's not very fair to ask them to conform to my ideas of the way the world should be."

"Pretty words." I leaned against the counter once I was on my feet. "So you're the philosopher and Emmory is the sword?"

"We take turns, Highness. I brought you breakfast, if you think you can stand it."

"Might as well try." I spotted Emmory by the door as I made my way to the bed and poked at the food on the tray for a minute before I looked up at Zin. "My mother has space madness."

Emmory nodded. "Yes, Highness."

"It's not public knowledge, though?"

"It is now," he said. "The news leaked a few hours ago at home."

"Does my mother know?"

"I believe Princess Cire was going to speak with her after we left, Highness. I am not sure if that happened."

"Bugger." Slowly I could feel the noose tightening on my neck. My plans to hunt down my sisters' killers and then leave hadn't included my mother's failing health. "Well, I'm going to need something to wear besides this, Tracker. I don't suppose you've got a spare uniform floating around?"

Zin frowned, glancing behind me at the now destroyed wardrobe. "You can't—"

"It's this or a uniform." I gestured at my now wrinkled pajamas.

"Highness, that's hardly appropriate attire." Emmory's voice was pained.

"I know, but unless you want to get into a wrestling match, I'm not putting on any of the clothing in there."

"Your Highness." He stopped and took a breath, letting it out slowly. I already recognized it as the sign of him struggling for composure. "We cannot present you to your empress-mother dressed in pajamas."

He sounded so exasperated, I had to bite back a snort of laughter. I wanted to let it loose in the air just to see what he'd do, but I didn't. I was the gunrunner they all expected to see and I'd bow to Mother in clothing of my choosing or not at all.

"You should find me something else then, Tracker. We're

about the same size." I waved a hand at him. "And it's better than pajamas."

"That is debatable, Highness," Emmory replied, but he vanished back out the door. He was right, of course. About the only way I could insult my mother more would be to show up dressed in the cheery yellow sari reserved for outcasts.

"Setting the tone early, Your Highness?" Zin hadn't moved from his spot against the wall. "Coming home in military dress is going to raise eyebrows."

"You probably should have thought about that before you came to get me. Bringing me home at all is going to raise eyebrows. Prodigal black sheep and all that."

"It was an order, Highness."

"Do you always follow orders?"

"Yes, ma'am."

"So if I ordered you to kill your partner when he came back in the room, would you do it?"

Zin froze, his eyes desperately seeking a sign that I was pulling a horrible joke on him, and when he couldn't find it, he fell back into the safety of formality. "Your Imperial Highness, I know my partner has behaved improperly to you, but he is only doing his duty." He dropped to his knees and bent over, arms outstretched and palms facing upward, his face against the floor. "Please—"

I immediately felt like an asshole, and the feeling grew exponentially when Emmory walked back into the room. He froze, a uniform in unrelenting black in his hand.

"Highness?"

The request for information was tentative, and the reality was that I didn't have to explain myself. Not only was I the Crown Princess, but I was a woman. I could do what I pleased and there was nothing these two could do about it.

I'd hated that twenty years ago and I still hated it. The inequality, the absolutism that bred contempt and hatred for a whole group of people simply because of the accident of their birth.

"Emmory, if I ordered you to not take me home, would you obey me?"

"No, Highness."

"You're going to want to explain why to your partner," I said, grabbing the uniform out of his hand and heading for the bathroom.

4

I muttered curses after the door closed, jerked off my pajama bottoms, and grabbed the uniform pants from the counter. They were long enough, and thankfully made of a material with some give—my hips were more generous than Emmory's. I tugged the black tunic on over the gray tank and plopped down onto the toilet seat to put my boots on.

First, I freed the hammered silver ring that was tangled in the laces of my boots and slid it onto my right hand. I unhooked the slender band of dark brown leather and wrapped it around my wrist.

"Take this." Cire pressed the leather into my hand and my eyes went wide.

"Father gave this to you, I can't—"

"Take it, Hail." Cire was almost twenty years old and already behaving like an empress; the frown on her face wasn't one to be argued with. "I want you to have it. To remember us. Just in case."

"I'm going to stay in touch."

"You might not be able to," she said too softly for our sister to hear.

"And this," Pace squeaked, waving a ring in the air. "I got it at

the market. The old man said it was a wishing ring. Turn it on your finger three times and whisper your wish into your hand."

I took the beaten ring of silver from her, not having the heart to tell her that wishes didn't come true. She'd learn it soon enough.

"Damn it." I was crying again, tears streaking down my face and dripping onto my shirt. I wasn't going to last five minutes in the palace if I couldn't get a handle on my ramshackle emotions.

Scrubbing my hands over my face, I peeked at myself in the mirror. Gods, I looked horrible. Even with the shiner gone, I looked precisely as exhausted as I felt.

"Let's get this shit over with," I muttered, heading back into the room.

Zin straightened when I stepped over the threshold.

"Highness," Emmory said, giving me a quick nod. He was back to the implacable mask. There was no hint of what he and Zin might have discussed showing on his face. "We're about to drop out of warp."

The warning chime sounded and I braced myself on the wall again as the bubble contracted back into the AWD, leaving us once more in normal space-time.

"We'll be in orbit around Pashati and on the ground within the hour. It's two a.m. at the palace, but they've word of our arrival."

"I'd like to watch the approach. Can we go to the bridge?"

My Trackers exchanged a glance and I suspected there was a whole conversation behind it. Emmory nodded finally. "If you'll give us a moment to talk with the captain. She's not aware you're on board."

"How did you talk her into making this trip in the first place? Royal starships aren't flown all over the galaxy without a good reason."

"Princess Cire authorized it," Emmory replied. "And the captain is Zin's sister."

Zin didn't say anything as he left the room, and Emmory watched him go, his eyes lingering on the door for a moment before he looked at me.

"I'm sorry I scared him." The apology tumbled out, surprising us both. "I was trying to make a point."

"The heir doesn't make points, Highness, she gives orders. Zin trusts that you know what you're doing. So if you ask him to commit suicide, he's going to take it personally."

"Maybe his mistake is thinking I know what I'm doing," I huffed, turning away from him and throwing my hands into the air. *Give it up, Hail. You're not going to win this one.*

Thankfully Zin came back before I could make a fool of myself and try again. "The captain said she would meet us in her briefing room and you could watch from there if that's acceptable." He wasn't any good at hiding his wariness, and I mentally punched myself in the head several times before I replied.

"That will work, thank you."

We left my room, the two ITS troops following behind us, and we passed through empty corridors until we got to the bridge.

Captain Hafin waited for us just outside the door to her briefing room. I could see the family resemblance immediately, though her eyes were darker than her brother's and her dreadlocked hair was long, twisted into a complicated knot at the base of her neck.

"Your Imperial Highness." There was no hesitation in her greeting or her bow, nothing to suggest that she'd been shocked by her brother's news. "It is a pleasure to have you on board. I apologize the accommodations were not better prepared."

There was the surprise. I caught the way her eyes slid toward Zin for just a second as she bowed and the frustration bled through the tail end of her sentence.

"It's no problem. They were just following orders, Captain."

"May I be the first to welcome you home, ma'am? And extend my sympathies."

I nodded sharply and went through the open doorway. Captain Hafin followed me, leaving my Trackers to enter last. The wide, opaque wall shifted to reveal the endless blackness of space and the twin stars of the Ashvin System.

Nasatya, the larger G-class star, and its companion, Dasra—a smallish orange dwarf—danced across their elliptical orbits. Dasra twirled closer to Pashati and then flung itself away on an eighty-year cycle like the whirling dervishes of old.

The other habitable planet, Ashva, orbited Dasra every five months, and it had developed into an ideal, if quiet, agricultural world for the empire.

"Jai maa," I whispered when Pashati, the crown jewel of the Indranan Empire, came into view. The years hadn't stolen her splendor. The massive blue-green planet hung suspended against the black, and I could see the traces of red appearing at the far edge. Pashati's sun was rising over the Great Desert, but its light wouldn't reach the capital city on the western edge of the Lakshitani Sea for several hours yet.

Welcome home, Hail.

The Ashvin System had been settled over three millennia ago by colonists from the Solarian Conglomerate. The first colony ship—piloted by my ancestor's husband—had set down on Pashati two Earth-Standard years before the other colony ships arrived.

There were fourteen other families on board, sacrificial lambs if one were to be honest. Colonization of other worlds was a brutal business in the early days. Long travel times from Earth coupled with unknown hazards meant the scout ships were on their own.

There was always a possibility that the first surveys and scouts missed something important after all, and Earth learned their lesson the hard way. Hundreds of thousands of people perished in the early days from a random strain of bacteria, oddly aggressive plant life, the air mixture shifting with the seasons. Any one thing or a combination of things could wipe out the settlers faster than they could call for help, and certainly faster than help could arrive.

The new system of sending down a small group of families was the easiest solution. If they were still alive when the other ships got there, it was assumed safe. If they weren't, the planet was X-ed from the habitable planet list.

For many families—mine included—it was worth the risk. Being a front family meant you were given certain privileges. First pick of land, a seat on the ruling council, a bonus payment if you survived until the ships came.

Or a death bonus for your family if you didn't.

My ancestor's husband and several other men didn't survive, succumbing to space madness; but their wives and children did, and my ancestor was savvy enough to keep her husband's spot on the Earth-appointed council.

She and her descendants held on to that spot and what amounted to control of the colony all the way up to the break with Earth, and after the dust from that ruckus settled, the empire was born: an empire ruled by women, my ancestor at the head, backed by the women of the other original families.

Those fourteen women made up the Matriarch Council; their daughters and other selected female nobles made up the Ancillary. Even today, this system held in place.

I understood what they'd been working toward. The gender politics of certain areas of the Solarian Conglomerate at the time weren't stellar, and colonization efforts tended to scrape from the more desperate levels of society. In the early days of colonization, women were treated more as breeding stock than explorers with equal rights. However, like so many great ideas, they took it too far.

I pressed my hands to the window as Pashati swelled until the blackness of space was lost to the dark blue of the night side of the planet. I was going back to everything I hated, and the thought of it was a fist around my heart.

"Highness, we should head for the cargo bay," Emmory said.

"Of course. Captain, thank you for the use of your ship."

"It's an honor to serve, ma'am." Captain Hafin saluted me.

"Lead the way, Tracker," I replied with a wave of my hand, privately horrified at how easily commands came out of my mouth in that frozen royal tone.

Time, it seemed, didn't change much at all.

I followed Emmory down the corridor, with Zin and the two ITS troops at my back and the familiar hum of a ship in spaceflight vibrating the floor under my feet. I felt it shift, the vibration growing darker, heralding our entrance into the planet's atmosphere.

We hit a set of stairs leading downward, and I stumbled as the ship shook more violently than normal.

Zin grabbed me by the upper arm to steady me. "Careful, Highness," he said.

"Thanks." I mustered up a smile.

Zin released me with an answering smile that was genuine. The man apparently didn't hold grudges. "Everything will be okay, Highness."

I wished I could believe him, but my stomach was a mass of

ugly knots and I'd survived for too damn long on my instincts to ignore them now. This whole thing was going to get far worse before it got better.

But I couldn't tell him all that, so instead I followed Emmory the rest of the way down, through another corridor, and into a wide bay.

Five people were already there, waiting. Their laughter cut off abruptly when someone spotted us and all of them jerked to attention. I spotted Fasé's red hair in the circle of ITS members.

"Your Imperial Highness." The voice coming from the stout woman was familiar as she greeted me with a surprisingly elegant bow for someone her size. "Captain Ilyia Gill. Allow me to apologize for pointing our weapons at you earlier. We were not aware you would be on that ship."

"Forgiven, Captain," I replied with a dip of my head.

"Trackers." She nodded sharply at Emmory and Zin.

"Captain," Emmory said.

The ship shook again, and both Emmory and Gill reached out to steady me this time.

Welcome to your old life, Princess.

I had to swallow my snarl at the thought. The captain didn't deserve it, and if I was going to be honest, Emmory didn't really either. They were just doing their jobs—their duty.

I wanted to scream.

"Highness?" Zin said as Emmory shook a cloak out, the flat black material eating the light that touched it.

"I'm skulking into the palace, Tracker?"

Emmory handed it off to Zin. Their hands brushed and the pair shared a brief smile. An image of Portis smiling at me like that swept through me and the ache almost put me on my knees.

"For your protection, Highness," Emmory answered, looking back at me. "Given the circumstances, we thought it prudent. We've tried to make your arrival as unobtrusive as possible, but word will get out. The press can't get onto the landing pad, but they will probably be as close as possible."

I felt a little trill of panic at his words. I hadn't read nearly enough of those files from Cire. I was walking blind into what very well could be a trap.

Wouldn't be the first time, Cressen.

I straightened my shoulders as Zin draped the cloak over them. He pulled the hood up, and must have spotted the expression on my face because his stone gaze softened. "All will be well, Highness. I promise you."

"You keep saying that. I hope you're right, Tracker."

Zin fell back behind me, while Emmory stayed at my side, just slightly in front of me, and icy fingers walked up my spine.

He'd take a shot for me.

He'd just met me, and even though we knew I hadn't killed his brother, he clearly didn't like me. Yet here we were. He'd give his life for me without hesitation. Either of them would. Buggered loyal fools. Those icy fingers wrapped around my spine and pulled.

Portis and I, we'd saved each other's lives more times than I could count. Because we knew each other, because we'd cared for each other—or so I thought.

This kind of blind devotion had been one of the many reasons I'd stayed away. I didn't want meaningless pleasantries to my face while someone stabbed me in the back. I wanted people who actually cared for me.

But I'd learned a long time ago that what I wanted and what the universe wanted rarely matched up.

Captain Gill's squad formed up around us. I couldn't stop the insane whirling of my mind as we disembarked the *Para Sahi* and crossed the tarmac at a speed just short of a run.

5

A wind as sharp as daggers drove through the fabric of cloak and clothing. It was winter in the northern hemisphere of Pashati. I was blinded by the lights of the landing pad, helplessly herded through the driving snow by the soldiers around me. Their shouted orders and the calls from the media just outside the fence filled my ears. Then we were inside, and a blessed silence descended.

"Keep it up," Emmory hissed when I moved to push my hood back. We marched forward, past the gawking onlookers, and into a side corridor barred with a heavy metal door. The two BodyGuards in battle armor didn't salute as we approached, and I heard the all-too-familiar whine of weaponry being powered up.

Emmory pulled down my hood and stepped forward.

"Scanning." The hollow voice came from one of the Guards, indistinguishable as female or male, though the former was more likely. "Confirmed, Tracker Emmorlien Haris Tresk, Level Eight."

Level eight? I nearly swallowed my tongue. Tracker levels were determined upon their entry to the program through a series of tests. It was less a rank and more a way to track the innate skill people like Emmory and Zin were born with.

Emmory was a damned expert tracker, the highest rank they had. Even if Portis hadn't ratted me out, Emmory and Zin would have found me eventually.

"Confirmed, Tracker Starzin Hafin, Level Five. Visual scan commencing. Cressen Stone, identified. Gunrunner wanted on seventy-eight counts of arms trafficking and three counts of petty theft by the Solarian Conglomerate, forty-three counts of assault with a deadly weapon by the Galactic Security Board in addition to another one hundred and six counts of—"

"We'll be here all night if you try to list everything," I said, holding my hand up to the Guard. "Get on with it."

"DNA scan commencing." The woman slid up her faceplate and pressed her gloved hand to mine. "Cressen Stone, identified."

The tension ratcheted up a notch. I examined my nails with a poorly concealed smile. Apparently, that mod was even better than I could have hoped for if it was fooling a palace Guard.

"I have record of a confirmed scan," Emmory said.

"Your scan cannot be counted as verified, Tracker. Commencing with deep scan." The Guard closed her hand around my wrist. The heat was immediate and intense and pretty much burned away any hope that had sprung to life about dodging this mess.

"Confirmed, Her Imperial Highness Hailimi Mercedes Jaya Bristol. Second daughter of Empress Mercedes Aadita Constance Bristol, and Heir to the Throne of Indrana."

"Gods damn, that's a mouthful," I muttered. Someone behind me choked on a laugh. The soldier frowned at me.

"You are cleared to enter the palace," she said. "Not the Squad," she continued when we all stepped forward.

"The ITS should have been cleared," Emmory protested.

"They are not. Proceed alone."

I dared a glance behind me, and caught Fasé's tentative smile. There was no time for one of my own as Emmory took me by the arm and propelled me through the now opened door. It slammed shut behind the three of us.

That frozen hand of unease was still wrapped around my spine. The booming sound of the door made it tighten further, and I felt my knees go weak.

"I don't like this."

"I'm in agreement with you, Highness."

I hadn't realized I'd spoken out loud until Emmory answered me. He released my arm and we continued in tense silence down the hallway, the rough-cut rock walls giving way to smooth-polished obsidian then white marble with bluish veins as we turned left, right, and then left again.

I'd taken this passage twice before in my life; the first time at the age of four after the state funeral for my grandmother. My father had carried me. Cire walked next to him, and Mother carried Pace until we reached the ornate double doors at the end of the tunnel.

She'd stopped just inside them and knelt on the ground, still holding Pace. Father set me down as Mother gestured us closer.

"I love you all," she said with a reassuring smile, still our mother even though she looked so regal in the heavy brocade of her coronation sari. "Remember that, and nothing's going to change."

God, how she'd lied. *Everything* changed when we walked through those doors. Everything.

The second time I'd walked this corridor had been for my father's funeral. A casket, my weeping sisters, and my granite-faced empress-mother, who had no time for softness in the face of a war.

I balked when we reached the ornate doors, bumping into Zin's solid chest. He closed big hands on my shoulders with a murmured apology.

These doors looked like pretty things, decorated with a painting of Indrana's break from the Conglomerate in the sixth century of *Gaia Diaspora*. But I knew from my long-ago studies that they were five feet thick, bonded metal, and virtually impenetrable.

"Highness?"

"Give me a moment, please?" I hated to beg on principle, and doing it to the men responsible for landing me in this mess seemed even more humiliating. But I needed a gods-damned minute before I walked through those doors and into the throne room. Even if all I could use it for was to lament the life I was leaving behind.

It's all gone, Hail. I heard my father's voice again, a long-forgotten memory shooting to the surface. *You can weep about it or get on with things. I can't make the choice for you, but for my part, I never much cared for crying over spilled milk.*

I threw my shoulders back, tipped my chin up, and let the royal mask slip into place. "All right," I snarled. "Let's get this fucking production over with." I took a deep breath and pushed the doors open.

The massive chamber was packed to the gills—even at 2 a.m.—with nobility and anyone else who could wrangle an invitation to my homecoming. Nothing like this had happened in the history of Indrana, and more than a thousand pairs of eyes stared at me in breathless anticipation.

The stillness in the throne room couldn't have been more absolute if someone had dropped a silencer-nuke.

However, the whispers started before I reached the halfway point, growing like a rolling wave on the Lakshitani Sea.

I kept my eyes fixed on the golden rays protruding from the top of the throne rather than looking at my mother as I walked over the slick white marble floor.

We hit the line of jagged black stone, the obsidian jutting up in sharp spikes from the smooth floor. No one, not even family, crossed the line without the empress's permission.

I dropped to my knees. Nearly twenty years of habit had me almost keeping my eyes up. A necessary requirement in Po-Sin's company, it would have really started things off on a sour note with Mother—the kind of sour notes that ended up with someone bleeding. So instead I lowered my eyes and bowed until my face was just a hairsbreadth from the sharp edges of the rock. Emmory and Zin flanked me, echoing the motion.

"Mother," I said, without looking up. "I am come home." My voice echoed throughout the room, silencing the whispers.

"Two deep scans confirmed and still we are reluctant to believe it." Mother's voice didn't sound any different, that same biting derision and weary annoyance I'd suffered for years. "Child, what have you done to your hair?"

There was more murmuring in the crowd, and I bit my tongue hard enough to taste blood. Answering that question would be a bad idea.

"Your Imperial Majesty—" a smooth voice started to speak.

"Yes, we know," Mother said under her breath. She raised her rich voice so it rang through the room. "You've seen her, vultures. Now get out and let us talk to our heir in peace."

I flinched at the word. *Heir.* I was the gods-damned Heir to the Throne.

My Trackers didn't move from my side, remaining still with their palms pressed to the white marble just in front of the barrier. I stayed on my knees, listening to my joints protest and trying not to drip sweat onto the jagged rock about to kiss my face while the royal court filed out, taking their sweet-assed time.

"Get up." The command was somewhat strained, and I rocked back on my heels, rising easily to my feet. Emmory rose with equal grace, while Zin pushed to one knee and then stood. I filed away the idea that his left leg might not support his weight. It could come in handy later.

Then I looked up, and it took every ounce of self-control I had not to gasp. This wasn't the loving mother I remembered from my childhood. It wasn't even the iron-cold bitch of an empress I'd come to despise.

Mother looked *old*, far older than she should have. There was silver woven through her black curls, and her dark skin was aged and creased with lines.

"Hailimi." Mother's cool greeting shook me from my shock.

"*Namasté*, Mother." I folded my hands together, pressing them both to my forehead as I gave the traditional greeting. It was an old ritual my ancestors had brought from Earth, resurrected here in our new home among the stars. "It is a great pleasure to see you well."

Ven wasn't in his spot. I longed to ask what had happened to Mother's *Ekam*. But I'd learned a long time ago that interrupting my mother fell in the category of Extremely Bad Ideas.

The new BodyGuard at her side was unfamiliar. His angular golden face looked like it had been fashioned by a lazy god with a razor. He raked unusual light blue eyes over me, and they were filled with disdain he couldn't quite hide.

"Since we are not well, we are also not surprised to hear you say that." Mother snorted, smoothing a hand over the skirt of her crimson dress, and flicked her black eyes to Emmory and Zin. "You've done us a great service, Trackers. How can we repay you?"

"We need no payment, Your Majesty. It was our duty," Emmory replied. "One we were happy to provide for the good of the empire."

I choked down the laugh at that cowshit. Always for the good of the empire. No one gave a shit about the good of Hail.

Mother's *Ekam* watched the exchange between my mother and Emmory with detached interest. A woman stood next to him. She was about my age, and stood at attention in a dress uniform of shimmering black and crimson. She was too damn pretty for her own good, with black dreadlocks pulled back into a short ponytail.

"Nevertheless." Mother smiled at Emmory, and I recognized the sly look as it slipped across her face.

Brace yourselves, everyone.

"You've already shown excellent judgment where our wayward daughter is concerned. We think we'll continue along that path. Bial, we will have Emmorlien take over BodyGuard duties for the princess. He shall be *Ekam*."

Oh, bugger me.

Emmory's head whipped up and he very nearly made the fatal mistake of arguing with my mother. I reached out, digging my fingers into his forearm, and cut off his protest.

Cire had said keep him close, and even though Mother probably meant it to be an insult, I'd take it. He couldn't get much closer than my damn primary BodyGuard.

Bial, mother's *Ekam*, looked equally shocked, and the face of the pretty BodyGuard standing next to him was so crestfallen I had to choke back hysterical laughter. No doubt she'd been the one picked to be my primary and thought it was some kind of honor.

"Swear on your life, Tracker?" my mother asked with a smile on her face. It was impressive how she circumvented the normal formality of the BodyGuard oath with those five words.

"Your Majesty, my partner." There was just enough desperation hovering behind Emmory's words to make me feel sorry for him, and out of the corner of my eye I saw how pale Zin was.

If she said no, this was going to get ugly. I was willing to put good money down that one or both of them would go crazy and die if they were forced to part ways.

"Ah, yes. A separation would be most unpleasant." A strange smile curved Mother's mouth. "Starzin may accompany you as BodyGuard also, Emmorlien. I will let you pick the rest of your team as you see fit, with the exception of Nalmari here. She shall be your *Dve*. As your second-in-command, she can help you learn the requirements of your role." She waved a hand at the woman to Bial's left. "Does that suit?"

"Yes, Majesty," Emmory said, because it was really the only answer he could give.

"Then swear on your lives."

"I swear, Your Imperial Majesty," Emmory replied. Zin echoed him just a moment later.

"Good. It is done then."

"Your Majesty." Bial was choosing his words carefully. "Tresk is an accomplished Tracker, a fine officer of the empire, but he has not been trained—" He broke off when Mother raised a hand.

"Nalmari can be his *Dve*, as we said. We are sure whatever gaps there may be in his outstanding abilities can be filled in quickly by a competent second-in-command."

"Majesty, it is traditionally improper to have a man guard the princess—"

"*Don't* argue with us, Bial," she snapped.

"I would never, Your Majesty."

"Good." She swayed in her seat for a moment, and I stopped myself from jumping forward. Mother closed her eyes, her face paling until the skin on her cheeks was like old paper. She opened her eyes and fixed them on me. They were fever bright.

"Your sisters have gone to temple, Hailimi. Best that you go clean up and present yourself to the priests. We will speak with you again at a decent hour." She rose from the throne with difficulty, grasping Bial's offered hand and using it to steady herself.

"Mother, I—"

I stopped myself, swallowing back the rest of the sentence, but it was too late.

"Your sisters have gone to temple." Now the cold, royal voice I'd always hated came from my mother's mouth. "Two loyal daughters lost to us. All we have left is one unfit, ungrateful daughter who wished to see the universe more than she loved her own flesh and blood. You are a disgrace to the *sahotra*. Know that we didn't want you back, but you are all we have left. Go see the fruits of your selfishness."

Her words punched the air out of my lungs, and I bit the inside of my cheek to keep from screaming as my mother turned her back on me and walked away.

6

I stared after my mother, my thoughts whirling as madly as Hassin Dervishes. Telling me I was a disgrace to the family wasn't a surprise, but it shouldn't have stung quite as much as it did.

Welcome home, Hail.

I was fucked. Completely and totally fucked. With two Trackers as my BodyGuards, the odds of me escaping once I'd dealt with my sisters' murderers had just dropped into the Underworld.

You gave your word anyway, remember? Or at least Emmory thinks you did. The voice in my head seemed pretty amused by my panicked thoughts and not at all shy in reminding me what I'd said to Emmory onboard the ship.

I promised to return home and do my duty. Just because my idea of duty and his were different didn't mean anything. But my new *Ekam* had done his research before he retrieved me. Promises might not mean much here at home—in fact, I was pretty sure that in the upper echelons of Indranan society people prided themselves on the lies they could tell and the promises they could break.

The world I'd grown up in was different. The gunrunners

who'd taken me in as family had a better sense of honor than any of the royal blood of Indrana and they'd instilled it in me.

The question was, which side did I count myself a part of: gunrunner or princess? It was with no small sense of irony that I felt guilty about the intent behind my promise.

"Your Imperial Highness, allow me to present myself." The voice of my *Dve* had the musical lilt of one of the island nations on the far side of the planet.

I turned to look into a pair of warm brown eyes. Nalmari bowed, all trace of her shock now hidden, and I hid my racing panic with equal skill.

Welcome home to the world where no one says what they mean or allows their emotions to show.

That was fine. I didn't need it. Court life was brutal, but it still maintained some semblance of civility. In my world— the world in which I'd spent the last twenty years—you either learned how to read people quickly or you died.

"I am Nalmari Zaafir Windhausen," she continued, bowing again with her eyes locked on the floor at my feet. The good news about this particular custom meant I could study her with impunity for a few seconds.

I eyed my second-in-command BodyGuard as my instincts set up a chorus of alarm bells.

Her shoulders were tense, for one. Now this could be a result of the shock of her sudden demotion, or it could be from something else. She looked earnest enough on the outside, but there had been a flicker of something unpleasant lurking in her eyes before the politeness dropped into place. At the moment, though, I was inclined to give her the benefit of the doubt.

Tradition held that the *Ekam* of the empress was male. My ancestor-grandmother's twin brother had miraculously avoided the Shakti dementia and taken over the role of protecting her when her husband died. The practice held throughout the years. The *Ekams* of the royal children were always female. No doubt my mother had thought to insult me by saddling me with a male *Ekam* instead.

She couldn't have known that it was probably my best hope for survival to have Emmory as my *Ekam*. I was suddenly grateful for my Trackers' presence. Maybe I couldn't trust them fully, but I could trust them more than anyone else in the palace.

"Nalmari." I dipped my head in greeting. I could play along with whatever game was under way here at the palace. I could also take this woman apart if it became necessary. I didn't need anyone to protect me. "I trust you know where my quarters are."

If she was put off by my liquid nitrogen tone, she didn't give me the satisfaction of showing it. "Of course, Your Highness. This way."

"You walk with me." I caught Emmory by the arm before he could fall into step with Nalmari. Zin took his place, his hand brushing over Emmory's forearm as though to reassure himself they were still together. Emmory met his gaze with a slight nod.

I let them get ahead of us before I spoke. "How deep are we in this?"

"I don't know, Highness. You rest first, then we'll deal with whatever we need to as it arises."

"Actually, first we need to go say good-bye to my sisters."

Emmory nodded sharply. We crossed the throne room, exiting out the same door as my mother. The plain steel hid behind a garish tapestry of white and gold, and I felt a bit claustrophobic as we left the massive, high-ceilinged room for the narrow corridor leading to the family wing.

Here in the enclosed space the familiar smell of sandalwood and Olbivai honey was stronger. The hand-rolled incense stuck in the brass holder threw lazy loops of smoke into the air beneath the statue of Nataraja. The base of the statue was buried in deep red flowers called *kislana*, which were similar to the Earth lotus.

I noticed that all three of my BodyGuards touched the statue and murmured prayers as we passed. Rolling my eyes, I resisted the urge to point out that none of Shiva's incarnations had done fuck all to keep my sisters safe. Instead I settled for giving the dancing god a cold look and headed on down the hallway.

The edges of my cloak brushed over the hand-painted tiles, dragging up memories better left floating in space with *Sophie's* remains. We passed servants who dropped into low bows and curtsies with murmurs of "Your Imperial Highness," but otherwise they went about their duties without paying me much heed.

I counted steps to keep myself from going insane. Seven hundred and eighteen steps later, Nalmari stopped outside a wooden door I knew was lined with polysteel. She pressed her palm to the panel set in the plastered wall, and gave Emmory an almost defiant look. "They expected me to—"

"It's all right, Nal," Emmory said, holding up a hand. "We'll get it sorted out."

Nalmari nodded, her dreads jerking with the movement, and looked at me. "If you will, Princess? So the computer can code your new readings."

I pressed my hand to the panel, felt it grow warm under my palm, and the door clicked open. Nal and Zin went in. I started to follow, only to be brought up short by Emmory's hand on my arm.

"You really want to find out what happens when you grab me again?" I asked dryly.

"When you learn to wait, I won't have to do it anymore. I'm your *Ekam*, and I'll grab you if it means keeping you safe. You're a princess, not a gunrunner," he countered. "Let your BodyGuards check it out first, Highness."

"They're my rooms!" I stared at him in shock. "If I'm not safe here—"

"Your sisters were murdered, Highness, one of them potentially in her rooms. Right now our job is to assume nothing is safe." He cut me off with a wave of his gloved hand. "Now will you stop arguing with me so I can listen?"

"If you stop calling me Highness every five minutes."

He gave me a flat look. I snapped my mouth shut, crossed my arms over my chest, and lapsed into silence. Several long moments later, Nalmari emerged with a nod.

"It's clear. You may enter, Princess." She gestured at the open door. I stepped past both of them into my quarters, barely resisting the urge to slam the door in their faces.

These weren't my old rooms—the ones I'd shared with my sisters—instead Mother had put me on the far side of the wing, in a suite of rooms normally reserved for visiting family.

Cute.

The doorway opened into a short, narrow hallway designed for ease of defense by only a BodyGuard or two. That hallway led to a wide, sprawling room with massive windows. One of the windows was open and I could hear the waves of the ocean roaring beneath the howling wind. A shimmering force field that kept the weather out and the heat in made its presence known only by the occasional ping of sleet that struck it, sending circles of blue belling outward across the surface.

A fire crackled in the copper-lined fireplace; I smoothed a hand over the rose quartz mantel, the stone warm to the touch from the heat of the fire. This palace had been built from the ground up with materials from Earth, and even after our break with the Solarian Conglomerate some twenty-five hundred years ago, we still bought materials from them for repairs. As far as I was concerned, tradition made people do silly things.

Three doorways led from the main room. I tossed cursory glances into the two bedrooms, but it was the bathroom that drew my attention.

A wide wooden tub, the polished surface dark against the cool blue paint above it, dominated the room, and a shower, lined in the same wood, was tucked into the corner. A low counter ran under a wide mirror, and a gleaming copper bowl stood on the far end under a spout that came directly from that slate-tiled wall. Behind another door was the toilet, and there was a connecting door to the larger of the two bedrooms.

I leaned over the tub, pressing a few buttons in the panel set just above it. Water began to bubble up from the bottom, and the air filled with the smell of eucalyptus and lemons.

Wandering back out into the main room, I caught the tail end of a conversation between Emmory and Nal.

"I'm assuming the empress had some people tasked for BodyGuard duty when she received the news that the princess was coming home. I'd like the files on them and get them into the BodyGuard quarters next door. I want to meet with them," Emmory said.

"Now?"

"Of course now."

Nalmari recoiled from the derisive lash of Emmory's voice, drawing herself up with a hiss of offended breath.

"The princess's safety won't wait for the sunrise, Nal. I need to be able to make a decision for a core team within the hour. Go get it done."

I watched her eyes narrow and her mouth thin. The hair on the back of my neck stood to attention as she saluted and walked out the door. My Trackers watched her leave, and shared a look.

"I'm going to clean up," I said.

"Highness."

I paused, but didn't turn back to Emmory. "Yes?"

"At the risk of being forward, I dislike the feel of this." His voice was soft, and my skin prickled at his admission. It was an odd thing for him to say and I wondered if it felt as forced as it sounded to my ears. We were stuck in roles as unsuited to our personalities as could be imagined.

He'd been right on the ship—I didn't have any choice but to trust him. It helped that my own intuition was screaming right now. "I'm right there with you," I replied.

"Zin will be here if you need anything. I'll be next door."

I raised a hand then continued into the bathroom and shut the door behind me. Scrubbing both hands over my face, I muttered a furious curse. The twist in my stomach became a vicious knot that lunged up and wrapped around my heart, its sharp wire teeth biting deep.

My heart shredded as the wire snapped taut. I didn't even try to stop the moan of agony that ripped through the air. My knees gave out and I sank to the floor, grief dragging sobs from me in painful gasps. I was grateful for the sound of running water to conceal my weeping as I wrapped my arms around my waist and curled into a ball.

They were gone. Really and truly gone. Mother's dementia would kill her. Portis was gone. Hao would probably kill me on sight if he saw me again for lying to him. I was orphaned.

Keep it together, Hail.

I didn't want to keep it together. I just wanted to hide in here until it all went away and I woke up back on *Sophie*.

It's not a nightmare. Pull your shit together. You can't come at this like some rookie. There was Hao again, reaching across space to slap some sense into me. It was thanks to him as much as Portis that I was still alive. They'd gotten me out of more scrapes and tight spots until I figured out how to do it for myself. He'd

75

taught me everything he knew, treated me with a patience he never showed to anyone else, and then had let me go to explore the universe on my own without a single word of protest.

He'd also never hesitated to kick my ass when it was called for and now it seemed like he was reaching across the stars to pull me up short.

You have a job to do here and dead sisters you should pay your respects to. I've never seen you back down from anything. Don't disappoint me now.

Toeing off my boots, I pushed to my feet, stripped, and tossed my clothes into the corner. A quick rinse off in the shower, and then I sank into the bath. The heat flooded through me. Closing my eyes, I rested my head back on the edge and let the water ease my tension.

The first order of business was to get hooked back up to the palace network. Until that happened, I was floating around blind. Of course, linking back into the palace would be both a blessing and a curse. I'd get instant updates about news across the universe without having to link into a news server. I could call up the names of people I encountered with just a thought.

But I'd be traceable. Linked to my BodyGuards, to the damn palace. Hell, probably to the planet. Emmory would have access to my vital signs as would the rest of my team.

A thrice-damned gilded cage. The development of the Brain Computer Interface started on Old Earth, before the SC, even before we hit the stars with serious intent. An array of five microscopic chips inserted into key areas of the brain used our own neurons and pathways as power and conduits to create a permanent interface. The BCI was a triumph of science.

Like most triumphs, it jumped the gun. The first versions were glitchy, prone to hacks, and something like the original spaceflight vessels. Far too bulky and dangerous.

Still, I had little problem believing that people jumped at the chance. The chance to increase one's cognitive abilities, to have instant recall of anything stored on your home system. For the ability to call or contact anyone just by thinking about it. Or to take a photo with the blink of an eye.

The SC called the tech NeuroNet after the antiquated Internet system on Earth. The Cheng called it simply *zhù*. The Indranan Empire called it *smati*.

My cyberware was better than average, possibly not as good as Emmory's military-grade ware, but still a damn sight better than most of the thugs I'd done business with over the years.

"No time like the present." I took a deep breath and connected. The network freaked on me for a few seconds as it tried to reconcile my new information with the data that had once been logged for Princess Hailimi, but someone had been on the ball, and after a moment it accepted my DNA log-in. Just like that I had access to the palace.

A lot of access, my gunrunner brain realized a little gleefully, and I had to shake some sense back into myself. We'd gotten ourselves into so much trouble at times, my sisters and I, when we'd been kids until Dad had locked down our access to the palace network.

I pinched the bridge of my nose, staving off the inevitable tears and grabbing for the towel by the side of the tub. "You're alone, Hail. Just suck it up and deal with it instead of flailing around like a useless git."

I dressed myself without much conscious thought, grabbing at the appropriate pieces with numb hands and somehow completing impossible tasks like minuscule buttons and side laces without the help of a maid. I was amazed everything fit, but my amusement turned to grief when I realized Portis must have passed my measurements on to someone here as they prepared for my return home.

I came out of the bedroom dressed in a blood-red corset, my skirts a wide circle of embroidered fabric in the same hue. A sari trimmed in golden tassels hid my hair, wound itself around my throat and waist, and hung down the back of my skirts.

My lips were painted crimson-gold, and a stain of black cut across my face, over my eyes. I'd had to fix the paint three times because of the damn tears.

The seven women and men sitting in my main room stared for a stunned moment—even my Trackers seemed shocked—before they scrambled to their feet and bowed to me as a unit.

"Highness." Emmory's dark eyes were unreadable.

"I go to temple to see my sisters," I said formally.

Emmory dipped his head, replying with equal formality, "I go with you, Highness. Zin, Cas, Jet, you will join us. Nal, you and the others get settled and see to the things we've discussed here."

My *smati* recognized the men as Emmory pointed at them. The baby-faced blond was Cas, and the man with the hard slate eyes was Jet.

Gesturing for me to follow the younger Guard out the door, Emmory moved into the space at my side with such ease that for a moment I found it hard to believe we hadn't been doing this my whole life.

If we had, maybe my sisters would still be alive. I clenched my hands against the guilt, wondering just what my Body-Guards would do if I put one of my fists into the mirror as we passed it.

"Are you all right, Highness?"

I managed to keep the burst of laughter in check, knowing it would sound hysterical. "Oh, I'm just lovely, *Ekam*. How are you?"

That earned me a look from Emmory. I ignored it and continued down the corridor.

We moved through the corridors, and I felt like I was floating through a dream—disconnected and disbelieving. The few servants out at this hour bowed out of my way, their eyes locked on the floor at my feet as I passed.

The family's private entrance to the temple was draped with filmy curtains of white gauze. They were streaked with red, signs that my sisters' journey was still within the three-moon mourning period.

The incense-laden air hit me like a slap as we passed through the curtain, the soft, everyday scent giving way to the heavier local Nag Champa. A red-robed priest met us at the bottom of the stairs. He bowed to me.

"Princess." It was Father Westinkar, his aged face grooved even more deeply than I remembered. The black mourning powder coating his eyes sank into the crevasses of his lined face—so dark against the paleness of his skin.

I didn't say a word, wasn't allowed to speak until I'd paid my respects. So I swallowed down the things I wanted to scream, and they burned like bile in my throat. Folding my hands, I pressed them to my forehead and bowed to him in return.

Emmory whispered orders to the other two Guards, then he and Zin followed me up the marble staircase into the temple itself.

Chanting floated on the air with the incense. A lone female voice, hidden somewhere among the carved and painted columns stretching back toward the altar, sang of loss with such aching clarity it cracked my heart.

Seeing the trio of clear caskets lined up on the altar broke it apart entirely. My sisters' faces were so peaceful and pristine, they couldn't be real. Ami looked like an exact copy of her mother. They were obviously holograms, digital projections for bodies that had been rotted away by a virus or reduced to vapor and ash by an explosion.

Just like Father. Gone. Erased from existence. It's too fucking easy.

"Mother Destroyer." I stumbled, catching my boot tip on the hem of my stupid skirt. Zin and Emmory both grabbed for an arm, keeping me from falling on my face. A wail struggled for freedom in my chest and I fought against it with a choked sob.

"Easy, Your Highness." Zin's voice was low, gentle.

"How could you have let this happen?" It wasn't a fair question. Neither of these men had been responsible for my sisters' safety.

Emmory, surprisingly, didn't chastise me as he released my arm. Neither did Zin. They didn't answer me because there wasn't an answer to be had.

I sank before the rows of flickering candles, the little lights throwing shadows through the multitude of colored glass holders. My hand shook as I lit a wax-coated stick and moved it to a row of unlit candles. I lit one, two, three. A blue for Cire. A green for Pace. And a white for the niece whose favorite color I would never know.

Pressing my hands to my eyes, I let the grief come. Now at least I could allow the scream that had been building in me to fly free.

It rolled out of my throat, bouncing off the marbled floor and shooting up into the gossamer web of the ceiling. There it stuck, quivering like a trapped fly, and I sent a second to a similar fate. I balled my hands into fists, feeling my blunt nails cut into my palms as I screamed a third and fourth time— inarticulate curses thrown like a gauntlet at the gods. My fifth scream trailed off into sobbing and I slumped back, exhausted.

The flames danced in front of me, oblivious to my grief. I

put a hand out, and watched the light flicker off my palm. It glimmered on the streaks of black and red. My blood mixing with the mourning powder. Heat prickled, then stung when I dropped my hand lower.

"I was not here," I murmured as the pain built. "Forgive me for being so selfish. I should have been here. I should have kept you safe."

Emmory closed his hand on my wrist, dragging it away from the flame. I jerked, staring up at him with tear-blurred eyes, and could have sworn I saw some sympathy hovering in his face. I'd forgotten they were there, standing guard still and silent.

"Enough, Highness. Your sisters are gone. It is done, but it was no fault of yours. Lay the blame where it belongs with those who did the horrible deed."

I pulled away from him—or rather tried to, but his grip on my wrist remained and I only ended up tugging him down toward me. "I want blood, Emmory. Do you hear me? I want the ones responsible at my fucking feet begging for mercy that will never come." I gritted out the last words, the hatred in them tearing at my throat like splintered glass.

He opened his mouth, but something in my face stopped him and instead he turned my hand over, scanning my burnt palm with calm dark eyes. Whatever he saw satisfied him and he let me go. "Yes, ma'am."

"Princess." Father Westinkar emerged from the shadows, his hands folded inside the voluminous sleeves of his crimson robe. "Have you paid your respects?"

"I have. Father—" I got to my feet. "It has been a long time."

"Too long, my child. I've missed you." Westinkar wrapped me in a hug. I buried my face against his shoulder and wept.

7

In what my mother had said was one more indication of my poor judgment, I'd always been fond of the priest who was in charge of the family temple at night. Since I was a member of the royal family, it would have been more proper for me to associate with the Mother Superior, but I—and my sisters—found a better connection with the kindly old man than the stiff and oh-so-formal head of the Indranan Church.

I couldn't afford to let my grief show for long and clung to the old priest for only a moment before I released him and stepped away.

"Father, what is going on?"

Black eyes flicked to my BodyGuards and then nervously back to me. "Not in the open, child. Even in this temple the things said reach more ears than just the gods'."

Translation: We were being watched. But by whom?

"Highness, we should go." Emmory's voice was pitched low and his hand was on my arm. Again.

I reacted without thinking, managing only at the last second to change from a jaw-breaking punch to an open-handed slap.

Mourning powder mixed with the blood from my palm glittered in a streak over his skin like diamonds on satin.

Emmory didn't react. Zin gaped at us, the look on his face clear that he was torn between defending his partner or keeping his mouth shut.

I was going to have to apologize for this anyway, so I settled on the option most likely to make anyone watching think I was still a spoiled princess, even after all my time away.

"I haven't asked for your counsel, *Ekam*, and *you* do not order me around."

Father Westinkar also looked between us, his black eyes wide in his wrinkled face. I kept my gaze locked on Emmory until he dropped his head in a barely civil bow I hoped was an act.

"My apologies, Highness," he said, raising his head. "I am concerned for your safety."

"Be as concerned as you want, Emmory. I have known Father Westinkar my whole life. He will not harm me. From now on, unless I'm actually in danger...you keep your hands to yourself."

"Yes, Highness."

I smiled at Father Westinkar and looped my arm through his, walking him away from my sisters' bodies and toward the fountain on the far side of the temple. The water should hide our conversation. "I'm sorry, Father. We're still working out the kinks in the chain of command."

The old priest's mouth twitched as though he was holding in a burst of laughter. Then he sobered, and said, "Before she lost her voice, Pace asked me to give you this—when you came home." He held out the charm suspended on a silver chain, a polished piece of shell wrapped in silver. It had a pearly sheen, and a thin spiral decorated the surface.

For an instant the world narrowed down to the space around the gently swinging necklace. I froze in the act of reaching for it, a thousand thoughts colliding in my head, all of them screaming for precedence. I took it, blinking away the image of my sister's face, and hugged Westinkar again.

"Thank you."

"When was the last time you spoke to a priest?"

"The day before I left home when I came to see you."

That wasn't technically true. A drunken, excommunicated cleric from the Holy Roman Republic was the last priest I'd talked with some six months ago, but I was pretty sure that wasn't what Father Westinkar meant since our conversation revolved around how the man had been dishonorably discharged for leaving his post during a firefight.

"There is more I must tell you, but we need to be careful." His whispered words were right against my ear and I stiffened.

"Highness, we should go." Emmory didn't grab me, but he was hovering so close I could feel his warmth through the heavy fabric of my sari.

I pulled away from Father Westinkar and looped the silver chain around my wrist so that it tangled with the leather already in place. Folding my hands, I bowed to him. "Thank you, Father."

He laid a gnarled hand on my head. "Bless you, child. I know you have had a long journey. I am sure the Mother Superior won't mind if I excuse you from Light Mass this morning."

I nodded, not trusting myself to speak, and with a final bow, turned and walked away.

The other BodyGuards were absent when we got back to my rooms. This time I stood quietly in the hallway with Cas and Zin while Emmory and Jet checked out the premises. When the all-clear sounded, I brushed past them all and headed for my bedroom without looking up.

I closed the door with a snap, cursed at my empty room as images replayed themselves, and jerked it back open.

"You two, in here."

"Highness, I apologize—"

"Stow it, Emmory. You're only apologizing because Zin just elbowed you," I said with a laugh. "Close the door." Turning my back on them, I unwound the sari. The patterns woven into the fabric caught my fingertips and I traced them absently as I stared unseeing at the floor and tried to collect my thoughts.

Rock and a fucking hard place, Cressen. Get a hammer.

"Or a plasma pistol," I muttered under my breath.

"Highness?"

"Sorry. Are we clear here? Or is someone listening in?" I shook my head and folded the fabric over a hanger, smoothing the wrinkles out to give my hands something to do.

"We're clear, Highness." Emmory turned his palms up, revealing the jamming device lodged in the wrist of his glove. It was flashing a series of green lights. "I haven't had a chance to check out all the surveillance on your rooms, but for now I can ensure at least a few minutes of privacy."

"I'm the one who needs to apologize. I'm sorry I hit you."

"It was your right, Highness."

"Oh, cowshit," I tossed back at him and he raised an eyebrow at me. "I'm on a hair trigger here and hit you because you grabbed me. I shouldn't have, you're trying to do your job, and it's my job to make that easier, not harder."

"I figured as much."

It was my turn for an eyebrow. A smile flickered at the corner of Emmory's mouth and then vanished.

"I did apologize because Zin elbowed me, Highness. I realized what you were doing when you slapped me instead of punched me. Zin didn't. Close your mouth and keep up." He reached out and tapped Zin's chin.

"I hate you both," Zin muttered, then flushed. "I'm sorry, Highness, I didn't mean—"

I raised a hand, cutting him off. "I need something from you two. I know offering unsolicited advice is against your nature, but—" I cocked an eyebrow at Zin's suspicious coughing fit. "I need you to be honest with me. This isn't going to work otherwise. We're soldiers, you and I. I need truth from you. Show me deference in public, whatever you need to do to play with these cowshit societal expectations of men keeping their mouths shut, but in private, I need to know you're not just agreeing with me to be polite."

Emmory, unsurprisingly, didn't even blink. "Done, Highness." He glanced at Zin and the pair shared one of those silent conversations that longtime partners often have. Zin nodded at me in wordless agreement.

"I need to get up to speed. I've been gone for a long time." I blew out a breath and forced a smile. "Which—" I stopped when Emmory raised a hand.

"Highness, Bial is here. Cas said he's asking to see you," Emmory said.

Sleep was apparently not in the cards right now. I hung up my sari in the wardrobe and started for the main room, but Zin stopped me with a half smile and a circle of his hand around his face. "Bad?" I asked and he nodded.

"I'll clean up. Have Bial wait in the main room. Are we sure he's not asking to see Emmory?"

"Yes, Highness," Emmory said, heading for the door. "Take your time. He can wait."

I didn't dawdle, but I did make sure every trace of my smeared makeup was off my face before I came into the main room.

And found myself facing not Bial, but Matriarch Desai, Dr. Satir, and a man my *smati* labeled as Prime Minister Phanin.

Zin and Jet were in the room, as was Nal. Emmory wasn't anywhere in sight, and since Cas was absent, I assumed my baby-faced Guard was getting his ass chewed for not telling Emmory how many people were actually at the door and for not announcing the matriarch properly.

Awkward.

Equally awkward was the fact that one of the matriarch's BodyGuards had come into my rooms with her and stood at her side with her hand on her gun. Nal was blank-faced over the obvious breech of protocol, but my other two Guards wore looks of stone-faced fury.

Bial and Emmory came into the room, my *Ekam*'s jaw tight as he crossed to me. I glanced his way only briefly, folding my arms over my chest and flicking my gaze at the others one by one. I finished, deliberately, on Desai's BodyGuard. Gun or no gun, I could take the young woman apart and we both knew it. I let a smile spread over my face and everyone except the Guards at my back shifted uncomfortably.

"So we're starting things off on the wrong foot bringing armed Guards into my living quarters. Emmory, an explanation?"

"I objected, Highness."

"And I overruled him, Princess," Bial said, somehow managing to make my title almost an insult. "The matriarch's Guard insisted on accompanying her and I felt—given your history—it was for the best."

I was a little startled that the choked-off snarls behind me were from both Zin and Emmory, but thankfully neither of them spoke.

I laughed. "That was a neatly dressed insult, Bial. But we don't need to stand on ceremony here; you can just say it's because I used to be a gunrunner."

Twitching my skirts out of the way, I took two steps until I was in his face. "It's the truth, so it's not much of an insult as they go. You know what insults me more? That you think you had the right to overrule my *Ekam* when it came to my personal safety and break the law by allowing someone armed into my fucking living quarters." I dropped my voice to a whisper and watched him flinch. "Don't fool yourself into thinking I am some uncultured gunrunner. Where I have been and what I have been doing since I left home haven't changed my blood. I am a Bristol, a princess of the empire. Don't think that I don't know the laws that were hammered into my head from before I would walk. And don't think, for one second, that I won't hesitate to shoot you myself if you break them again. Am I understood?"

"Yes, Highness."

"Good. I'm going to assume we don't actually need you for anything. Get out of my rooms."

"Princess Hailimi." Clara Desai, an older woman built like a DLine pro-baller, smiled and folded her hands together as she bowed. I remembered being terrified of her as a child and how Mother would frequently threaten to bring Desai in to discipline us if we wouldn't behave.

Clara was the head of the Matriarch Council, the fourteen women—one from each of the founding families—who would approve me as heir.

"Matriarch Desai." I dipped my head. "With my apologies, we can either move this meeting to another venue, or for the sake of my *Ekam*'s blood pressure, I'm going to have to insist the law is upheld. Your BodyGuard can either leave or present her weapons to my man at the door."

Clara studied me for a moment, her eyes dark in a smooth face that belied her age, and then nodded. "Trisa, wait outside, please."

"Ma'am—"

"Don't argue with me. I'd like to think at least one of the BodyGuards in the room is capable of following orders without fussing over it. I'm perfectly safe, and I'm sure the prime minister will jump to my defense if necessary."

The man on Clara's other side was as tall as I was but didn't look like much of a threat. His graying hair lay short to his scalp in what seemed to be the latest fashion of the empire. His white kurta and black pants were plain but cut from expensive fabric. He swallowed nervously, looking between me and Clara like a rabbit trapped between two wolves.

Trisa left the room, but not after shooting me one last look. I just grinned and rubbed my hands together. "Dr. Satir, it's been a long time," I said.

Dr. Satir's smile creased her weathered face. "Welcome home, Your Highness. It is a great blessing to see you well."

"Highness, if you'll allow me to present to you Prime Minister Eha Phanin," Clara said.

The Assembly General was open to anyone via a public election held every five years for one-third of the assembly. The prime minister was elected from the ranks of the AG by popular vote. It was a position that, admittedly, had little influence and was more a way for the ruling class to keep an eye on the mood of the rest of the populace. In a world ruled by women, the majority of the assembly was female so it was a bit of a surprise to see Phanin in the position.

And it didn't explain why the man was here now.

"Your Imperial Highness." The bow was elegant for a man with no noble blood, perfectly executed.

I hated him immediately. Worse, I couldn't put my finger on exactly why. Something about the man made my skin crawl. My reaction wasn't fair in the slightest, and I stepped down hard on my snarky reply. "Prime Minister, it's a pleasure."

"I wish I could say the same, Highness."

Emmory shifted in front of me and I found myself wishing again for a weapon. *Twice in ten minutes. Welcome home, Hail. Bugger it all.*

But Clara held her hands up. "Apologies, Highness, *Ekam*. For a politician, Phanin can be entirely too blunt at times."

"I prefer blunt and given the hour…"

"Yes, of course, you've had a long day. You know of the empress's issue?"

"She's got space madness."

"Yes, Ven noticed some odd changes in her behavior and brought it to the attention of the Crown Princess. Your sister had Dr. Satir run the tests, and when the answer came back, she decided it would be in the empress's best interests not to let her know."

"Sometimes the knowledge of the diagnosis can make the disease progress faster," Dr. Satir added. "When the news leaked to the public this morning, though, I informed the empress of her diagnosis. We are doing what we can to stop the spread, but it is difficult."

"Plans were under way to convince your empress-mother to abdicate the throne to Cire, but then—"

"My sisters were murdered."

"Yes, Highness." Clara frowned and bowed her head. Not fast enough for me to miss the uneasiness in her eyes and I braced myself even as I asked the question.

"So what's the plan now?"

"Mostly unchanged, Highness." It was Phanin who answered me. "Since your sister was unsure if you would come home, it was decided to follow the line of succession and name your cousin Ganda as next in line. Since the chaos she has been handling the day-to-day issues for the empire when it is obvious the empress cannot keep her normal schedule." Phanin bowed his head. "Now that you are home, things will, of course, change."

I swallowed down my hatred, and it burned all the way into the pit of my stomach. Ganda Naidu was my cousin, the eldest daughter of my uncle. Succession through the paternal line wasn't ideal, but it was better than nothing if the family wanted to hold on to the throne.

The fact that I hated the spoiled, treacherous, conniving brat didn't really factor into succession protocol.

Especially since everyone else loved Ganda.

She was the ideal princess. Prim and proper. She smiled when required and kept her mouth shut the rest of the time. As kids we'd tangled repeatedly and I'd always come out on the losing end because no one realized what a snake she was.

Tell them, Hail, the voice in my head screamed. *Just tell them to let Ganda keep doing what she's doing and you'll get out of their way. You don't want to be heir. You can go back to your life.*

Back to my life without Portis.

My heart broke again, falling out of my chest and shattering on the rose quartz hearth at my feet.

"Well—" The word came out rough and I had to clear my throat and start again. "Yes, I'm back. So Ganda can go back to whatever it was she was doing before she got dragged into this. I'm sure she'll be relieved."

"Of course, Highness." Phanin bowed again. "I will see to it."

"You'll need someone to organize your schedule for you. I can send you several candidates for a chamberlain if you'd like to choose yourself?" Clara asked.

"I'd like that very much. Thank you."

"I realize it will probably take you several days to get up to speed. If it is acceptable, we'll keep Ganda on her scheduled appearances for this week."

I nodded again. "Yes, that's fine."

"We'll leave you then. Sleep well, Highness."

"Matriarch, if I might beg a moment of your time?" Emmory held up a hand with a quick bow of his head. "In the excitement of the princess's return home, something was overlooked. If you wouldn't mind witnessing for us, it would be appreciated."

At Clara's nod, the door opened and my BodyGuards filed in—or what Guards had been collected so far. They were a motley group, some still in street clothes, others in military uniforms of various branches.

"Highness," Emmory said, and I managed somehow not to let my mouth fall open when he dropped to a knee in front of me. "We didn't do this properly," he said, taking my hands. He'd removed his gloves, and the hard calluses of his palm scraped over my equally rough knuckles.

Gunrunning didn't give a girl ladylike hands.

"Didn't do what properly?" I asked warily.

He smiled and the brief flash of emotion showed his dimple. He composed himself, looked right into my eyes, and spoke, "Hailimi Mercedes Jaya Bristol—I swear my loyalty to you. Your life I will defend until my last breath if there is need."

I stiffened when the formal words of the BodyGuard oath hit me with all the force of a sledgehammer swung by one of those muscle-bound guys at the circus. Emmory tightened his hand over both of mine, holding them in place when I tried to pull away.

"I give myself willingly to you, Heir to the Throne of Indrana. You are the shining stars in the blackness of space. The hope of the lost and forsaken. The spark that must not be extinguished. So I pledge myself to you—loyal subject, protector, and BodyGuard."

"Gods help you." The comment slipped out and I bit my tongue with a mental swear.

Emmory was unfazed by my rudeness. He smiled, releasing my hands. "Yes, gods help me, Highness." Then he sobered, the amusement sliding away like the rain off the windowpanes. "Gods help all of us."

Before I could say anything else, Nal had taken Emmory's place. She recited the oath in a clear voice, though the words were devoid of any emotion at all. One after another the Guards followed suit, until at last Zin slowly lowered himself to a knee and took my hand.

His hands were cooler than Emmory's had been as he folded them over mine and repeated the oath without ever taking his eyes off me.

Zin's hands tightened briefly as he got to his feet.

"Very well done." Matriarch Desai nodded in approval. "Good night, Highness. I'm sure I'll see you soon."

Hating the arrogance of the gesture, I waved a hand toward the door and turned to the windows. I couldn't have said anything if I'd wanted to. Not without breaking down into tears. I heard Emmory's voice mixing with Clara's and then silence as the door closed.

My *Ekam* hadn't left me alone, though. He reappeared at my side as I was wiping the tears from my cheeks with the palm of my hand.

"I'd like to pull a few candidates for your chamberlain position and do a background sweep on the ones Matriarch Desai sends over."

"Agreed." I'd be spending a lot of time with my chamberlain and I'd need to be able to trust her. "Speaking of backgrounds, what do you know about Phanin?"

"Very little. He was elected two years ago. Seems to have done a decent job as prime minister."

"Odd that he was here tonight."

"Not as such, Highness. Princess Cire did quite a bit of work to make the prime minister more involved in the day-to-day affairs of the empire. She felt it kept her more in touch with the people."

I was wiped, and even though he wasn't showing it, I figured Emmory was at least as tired as I was. "What have we waded into here, Emmy?"

"I don't know." He wasn't prevaricating or trying to placate me. As hard as Emmory was for me to read, I was able to figure out that much from his open stance. "I think it is suspicious enough to have the empress's *Ekam*, two of her daughters, and a granddaughter die within two months of each other. Even without all the other troubles facing the empire, that spells trouble of the worst kind."

I whirled away from the window. "Ven is dead?" More crushing anguish landed on my shoulders at Emmory's solemn nod.

Scattered memories of Mother's *Ekam* rushed through me—his bright smile and a laugh that rolled on the air like colored candy falling off a scoop, the way his face went from open to deadly the day someone from the *Upjas* had tried to kidnap Pace. The time he and Father had found me trapped in that tunnel—I shuddered and fought the memory off.

"Ofa? Tefiz? You said she'd sent Portis after me."

My *Ekam* and *Dve* had been a wife-and-wife team. I'd looked to Ofa like a mother when my own was too cold and royal, but it'd been Tefiz I'd really bonded with. The thought that either had been punished for my flight from home was almost too much to bear.

"They were both officially dismissed, Highness, but still on the BodyGuard payroll—tasked with keeping tabs on you after you left home. They were in the aircar with Ven when the accident occurred."

"Still dead then, just not my doing." Grief welled up again. "I don't trust Bial. Do you know him?"

"Not now, Highness. You need your sleep." Emmory headed for the doorway with Zin on his heels. "I'll find out what I can and we'll talk about it in the daylight."

I sighed and reached behind me for the ties of my corset as I headed for the bedroom.

"Highness, will you need assistance with that?"

"Are you offering?" I watched in the mirror as he paused, and a dark eyebrow arched upward.

"I'll call a maid, Highness."

"I don't need—" I stopped at his look and sighed. "Call a maid. I honestly have no idea how I managed to get into it in the first place."

"That doesn't surprise me," he said and continued out the door.

8

The sun was shining in through the stained glass of my bedroom windows when I awoke the next morning. Exhaustion had dragged me into a dreamless sleep, and I felt a little more like myself as I stretched.

A riot of colors danced over the white linens, and I lay for a moment on my back, tracing my fingers through wavering diamonds of green and blue.

It reminded me of the waters on Calpis VII, a resort planet we'd stayed at once after a successful drop-off. After several months with Hao, and a brutal induction into Po-Sin's employ, it had been our first big score as official members. We'd spent a blissful week soaking in the warm waters and dozing on the pink sand.

It was there, floating in the waves, that Portis had told me he loved me for the first time. I could still remember with painful clarity how gentle he'd been that night. How his hands swept over my skin, followed by his mouth, shooting trails of fire through me. We'd gotten along so well, right from the beginning, and now I knew it was because he had known exactly who I was.

"I miss you, you bastard," I whispered.

"Your Imperial Highness? Are you awake?" My new maid, Stasia, poked her head into the room. Her golden curls bounced merrily around a cherub-like face.

"Come on in," I replied, sliding from the four-poster bed and padding across the floor. The moment was gone and there wasn't any point in terrorizing the girl just for having bad timing.

The satin wood covered a complex system of water pipes that kept the floors warm in the winter seasons and cool in the summer. I sighed at the heat under my bare feet.

I'd forgotten about little luxuries like this. *Sophie*'s always-freezing steel floors had kept me from going barefoot that often.

Stasia averted her eyes at the sight of me naked. I rolled my eyes and headed for the bathroom. Hot water already steamed in the tub, and the smell of lemon and spearmint dragged away the last vestiges of my sleep.

"I've brought you breakfast, Princess, and your empress-mother wishes to see you once you've eaten."

"How generous of her," I muttered, and watched Stasia's reflection in the mirror wince. "What time is it?"

"Half past ten, ma'am." Stasia kept her gaze on the floor, her hands clasped at her waist. Skin the color of cream stood out against the drab gray uniform.

"Stasia, look at me," I said.

She raised her head, and I raised an eyebrow at the vivid blue eyes she'd kept hidden from me the night before. As clear as the Hini sapphire and twice as brilliant.

"Orphan?"

"Yes, ma'am."

Most of the servants in the palace had no *sahotra*. A position in the palace meant a better life for them since businesses tended to hire within the family or upon recommendations from very good friends. A person without family was lost in Indrana, with very little chance to change their fate.

I added this to the list of things I intended to change if I was going to be in charge around here. *You're just pretending, Hail, remember?*

"We have cycled through three different titles in less than three minutes," I said, keeping my voice gentle. " 'Imperial Highness' is fucking cumbersome and I'll forget to answer to 'Princess.' My name is Hail."

"Highness, I couldn't."

I smiled. "So let's stick with 'ma'am' for the moment, okay?"

"Yes, ma'am."

"Good." I nodded and waved a hand. "I don't need an audience. Go entertain my BodyGuards."

What I did need, I realized when Stasia paled, was to think before I attempted to issue orders. Rumors about the gunrunner princess were no doubt flying with reckless abandon. And the horrified look from my maid told me more than enough what some of them might entail.

I closed my eyes and cursed, opened them just as quickly to look at Stasia with an apologetic smile.

"Poor choice of words. That wasn't what I meant."

"Yes, ma'am."

I waved a hand, swallowing back the need to apologize again. "Go find something else to do besides stand there and watch me." I gave her a second smile, which she hesitantly returned before she bowed and left me alone.

I sank down under the water, letting it close over my head and cocoon me in silence. The beating of my heart throbbed in my ears as I floated to the surface and took a breath.

All your running, Hail. All your attempts to get away led you right back here. There's a reason for it, don't waste it. My father's voice in my head was kind, but firm as it always had been.

I pulled up the local news reports using my *smati* and started piecing together the timeline as best as I could.

Just a little under three months ago my baby sister had died of ebolenza. There'd been a huge outpouring of grief from the people, but little to nothing reported on the strange, isolated outbreak by the palace-controlled news stations. Two of her BodyGuards and a servant had also died, but for so virulent a disease, the spread had been stopped quickly.

A month after Pace's death—the empress's *Ekam*, four other BodyGuards, and the dismissed *Ekam* and *Dve* of the runaway princess were killed in an aircar accident.

Grief ripped through me again at the familiar faces in the news report. Ofa and Tefiz Ovasi had been my BodyGuards from the moment of my birth. When I'd left, they'd been officially dismissed from service for failure to perform their duty but had stayed on in secret to help me with my search.

There'd been a great deal of speculation by the press about why they'd been in the aircar with Ven that day, but no concrete answers.

Then, not even forty hours ago my older sister and niece were killed in an explosion while out on a shopping trip. That, and news of my mother's dementia, was all the news stations were talking about.

Well, and the return of the runaway princess. Though the off-planet news was by far more amusing. A severe-faced man with shocking purple hair waved his hands in the air on the set of *Interstellar Daily*. "Cressen Stone, feared gunrunner, is revealed as the daughter of the Empress of Indrana. Is this a plot by Chang Po-Sin to take over Indrana?"

I snorted with laughter, accidentally sucked water down my

windpipe, and surfaced in a spray of water and curses. The door to my bathroom slammed open, Emmory and Zin bursting through.

I blinked at them in shock as both men turned their heads fast enough to get whiplash. Stasia came in through the other door and my giggles broke free at the sight of the wicked knife in my tiny maid's hand. I finally got control of myself enough to gasp, "Emmy, I admire your diligence, but you really need to not burst into my bathroom without permission."

His face didn't change expression as he pushed Zin out the door. "Perhaps you would be kind enough to not shout in the bath, Highness. I take it you're all right?"

"I'm fine; apparently being heir doesn't mean I can breathe underwater." I exhaled slowly, pinching the bridge of my nose again with one hand while I waved at Emmory with the other. "I'm fine. Go on."

He bowed and retreated, closing the door behind him.

"Ma'am?"

"Thank you, Stasia." I took the towel from her, wrapping it around my soaking hair. I climbed out of the bath, taking the second towel with a smile.

I stopped short in the doorway to my bedroom, eyeing the clothes Stasia had laid out on the freshly made bed. The white skirt and top all but disappeared against the linens, only the golden embroidery giving away their presence.

I took the new robe Stasia offered me and sat down in the plush chair by the windows. I grabbed for the blue-handled mug, sinking back against the garish paisley upholstery.

"I'm not wearing that." My hand shook and I barely kept from spilling coffee on myself. I sniffed at it, grimaced, and set the mug aside.

"Ma'am, you must wear white to see the empress," Stasia replied.

"The dress," I agreed. "Fine. But the sari will be red—the

darkest one in there." I waved my free hand at the wardrobe. "Don't argue with me on this, Stasia, you won't win. My sisters were murdered and I will not let anyone forget it."

A frown worried at the space between Stasia's pale eyebrows, but she obeyed, and I turned my attention to my breakfast as she flipped through the many saris in the wardrobe. I nodded in approval when she produced the one I'd worn the night before, crimson so dark it looked black. Golden tassels danced from the ends.

I finished eating and got dressed. Stasia urged me down onto the vanity seat, and fixed my hair with startling efficiency.

Twitching my skirts out of the way, I took the sari from her and flipped the end over my left shoulder, winding it around my waist so the extra fabric draped over the white silk of my skirt like pooling blood. I wrapped the other end over my head and my right shoulder, giving Stasia a tight smile.

"Shoes, ma'am?" She hit the panel near the wardrobe, and the door slid open to reveal rack upon rack of shoes.

My laughter was sharp. I grimaced, rolling my shoulders and shaking my head. "I'll go barefoot. Thank you, Stasia. I'm not sure how long this audience with Mother will take. I'll call you if I need you."

She dropped into a curtsy. "Yes, ma'am."

Marshaling my courage, I strode into the waiting room. Emmory and the other four BodyGuards came to attention. I already knew Nal and Zin, and my *smati* identified the other men at the same time Emmory introduced them.

"Highness, your BodyGuards—Pezan and Salham." He pointed at each in turn and the men bowed low.

They were all dressed in the standard matte black uniforms, a crimson piping along their cuffs and worked into the detail of the intricate star pattern on their left breasts.

It was similar to the one on Emmory's left cheek. I pressed a hand to my stomach and stared out the window as I wondered what deadly honor had garnered him the Imperial Star.

The Imperial Star wasn't issued for just any act of valor, but something above and beyond the call of duty that caused the recipient to walk the road to temple. That award was normally given posthumously and I knew firsthand how that trip changed a person. I'd nearly died so many times over the years, but the most recent experience had been the closest I'd ever come. I'd died twice on that backwater planet and still wasn't sure how Portis had brought me back. Through sheer force of will most likely.

"Are you all right, Highness?" Emmory asked. I was normally so good at reading people, but he was a challenge, and the concern in his voice seemed genuine. "Your empress-mother wishes to see you this morning."

"Of course she does." I saw the flicker of disapproval in his eyes and softened my snappish tone with a smile. "We shouldn't keep her waiting, Emmory. Shall we?"

He nodded, looking at Nalmari and Zin. "You're with me. You two stay here." The other Guards saluted. Nal headed for the doorway, exiting my room first, and Emmory fell into step beside me.

A thousand questions raced through my mind. Who was this man who'd pledged his loyalty to me with such quiet determination last night? How had he gotten the Star? I longed to ask him, but with Nal trailing ahead of us, any conversation was unwise—at least until we figured out if we could trust her.

At this point the odds for that seemed pretty astronomical.

Dad was right. All the work I'd done, all my running and hiding, had been useless. Here I was, right back in the gods-damned intrigue. The bitter thought made me sigh, and Emmory shot me a curious look as we marched down the hallway.

We passed several servants and one caught my eye. A younger man, head down and shoulders tight. His hands were bunched in fists.

"Her Imperial Highness, Princess Hailimi, to see her Imperial Majesty." Nal announced me to the pair of Guards standing like chess pieces in front of my mother's doorway and jerked my attention away from the servant.

The door Guards conferred with the ones inside Mother's rooms over the uplink. Then they pushed open the pockmarked metal door and gestured us inside. My BodyGuards handed over their weapons as they crossed the threshold.

I trailed a hand over the damaged door as we passed. The marks on the surface were from a failed coup attempt in 1990 GD. Princess Kastana hadn't been happy with the idea of being second fiddle to her older sister, Empress Ilenka, for the rest of her life. She convinced her BodyGuards and a large chunk of the regular Imperial Guard to join her cause, and they assaulted the empress's quarters.

Empress Ilenka's BodyGuards, her husband, and her two youngest daughters held out against overwhelming odds until reinforcements arrived and shredded the traitors against the very same door they'd been trying to breech.

Princess Wei had earned the Imperial Star in that battle, fighting like a terror as she bled out from a host of wounds. She had not returned from her walk with the Mother Destroyer, dying in the empress's arms on the other side of this door.

Kastana was executed and her family cast out of the royal city. And the law forbidding weapons in royal chambers that I'd quoted to Bial last night had been enacted.

The door had never been replaced, but instead stood as a warning to those who would raise a hand against their empress.

"Bet you fifty ravga the first words out of her mouth are

critical," I muttered. Emmory pretended not to hear me while Zin turned his laughter into a choking cough. It appeared my *Ekam* was taking his new position very seriously while his partner was loosening up. Though neither of them took me up on the bet.

"Your Highness." Mother's chamberlain, a young, dark-haired woman named Tye, bowed low to me. "Welcome home. Your empress-mother is doing well today."

Translation: She was coherent today.

I gave Tye a smile and headed into the sitting room—a smaller room off to the side of the large waiting area.

Mother did look healthier this morning, the mahogany gleam back in her cheeks as she sat in a pool of sunshine. The light reflected off the golden embroidery work on the voluminous sleeves of her heavy robe and the crystal cup in her hand.

Bial stood by the window, his hands clasped behind his back. The sunlight threw red highlights into his blond hair. He didn't turn to look at us when we entered, but I got the distinct feeling he saw everything that happened.

That was fine. I could see things, too. The man was tense but trying to hide it.

I dropped into a curtsy in front of my mother.

"Get up, Hailimi." Mother's voice was sharp with an all too familiar annoyance. "Have a seat and have something to drink. There's no liquor, you'll have to make do."

I ignored her sarcastic comment, resisted shooting Zin a look, and took the farthest seat from her even though it put my back to the door. My Trackers settling in behind me was enough to put me at ease.

"Your choice of color is duly noted," Mother continued with a sniff as I reached for a crystal glass filled with the pinkish juice of a water-orange. "Even if it is too late as usual. The terrorists responsible for the deaths of the princesses have already been executed."

"What? What terrorists? Who was responsible? How did you find them so quickly?"

"What do you mean what terrorists?" Mother snapped. "Those who would undermine the empire, Hailimi. Those damn *Upjas* murdered my niece, my daughter, and the Crown Princess!"

I winced at the fury in her voice, and swallowed back the protest that automatically rose in my throat, pleased with myself for not falling straight back into our old pattern of bickering with each other.

The *Upjas* were a Gordian knot of rebels in the heart of the empire who called for a relaxation of the class system and a return to what they saw as the days of equality when the empire had been a member of the Solarian Conglomerate.

Social, economic, and political equality of the sexes.

I didn't agree with their demand to abolish the monarchy, but there was also no way in hell I'd ever admit to my mother that the *Upjas* had a point about some of the more archaic social laws in the empire. Or that both Cire and I had been in contact with them before I'd left home.

Instead, I asked the question I knew put me out on a limb. "You don't think that's the slightest bit suspicious? Why didn't they try to kill you? If they infected Pace with ebolenza, don't you think they could have struck down the whole palace? It doesn't make any sense. The *Upjas* have never wanted us dead. They just want change—"

"They want revolution!" She cut off my protests with a sharp look and a wave of her hand. "We didn't ask for your return home so we could speak to you of your sisters. They are dead and gone. There is nothing more to do. If you'd cared about them at all, you wouldn't have left in the first place."

A cold weight settled into my stomach, and I stifled the smart remark even though it hurt. "Why did *you* ask for my return home, Your Imperial Majesty?" I didn't bother to keep the sarcasm out of my voice as I echoed her words. She and I both knew who'd really wanted me back and who'd sent my Trackers after me. Her eyes narrowed at the veiled insult.

"Leave us, all of you," she said.

That was enough to get Bial away from his contemplation of the window. "Your Majesty—"

"Don't argue with me, Bial. I'm perfectly safe in my own rooms, and my own daughter isn't going to try to kill me. It would just bring justice down on her head that much swifter." Mother smirked a mirthless smile in my direction and I tightened my grip on my glass until I was afraid it would crack in my hand.

She was right, of course. I kind of wanted to smack her senseless, but I wouldn't kill her. That would just be rude. Not to mention it would immediately elevate me to a position I didn't want.

"Very well, Majesty." Bial bowed stiffly and headed for the door.

"I'll be right outside, Highness," Emmory murmured.

"Mother—"

"To answer your question—the future of this empire is my concern, Hailimi. As my primary heir—gods help us all—so it is also yours."

I choked on my juice, just barely swallowing it instead of spraying it all over my dress. Oh, bugger. There was that spark in Mother's eyes again.

"I've assembled a group of suitors for you, daughter. Pick one. Marry him or not, we don't care. Don't feel you need to wait for the ceremony, though, if you do. I expect you to have a daughter of your own before the summer comes. The least you could do for our *sahotra* is to make the same sacrifices the rest of us have."

9

The *sahotra*; always the family. It was all she'd thought of since she'd put that damn crown on her head. If only she knew what I'd done for the family, everything I'd given up. Hatred welled up in me again as I stared at my mother's implacable expression, and any plans I had not to let her goad me back into behaving like the bratty daughter she remembered went up in smoke.

"I don't fucking think so." I was kind of shocked by the cold curse, but Mother was surprisingly unfazed by my behavior.

"*Uff.*" Mother exhaled the annoyance. "Be grateful we will give you leave to choose your own betrothed. We believe that was your issue the last time, was it not?"

"You can't do this!" I knew I shouldn't have said it the moment the words slipped out. Mother would let my cursing slide more often than not, but questioning her authority had always been treading on the edge of treason as far as she was concerned.

Never mind she was completely off the mark. I'd left to hunt the last man of the trio responsible for my father's assassination. I'd stayed away because I'd been done with someone else picking my future for me. I'd been finished with the idea that my mother got to dictate my entire life. Tired of Indranan society not valuing people for who they were, only caring about what they could provide for throne and country.

"We can do whatever we please, ungrateful child!" Immediately it was the empress speaking and not my mother, and that cold, formal royal "we" was a fist in my stomach. "Hope is gone— lost with the death of your sisters. We are stuck with you, but we will do what is necessary to save this empire and so will you."

Even had my mother known why I left, she wouldn't have cared. She hadn't wanted me looking into my father's killers in the first place. She thought I was a spoiled brat, just like Emmory did. I couldn't stop my tongue. "You forget. I left. I don't care about this empire. I'd just as soon watch it burn."

Fury raced over Mother's cool features, putting even more color on her cheeks and a fevered light in her eyes. She lurched to her feet. "Watch your tongue or I'll have it removed."

I got to my own feet. "You'd like that, wouldn't you? No one around who'd dare tell you no. No one to tell you you're inhuman. Go ahead, Mother, if you think you have the stomach for it, I dare you to take it out yourself."

I did not expect her to hit me, so the slap caught me right in the cheek, whipping my head to the side. I stumbled into the table, knocking glasses to the floor before I righted myself.

That crashing, predictably, brought the BodyGuards back into the room.

"Highness?" Emmory's voice was wary with concern.

"I'm fine." I stared at the blood smeared over my fingertips with amusement. "Just a family feud. I've been hit harder by boys barely old enough to shave."

"Hailimi, you are going to produce a child and save this family's claim to the throne."

I looked away from Emmory. Mother was pale again, leaning heavily on Bial, who watched her with a frown. The slap had shaken some sense back into me and I retreated back into the habits I'd acquired with Po-Sin. Considering my options, I went for the one that was the least offensive—not that anyone would believe it.

"Over my dead body, Your Majesty."

"That can be arranged," Mother snapped. "I'll speak to your father about this."

My father?

Bial's quick shake of his head and the sudden tension in Emmory's hand stopped the question before it could slip out. Bugger me, I'd pushed her too far. There was a moment of silence as we all stared at each other.

"Bial, I'm not having a maid with green hair. Tell that girl to go," Mother said.

"Curtsy, Highness."

I was too shocked to do anything but obey Emmory's whispered order and dropped into a quick curtsy. As Emmory hustled me from the room, I caught sight of my mother chattering away at her *Ekam* like a schoolgirl.

My victory over dodging a royal order tasted like ash in my mouth as the full weight of my mother's predicament—and mine—settled onto my shoulders.

I'd probably adjusted the best out of all my sisters to the transition of Mother becoming empress. I was used to going my own way, and I'd spent more time with Father anyway, so the sudden demands which dragged her away didn't reduce me to sullen silence like Cire or fits of temper like Pace.

No, I just went on about my business as though nothing had happened, and for a few years that worked perfectly. Then some hideous soul decided we had to start going to court with Mother, and my misery was found in spending hours bored out of my mind as my ass slowly went numb in the gilded chair that had been made for me.

That was when the trouble really started. It only got worse after Father died. I'd thought tracking down his killers would convince Mother to allow my early entrance to the Naval Academy. Instead it earned me an arranged marriage and Mother's refusal to let me into the Academy at all.

No one said a word as we exited Mother's rooms and headed back down the hallway. Nalmari was in the front again, Emmory beside me, and Zin brought up the rear.

I was so distracted by the scene I'd just witnessed, trying to reconcile this woman with the one I used to know, that I almost missed the attack when it came.

The same servant I'd noticed on my way in was still there and he lunged at me.

"Knife!" Emmory shouted, spotting the weapon at the same time I did.

Instinct kicked in. I avoided the man's first swing, moving toward my attacker and landing a blow to his ribs with the side of my hand. Before I could hit him again, Emmory shoved me back into Zin. We cracked heads. Stars floated in front of my eyes and the scene played itself out in slow motion as Zin covered my body with his own, turning us away from the danger.

Emmory slapped the black-bladed knife to the tiles. He caught the young man's arm and struck him in the face with an open palm, snapping his head back.

"Princess, back to the empress's quarters," Nal ordered. She had her gun out, but with Emmory in the way, there wasn't a clear shot. I saw her jaw tighten and she raised her weapon anyway.

I lunged into Zin, knocking him into Nal and nearly sending all three of us into Emmory and my attacker. Zin swore, righting himself and propelling me back toward Mother's door. I didn't fight him; that had been enough to disrupt the moment and any potential shot Nal had.

Emmory caught the attacker by the throat and swept him to the ground.

My attacker landed on his back, and a shudder ran through me when I locked eyes with him over Zin's shoulder. "Long live the revolution. Death to the throne," he said, and clamped his mouth shut.

"Poison!" Emmory grabbed the young man's head, trying to force his mouth back open, but it was too late.

My would-be assassin was convulsing against the tiles, his face gray, and his eyes rolled back in his head. His heels drummed a strange pattern before stilling, leaving me with my heart pounding in my throat and the hollow echo of his words ringing in my head.

Emmory swore, glancing up as other Guards pounded down the hallway toward us. The pair at Mother's door hadn't moved; it was Imperial protocol in case the attack on me had been a feint and the real attack was directed at the empress.

Blond Cas and another man with green eyes and sharp cheekbones—who my *smati* identified as Adail—skidded to a halt at my side. The moment they arrived, Nal moved to Emmory, looking down at the young man on the floor in disgust.

"Blasted *Upjas*," she muttered.

"Maybe," Emmory said and rolled his shoulders.

"Highness, are you hurt?" Zin's hands were warm on my arms, the textured material of his gloves catching on the long sleeves of my dress. "Look at me," he urged in a low voice. "Did he cut you?"

"I'm fine," I replied, forcing out a smile as Emmory approached. "Survived the first assassination attempt. I wonder what the bookies' odds were for that."

This time Zin couldn't stop his laughter. And even Nal smiled, though she looked more confused than anything. Emmory closed his eyes briefly, his throat working as he swallowed back his reply. When he opened them again, the expressionless mask was back into place, but not before I caught the spark of relieved humor in those chocolate-and-silver depths.

"Take the princess back to her rooms, Zin," he said. "Cas, you and Adail guard the outside door until Nal and I return." Both men saluted, and Emmory turned back to me. "Highness—"

I forced another smile past the hammering of my heart. "Don't worry, Emmory, I'm not going to argue with you on this one." I dipped my head at him, and turned for my rooms.

"Do not ever do that again."

I didn't turn from the open window at the sound of Emmory's voice, but continued to watch the dolphins play in the azure waters of the Lakshitani Sea. The gorgeous creatures thrust themselves high into the air over the water's surface, twisting and spinning in a dramatic acrobatic display.

Bearing the same name as Earth dolphins, and much of the same sleek, pointed nose physiology, Indrana's dolphins were more intelligent than their cousins across the universe. Their coloring was a darker gray, more like gunmetal, with white shimmering markings that were unique to each dolphin. They could also survive the freezing temperatures of the sea in this area of Indrana.

"I was wrong back there. Technically that was the second attempt on my life."

"Highness." The bite of annoyance in Emmory's voice dragged me away from my contemplation of the dolphins.

"Of course," I said, just to throw him off balance. "You're absolutely right."

"You are no longer a gunrunner," he replied.

"Princess, gunrunner—let's be honest—they're two sides of the same coin. For twenty years I was, Emmy," I continued before he could interrupt me. "It was instinct. I'm sorry. I promise that I'll work on it." I offered up a blinding smile, but he didn't react. "Wouldn't you rather guard someone who knows how to defend herself? I'd think that would be preferable to a simpering girl cowering in the corner."

"It isn't your job, Highness. It's mine."

"I was joking—sort of. Did they take out your funny bone when you joined the Trackers?"

"Just temporarily. I got it back after I passed basic."

I looked back out the window with a choked laugh. "Convenient that I was just attacked by a member of the *Upjas*."

"They are looking to do away with the Throne, Highness. It's not much of a stretch." He braced his hands on the windowsill. "May I ask why you pushed Zin into Nal?"

"She was about to shoot you in the back." I answered Emmory's raised eyebrow with a lifted shoulder. "That's what it looked like. I'm sure there would have been a lot of discussion about split-second decisions and horrible accidents. I didn't feel like dealing with it. Plus, you haven't annoyed me yet today." I tried to sound flippant, but I wasn't sure I fooled him. The truth of the matter was the thought of losing Emmory put a lead weight into my stomach. I was stuck here. No backup, no intel. Cire had said to trust him, that he could keep me alive and that was something I was seriously interested in.

"I don't trust her, Emmy." I pushed away from the window,

pacing the length of my sitting room. The movement startled Cas, who was standing by the inside of the door, but I waved a hand at him when he snapped to attention. I wasn't sure if Emmory trusted my baby-faced Guard, but my instincts didn't scream warning bells at me, so I figured he was safe for now.

"Are we clear?" I asked Emmory, and to his credit it took him a fraction of a second to realize what I meant.

"Yes, Highness. We swept the suite last night." Emmory glanced over my shoulder and dismissed Cas with a jerk of his head.

"Don't trust him?"

Lifting a shoulder in a shrug, Emmory crossed the room and locked the door. "I picked him, but putting a team like this together should take months, not minutes. I trust Zin, that's it."

"You don't trust me?"

"With pardon, Highness. I can't figure you out. Everything I read about you said you'd keep your word, but I get the feeling you're only here to find out who killed your sisters, and once that's done, you'll run."

I blinked at the brutally honest reply and at the fact that there was no judgment on Emmory's face. It stung more than it should have that he doubted my honor and that once again he'd hit the mark about my intentions. I couldn't think of anything to say, so I stood there for a few seconds looking like an idiot with my mouth hanging open.

"So let me get this straight. You don't trust me to keep my word, but you want me to trust you?" I crossed my arms over my chest.

He rolled his shoulders, looking uncomfortable. "I could say the same about you, Highness."

"Touché."

We stared at each other, stuck at an impasse as the heartbeats ticked away. There wasn't any point in sorting through my options. What it boiled down to was this: I either trusted him or not.

He gave his life for the empire, Hail, and you gave your word.

I looked at the star on Emmory's cheek. The man had already lost a brother. He'd given his life, dying in whatever incident had garnered him that damn star, coming back to life through some miracle and sheer stubbornness; and then he'd gotten on his knees and agreed to do it again.

"Thank you for last night." The words sounded forced, stupid. I cleared my throat and tried again. "It meant a lot to me that you felt like the oath was important enough to take."

"I meant it, Highness. I don't say things like that lightly."

"I guessed as much." I touched a hand to my own cheek. "That star says it all."

The tension in his shoulders dropped away and a ghost of a smile graced his mouth. Emmory nodded once. I exhaled, amused to note that my hands, which had not shaken with the attempted assassination, were now trembling. "How bad are things?"

"You mean for us, Highness? Or the empire as a whole?"

I stopped my pacing and sat on the couch. "Let's start with us. After we get a handle on that, we'll worry about the empire. How did you know Cire? How did you get involved in all this?"

Emmory rested his hands on the ornate back of the couch opposite me, fingers digging into the pale stripped fabric. "Ven brought a number of us in on the situation four months ago when the empress started acting strange. After his death, your sister asked me to bring you home. She felt it would be necessary to have you at her side."

"It didn't quite work out that way, did it?" I muttered bitterly, biting my lip to hold back the tears. I was going to have to come to terms with the fact that I'd be running into reminders of my sisters every time I turned around. Crying when it happened wasn't going to serve anyone, least of all me.

"No, Highness."

"And no one told you the real reason I left home."

"The real reason?"

"I didn't run away, Emmory. I may have stayed away for personal reasons, but I left because I was following my father's killer."

"Highness, they caught your father's killers." He frowned at me.

"*I* caught my father's killers, Tracker. One of them anyway. There was a third man. A man I saw the day my—" Bugger me, but it was still hard to say out loud after all this time. "I saw him in the crowd. Jagjit admitted that he and Wayla were working with a third person, but he couldn't give us more than a name—Wilson."

"Who knew about this, your empress-mother?"

I shook my head. "She knew about my investigation after the fact, and if Ven told her the rest, it's lost to her dementia because she didn't say a word about it in there. Ofa and Tefiz were involved, and the head of the GIS—Fenna Britlen. I don't know how much it matters."

"It matters, Highness."

"I lost the trail about sixteen months out. Whoever he was, he vanished like he went into a black hole. I decided not to come home, but I never stopped looking for him. I have the files, I could send them to you."

"Let me talk with the GIS and we'll discuss it more later."

"Right." I dragged the word out as I got to my feet. "I need to get up to speed. I've been gone for a long time." I blew out a breath and forced a smile as I looked toward the windows.

The sun was shining, lighting up the whitecaps and tossing

rainbows into the air. But I knew from experience the air was probably frigid. It was Paush, and we were in the depths of winter. Just three weeks away from Pratimas, the holy light festival.

Just three weeks away from a wedding to a total stranger—or worse, going through the utterly useless motions of trying to have a child.

Oh, bugger me.

Mother's insistence that I marry was pretty much a moot point, while her declaration about being saddled with a useless daughter was the truth.

I could have sex until our sun died out, but there weren't going to be any more little Bristols running around this palace. That hope had died with Atmikha.

Seven Indranan years ago, on one of the wilder outlying worlds at the edge of known space, we had a deal go horribly wrong. We were ambushed by the gang who'd contracted us for a load of neoprene explosive. They'd decided it would be easier to liberate it from us prior to delivery rather than paying the fee. Our navigator, Jexen, was killed, and I took an old-fashioned bullet to the gut. Which, ironically, saved my life while ruining any chances of saving the empire.

Thanks to the royal gen-manip done before my birth, I hadn't died right there in the dirt of that shitty little world, but it had been touch and go for a month and more than a year before I was well enough to track down that gang one member at a time and burn them to the ground.

None of it changed the outcome. According to the doc, the bullet had been designed to fragment and the main piece destroyed one ovary while the shrapnel damaged the other beyond repair, killing any hope I had of bearing children. Even if we'd been able to find a Farian, they couldn't replace dead tissue.

Mother was righter than she knew when she'd said she was stuck with me and that hope had died with my sisters.

I was barren.

It was a secret that could bring down the empire. The only people who'd known it were all dead, but I didn't know if Portis had passed on the information. The fact that Emmory came to get me at all suggested Portis hadn't breathed a word of it.

"What are your intentions, *Ekam*?"

"Highness?"

"I meant what I said. I'm not getting married and I'm not a damn breeder." I tried to sound casual, but the moment hung on the tip of a knife. If Emmory backed my mother's demands…

"Of course you're not." There was no derision in his voice. Emmory shrugged and a second flicker of a smile poked through his stone expression. "I can see the need for an heir, Highness, in the long run. But things are volatile right now, and from a security standpoint, I'm not in favor of putting a stranger in your bed."

"I'm pretty much never in favor of that, unless I've had too much to drink."

Emmory winced and I snorted a little laugh.

"As entertaining as it is to have this extremely awkward conversation with you," I continued, "let's move on to something important. Do I have some chamberlain candidates to interview?" The list from Clara had been waiting for me when I woke up this morning and I'd passed it on to Emmory before even getting out of bed.

"Yes, Highness. I didn't care for two of the suggestions from Matriarch Desai, so unless you have objections, we won't bother with them. I passed the other names on to General Saito and she sent me files a half hour ago."

"That's fine. We're in a time crunch here anyway." I needed someone to handle my schedule; there wasn't any way I could do it on my own. General Saito was Emmory's former commander with the Trackers, and if I couldn't trust her information on these people, I was better off putting a gun in my mouth and pulling the trigger.

Accepting the amended list he sent me, I moved away from the window and settled onto the couch. "Will you have Stasia bring me something to drink? And who on this list is in the palace?"

"Louis Winston, Alba Tanaka, and Hanna Obedai. The other four on the list we could vid-conference with if you wish."

"Have those three come here. We'll start there. The questions I ask might seem strange, Emmory, but just trust me on this."

"Of course, Highness."

Two hours later I had a headache and a new chamberlain.

Alba Tanaka was a twenty-three-year-old who'd formerly been in Matriarch Desai's employ as the assistant to Clara's household coordinator. She'd answered my rapid-fire questions in a calm, even tone and hadn't seemed the least bit intimidated by me. Which was more than I could say for the other two interviewees. I didn't need a chamberlain who was terrified of me. I needed someone who could manage my schedule and—quite frankly—me should the need arise.

The best part had been right toward the end of the interview, and clinched the job for her.

I rubbed a hand against my temple. "So, Alba, do you think that this is a position that will suit you?"

"I'm sorry, Highness. If I could beg your pardon for just a moment?" Alba gave a quick bob of her head. "*Ekam* Tresk. Has someone seen to lunch for the princess? It's been quite a while since breakfast and her headache is probably from hunger."

I blinked at her, laughed, and waved a hand at Emmory. "She's right, I'm starving."

"I'll have something brought right away, Highness," he said.

"Some more blue chai for you would be a good idea in the meantime." She got easily out of her seat and took my cup, handing it off to Stasia with a smile.

"Do you want the job?" I asked with an eyebrow. "Because you just got it."

Alba's smile spread and she bowed so low her straight black hair touched the ground. "Thank you, Highness. Thank you."

"Go take care of what you need to. Zin, go with her and help her get settled."

"Yes, ma'am." Zin bowed and followed Alba from the room.

"Do you trust her?"

Emmory shrugged a shoulder. "Background was totally clean. She'd already passed all the basic requirements to be in the matriarch's employment anyway, so it was a relatively easy process."

I raised an eyebrow at him.

"She doesn't set off any of my alarms, Highness. I'd be careful for a while until I get word back from some of my contacts."

My food arrived shortly, and after Emmory murmured something about sorting out shift issues with the BodyGuards, I was left alone to eat.

Nal stood by the door with her hands clasped behind her back. I studied her out of the corner of my eye as I ate. She wore the same mask Emmory had perfected, seemingly staring into empty space, but I knew if I moved in her direction, she'd focus her attention on me in an instant.

"Where are you from, Nal?"

"I grew up on Deepai, Highness."

Deepai was the largest island in the Kormekain chain, a long string of islands near the equator. "I remember a visit there when I was about eight, I think."

"My sisters spoke of it, Highness. I was just a baby."

"How many sisters?"

"I had five, Highness." Nal's eyes darkened with pain and I knew what her next words were going to be even before she said them. "They were all lost to the war."

"*Uie Maa*," I murmured with a sigh. "I am terribly sorry."

"It was long ago, Highness."

I returned to my food, appetite lost. So much for an attempt to connect with my *Dve*. Had I been imagining that incident in the hallway? Maybe Nal had only been concerned for my safety and had the gun out as a precaution in case Emmory couldn't subdue my attacker.

No. I tossed my fork onto my plate in annoyance. I knew what I'd witnessed. Twenty years I'd survived in the underbelly of the universe because of my gut. I wasn't going to start second-guessing it now just because I was in a world covered in a thin veneer of civility.

"Is everything all right, Your Highness?" Nal hadn't moved, but she was watching me.

"Fine, thank you. I'm finished." I pushed away from the table.

"I'll have someone clear it away."

"I'm going to lie down for a bit. Please let Alba know I'd like to see her after she gets settled." I didn't wait for Nal's reply and headed for the bedroom.

10

Alba, bless her, let me sleep for almost two hours before she knocked tentatively on my bedroom door. "Your Highness?"

"I'm up." I rolled out of bed, rubbing at my face. "Give me a minute."

"How's your head?" she asked when I emerged from my room.

"Better, thank you. How are your quarters?"

"Just fine, Highness. Thank you."

We stared at each other for a second and then I snorted a laugh. "Okay, enough of the awkward small talk, Alba, you'll find I'm not a fan. I assume your position was activated in the palace system and your *smati* has probably blown up with incoming messages."

"Yes, ma'am."

I smiled. "I have a request for you. Don't be afraid to say no to me or anyone else. Okay? You are the gatekeeper and I trust you to organize my schedule in the best manner possible. Obviously I'd like some input on where I spend my time and with whom, but I will let you do your job as long as you prove to me you're competent."

Alba nodded. She hadn't changed out of the dark suit she wore for the interview. The skirt hung down to the floor, and her jacket had sleeves that stopped at her elbows and flared out when she moved her arms.

"Okay, so what are we starting with?"

"I received a message from Chamberlain Tye. Your mother says to have your hair fixed immediately."

I smothered the second laugh. "That took longer than I thought it would."

Alba gave me a curious look but didn't say anything. I waved a hand at Cas and grabbed for the dark red sari I'd tossed onto the back of the couch earlier. With Alba's help I got it back on, straightened it, and fixed my hair in the mirror.

"Alba, make a note to get with Stasia about some improvements to my wardrobe."

"Yes, ma'am."

"Highness, Cas said you needed me?" Emmory asked as he came into the room.

"Mother wants me to fix my hair." I tugged on a green curl with a depreciating smile. "I don't think it's possible, but we may as well go try."

"Highness?" He frowned at me.

"The modifications are permanent. I'm stuck like this."

Emmory's mouth dropped open, and I couldn't stop the giggle that bubbled up in my throat. Surprised my unflappable *Ekam* twice in one day. That was probably going on the record books.

"Anyway," I continued through the giggles, "I'll go make an appearance at the modification shop so some poor technician can tell Mother about the problem instead of me having to do it. She'll probably still accuse me of doing it just to upset her, but at least I'll have some witnesses."

We left my chambers again and headed out of the royal wing

toward the mod-center. There were more people out in the early afternoon than there had been during my arrival in the dark of night, but thankfully the grim-faced cadre of Guards around me stopped anyone from approaching for a chat.

Alba trotted along at my side and I shortened my stride a little. The poor girl was going to end up with blisters from those heels of hers if I made her run all over the palace. And it wasn't like I was in a hurry to get this done.

Or not done. A tiny sliver of worry had burrowed into my brain. Sure there'd been places where underbelly tech was often just cobbled-together scraps, but on the whole, the kinds I'd had access to courtesy of Po-Sin were probably better than any top-of-the-line equipment from the SC. We were in the heart of Indrana and I doubt the palace spared any expense for their modification equipment; however, there was no way it was better than anything Po-Sin had.

What if they could change me back?

I didn't want to go back. I didn't want to blink and have Cressen Stone and all those years of my life vanish. I didn't want to go back to being Princess Hailimi with all the confines that life entailed. I didn't want to go back to being eighteen and fighting with my mother all the damn time. It was hard enough to remember who I was when I was in the same room with her—what if I went back to looking like my former self, too?

I could do this if I could hold on to my past—and to Portis.

Emmory stopped outside a pair of steel doors. "Stay here, please," he said, and slipped inside without waiting for an answer.

Several white-coated techs filed out and I couldn't help but notice the way Zin's hand strayed to the gun at his hip each time.

"Easy," I murmured, trying to stave off some of my panic

with humor. "You'll get gray hair if you keep jumping at everything."

He flashed me a grin, the dimple in his cheek winking into existence. "Something tells me I'm going to get gray hair anyway, Highness."

"That's unkind," I replied, reaching out to tweak one of the short dreadlocks on his head and mirth sparkled in his gray-green eyes. But before Zin could say anything, Emmory reappeared.

"Alba, if you'll stay outside please. Jet, you and Cas stay with her. No one comes in."

"Sir." The older Guard snapped a nod in acknowledgment. He and Cas slipped into position on either side of the steel doors as they closed behind me.

"Your Highness," the young technician stammered out my title and tried to bow at the same time. He was pale-skinned with a shock of black hair that kept falling into his thin face. "Tech Samuel Parkins. If you'll step this way, we'll get you put back to rights—uh, fixed up right away."

The poor man was already on the verge of panic and I mouthed a silent apology at the ceiling as I stepped into the mod-chamber. This wasn't going to go at all well for him, but there was very little for me to do except play along.

I hoped. *Bugger me, please don't work. I don't want to go back.*

The doors closed around me, and the suffocating feeling was only somewhat mitigated by the fact that I could see through the polyflex surface. I fisted my hands and concentrated on looking through the clear partition at Emmory and Zin.

"If you'll press your hands to the indicated spots and watch the screen in front of you."

"I should warn you, Samuel. I had a kill switch installed in my *smati*. If my mother thought about trying to download any submission programming, it's going to end badly." I kept my tone pleasant as I uncurled my fingers and laid my hands on the smooth surface in front of me.

"No! Of course not, Your Highness." The tech jerked as if I'd slapped him and craned his neck around to stare at Emmory. My BodyGuard hadn't moved a muscle and kept his eyes on mine for a long moment before looking at the technician.

"Proceed, Samuel," he said.

Samuel swallowed and began tapping buttons on the panel in front of him.

There was a flare of heat through my palms as the chips imbedded there began receiving a signal. I closed my eyes and exhaled slowly. When I opened them, the string of code flying across the space in front of me was faster than my eyes could track. My *smati*, however, suffered from no such limitation and processed the code as fast as it appeared.

I locked my knees to keep myself upright as the vertigo set in. I knew it would fade in a minute or two, but for the moment I clenched my teeth against the nausea and concentrated on the simple task of breathing.

"Highness?"

I refocused my eyes and found Zin standing just outside the chamber. Forcing out a smile, I said, "Dizzy."

"Not surprising." He nodded in understanding. "It should fade quickly."

I glanced past his shoulder where Emmory stood next to the tech. "I'm fine. Bet you twenty ravga it doesn't work, Emmy."

"I don't think I'll take that bet, Highness," he replied without looking up.

I grinned again and settled back against the far wall of the chamber as Samuel starting tapping in commands to return me to my "original" look.

Gene manipulation for cosmetic uses had been big since the early days of the SC. While governments and researchers were still wrestling with curing diseases and preventing defects, the private companies turned their focus toward more profitable applications.

Now women (or men for that matter) could change their hair color on a whim. Or their eye color, height, or body type. You name it, it was doable.

The process fell out of favor here during the empire's break with the Conglomerate. After our split it became a point of pride to lay claim to "natural" features rather than some bio-sculpted façade you could find in the Conglomerate.

The modification I'd gotten after fleeing the palace had been anything but cosmetic. The gene-manip in a shady back-room in Delhi just before I'd met Portis had been more than skin deep. In fact, it had been so good that it had fooled all the thousands of DNA scanners I'd been through for the last twenty years.

Until I'd run afoul of one Tracker named Emmory Tresk.

The price for that kind of security had been a permanent modification. I hadn't realized the extent of it until a few months later when Portis and I had tried to change our appearances for a job and nothing the mod-techs did would change my green hair and tall, rangy build.

Please don't change back. The mantra repeated itself over and over in my head as the lights flickered through the chamber.

"Uh, Your Highness? It's not—"

I couldn't stop the grin from spreading over my face. "Working?" I supplied cheerfully when the tech stuttered to a halt. The stoic expression on Emmory's face didn't shift at all, while Zin looked vaguely impressed.

"I could have told you that. The modification was permanent.

I could have told Mother that, too, but I didn't think she'd listen. It's easier to just have it on record."

"Permanent? But, Your Highness, I—"

I choked back a laugh. It wasn't all at Samuel's panicked flailing. Part of it was pure joy, and my hands were shaking with relief. It wasn't very nice to laugh at him, especially since I was sure he thought he'd get the short end of the stick for this snafu.

Not that I'd let that happen. It wasn't his fault, after all. Letting him run through the process a handful of times so that it was on record seemed the kindest thing to do. So I did, until my claustrophobia got the better of me. Feigning a yawn to hide my panic, I shouldered the door open and caught a glimpse of my green hair in the reflective surface of the metal band around the glass. I was still me.

"Your Highness—" the tech protested, but I waved him off.

"That was seven times, Samuel. I think even my mother will realize that it's not your fault." I crossed the room and patted him on the cheek, hoping he'd been so distracted by my stubborn appearance that he hadn't run a full scan.

The last thing I needed right now was someone finding out about my problem.

"I'll be sure to tell her you tried everything." I smiled again. "Come on, Emmory. Let's go."

"I'll be right behind you, Highness." Emmory gave Zin a look and I raised an eyebrow as I was ushered from the room.

"What's that about?" I asked Zin, who merely shrugged in reply.

The hallway juncture at the mod-center widened and split off into several different corridors. Opposite the steel doors was a bank of rounded windows with the same view of the ocean as my rooms. I grabbed my heavy skirts in my hands and padded over across the open space. The slate tiles were cool under my feet.

The tech hadn't said a word, but I didn't know if that was a good or a bad thing. Right now I reveled in the fact that I got to stay me and that I wasn't going to lose the ties to my past. I'd worry about the rest of it later.

"Cousin!" The unpleasant voice, high-pitched and nasal, hit me just seconds before the tiny blond whirlwind did. Twenty years gone, and my spine still tried to crawl up out of the top of my head at the sound.

"You're home! They said you were but I needed to see you with my own eyes. I was on the other side of the planet at a function when you arrived and missed your homecoming."

I wiggled free, choking back the snarl in my throat. My cousin smoothed her blond hair down as she babbled at me. "I'm so sorry about your sisters, Haili. It was simply awful." She moved to hug me again and this time Zin blessedly intervened.

"Ma'am, I'm sorry. You need to back away from the princess."

"Oh? Oh! Sorry. We're family. I wouldn't ever hurt her." Ganda waved her hands in apology, giving Zin a bright smile. "BodyGuards, right. Male BodyGuards." She made it sound like the insult it was supposed to be and I struggled to keep my face blank.

For a nanosecond I'd started to wonder if Ganda had finally grown up and if the severity of the situation had changed her. But when she'd said "hurt," I saw the flicker of malice in her gemstone bright eyes and knew that nothing had changed at all.

"Well, they're attractive at least. You'll have to let me borrow them."

"I haven't gotten any better at sharing, I'm afraid." I almost choked on the words and Ganda's delighted snicker made my skin crawl.

Ganda's Guards were all women—of course—and they

eyed my Guards with a wary distaste that made me want to grab Zin's gun and start shooting.

Temper, Hail.

I wondered if Zin had seen the look in Ganda's eyes, too, or if I'd once again be alone in my battle against my cousin. The good news was that I'd learned some tricks and some self-control in the last twenty years.

Now would be the time to show it.

"It's all right, Zin. She's right, we're family. You look good, Ganda."

"So do you." She reached out and tugged on a curl. "Luckily the Crown Princess gets to set fashions. We'll be seeing green hair all over soon."

"I think a nice blue would suit you better. Something icy and frigid."

Her hand fisted briefly on her skirt, but her smile never wavered. "I'll have to try that. It was lovely to see you. I really must go. It's been frightfully busy around here helping out the empress."

"We'll get you a break here soon. Don't worry." I patted her on the arm.

"It's a pleasure to serve the empire." She beamed at me. "We should have lunch, Haili, get caught up. Have your chamberlain buzz mine. I have to go; I'm going to be late."

"Of course."

Ganda gathered up her emerald-green skirts and hurried off.

"Well, *that* was interesting." I rolled my eyes, and offered up a smile to Zin, who watched me carefully.

"Highness?"

"Let me enlighten you. Beware of my cousin. She will smile and flatter you until the moment she drives a knife into your back. Please tell me you are all smart enough to recognize that."

No one said a word. Cas looked at me with nervous confusion, darting glances back to his fellow BodyGuards. The two older men were watching me, not a hint of their feelings showing on their faces. Alba's frown might have signaled confusion or consideration.

"Highness, time to go." Emmory interrupted the lesson and I couldn't stop myself from snarling at him.

"Let's go back to my cage, boys." Grabbing my skirts, I started down the hallway, leaving my Guards to catch up with me.

Back to your cage, the voice in my head hissed the words. *Back to being the powerless, useless princess.*

Bugger me.

I wasn't going back to that. I'd spent too long building my life, my reputation from the ground up into something that meant more than all this fluff and nonsense. If they wanted me as the damn heir, they were going to have to take the gunrunner.

Zin and Cas checked out my rooms. Emmory was already looking at me strangely, so I waited until his back was turned before I slipped the knife out of Jet's belt and stashed it in my sleeve.

"Okay, everyone in," I said, shooing Jet's bulk ahead of me. "We need to have a conversation." Perching on the arm of the rose-colored couch, I folded my hands in my lap as Emmory closed the door.

"Highness?"

"I realize we're all just getting to know each other here, but if we're going to make this work, I need some help. First thing is that I need to trust you. Second is that I need actual living people around me who are willing to offer up their opinions when I ask for it. Emmory and Zin can tell you that when I ask for your opinion on something, it means I want it. Whatever experience you've had with royalty, I'm not them. I don't want you to blow smoke up my ass."

Cas's eyes flew open and I had to smother a grin. That poor kid was in for an education.

My *Ekam* didn't blink. "Highness, perhaps—"

"No, we'll do this now, Emmory. You picked these two to be on my primary team for a reason. I'm not going to settle for the status quo here when my life is on the line. My cousin might seem sweet and empty-headed, but she is not." I pointed at Zin. "So here's your first lesson. I want honesty from you. Opinions on my cousin. Zin, you're first."

Zin sighed audibly. "Highness, you're asking us to talk about a member of the royal family. It would take me all day to list the number of reasons this is improper."

"Thank you for restating the obvious. Zin's taken a pass, which means Caspian Yuri Kreskin, you're up." My *smati* gave me Cas's full name. That and his blond hair marked him as part of the influx of Saxon refugees the empire had seen over the last sixty years.

"Emmory, why did you put a Saxon on my primary Body-Guard team?"

"Your Highness?" Cas's voice cracked and he gave me a nervous smile. "My family has been members of the empire for more than five hundred years. We actually came from the Conglomerate. Kraskey-Ploha was settled primarily by people from Russia and Eastern Europe in the Great Flight." He had pretty eyes, which shifted in the light to a deep blue.

"Everyone is calling you Cas. Do you prefer that or Caspian?"

Surprise made his eyes widen and a blush appeared high on his cheekbones at my question. "Cas is fine, Your Highness."

"All right then, Cas. What did you think of my cousin?"

"She seemed nice, Highness."

"Oh, for fuck's sake." Throwing a hand in the air, I turned to the last of my BodyGuards. Jet was watching me, his face as blank as Emmory's.

"Ojayit Uli Gaiden," I said, using Jet's full name from the label that flashed over him courtesy of my *smati*. "You're up."

"Your pardon, Your Highness," he replied with a bow that was surprisingly elegant given his blocky frame. "But our job is to keep you alive, not to give you advice."

"Your job is what I say it is. Besides, it makes me happy."

"That's not our job either, Highness," Jet said with a trace of amusement in his accented voice.

I slid off the couch with a smile and crossed the room. "Jet, if you're not going to keep me happy, you're going to want to keep a closer eye on your weapons."

Confusion flashed through his eyes and was quickly overtaken by surprise. I gave him a broader smile and flipped his knife over my fingers.

He studied me for a moment, tilting his head to the side as he spoke. "Her greeting was strained, Highness. Too high-pitched to be genuine. She was surprised by your controlled reaction to her insult and confused by how calm you were. I take it you weren't always so cool around her.

"She could be dangerous given how her influence has grown in the short time since Princess Cire's death. But she's worried by your return, which means she hasn't consolidated enough power yet to challenge you outright for position as Heir Apparent."

The knots in my stomach released themselves so abruptly, I almost collapsed in relief, but I hid it and handed Jet's knife to him with a wink.

"I like you."

"I'm terrified to hear it, ma'am."

I punched him in the shoulder. Everyone froze. "*Uff*," I muttered, seeing no graceful way to move on from my decidedly gunrunner behavior. "Alba, your thoughts?"

"With apologies, Highness." My heart sank at my chamberlain's reply. "But Ojayit has stolen my answer."

Jet raised an eyebrow in her direction, and Alba only allowed a tiny smile to peek through in return as she dipped her head in his direction.

"That's my girl." I clapped my hands and grinned at her. "Okay, Alba, you stay. I'm sure we have things to go over. Body-Guards can go now." I winced at the awkward dismissal. My BodyGuards weren't the only ones who needed to get used to things apparently.

No one seemed to mind. Emmory merely gave me a look as he headed for the door. As soon as we were alone, Alba jumped right into my schedule.

"Matriarch Desai sent me a message, ma'am, saying they'd keep Ganda on the schedule for the week and give you a chance to get your feet under you. She would like to meet with you when it's convenient."

I nodded. Clara had copied me on that message as well as attaching a file summarizing the current political climate. "Who's the head of the Ancillary Council right now?"

"Juna Saito has held the spot for several years now."

The AC was made up of the daughters of the matriarchs as well as daughters of several other noble houses, and the head was elected by majority vote. I remembered Juna; she was several years older than me and had been a friend of Cire's. She was a tiny thing with curly black hair and pale skin. I wondered if she was still quiet and serious or if time had changed her.

"When's their next meeting?"

Alba's eyes unfocused as she checked her calendar. "Right now, I'm afraid, ma'am. Just their normal weekly meeting, though I suspect things aren't the least bit normal given recent events. There's nothing else scheduled until next week."

"Make a note that we should stop in and say hi if we have time." Cire wouldn't have had much to do with the AC. Her duties as heir would have kept her too busy, but they were her social peers, and Pace probably had sat on the council. It would be important for me to get to know these women as many of them would end up in the Matriarch Council during my reign.

Look at you, Hail, settling right into this.

"I also have a message from Admiral Hassan requesting a meeting as soon as possible." Alba had moved on to the next item without realizing my distraction and her announcement pulled me out of my self-pity.

I pulled up the files Alba sent to my *smati*. Inana Hassan was Mother's age, a graduate of the Naval Academy who'd worked her way up through the ranks until her appointment as Admiral of Home Fleet five years ago. Her elevation also garnered her control of the Raksha—the military council for Indrana.

This woman had power, and the fact that she wanted to talk to me was a good sign. I knew my priorities. Hao used to go on and on about how there were three things a gunrunner needed to pay attention to before entering into a deal with anyone: their politics, the cost of the deal—not just financially but everything else—and the mood of the locals.

It wasn't much of a stretch for me to translate that into my situation here. The top three pressing issues were politics, the economy, and the state of my people.

I wasn't even close to being caught up on everything that had happened in the last few months, but what little information

I'd scraped together in the hectic hours since my return was all bad news.

Economics wasn't my strong suit, and I was reluctant to involve myself and potentially make the mess worse. But the political situation—specifically the mounting troubles with the Saxon Kingdom—and the growing popular unrest? Those I could handle.

I remembered Hao's favorite saying: *Concentrate on what you know. The rest will sort itself out, or it'll kill you.* It had always been delivered with a grin and a wink, typical of Hao's easygoing attitude.

"Make her a priority, Alba. If she can't make a meeting today, schedule something for tomorrow. I'll meet with Matriarch Desai tomorrow morning if that works for her.

"I'd also like to talk with Fenna Britlen. Emmory may have already sent her a message."

"Fenna retired last year, Highness. Caspel Ganej is the new head of Galactic Imperial Security."

"Interesting. Is Fenna still in the capital?"

"No, ma'am."

"I'll compose something myself then, if you'll get me her contact information. No one else gets audiences, but if you aren't sure about someone, feel free to double-check with me. I want to spend the next two days getting up to speed on the situation here."

And start figuring out who killed my sisters, but I wasn't going to share that with Alba just yet.

11

Admiral Hassan was able to meet with me later that evening. It hadn't occurred to me that people would scramble to rearrange their schedules on my account.

"You're the heir, ma'am," Stasia reminded me with a smile as she deftly looped my hair into a massive braid. "Of course they're going to do what works best for you."

I'd changed from the white silk dress I'd worn to see Mother into a dark blue sari. The slubbed fabric had a slight sheen to it. The pants and *choli* were black and the whole thing was far more comfortable than my earlier dress.

I waved off Stasia's attempt to put jewelry on me. This outfit was the best I could find to mimic the naval uniforms and I wasn't about to ruin it by jingling every time I moved.

"Highness, the admiral is here." Emmory's voice was soft over our private comm line. I let Stasia have one more moment to fuss over my outfit before I headed into the main room.

"Your Imperial Highness." Admiral Hassan was several inches shorter than me but not at all intimidated by it. The dark-haired and dark-skinned woman saluted me, her uniform immaculate, and I felt a strange pang of jealousy as I nodded at her in return.

I'd wanted to join the Navy for as long as I could remember. My father's Saito bloodline had granted him entrance into the Naval Academy, and his marriage to the heir furthered his career in ways Indranan society never would have allowed otherwise.

He was a brilliant strategist, my father, and it was because of him that we'd taken as much territory in the war with the Saxons as we did. After his death it was all we could do to hold back the Saxon tide until the peace treaty was signed.

"Allow me to introduce my aide—Commander Cole Hamprasade."

"Admiral. Commander." I returned the nod. "Have a seat, won't you? Would you like something to drink?"

"I'm fine, thank you. I thought Commander Hamprasade could meet with your chamberlain. There are several important briefings I think you should attend, with the empress's permission."

"Of course."

"We'll be in my office, ma'am. Call if you need anything," Alba said.

Hassan smiled tentatively a moment after Alba left. "Welcome home, Your Highness. I was relieved to hear you were uninjured in the attack this morning."

"Join the club." I jerked a thumb at Emmory as I sat down and picked up the cup of chai that always seemed to appear when I needed it. Stasia had figured out my dislike of coffee with surprising speed. "Thankfully Emmory is on the ball. So, Admiral, I don't need a detailed breakdown of what we're looking at just yet. How about you just hit the highlights on the state of our military?"

Hassan blinked at me and I felt a little sorry for her. No doubt she was used to Cire's quiet demeanor. My sister had had

ЋЋЋЋЋЋ

ЋЋ

a fine knack for politics, but where military matters were concerned, I think she'd been more willing to let others handle it.

"Admiral, is my sister's husband still in the capital?"

She blinked again, but recovered more quickly this time. "He left, Your Highness, with Admiral Shul's fleet. Just this morning. We offered him bereavement leave, but Shul's fleet is going to the Saxon border and Major Bristol felt it would be better for the empire for him to do his duty."

"My nephews?" Cire had had two boys, one older and one younger than Atmikha. I didn't know what kind of reaction I was going to get from them. They might not want to see me.

"Laabh recently graduated from the Academy and was posted on his first ship. I am considering transferring him to my ship, Your Highness, so he can stay in-system and be close to his brother."

"Where is Taran?" Laabh had just turned twenty-two if my records were correct and his younger brother was only eight.

"With Leena Surakesh, ma'am."

I nodded. My older nephew had married into the Surakesh family less than a year ago. It wasn't common practice for Leena to take Taran in, but I was grateful for her kindness. "Give me a chance to talk with Laabh, Admiral? I'll see how he feels about it."

"Yes, ma'am."

"All right, back to the issue at hand." I leaned forward, resting my forearms on my knees and watching Hassan closely. "How is Indrana's military?"

"We are stable, ma'am. Recent budget cutbacks and concerns over the last five years have cut into our research and development as well as some of our operational capabilities."

"What kind of cutbacks?"

Admiral Hassan named a figure that made me whistle. "It

hasn't affected our ability to carry out our mission, ma'am," she hastened to add.

I heard the unspoken "yet" at the end of her sentence. "Tension with the Saxon Kingdom?"

"Trade disagreements mostly and the occasional small skirmish on border worlds they lost in the war. King Trace seems the cautious sort. I think he wants to keep the peace. Lately it's gotten worse, though."

"Do you think the Saxons are responsible for my sisters' deaths? Mother claimed the *Upjas* responsible had already been found and punished but I'm having a hard time finding any arrests or legal action in the system."

Hassan froze, swallowed, and then answered me with extreme care. "I can't say for sure, Your Highness. I would recommend speaking to Caspel Ganej, Director of Galactic Imperial Security. He would know better."

Translation: My mother had interfered, and if I wanted answers, I was going to have to either go to her or find someone else.

"Yes, Alba mentioned Fenna had retired. I'm surprised they named a man to the position."

Hassan smiled. "Your sister talked your empress-mother into appointing him after Fenna's retirement, ma'am. Caspel is good at his job."

"Interesting." I settled back against my couch with my cup cradled in my palms. Hassan mirrored my posture, yet somehow kept her military bearing. She studied me with her brown eyes and just the slightest hint of a smile on her narrow face.

I smiled back. "Are you loyal to the throne, Admiral?"

The admiral, to her credit, didn't even blink.

"I am, Highness. To the death and after if necessary."

I gave her a nod and leaned forward to set my cup down on

the table. "It's obvious even to an idiot that things are circling the drain around here. I'm not an idiot."

"Of course not, ma'am. Am I correct in assuming you don't believe the princesses' deaths were accidents or terrorism?"

"Terrorism, yes. Just not the kind the palace announced. The *Upjas* are the easy answer. Until I have a chance to talk to them, they're nothing more than one more name on the list."

"You're in contact with the rebellion?" Hassan arched a dark eyebrow.

"I am not," I replied carefully. At least I hadn't been since I'd gotten home. I knew I was treading very closely to the edge of treason, a treason the admiral would be forced to report if I wasn't careful. "We don't know yet who's behind this, Admiral. I need to know if you're going to be on my side when this explodes."

Hassan steepled her fingers. "If I say no?"

I let a smile flicker to the surface. Emmory didn't move, but Admiral Hassan inhaled. I watched her tense like a *karegosh* spotted by a panther. "There'll be an unfortunate attack tonight. Another assassination attempt on the heir. I'll survive, of course, thanks to the sacrifice of a very brave naval officer."

I'd talked this over with Emmory before the meeting. He hadn't liked the idea of threatening an officer who was possibly loyal to the crown, but in the end had seen my reasoning for it.

Hassan didn't react, didn't move a muscle, and kept her hands well in view.

"I wondered how true the rumors were, Highness."

"Gunrunner," I replied, spreading my arms wide and smiling. "Someone killed my sisters. My mother is dying. I don't have a good temper at the best of times, Admiral, and all this is straining my limits."

"You ran away from your duty."

Out of the corner of my eye I saw Emmory stiffen.

Picking up my cup, I took a sip out of it to hide my smile. The admiral was willing to play hardball. I liked her.

"I did," I admitted, not willing to tell her the truth just yet. "I wasn't interested in spending the rest of my life being useless and playing dress-up at social functions. I was only the second daughter, Admiral, not fit for much besides a backup, and an unwanted one at that. Cire was supposed to be empress, not me." It was as good as I could do without sounding like a whiner, but from the expressionless look on Hassan's face, my explanation wasn't worth the effort.

"The day you ran away, Highness, I met with the empress." A strange look of sympathy crossed the older woman's face. "She was concerned for her second daughter. Afraid you couldn't see your place in the empire, because she had let her emotions overrule her reason."

I choked back the bark of laughter at Hassan's words. My own reply chilled the room. "My mother never let emotions get in the way of her duty, Admiral. That was one of her major issues with me."

"The empress was afraid her actions had prevented you from seeing what good you could bring to the empire. She regretted forbidding you from joining the Academy and asked me if I would sponsor your entrance. Take you under my wing, so to speak."

I almost dropped my glass in my lap. "The *Naval* Academy? But she'd—"

Hassan's smile was almost kind. "The empress was trying to protect you, but she realized it was strangling the life out of you. You have a great talent for the military side of things, Highness. You always did have a better grasp of how to keep the empire safe than your sisters did. Princess Cire was too kind for her own good, if you'll forgive my bluntness."

I shoved to my feet, startling both Hassan and Emmory, and threw up a hand before Emmory could open his mouth. I needed to move—it was that or scream.

All this time. All my life I'd thought staying away was the only chance I'd have to live my own life. Now I was finding out that my timing was as shitty as my judgment. No fucking wonder Mother had let me go in the end.

Military service was traditional among the noble families, and as the second daughter I'd been well prepared to follow my father into the Imperial Navy.

When he died, everything fell apart. I did everything I could think of to make her proud of me, to show her I was capable enough to handle the Academy. She shot me down, and more than anything, I had to admit that was the reason I hadn't come home when the trail went cold. There wasn't anything left for me here because she'd taken the only thing that still connected me to Father. Now I find out that she'd changed her mind?

In a flash, a whole other life played itself out before my eyes. I saw myself standing straight and tall in the same uniform Admiral Hassan wore, commanding respect from nobles and troops alike. I saw myself in a better position to protect my sisters, to protect the empire from the worms wrapped around her heart.

"'There is neither this world nor the world beyond nor happiness for the one who doubts.'" Emmory's quoting of the *Gita* broke me out of my daze. The words shattered the life that never existed and I blinked away tears before I turned to face my BodyGuard.

"We've been down this road already. It's over and done, Highness. There is no changing it, and you are just as well suited for the task at hand as that other you would have been," he continued.

"Why did Mother let me go?" I couldn't stop the desperate whisper from slipping out. "She didn't say a word about it. If she'd told Ven, he could have had Portis tell me. I could have come home. My whole life could have been different."

"You are not the only one, Highness." Emmory's reply was gentle, almost startlingly so. "We all live with such a burden."

I dragged my hands through my hair, disturbing Stasia's carefully constructed hairdo, and turned back to the fireplace. Admiral Hassan was on her feet.

"Your Highness, it wasn't my intention to upset you." There was genuine regret in Hassan's brown eyes.

"No, your intention was to discover if I'd known that little gem before I left." An unwilling smile made its appearance on my face and Hassan paled a bit. I ignored it, and settled back into my seat. "You have your answer, Admiral. Do I get mine?"

Hassan started to say something else, thought better of it, and folded her hands in front of her with a sharp nod.

"Good," I said. "Let's get to work then."

Face it, Haili, you'd rather have been a gunrunner anyway. Portis's voice echoed in the back of my head.

With an almost imperceptible exhale, I let go of the life I could have had as Admiral Hassan steered the conversation toward the Saxon Alliance's military strength and our own current R and D projects.

By the end of the hour, my brain swam with names and numbers and locations; even with the help of my *smati*, I was hard-pressed to keep track of it all.

"Please call me if you have any questions, Your Highness." Hassan passed over the tablet and dipped her head. "I'm available at any hour."

"Thank you. I'll read through the files."

Hassan bowed lower, came up, and nodded at Emmory with

sharp military precision and headed for the door. My *Ekam* didn't move and I cast him a curious look as I headed toward the window.

A quick, brutal storm had swept through as the sun set, dropping no snow but leaving the temperature just above freezing. We'd probably get snow before the hour was out.

The dolphins in the bay jumped and played, unaffected by the cold. Had we been closer, we could have heard them singing. It was a sweet song, another thing that separated them from their Earth-born cousins. Not a series of clicks, whistles, and sounds too high-pitched for human ears to hear, but a song like a chorus of angels. I used to love going to the beach with my father. Getting out of the palace was always a treat, and after his death I clung to the memory of those conversations.

Dad and I walked on the beach, hand in hand, our BodyGuards trailing after us like silent shadows. "Your mother is going to need all our help, Haili," he said, staring out at the waves. His dark green eyes were hidden behind mirrored sunglasses, but I could feel the tension in the hand that was wrapped around mine.

I tried not to sigh, not to have the next words out of my mouth sound sullen, but judging from the slight smile on Father's face, I only partially succeeded. "It's boring."

"It's necessary."

"Why can't I go to the War Room with you? I'd rather know what the damned Sax are trying to pull."

One of Father's dark eyebrows winged up and he laughed. "Oh, my brilliant little soldier." Dropping to a knee, he scooped me into a hug, his arms closing fiercely around me. He released me, holding on to my shoulders as he pulled back. "No more cursing though, okay? You're only twelve and your mother would kill me if she knew you were doing that."

"If she bothered to pay attention."

"Haili." Father slid his sunglasses off and cupped my face in his hands. *"You're right about the Saxons. They're up to something. Your mother is under a lot of pressure to keep us all safe. Let's help her out with that, okay? Like good soldiers?"*

"Yes, sir." I hung my head, watching my toes as I dug them into the gray sand. Father laughed again, but the strains of tension woven through his amusement were now evident to me, and when I launched myself into his arms, I clung to him with all my strength.

"Could we go down to the water?" The question slipped from me, and Emmory's reflection jerked in surprise. All my attempts to get a reaction, and he was surprised by a request inspired by a stupid childhood memory—that figured.

"Highness, it wouldn't be safe."

"What's safe? Cooped up in a cage?" I hoped my smile softened the teeth in my voice. "You know I'm not going to stand for it. I've spent a large chunk of my life with people trying to kill me, Emmory. The only difference between my life there and the one here is that I'm not armed right now. Which is something I've been meaning to talk to you about."

"It's safer for everyone if you aren't armed."

"Please." The word was followed by snorted laughter. "You're not believing the stories about me, *Ekam*?" I couldn't resist the tease.

"You just threatened to kill the head of Home Fleet if she wasn't loyal to the throne." He gave me a look I was fast beginning to recognize: one mixed between frustration and amusement. "Highness, I know which ones are stories and which ones are truth. That makes it worse somehow."

"Yes, but then you know I'm a hell of a shot, and despite rumors to the contrary, I have very good control of my temper."

"It's against protocol," he said and my heart sank. "But I'll think about it."

I resisted the urge to hug him, settling instead for a beaming smile Emmory did not return.

My smile faded, and I glanced out the window once more. "Who killed my sisters, Emmory?"

"Highness, we've been home less than a day. I will need a little more time."

"I want to see any information you have."

His expression didn't change. "You have enough on your plate."

"Emmory, don't try to tell me what to do. I want that information and I'll have it with or without your help. They were my sisters, I have the right."

Emmory dipped his head, his face still unreadable. I wished I could crack my BodyGuard open and figure him out, but I doubted even that would give me the answers I wanted. I pushed away from the windowsill with a sigh.

"I'd like to go to temple and visit my sisters, *Ekam*."

I didn't change clothes or mess with makeup for this trip. It wasn't required after the first visit and I wasn't in much of a mood to go through the fuss of a ceremony.

Shift change for my BodyGuards had been hours ago, but Emmory hadn't quite settled on the members of my other teams so I was escorted to the temple by Willimet and Kisah.

The two women provided a study in polar opposites. Where Kisah was tall and blond, Willimet was tiny and dark. They both greeted me easily with smiles and quick bows.

The third member of their team, Rama, was younger than both of them. He bowed his dark, curly head as I came out of the room. "Your Highness."

I smiled and resisted—only barely—the urge to pat his head. "Good evening, Rama."

"Rama, stay on the door. You two are with us." Emmory gestured down the hallway. Willimet took the lead and Kisah fell into step behind us.

If Nal had been by my side instead of Emmory, we'd look like a proper princess and her escorts.

Do you want to be proper, Hail, really? Thankfully my follow-up thought quashed the spike of guilt. I wasn't ever going to be proper and I didn't care about the gender of my BodyGuards.

"Fuck this place." The words hissed out of my mouth before I could stop them and there was an audible inhale from behind me.

"Highness?"

"Nothing." I cleared my throat and picked up my stride, forcing poor Willimet into a jog to stay ahead of me. People scrambled from my path so quickly I barely caught their rushed greetings.

Those are your people you're trampling in your temper.

I came to such an abrupt halt that Kisah crashed into me and Emmory took several steps before he realized I wasn't right beside him. The old man who'd just bowed out of my way looked up with something very close to terror on his face.

"Forgive me my haste, grandfather." I hoped my smile eased his nerves. "What is your name?"

"Garuda, Your Highness." He glanced at my BodyGuards, but smiled in return.

"That is an honorable name. It's a great pleasure to meet you, Garuda."

"My mother had high hopes, Your Highness. Sadly, I only spent my life in the kitchens."

"We all need to eat. There are less honorable pursuits."

"Truly spoken, Your Highness." He bowed. "I shouldn't keep you."

"Have a good evening."

"You as well, Your Highness. May the gods keep you."

I nodded and headed down the corridor again, this time taking care to smile and speak to the few people I encountered along my way.

The temple was silent when I entered. The wire wrapped around my heart tightened again at the sight of my sisters and niece, their illusions still lying silently above the bank of flickering candles.

You were expecting them to wake up? The voice in my head bit hard. *Get you out of this mess maybe? Or maybe you should grow up, Hail, and realize that this isn't a dream and there's work to do.*

This time I was able to hold my cursing back and instead knelt wordlessly at the altar. I stayed there, silent, until my feet went numb and the candle flames blurred. I stayed there, frozen in grief, some kind of strange penance for running away in the first place.

If I'd stayed. If only I'd stayed, maybe they'd all still be alive.

"Announce yourselves." Emmory's order jerked me out of my guilt and I stumbled to my feet with Willimet's help.

Father Westinkar emerged from the shadows, two young women behind him. "With my apologies, *Ekam*. We didn't mean to startle you."

"This is the family temple, priest."

"Yes, however my office is open to all. I was counseling this couple. Go on, children." He sent the pair off and bowed, looking straight at me as he did. "Some need the quiet voice. Especially those with unquiet hearts."

"Emmory." His name was an exhale as I grabbed for his arm. *"Tefiz used to say that to me."*

"Be at peace, *Ekam*. I am ever the empire's loyal servant." Father Westinkar didn't say anything else, just disappeared around the massive columns to his rooms at the back of the temple.

I started to follow him.

"Highness."

"I have to know. Call off Zin and whoever else is running this way. Father Westinkar would never hurt me in a million years."

"I am not worried about one old priest—"

"Good," I interrupted him. "Let's go then." My heart was hammering in my chest, but I headed into the shadows.

Golden light spilled from the doorway of the priest's office and living quarters. I followed it like a beacon. Part of me hoping I wasn't giving Emmory a reason to say "I told you so."

The two women, older than the ones who'd been in the hallway, turned from the fire as I came through the door. Tefiz hadn't changed at all. Her hair still black as the sea at night and her diminutive figure still imposing through sheer force of will. The woman at her side wasn't her wife, but Fenna Britlen. The former head of the GIS had gray streaks in her red curls and more laugh lines around her blue eyes.

"Highness." Both women kept their hands visible as they dropped to a knee.

I was only dimly aware of the sound that clawed itself from my throat as I crossed the room and wrapped Tefiz in a hug. "Dead. I thought you were dead."

"Almost, *Ata*." She squeezed me once and then urged me to my feet. I dragged her up with me. Cupping my face, Tefiz shook her head. "I never thought I'd see the day. I'll bet that hair is driving your empress-mother wild."

"Probably." I laughed. "Nothing to be done about it. Ofa?"

Tefiz shook her head. "Dead in the wreck, Highness. I almost followed her." She made a curious gesture of interlocked fingers I'd only ever seen her make once before. In the car after my father died.

I sank into the soft red chair by the heating grate and took the cup the priest pressed into my hands.

"We will be outside if you need us, Highness." Emmory, in a move so shocking I nearly dropped my cup, closed the door behind him and left me alone with Tefiz.

"Drink up, Highness. I suspect you need it."

I was expecting tea, or coffee, anything but the sharp sting of brandy. It kicked me in the back of the throat, and when I got done struggling for breath, I looked up to find Tefiz smiling at me with a mischievous twinkle in her dark eyes.

"The Father keeps some good stuff on hand."

"I'll say. What are you doing here?"

"You're in danger, Highness."

This time my laughter was humorless. "Someone's tried to kill me twice in the last few days. I'm pretty aware of the danger. I'm also pretty sure we can handle it."

"Don't underestimate these people, Highness. They have spent your lifetime putting into action a plan to tear this empire down to its foundations. They have nearly wiped out your family. They managed to kill almost all the loyal Body-Guards. They have made the people frightened—not only of what's out there but of the very people they should be looking to for guidance." She pointed a finger at me.

"Knowing who these people are would help."

"*Hai*, if I knew that, we'd be talking with your sister." Tefiz made the gesture again and looked at the floor. "I've failed you.

I've failed your family. I failed my wife. The only thing keeping me going right now is the thought of revenge."

"I'm still alive." I came up out of my chair and grabbed her by the wrists. "You didn't fail me."

"I can't recognize a single thing about you," Tefiz whispered. Sadness was heavy in her eyes. "I let you go into the blackness of space alone. The Haili I knew may as well be dead."

Of all the ways I'd imagined this reunion would go, this had not been on the list. "Maybe she is," I said, releasing her and moving back to my chair. "Bugger me, maybe the Tefiz I knew died in the wreck, because I never thought I'd hear her give up so easily. I'm not an uncertain eighteen-year-old anymore."

"You weren't uncertain then either," she said. "Determined, rash, intelligent, but not uncertain."

"And you didn't let me go into space alone. You and Ofa sent Portis with me. I can't ever thank you enough for that." The ache in my chest grew and I rubbed a hand over the spot. A smile ghosted across Tefiz's face as she echoed the gesture.

"I'm glad my instincts were right on that at least."

"I wish things could go back to the way they were." I wasn't even sure if I meant back to my gunrunning or back to my childhood.

"It's over and done. The gods had a different plan for you."

"You already know I stopped believing in the gods the day my father died." I shook my head before Tefiz could protest. "That hasn't changed in twenty years, except maybe I've grown even more bitter on the subject."

"Whatever rot this is, *Ata*, it goes deeper than any of us fear and has consequences more terrible than any of us can guess. It's no exaggeration to say you are the last hope of the Indranan Empire."

"I'm a gunrunner, Tefiz, not an empress."

"I am no politician, just a cast-off BodyGuard. However, I would hazard a guess that what Indrana needs right now is someone who can be more than an empress." She pushed out of her chair. "I suspect your *Ekam* is getting restless and I need to get out of here before someone spots me."

"You're not staying?"

Tefiz smiled. "I was relieved of duty, Highness, and I'm supposed to be dead, remember? I think there's quite enough for people to chatter about without tossing me into the mix. We'll stay in touch through Fenna. I'm sure she gave your *Ekam* all the information we have on the bastards who did this—admittedly it's not much, but maybe you can find something new."

"Did anyone tell Mother why I left? Or does she really think I ran away?"

Tefiz blinked and shook her head. "I don't think anyone told her, Highness. Ofa thought it best. Ven didn't agree but I don't know why he didn't overrule her and tell the empress anyway. Maybe he thought with her illness it wouldn't matter."

I hugged her tight. "Everything has changed, but I'm still me and I missed you."

She hugged me back. "I missed you, too, *Ata*. Watch your back and try not to give that *Ekam* of yours as much trouble as you used to give me."

I nodded, too choked up to reply, and slipped out of the room. Emmory and Fenna turned, their conversation coming to an abrupt end.

"Fenna, it is good to see you again." I took her hand and squeezed it. "Did you fill Emmory in on the reasons for my disappearing act?"

"I did, Highness. Did you get caught up with your friend?"

"Yes. You should go. I'll speak with you both later."

Fenna and Father Westinkar bowed. I tapped Emmory on the arm and headed back down the hallway where Willimet and Kisah waited. Neither of them gave any indication they'd heard anything out of the ordinary, but I was starting to see danger everywhere.

12

I owe you an apology, Highness."

I staggered into the back of the rose-colored couch in my apartments and blinked at my *Ekam*. "I'm sorry, what?"

He gave me a look as he reached around Zin and pulled the door closed. Spinning a finger in the air at his partner, Emmory settled into parade rest and bowed his head. "I would beg your forgiveness for my cruel and hasty words."

"We're clear," Zin said, looking between us with a frown. "What happened?"

"You're serious." I leaned against the couch, my surprise no longer feigned. "You didn't know. You were angry. It's fine."

"When I'm wrong, I say it, Highness. Fenna told me what you did. What you gave up."

"Now you make it sound like some noble crusade." Snorting, I shoved away from the furniture. "I was a grieving teenager who wanted revenge, Emmy. Then I was a young woman who didn't come home because, as my mother so succinctly put it, I wished to see the universe more than I loved my own flesh and blood."

Emmory actually flinched. "Highness, your empress-mother is not herself."

"Will someone tell me what's going on? Or am I just here to witness this cryptic conversation for posterity?"

The sarcasm was surprising coming from Zin. I suspected the sharp tone in his voice was directed more at Emmory than me and so I waved at hand at my *Ekam*. "I assumed he'd told you while we were on our way back here."

"It took that long to encode the files. You've both got incoming," Emmory said to his partner. "I just spoke with Fenna Britlen, who confirmed that the princess left home in search of an unknown man they think was behind the death of the prince consort."

"Why didn't they send Trackers after him?"

"They did. A sister team. They're in the files. Last report from them was about six months after the princess lost the trail."

The ping of an incoming message rang in my ear and I downloaded the files. "Do I get the decode key for this, too?"

"If you behave yourself, Highness."

I arched an eyebrow at Emmory. "You'll learn, *Ekam*, I am good at many things. Behaving is not one of them."

"Gunrunner," he countered dryly and I grinned.

Zin's whistle cut the air. "The director has an impressive list of suspects, most of whom we can't accuse without ending up dead. I'm sorry to say Your Highness's brother-in-law and nephew are on the list."

I frowned. "Laabh, I'm assuming?" I hated that I even had to clarify, but eight years old was plenty old enough in the palace to get involved in intrigue and I couldn't discount Taran just because of his age.

"Yes, ma'am." Zin held a hand out. "I can give you the key if you'd like."

I took his hand, a little shiver arcing as the data was passed. "How'd you get yours to decode so fast? This says it's going to take ten minutes."

"I don't need it, ma'am."

"Zin has an aptitude for code, Highness." There was a quiet note of pride in Emmory's voice. "We haven't come across one yet he can't read."

"That's handy. I could have used you a few times over the years." I tapped him on the arm with a smile. Zin swallowed and returned it—cautiously. He was loosening up, but still wasn't nearly as blunt as his partner.

"I need a full day to get through all this, Highness. Can I give you a report tomorrow?"

"Sure. I'll read through it, too, as time allows. Do we have a plan here, Emmory?"

"Fenna gave me some leads, Highness. I'm going to com General Saito and ask for the Labrinis' files. I'd like to know whatever I can about their disappearance."

"Why didn't the general send someone after them?"

Emmory shrugged. "There might not have been a team available. Depending on the circumstances, if the general thought they went native, there wouldn't have been a point. If Trackers don't want to be found, they won't be."

"Even by other Trackers?"

He shrugged again. "I could probably find them, given enough time and resources. But that's another issue—they disappeared at the worst of the fighting with the Saxons. It was likely decided that we couldn't spare the resources."

"Because finding my father's killer wasn't a priority." I wondered if that bitter wound would ever heal and fade.

"Because a lot of things weren't a priority, Highness."

"True." I rubbed a hand over my forehead. "*Hai Ram.* It's late and my brain is scrambled. I'm going to bed."

"Should I call Stasia for you?" Zin asked.

"No thanks, I've got it." I waved a hand at both of them as I slipped through my bedroom door. Several moments later my clothes lay in a pile on the floor and I crawled into bed with a weary sigh.

I woke up early the next morning, clawing my way free of a nightmare that involved Portis dying in my arms.

Lying in the dark, I waited for one of the BodyGuards to check on me. My heart hammered so hard in my chest that even if they weren't linked through the palace network, they had to hear it out in the next room.

I rolled over in bed and hit the light switch just as the door cracked open.

"Your Highness? Are you all right?"

"Nightmare, Zin," I said and grabbed for my robe. "Give me a second then you can come in."

"No, it's all right, Highness. I just wanted to—"

"*Dhatt*," I sighed in frustration. "Come in, please." I managed to keep most of the exasperation out of my voice as I slid from the bed and finished tying my robe. "You know what I miss the most?" Tossing the question over my shoulder, I crossed the room and curled up in one of the ornate chairs by the fireplace. The carved wood was smooth under my fingers.

"What's that, Highness?" Zin moved away from the door, leaving it open, and dropped to a knee by the fireplace.

"Conversation. No one talks to me here. They either talk at me, or to their own damn feet. When nobody knew who I was..." I stopped and laughed softly. "Or I suppose when Portis was pretending not to know; either way I miss having people actually talk to me. It's been almost a week since I..." I swallowed back the rest of my sentence. It sounded too much like whining to my ears.

Zin coaxed the embers back to life with a few pieces of wood.

The fire wasn't necessary, but the crackling flames and red-gold glow chased away the last bits of my nightmare.

"You knew him, didn't you?" I said finally. "You had to have known him if he was related to Emmory."

Zin hesitated as he got to his feet, and I noted again the stiff way he moved. Whatever injury he'd sustained to his left leg had either healed before a Farian could get to him or was so damaging they couldn't encourage the tissue to repair itself.

"We grew up together, Highness." He braced a hand on the mantelpiece, staring into the fire.

"Why weren't you mad at me earlier?"

"I was, Highness. I'm just better at hiding it than Emmory."

"Are you still mad?"

Zin looked away from the fire, tilting his head in confusion. "You didn't kill him, Highness. He knew the risks. Portis and Emmory were like twins, despite the year separating them. Portis swore an oath to protect you with his life and he followed that to the end. Emmory and I will, too, if it is necessary."

"Was he really eighteen when I met him?" I wasn't sure why that was the next question out of my mouth, but it put a smile on Zin's face.

"Twenty, actually. He always looked younger. Our families are all out in the Southern Provinces. My family owns most of the fishing fleet in the area. Portis's mother is a spice merchant."

"His mother..." A sick feeling landed in the pit of my stomach. "Does she know?"

"ITS notified her the day you got back. Good news is she doesn't think Portis got thrown out of the service anymore."

I turned my face away from him, the grief flooding back to the surface.

Zin muttered a curse under his breath. "I have a big damn mouth. I'm sorry. Highness, it has been hard. Until about four months ago even Emmory and I didn't know what Portis had agreed to. His mother will get his death benefits and all his back pay."

"I did kill him."

"You weren't responsible for his death. Portis made his choices, just like the rest of us did."

"Portis…" I choked out the confession. "I'm sorry I messed things up. If I had taken that job like Portis wanted, we would have met up with you in Hortsmith."

Zin nodded, confirming my suspicions, and my gut twisted again.

"I killed him, even if I didn't do it directly. If I had taken that damn job, Portis would still be alive."

"You can't know that for certain, Highness." There was such quiet confidence in Zin's voice that I turned around to stare at him. "Portis clearly adored you. I know…" He cleared his throat, looking uncomfortable. "I know how hard it was for him to lie to you, especially closer to the end. He wanted to tell you the truth, convince you to come home. He had a great deal of faith in you, thought you would do the right thing."

I had no response for this; no clue what to do with this information as it all collided in my head. I didn't want to know just how much detail Portis had gone into and I suspected Zin didn't want to tell me even if I asked. I couldn't be mad at Portis about the lying anymore—I'd lied to him about who I was, too.

"I'm sorry about breaking your nose." I blurted out the apology instead.

Zin's laughter was startled, but pleasant. It bounced off the smooth granite of the mantle and danced around like the snow outside the windows. I grinned a little in response, the knot in my chest loosening until it felt like I could breathe.

"I should have known better," Zin said when he got his laughter under control. "It was a rookie mistake."

"Was the leg one, too?" I regretted the question when all the amusement drained from Zin's face.

"Highness—"

"Zin doesn't like to talk about the leg; it brings up bad memories. He's just too polite to tell you so," Emmory said from the doorway.

"Does it have to do with how you got the Star?" I was in deep already. I figured there wasn't any harm in getting that question out of the way. The way Zin winced told me enough, even if Emmory hadn't nodded in the affirmative.

"It does. Maybe someday we'll share that story with you." He leaned against the bedpost and crossed both arms over his chest. "You want to tell me why you're awake at this hour?"

I shrugged, tugging the blue silk of my robe back up when it threatened to slide off my shoulder. "Bad dreams. What about you, *Ekam*? Or do you just never sleep?"

"Not since I met you, Highness."

Zin snorted. I grinned at Emmory's straight face, relieved the awkward moment seemed to have passed.

"Actually," Emmory said, "I was in a meeting. There's an event in a few days the empress was supposed to attend. Bial doesn't think she'll be well enough and asked if you would go instead. I don't like it, but I wanted to run it by you first. If you think it's a good idea, we'll see if we can make it work."

"I appreciate that." Actually, *appreciate* didn't begin to cover it. I was thrilled that Emmory seemed to get my need to be involved in my own protection. "I need some chai before we get into that discussion, though." Pushing myself to my feet, I sent Stasia a message with my *smati*. "Let me get dressed and I'll meet you both in the sitting room?"

"Of course, Highness." Both men bowed and headed for the door.

"Emmory?"

He stopped in the doorway, his hand sliding off Zin's shoulder. "Highness?"

"We'll probably do this, unless you think it's really too dangerous. Someone killed my sisters," I continued. "We don't have a clue who we can trust and it only makes sense they'll keep trying to kill me, too."

"They won't kill you."

I had come to realize that tone of voice from Emmory wasn't something to be argued with, especially when coupled with a feral dog snarl in the back of his throat. Not that I was going to argue with him—I didn't *want* to die.

What I wanted was to run, as fast and as far away from this whole mess as I could get. I didn't want to be empress. I wanted to wake up from this horrible dream, safe in Portis's arms. But I couldn't fucking run. I couldn't let my sisters' deaths go unavenged, and like it or not, I was going to be empress.

Gods help us all.

The "event" Emmory mentioned so casually turned out to be the lighting of the lamp in the public temple. It kicked off the celebrations leading up to Pratimas and could only be done by a member of the royal family. It was the only light that would stay lit the night before Pratimas, a beacon in the dark, serving as a reminder to all that the light would triumph. Shortly before the dawn on Pratimas morning, people would light their own lamps to wake the sun. It was magical to watch the spread of the flames from the palace along every street and on top of every building. I'd even heard on some planets in the empire that they lit lanterns and released them, but I'd never seen it in person.

The lamp lighting at the temple would start it all. Which meant I was up if Mother couldn't do it.

Alternatively, I could have let Ganda do it, if the very thought of it hadn't made the spot between my shoulder blades itch. I'd managed to avoid having to suffer her presence thanks to her busy schedule, and if I had any say about it at all, once her schedule became mine, I'd have Ganda shuffled away from the palace so I didn't have to deal with her.

Our plan, like so many others before it, fell apart the minute it contacted reality. We'd wrapped up the briefing about the lamp lighting and I was getting ready for a full day of actual meetings when the ping of an incoming message from my mother sounded on my *smati*.

"Good morning, Mother."

Her eyes seemed clear enough, though her hand shook as she reached up to smooth her hair back. "Hailimi, you are late for breakfast."

"We're having breakfast?"

"You're the one who insisted. If it was so important to have a family meal with me and your cousin you could at least be on time for it." Her annoyed sigh cut off with the disconnecting line and I muttered a curse.

"Ma'am?" Stasia paused, a twist of hair in one hand.

"Wrap it up and get me a green sari." I looked down at my black choli and pants and rolled my eyes at the ceiling. "I'm apparently late for breakfast with my mother. Alba."

My chamberlain came into the room. "Ma'am?"

"Did I have breakfast scheduled with my mother?"

"No, ma'am, you have a meeting with the labor union heads."

"You're going to have to make apologies for my tardiness. I have no idea how long this will last."

Alba bit her lip. "Dressed like that, Highness?"

"I'm already in trouble. If I take the time to get dressed, I'll never hear the end of it." I raised my arms as Stasia wound the sari around me, and I took the loose end from her with a smile. "Emmory, we're late for breakfast. Come on."

"Yes, Highness."

"Ganda screwed me, Emmy. Told Mother I wanted to have breakfast but neglected to let me in on the plans." I subvocalized to Emmory as I marched down the hallway, bare feet slapping on the stone tiles. *"She used to pull shit like this all the time just to get me in trouble. And I swear, if you tell me I'm being paranoid, I'll kneecap you. You watch her when we come in the room and Mother starts in on me, watch her face and then tell me I'm wrong."*

I wasn't sure why I so desperately needed my *Ekam* to believe me on this, or even why I was convinced Ganda was bad news. My instincts were screaming at me, and they were rarely wrong.

Mother looked me up and down as I came in the room and curtsied, her silence a deafening disapproval broken only by Ganda's greeting.

"Haili! Good morning!" She wrapped her arms around my neck and squeezed. "You look wonderful, so nice to be able to buck trends and just slap clothes together, huh? Let's take a digital. Smile." Pressing her cheek to mine, she held up her hand, taking the photo with the tech embedded in the tips of her fingers. "I'll post it on Hansi."

I barely, only barely, kept from punching Ganda in the kidney before I disentangled myself from her. "Hansi?"

"All the rage, you should get your chamberlain to set you up an account. I'll send you the link since you're not on it yet."

My *smati* pinged with her words, revealing the picture with a caption "So happy my cousin is home!" and I resisted the urge to shoot Ganda a dirty look. "Good morning, Mother. Sorry I'm late, our briefing ran long."

"We didn't wait for you," she said, returning to her food. "However, at least you're being responsible."

I swallowed back my snarky reply, Admiral Hassan's words from earlier still echoing in my ears. Whatever was plaguing Mother now, she'd tried to do the right thing and the least I could do was make things easier on her. I sat down, smiling at Emmory when he pushed my seat in for me. He nodded back and settled near the window in parade rest.

"Briefings are exhausting, aren't they?" Ganda asked, plopping back into her own chair and arranging her cream-colored skirts before she picked up her silverware again.

"They're interesting." I glanced past her at the screen on the far wall. Mother was old-school and, rather than keeping up on things with her *smati*, had always preferred having it up on the wall of her apartments. It did make things a little easier in terms of keeping everyone in the room in the loop rather than having to explain what you were looking at.

I tuned out Ganda's prattling and focused on the news story currently running. It only took me a few minutes to find the same story with my *smati* so I could actually hear the audio.

"...joining us in the studio is noted historian Juna Manne. Her book, *Stars in the Night*, was on the Empire Bestseller List for twenty-two months. It details the assassination of Prince Alix and how that influenced the empire's policy in the final years of the Saxon war." The news anchor smiled at the camera. "Juna is here today to talk with us about the worsening tensions with the Saxons and what it spells for Indrana."

"Hailimi."

I hit record and blinked. "Yes, Mother?"

She set her cup down, the china rattling a bit as it hit the saucer. "I asked how Admiral Hassan's visit went. Nal mentioned that you spoke with her."

"Is my *Dve* reporting on my activities?"

Mother waved the comment away. "She mentioned it in passing to Bial. I'm pleased you're taking an interest in our home defense; just remember not to meddle."

Stuffing food in my mouth seemed a better response than the words I wanted to say.

"Haili," Ganda said. "I was thinking of having a dinner party for you. It would be a good way to meet the eligible bachelors in the capital. Would tomorrow night work for you, or should I get with Alba to see what your schedule is?"

I wondered what the reaction would be if I threw my knife at Ganda's smirking face, decided against it only because it'd make me really late for my meeting. "Tomorrow night won't work."

"I'll get with Alba then."

"You do that." I shot Alba a note to ignore any and all requests from my cousin and not to schedule anything without my approval.

"You should make time, Hailimi. It's important," Mother chimed in and I cursed under my breath.

"Yes, Majesty."

"Don't you brush me off, child. You need an heir."

Carefully setting down my silverware, I pushed away from the table and gave Mother a sharp nod. It didn't escape my attention the way Bial stiffened or Ganda's *Ekam* moved her hand to the empty spot at her hip. Only Emmory hadn't moved.

"Thank you for breakfast, Mother. Now, if you'll excuse me—"

"You're not dismissed, child."

"I'm not a child, Your Majesty. I am your heir and it's best if you let me do my duty. I have a meeting to get ready for that's more important than sitting here quibbling about babies."

Her sputtering followed me out the door, rising in volume as I hit the hallway and cut off only by the door that Bial closed behind us.

"It would perhaps be better if Your Highness just didn't answer your empress-mother's summons for a while."

Bial phrased the sentence with such delicate care, I had to raise an eyebrow at him.

"I'm not sure that's something I can legally do."

"Just until she calms down, Your Highness. You have enough to focus on right now without..." He shook his head as he trailed off, awkwardly searching for a word that wouldn't make him into a traitor.

"Dealing with my mother's crazy?" I regretted the words as soon as I said them. "Never mind me, Bial. I get what you're saying. I'll make myself scarce."

"Thank you, Highness." He bowed to me, his blue eyes never leaving mine. He'd gotten better at hiding his unease with me, but it was still there lurking at the edges.

I returned his gesture with a sharp nod of my own and walked away with Emmory in tow. "Nal's reporting on my activities?"

"It would appear so, Highness."

"That makes me unhappy, Emmory." I tapped my fingers on my lips. "I trust you know that's not a good thing."

"I do have a file on you, ma'am."

"Right." I laughed. "You might want to let Nal have a read on that when you tell her to keep her mouth shut."

"I think I'd prefer if she doesn't have the warning. I'll speak to her, ma'am. It won't happen again."

"See that it doesn't." I didn't voice my concerns about Bial as we continued down the hallway. The man had seemed solicitous enough of Mother; maybe he only had a problem with me.

13

Two days later I was hanging out in my apartment replying to comments on my Hansi account. Hao had always said I was good at interacting with people and the social media platform that dominated the empire was a perfect setting for me.

"Good afternoon, Mother," I answered the pinging of my *smati* with a smile.

"Hailimi, you are confined to your quarters until I inform you otherwise."

"Excuse me?"

"You heard me," she snapped. "I am the empress. You are the heir only because I say so, and if you continue to be defiant and willfully disobedient, then I will *not* say so. You will be released from your rooms when you agree to provide this empire with what it needs—namely a daughter. And when you have provided us with that daughter, then you will be named heir."

Bugger me. I almost spit out the curse, only just managing to hold it back behind my teeth. Thankfully, Mother clicked the vid off without saying anything else, leaving me staring at the wall. I sat there a moment, fury brewing an acid soup in my stomach, as I tried to digest the mess Mother had just thrown at me.

I shoved out of my chair, startling Alba with my sudden movement and the string of curses I finally released.

"Emmory!" I pushed past Zin on my way into the main room. "Where's Emmory?" Without waiting for an answer, I headed to the bar in the corner. It was 1600, but I needed a drink.

"Highness?" Emmory appeared in the doorway.

"That b—" I swallowed back the insult that would likely have resulted in all of us getting shot along with the whiskey I'd just poured. "My empress-mother," I said through gritted teeth as I struggled for composure. "Has just confined me to my rooms."

"I know, Highness. I just got off the com with Bial. He tried to talk her out of it."

"I'm sure that went over splendidly." Pouring myself another drink, I tried to find the words I needed. I was going to have to tell Emmory about my little problem. "What in the hell precipitated that?"

Gods damn it, Hail. This is your out. Don't you get it? Let Ganda be all prim and proper and locked in this place. You can go back to your old life.

Except I couldn't. It was likely by now that everyone in the known universe knew who I was. I couldn't go back to my old life. The stream of Cheng curses I spit into the air was particularly vile. Emmory didn't flinch, but Zin's gasp was strangled.

The ping interrupted my tirade. Rubbing a hand over my face, I took a drink and then answered the call connecting Emmory in as well so I wouldn't have to repeat the conversation. "Good afternoon, Clara."

"Your Highness, I just heard about your empress-mother's order." Matriarch Desai's face was carved into a deep frown.

"Can you talk to her? There are slightly more important

things to deal with right now. I have the lamp lighting tomorrow."

Clara dipped her head in agreement. "Be that as it may, your empress-mother is not to be argued with."

I could argue with her; it just wouldn't end well. I made a face and dragged my hands through my hair.

"There isn't anything I can do about the briefings, Your Highness. She'll attend many of them, and obviously, if you were caught disobeying her orders, things could get worse. We have no idea what her reactions will be right now. However, your *Ekam* has pointed out, and I happen to agree with him, that having Ganda do the lamp lighting tomorrow will cause unnecessary confusion among the general population. You are the heir; whatever contentions exist between your empress-mother and yourself right now are not the real issue. She has already acknowledged you as heir, and though the Matriarch Council has not yet given their approval, it's not something that can just be taken away."

Clara looked away for a moment, her jaw set, and then sighed softly as she faced me again. "Indrana is unstable, Your Highness. The last thing we need right now is a debate about who belongs on the throne. Your empress-mother is no longer capable and we need a clear line of succession. I understand your hesitancy about providing an heir of your own, and I agree there are far too many other pressing issues at the moment. However, the Bristol line must continue. I suggest you start looking. At the very least it will help placate your empress-mother.

"You will do the lamp lighting tomorrow—that is an order from the council. If we get lucky, your empress-mother will slip back into her dementia for a while and it will pass unnoticed. Bial will do what he can to keep her from the news coverage for the day."

"And if we're not lucky?" I didn't particularly want to be shot for doing what the council said.

"I will handle it." Clara smiled, and for a moment she looked as tired as I felt.

"Thank you." I rubbed at the back of my neck with my free hand. "I appreciate all your support here, Clara, you didn't have to—"

"You are the heir, Your Highness. I was there when your empress-mother birthed you. I know you are her blood and I know you can rule this empire as well as your mother has."

Her words were honest, not pandering or an attempt to curry favor with me. I was grateful for them but couldn't find the words to say just how much.

Clara smiled again. "Your empress-mother didn't say anything about you not being allowed visitors. If this stretches beyond today, I'll see about sending someone to keep you up to date."

I nodded and cut the connection. Alba was whispering quietly with Zin by the door and I could feel Emmory's eyes on me as I wandered to the windows and cracked one open. Cold air rushed in, alleviating some of the claustrophobia that had already gripped me tight.

There was access to the tunnels my sisters and I had used for years to sneak out of the palace in these rooms. It was buried in the back of my wardrobe. If we needed to, we could still get out of here. The thought helped calm me down as much as the air did, or maybe it was the second glass of alcohol. I rolled the empty glass between my palms and watched the waves crash on the shore.

The words I needed wouldn't come. How did one admit to being useless?

You'll have to do something, Hail. There's no point in a farce of a marriage since you can't have a baby.

Cloning was illegal, but maybe I still had viable eggs in my damaged ovary and I could have a tubed baby. Tubed babies were commonplace in the Solarian Conglomerate, where women preferred to keep working rather than deal with the mess of pregnancy and childbirth. They claimed lost productivity wasn't worth the experience.

In the empire it was frowned upon, especially among nobles, and I couldn't think of a point in our history where the royal family had had to stoop to something so unnatural.

"Desperate times call for desperate measures," I murmured.

"That they do, Highness."

I jumped, squeezed my eyes shut, and cursed Emmory in Cheng. He laughed and said, "Actually, Highness, my grandfather was a very attractive man."

"I shouldn't be surprised you speak Cheng," I replied and went back to watching the waves crash on the shore.

"Likewise, Highness. Your ability with languages puts mine to shame."

I felt a smile hovering just out of reach, but didn't look at Emmory as I asked, "How many do I have you beat by?"

"Three and a half," he said. "I speak passable Svatir, but I'm not fluent in it."

"The verb conjugations are a bitch." I let my smile show as I glanced over at him. "And they're so quick to take offense if you mess up. I guess I'm stuck in here for the day. Give the Guards a rest. I'm safe enough in my rooms with someone on the door, and if you leave someone in here with me, it'll just make the rooms seem even smaller."

"All right, Highness."

I didn't tease him for the lack of argument even though it surprised me. If I hadn't been spinning possible solutions to this trouble with Mother, I probably would have realized what my *Ekam* was up to.

Cire had chosen better than she could have imagined, for there was no one better to find the people who murdered my sisters and my niece than Tracker Emmory Tresk.

The sun shone in a clear sky as I exited the aircar, smiling and waving to the crowd who'd gathered to see the flame lit. My BodyGuards followed in a tense formation around me, and I elbowed Jet lightly. "Smile, for fuck's sake, you're all scaring the crap out of people."

"We're your BodyGuards, Highness. We're supposed to scare people," he replied, his gray eyes never leaving the crowd.

"Not like this," I murmured.

Fear tempered the ground ahead of my BodyGuards. A bystander might not have noticed, but I was looking for it, so I saw how people shifted out of the way of Nal, who led my black-clad Guards toward the temple. The look of wary suspicion they couldn't quite hide dampened the joy in the air like a wet blanket. They weren't afraid of me; people still called my name and smiled in my direction. It was my Guards who garnered the reaction.

"Emmory."

"I see it, Highness," he replied from just behind me.

"What's going on?"

"Not now."

I gathered up the heavy fabric of the traditional white sari I wore and mounted the steps. "Fine. Later, though, and for right now, tell the others to smile. Or at the very least to stop looking like they're going to eat someone." I hissed the last bit, pasting a smile on my own face and holding out my hands to greet Mother Superior Benedine.

She'd become the head of the Indranan temple when I'd been just a girl. Now there was gray in her brown hair and lines around her serious eyes.

"*Anand*, Your Highness," she said, kissing my forehead.

"*Anand*, Mother Superior." I returned the greeting and sank down to my knees in front of her.

I wouldn't admit it to anyone, but I'd missed this ceremony. I missed the smell of incense hanging heavy in the air, missed the cool drops of lemon-scented water she shook onto me as she chanted the blessings.

"May your light be stronger than the darkness," the abbess murmured as she pressed her thumb to my forehead. The precious sandalwood paste filled my nose with its sharp, woody smell.

She moved past me and I hid my surprise when Emmory allowed the mother superior to bless all my BodyGuards in the same manner. It was just as well I did because the media cameras were hanging in the air like flies, recording everything.

Smile for the cameras, girls. My father's voice whispered in my ear and my arm was moving before my brain caught up with it. Dropping it again would have looked foolish. So I pasted a smile I hoped looked somewhat genuine onto my face and waved.

The crowd roared in approval. This was no snotty gathering of nobles. It was the backbone of Indrana: the workers, the merchants, the businesswomen—all the people who made up the empire.

In truth, who *made* the empire.

My stomach cramped as I looked out at the sea of faces,

174

and the reality hit me square in the gut. If I left the care of my empire and my people to someone like Ganda...that was something I couldn't do.

Oh, bugger me. I am well and truly fucked. They need this, need me.

None of this showed on my face as I continued to smile and wave to the assembled crowd. Mother Superior Benedine stepped up to my side and raised her hands, quieting the cheers.

"There has been a shadow in our hearts and a grief coating this empire. Now, as we enter the holy festival time, we look to the return of the light.

"It is a fateful time, for another light has returned also, the shining star of Indrana. I give you the Heir to the Throne; may her light banish these dark times!"

The crowd roared its approval.

She turned and pulled the torch from the Dark Mother's lower right hand. I was supposed to take it from Benedine, light the massive copper basin at the Dark Mother's feet, and then replace the torch in Her lower left hand.

Instead, when I reached for the torch, I spotted a familiar face in the crowd. My breath ghosted out of my lungs as if I'd been spaced. The next few moments played out like a corrupt digital video, all jerky and disjointed.

A split second later I saw another man with a gun off to the left. Emmory shouted. Nal froze. Jet, already in motion, tackled me. We went spinning off to the side of the statue, the first shot hissing through the air at us.

I felt the sting when the shot passed through Jet's upper shoulder and nicked mine. The jolt of current that followed had me throwing curses into the air as my *smati* blacked out from the interference.

We hit the stone floor with enough force to eject the rest of my air, sliding to a stop before I bashed my head on the base of the statue.

Jet went limp when he cracked his temple against the marble corner. I swore, fumbling at his belt for his gun, as a second gunman sprinted across the stage.

I jerked the gun free and squeezed the trigger. My would-be assassin crumpled to the floor missing a chunk of his head.

"Jet!" Keeping one eye on my surroundings, I felt around his head and breathed a sigh of relief when my hand came back clean. I was not so lucky with his shoulder, but I decided I'd gladly take the bloodstains on my sari in exchange for his moan of pain.

"Wake up," I said, unwinding my sari and pressing it to the wound with my free hand. "You're not allowed to die for me."

Jet cracked an eye open. "Sorry, Highness, that is in my job description."

"Not funny."

His sharply angled face transformed briefly with a quick grin. "What hit me?"

"More like you hit this." I gestured up at the statue of the Dark Mother with his gun.

"Help me up." Jet groaned, ignoring my protests. He froze when he spotted the dead body near us. "Mother of all. Highness, did you shoot someone with my gun?"

"He was going to kill me," I replied with a tiny shrug.

"I'm going to get it from the commander for that."

"Sorry, it seemed like the best—" I jerked the gun back up, but it was Emmory who skidded around the corner.

"Highness, are you all right?"

"I'm fine. Jet needs a Farian. Is anyone else hurt?"

"Why didn't either of you answer your com?"

"Disrupter shot," I replied. "I just took a piece of it. Jet got the worst."

"Sunshine is safe. I repeat, Sunshine is safe." Emmory dropped down into a crouch next to me.

"Sunshine?" I groaned. "You're fucking kidding me." They'd apparently kept the old codename from my childhood.

"It seemed appropriate, Highness," Zin said, sliding to a halt with Cas on his heels. "Nal and Salham went after the third shooter, Emmory."

"Good. I've got an ITS transport on the way. We need to get her out of here."

"I'm not going anywhere."

That made Emmory blink. "Excuse me, Highness?"

"Was anyone else hurt?" He shook his head and I glanced over his shoulder as Zin and Cas came around the corner of the statue. "Jet will be okay," I continued, finally releasing my grip on his gun so I could reach for the knife at the small of my back. I ignored Emmory's look and sliced through the top piece of my sari that was pressed to Jet's wound, unwinding the rest and rewrapping it around my waist. The long-sleeved white shirt I wore underneath was streaked with blood, but there wasn't anything to be done with it now.

"I'm not letting some idiot ruin this ceremony," I said and got to my feet. "Get that body off the stage. You do what you need to, *Ekam*, I'm going to light that damn flame."

"Highness, you should go," Benedine said.

I touched her shaking hands. "Are you all right?" At her nod I smiled. "Then we'll do this. Bristols aren't afraid of a little gunfire and I'll be damned if I let someone interrupt this for my people."

Somehow the torch hadn't gone out when I dropped it, and

with Emmory and Zin flanking me, I held it aloft until the crowd quieted from their panic.

"People of Indrana, know this—I will never back down from a challenge. I will never forsake you. Our light will shine through the stars now and forever." My words echoed through the air. I thrust the torch into the copper basin and the flames roared up.

"Okay, you've lit the damn thing. Now move." Emmory grabbed my arm the second I got the torch back into its holder and practically dragged me to the waiting transport.

"He's mad at himself, not you, Highness," Zin murmured after Emmory barked an order at me to "sit the hell down" and strode out of the room snarling for Nal.

"It wasn't his fault." I pulled on the tear in my choli, trying to get a look at the shallow furrow in my shoulder.

"Don't mess with it." Zin slapped my hand and winced. "Sorry, ma'am. Let the doctor look at it."

I grinned at him. "You have younger sisters, don't you?"

"One older and three younger, ma'am. Captain Hafin on the *Para Sahi* is the eldest. Can I see if your *smati* will link?"

I nodded. The damn thing had been flickering on and off since I'd been hit. I felt trapped in a black hole, no light or sound, cut off from the world around me with only my pitiful gods-given senses to manage the deluge.

With any luck, Zin might be able to jolt it back up fully and save me from another trip to the plastic coffin at the mod-center. The easiest way to facilitate the process was for me not to think about it.

"How's Jet?"

"He's fine," Zin replied. "Fasé saw to him on the way back to the palace and they've got him at the mod-center to get his gear back up and running."

"Good." A shudder crawled through me as Zin's *smati* tried to make contact with mine. It was like ants running on my skin, and I wondered briefly how people had stood it before this technology was commonplace.

Zin muttered a curse under his breath and frowned. "Why won't that... There you are. Give me a second, Your Highness."

I tried not to hold my breath and closed my eyes to the wave of dizziness as my *smati* came fully back online.

"That's better. Thanks."

"You're clean." He smiled at me and got to his feet. For some stupid reason it reminded me of Portis and the pain that shot through me had nothing to do with my injury.

I faked a smile—poorly—and ignored Zin's concerned frown as I tucked my feet up under my skirt and rested my head on the back of the couch.

It was quiet enough in the room that I let myself slip into a doze until Emmory returned with a nervous-looking doctor. I resisted the urge to tease him about being new as he cleaned and bandaged the shallow scrape with shaking hands. The bandage melted into the wound and within moments the stinging pain was gone as the skin fused itself over the cut.

"Thank you."

"My pleasure, Your Highness." Zin led the man out, holding the door open for Stasia as they crossed paths.

My maid slid a large tray onto the table in front of me and I shot her a grateful smile when she poured me a mug of blue chai and passed it over.

"You're a blessing," I said, holding the steaming mug up to

my face. The adrenaline had worn off and now I felt disconnected and as shaky as that young doctor.

"Do you want me to start a bath, Highness?"

As tempting as it was, I shook my head. "No, but if you'll lay out a change of clothes for me, I'd appreciate it. Don't go anywhere," I said to Emmory. "I want to talk to you."

I reluctantly pushed to my feet with a groan, still holding my chai. "I'm all right." I waved off Emmory before he could help me up. "That man hits like a professional baller."

"I believe Jet played in college, Highness. Turned down several pro offers to join the military," Emmory replied with a straight face.

"I'm not surprised by this at all." Shaking my head with a laugh, I made my way to my room. Indranan rugby was an odd mishmash of old Earth rugby and cricket—thankfully without the bats the later sport employed back in the SC. It was a way for men to get their aggressions out and also served as a showcase for women to admire the physique of the players. The whole thing made me uneasy, even though I'd enjoyed it when I was younger.

Ten minutes later I was cleaned up and dressed—at my insistence—in black pants and a long-sleeved shirt. Stasia left my hair in the intricate braid but took out the heavy diamond tiara that had miraculously stayed in place throughout all the excitement. I refused her offer of shoes and padded barefoot back into my waiting room.

Emmory backed away from Zin where they'd been in quiet conversation.

"First things first," I said as I curled back into the corner of the sofa with a new cup of chai. "Jet's really okay?"

"Yes, Highness." Emmory didn't smile, but his reply eased my nerves.

"Good. Did you get an ID on the first shooter?"

"We'll handle it, Highness."

"Is that a nice way of telling me to mind my own business?" I smirked at him when he raised an eyebrow. "I realize it hasn't even been a week, Emmory, but you should realize that it's not going to happen. This is my business. You know this wasn't your fault, right?"

"I shouldn't have let you go."

I bit my lip to keep from laughing at Zin's stunned look and busied myself with putting my cup back on the table as I hunted for the right response.

"Sit down, both of you. Come on, it's awkward to have this conversation with you looming over me and I don't want to get up." I pointed at the couch and gave Emmory a look of my own. "Sit. Down."

Zin moved first and only then did Emmory budge. I was pretty certain if it had been just me and him, we'd have stayed in deadlock for a few days before someone—me, more likely—passed out from thirst.

They dwarfed the delicate, rose-colored couch and I had to press my lips together to hold in my laughter. I leaned back and crossed my arms.

"Not your fault," I repeated. "You're going to have to trust me on this one, Emmy. Whoever is behind this isn't going to quit. They're going to take shots at me. They're going to try and kill me. It's not the first time in my life that's ever happened. If Portis was sending reports back, you know that already. I'm not going to cower in a cage thinking it will somehow keep me safe. Mother's sick and I have to step up and take the brunt of the responsibility."

I leaned forward. "What in the hell was with everyone being so scared of you guys?"

"There were reprisals, Highness," Emmory replied. "After Pace succumbed to the ebolenza and then again after the explosion. Bial sent Guards into the streets, presumably on the empress's orders, to find the men responsible. Several people were executed in the main square the day you arrived home."

"Without a trial? By BodyGuards?" I snapped my mouth shut as my exclamation came out louder than I'd wanted it to. "Emmory, they are not meant to be used as—"

"Executioners?" Zin finished my sentence, his face hard with fury. "The empress used them as such. The news of it was all over the empire. Hundreds of people were rounded up in the weeks following Princess Pace's death. Princess Cire protested, but your empress-mother refused to listen to reason. We have no idea what happened to them."

A horrible chill crawled over my skin. I pressed a hand to my mouth, struggling with the now familiar surge of guilt that mixed with my outrage. This was my fault. Because I had been stupid and selfish and—

"If your empress-mother gave such an order, it was because of the dementia, Highness." Emmory's reassurance was off the mark, but it helped derail my self-loathing nonetheless.

"Maybe," I murmured sadly, unable to look him in the eye.

"It's more likely that Bial or your cousin gave the order. He also knew of our orders to go get you. After Princess Cire was killed, I felt it was best to notify him we were en route to retrieve you. There's a good chance that he told Ganda." Emmory shifted uncomfortably in his seat.

"Yet another reason not to trust him. You think that's why Memz tried to kill me on *Sophie*? She'd been with me for six years, Emmory." I wouldn't have put it past her to sell out to someone, but how did they know where I was?

"I don't know, Highness. Only a few people knew where you

were. Most of them are dead," Emmory continued. "Which is why the majority of the BodyGuards are not to be trusted, Highness. I am weeding out the ones on your team as fast as I can, but there are some I have no control over."

"Nal," I said, just as she came through the door. "Speak of Kroni and she appears," I muttered under my breath as Emmory and Zin got to their feet.

"Your Highness." She bowed low without so much as a glance in Emmory's direction. "Your empress-mother is headed this way."

"Hailimi!" The shout echoed from the hallway.

14

I was on my feet before Mother got into the room. Blocking the slap would have been easy, but I braced myself and took it. The impact stung, snapping my head to the side.

"Disrupting a sacred ceremony with bloodshed. What the hell were you thinking?"

"I'm fine, Mother." I rubbed at my cheek. "Thanks for asking, and if you don't mind me pointing it out I wasn't the one disrupting anything. Someone tried to kill me. Typical luck for this family lately." I mentally winced at my snide tone.

"You shot a man, Haili!"

"He was trying to *kill* me." My grip on my temper slipped precariously at the condemnation in my mother's voice. There was no sympathy, no concern. Dementia or no, you'd think she'd be a little worried about me.

Get a grip, Hail. She doesn't get to pick and choose when she's lucid.

"The media—" Mother sputtered, waving a hand in the air. "Hailimi, you were caught on camera murdering a man!"

Even Bial winced at that one and surprisingly defended me. "Your Majesty. The princess did not murder—"

"Fine, killed. Whatever," Mother snapped at him. "We don't need the reminder that our daughter was a criminal. Which is exactly how those jackals will use this."

"I'm sorry, was I supposed to let him kill me?" The second slap wasn't even as hard as the first, but I thought I showed admirable restraint by not hitting her back. I was, however, at the end of my patience. "Mother, I'd suggest not hitting me again."

"Don't threaten me, child." The command and the imperial set of her spine were ruined by the fact that she took an immediate half step away from me.

"It's not a threat," I said, keeping my voice even through sheer force of will.

Bial's hand twitched toward his gun and the tension in the room ratcheted up several notches.

"I told your father we should have hit you more. Shouldn't have let you play with those hooligans. It's distressing I have no proper daughters left. I should have formally adopted Ganda as was suggested."

Now Mother was rambling, starting a slide away from coherence that was becoming familiar, but I raised an eyebrow at the last bit. If we'd been alone, I would have pushed her a little about just who'd suggested she adopt my cousin, but I wasn't about to grill my mother in front of everyone.

"It's a little too late for that. I supposed you could join forces with whoever is trying to wipe out our family. Though they're three and zero with me, I'm not sure I'd put money down on them just yet."

Bugger me, Hail. Could you stop sounding like a petulant child every time you speak to your mother?

Mother didn't notice my grimace. She grabbed me by the shoulders and jerked me close. "I am betrayed by those closest to me, my little terror. I'm sorry. You are the only one left," she whispered.

This wasn't dementia ravings. The haze of sickness had lifted from her eyes, replaced with a determined desperation blazing within. For a moment I saw the mother I'd worshiped, the one from my childhood who could do no wrong.

Just as quickly, the mother I remembered was gone, replaced by the cold empress I hated. She shoved me away, turning her back on me as if nothing had happened.

Emmory caught me before I tripped over the couch in my shock, his hands squeezing my upper arms lightly before he let me go.

"You have BodyGuards for a reason, Hailimi." Mother sniffed, gathered up her gray skirts, and marched out of the room without another word.

"Highness, I am sorry." Bial murmured the genuine apology to me and followed her from the room.

"At least she seems to have forgotten that I wasn't supposed to leave my rooms." I rubbed at my face, trying to decide which problem to tackle first. I didn't want to talk about what had just happened. There were too many ears around, even with Emmory's surveillance-blocking abilities. "Did they really catch me on camera?"

"I'm afraid so, Highness."

"Is the response bad?" I bit my lip as I turned to the window. The last thing I needed was bad press. Not that it was worth trading my life to avoid, but Mother was right about one thing in that we couldn't afford any more bad press for the throne right now.

"Actually most of the major networks are being very sympathetic about it. The spin at the moment is of the 'thank the gods she's okay' variety. The fact that you still lit the flame helped with that," Zin replied. "We'll see if that holds."

"I didn't do it for the brownie points," I muttered, swiping both hands over my face.

"Highness."

The sympathy in Zin's voice threatened my already tenuous grip on my emotions. "Don't." My voice was too sharp, cutting through the air like a laser-blade. "Sorry. I'm sorry. Just give me a minute, okay?"

I turned toward the windows and gripped the sill so hard it was a miracle the wood didn't splinter. *Snap out of it, Hail. You can't fall apart now.* Killing someone wasn't easy and I saw the man's sightless eyes when I closed my own.

Zin gave me space. Emmory, unsurprisingly, didn't. He'd taken me seriously when I said I wanted honesty.

"Let it go, Highness. You were protecting yourself. It's obvious the empress isn't herself."

"I think you'd be surprised how close that was to the arguments we had before I left," I said. My reflection smiled wryly back at me. "She hit me less then, but that's about the only difference."

"With respect, Highness, she might treat you less like a wayward daughter if you stopped giving her the opportunity."

"I know," I sighed. "I'm trying, it's just... She brings out the best in me apparently." I forced a smile. *"It's not the violence that bothers me, Emmory."* I used our dedicated com on my *smati* for the first time since this whole thing started. *"Did you hear what she said to me?"*

Emmory didn't even blink. *"No, Highness. What did she say?"*

"Not here. We need to get out of the palace. The ocean would be best." The roar of the waves and the song of the dolphins

would give us the perfect cover for a conversation that had to be private.

"You're not going out in the open again."

"I'm not staying trapped in here for the rest of my life, however short it might be." I didn't miss the fury that ripped through his face at the suggestion he couldn't keep me alive, but I wasn't about to back down. *"No one knows I want to go. It's not like some dolphin will be lying in wait to try and kill me. And we have to talk."*

"Fine," he said, surprising me with his abrupt agreement. "Zin, tell Jet to come in."

I turned away from the window with a frown at my *Ekam*. "He's not coming back on duty, is he?"

"He asked if he could speak with you, Highness."

Jet came into the room, looking weary but healthy, and dropped to a knee in front of me. "Highness."

"Fasé took care of you. Did they get you hooked back in?" I smiled, shoving aside my worry.

"Yes, ma'am."

"I think we can spare you for the day, Jet. Get up, man. Get some rest. We'll see you tomorrow."

He looked up at me in surprise. "Ma'am?"

"Was I not speaking Indranan?"

"Your Highness, I've come to give you my resignation."

"Excuse me?"

"I failed you." Jet dropped his eyes to the floor. "Your blood was spilled. It's unforgivable."

I whirled on Emmory. "Did you tell him he had to do this?"

He looked just as startled as I was. That wasn't good.

"No, Highness. I don't think—"

I waved a hand, cutting Emmory off, and turned away, casing the room as I did. Zin and Cas had the same looks of poorly concealed shock as the rest of us, but there was a smug look in Nal's eyes that I didn't like at all.

My brain raced through my options at lightning speed. If Jet had been on my crew, I would have bought him a drink and given him my share of the profits from the job. I learned early on from Po-Sin that fear was a great motivator but that it didn't inspire much loyalty. That came from praise and tangible rewards.

Rewards happened in front of the rest of the crew. Ass chewings were private affairs. I nudged Jet with a bare foot. "Get your ass up."

"Highness?"

"You heard me, get your ass up." I let him get to his feet and then grabbed his face with both hands. "Ojayit Uli Gaiden, I realize you hit your head today; however, I doubt very much it scrambled your brains enough to make you believe I would let you walk out of here in disgrace. You saved my life." I shook him, the bracelets Stasia had forced on me in a desperate attempt to break up my severe outfit jingling with the movement; then I released him with a smile. "I would be a fool to let you go. I thank you for it and I owe you for it."

Jet was still staring at me, confusion etched into his weathered face. His dark gray eyes darted between me and Emmory. "Your Highness, I—"

"Highness, your empress-mother will object."

"You will hold your tongue, Nalmari. I haven't asked for your opinion." I didn't raise my voice but my *Dve* jumped like she'd been stung.

Okay, so most of the time ass chewings happened in private.

"You think on it," I said with another smile at Jet. "My influence sucks at the moment, but that'll change eventually. If it's in my power, I'll grant you whatever you ask. Now, go get some rest." Winking at him, I gave him a little shove toward the door. "You say, 'Yes, ma'am,' and get out of here."

"Yes, ma'am," Jet echoed, still looking utterly baffled as he left the room.

"Zin, out." I waited for the door to close before I turned on Nal. "Do we have a problem?"

"No, Highness."

"I welcome suggestions, Nal, but not if they are prefaced by 'my empress-mother objects' or 'my empress-mother will be offended' or any variation thereof. I don't care about what my empress-mother would do. I am not her. Is that clear?"

"Perfectly, ma'am."

"Get out of here." I watched her go and muttered an unpleasant word under my breath. "Emmory, when you have a moment, I'd like the files on all my BodyGuards," I said, and headed back to the window.

"May I ask why?"

"I'm not going to interfere with your choices." I grinned at him and leaned against the sill. "But I think it's only fair I know something about the people who are risking their lives for mine. You included."

"I think I've misjudged you."

"I'm not even going to ask what that means," I replied with a laugh. "Let me get my boots, Emmory, and we can go to the beach."

We avoided the throng of media at the front gate and took off in an aircar for the coast. Cas and Zin stood like the statues around Balhim Bay, silent sentinels against the chill winds that cut in off the water. I huddled deeper into my heavy coat, burying my nose in the pristine fur of a silver tigerfox as I walked along the shoreline.

I could see the palace from here. The bright blue domes and intricate windows peeked out from among the tall buildings of Krishan's downtown. The winter sun flashed off the steel surfaces, bouncing around and making the gold accents on the palace walls gleam.

Our ancestors had carried the plans and designs of their forefathers to this strange planet, surrounding themselves with memories of India in every rounded archway and curved dome they constructed.

The architecture of our capital reflected our roots at the core and then became more and more modern as it splayed outward toward the sea.

Emmory stood at my side, unaffected by the cold, in nothing more than a heavier version of his uniform jacket.

"Nal's right. Your empress-mother will not be happy about you keeping Jet." The wind and the song of the dolphins grabbed at his words with greedy fingers, tearing them into shreds almost as fast as they left his mouth.

"She'll deal. He saved my life, Emmory. I'm not going to can him just because I got hurt in the process. By that logic I should toss the lot of you." I trusted them now, and I didn't want to have to try and forge ahead without them.

I swore as I connected the dots. "That's why I don't recognize any of her Guards, isn't it?" All the familiar faces around my mother were gone and it shocked me to realize how much I cared. I'd seen the fear in her eyes when she grabbed me. She was sick, isolated, and I had no clue how to help her.

"I suspect so, Highness. Bial replaced Ven after the accident."

"Convenient."

"He was on the short list, Highness."

I made a face and didn't look Emmory's way. Every *Ekam* had a short list of replacements that could be trusted to take over if they were killed in the line of duty. Given how few people he trusted, I wondered if he had more than just one. "Doesn't mean I have to trust him, too. Ven's dead, Bial could be responsible."

"Bial picked the three Guard replacements for those who'd died with Ven. Then either he or your empress-mother replaced her other Guards one after another. She is extremely ill."

"She's slipping into paranoia." I tried hard to keep the tears out of my voice. Now wasn't the time to remember the scared little girl whose mother had suddenly become empress and left her alone. "She said she couldn't trust anyone around her." I recounted her words.

"I know that paranoia can manifest at the end, Emmory, but she didn't seem sick. If anything, it was the most lucid that I've seen her since I got back. It doesn't make sense."

"What are you thinking, ma'am?"

"I don't know. Something is off." I squinted out at the ocean. "I can't put my finger on it." Shaking my head in frustration, I crouched to examine the shimmering gray sand. I tugged off my glove and stuck my fingers into it. The cold burned, a thousand slivers of glass, but even that pain didn't ground me and I couldn't wrap my head around whatever was bothering me.

The desperate pleading in Mother's voice during that brief moment of sanity had jammed a knife into my chest and twisted it sideways. She'd given up any hope of surviving, laying all her faith on me instead. The one gods-damned daughter who'd failed her time and again.

"That doesn't give me a lot to go on." Emmory crouched at my side, dark eyes still tracking the space around us, ever alert for any sign of a threat.

"I know. I'm sorry." I looked up from the sand. Emmory's face was expressionless, and I knew anything I told him would be calculated and analyzed with the speed and precision that only a Tracker could manage.

But there was something else, a flicker of concern in the depths of his eyes that gave me the strength to bare my soul to him. He was my last link to Portis—if I couldn't be honest with him...

"I saw an old friend at the lamp lighting." I swallowed. "Taz was in the crowd. I spotted him just before the shooters appeared."

Trust was a double-edged sword here. Tazerion Benton Shivan had been my best friend and the man Mother wanted me to marry. Of course, if she'd suspected he was a member of the *Upjas*, I doubt she'd have been so excited about our marriage.

"I don't know why he was there. He wasn't one of the shooters." The words tumbled out of my mouth as I watched suspicion cloud Emmory's face.

"I don't believe in coincidences."

"Neither do I, but he wasn't pointing a gun at me, Emmory. And he seemed just as surprised as everyone else when the shooting started." I shook the sand off my hands. "You think I'm stupid for defending a man I haven't seen in twenty years."

"I think," Emmory replied, clearly choosing his words with care, "you are quick to discount the *Upjas* when you haven't been home for a long time. There is no doubt of their goals, Highness. All their propaganda for the last year has been about removing your mother from power."

"He helped me find Father's killers; did Fenna mention that?" I looked away and changed the subject with the kind of ruthless disregard only a royal could get away with. "Mother and I had a decent relationship up until she was crowned. Even after, it was strained by the necessities of life at court, but we still managed to get along well."

I wasn't ready to talk about the *Upjas* with Emmory. I wasn't ready to admit to him that my sister had been in love with one of their leaders, or that both of us had been involved with the rebels before I ran.

"When Father died... things got bad. I was"—I dragged in a breath—"I was unmanageable."

"I remember the day we lost him, and I've seen the footage. You reacted with astonishing calm, Highness."

"He made me leave him. I should have stayed until the end." The confession was hoarse and I blinked back tears. "I idolized him. It drove me crazy the way people treated him. Even after everything he'd done, he was still nothing more than the empress's husband." I couldn't believe the bitterness in my voice. "He was a hero. A genius. We would have beaten the Saxons if he hadn't—" The words lodged themselves in my throat. I surged to my feet, needing to be on the move, and started down the beach with my skirts held in my hands.

"I wanted to follow in his footsteps. I wanted to join the Fleet. Join ITS. Anything to get me out of the damn palace and the bullshit restrictions that were strangling me. All the politics and lies. But Mother didn't want me in the military. She wanted me married and out of her hair."

"Highness, can you see it from your empress-mother's position? She'd just lost her husband. Perhaps she wouldn't send you into the war because she couldn't risk losing you, too."

Whirling on him, I threw my arms out wide in an extravagant gesture. "She lost me anyway! I thought if I hunted down the bastards who killed him, she'd at least let me live my life, but it wasn't good enough. Nothing I ever did was good enough."

I dropped my arms, my anger vanishing so abruptly my knees

almost gave out. I locked them, smiling sadly at Emmory. "Did you know Mother never said 'I'm sorry'? From the moment Daddy died, she never said those words again," I murmured. "Until today. I can't help her. I can't save her. I can't fix this. I've failed her again."

"Not your empress-mother, no. But you can help your people, ma'am. You can fix what's wrong here. Or at least get things started."

"She's going to get worse, Emmory."

"Most likely."

"I need some allies in court. Whom do you trust?"

He shook his head with a slight smile. "I don't trust anyone except Zin."

I gave him my best hurt look. "You still don't trust me?"

His smile grew and he dipped his head. "Maybe just a little, ma'am."

It was just the thing I needed to shake me out of my misery. "That's something, I guess." The laughter snuck up on me, spilling out of my mouth and into the freezing air. I bumped him with my shoulder, still giggling, and was rewarded with a little answering chuckle from my BodyGuard.

"Well, you're kind of stuck with me, seeing as how I'm the heir and all," I said once my laughter died out. Emmory didn't say anything to that declaration and I felt oddly vulnerable for a moment.

"I need your help, Emmory, especially if Mother is going to keep me out of the briefings. I need your help navigating this mess. You've been around court more than I have. Everything I know I learned from gunrunners and criminals..." I trailed off, uncertain how to continue.

"It's not true, ma'am. You learned plenty before you left

and..." Emmory shrugged. "I'd deny it in public, but you weren't far off the mark when you said there wasn't much of a difference between a princess and a gunrunner."

"Yes, but I was trying to persuade you to give me a gun at the time. I'm not sure I really meant it."

"Lying, manipulation to get what you want; see, you're already more than prepared for everything this planet can throw at you."

"If I didn't need your help here, I'd suffocate you in the sand."

"Yes, ma'am."

I tugged my gloves back on. "I guess we're stuck with each other then. I'm freezing. Let's get back to the palace."

15

The sun rose over the horizon as I sat curled up on one of the chairs in my room, blessedly alone for the first time in what felt like forever. I'd followed Mother's edict about not leaving my room since the flame ceremony, but it hadn't prevented me from having an endless parade of visitors to my room for the past four days. Admiral Hassan had been by to see me twice and Matriarch Desai had caught me up on the council meetings I was barred from. There had been a dozen other meetings with various people in the palace and two short interviews with carefully selected members of the media.

The remains of my breakfast were on the coffee table, and a fresh cup of blue chai threw steam up into the air. The fire Stasia had thoughtfully built up before she left roared in the grate.

I wrapped my hands around the mug, inhaling the sharp spice until it brought tears to my eyes. The sweet scent of clove reminded me of better days; of trips to the far North, where there were snowdrifts deep enough to bury myself in, of long days playing with my sisters in the snow and coming back inside to warm ourselves by the fire.

I put my cup down on the delicate glass table to my right,

noting in a kind of detached amusement that my hand was shaking. *Fiendishly difficult* didn't even begin to describe this situation. *Death trap* might be more accurate in the long run, and I still had no way to get free of it.

The burst of clarity in my room last week and my mother's desperate plea continued to haunt me. I'd pored over Dr. Satir's reports, trying to find something that would explain my nagging doubt. I didn't have a *reason* for it, which was the messed-up part.

Between my conversations with Clara and the admiral, plus all the information Alba was feeding me on a daily basis, it was clear the empire was in trouble. There'd been riots and unrest before my sisters' deaths, and they had only gotten worse since then. Things seemed to have died down somewhat with my arrival and the approaching holiday. It was almost as if the whole empire was holding its breath and waiting to see what I would do.

My standoff with Mother over the baby wasn't helping matters. Despite Clara's best attempts, she'd continued to insist Ganda be the official liaison with the heads of the three councils. Until we got this sorted out, I couldn't meet formally with the Matriarch Council and receive their confirmation of my position. This meant that even though my public stock had risen after the assassination attempt, within the palace I had less power than Mother's cats.

They got to go out whenever they felt like it.

Unless I fixed that, consolidating my position was going to prove difficult. Of course, I could just walk into a meeting and see what happened, but I wasn't certain going head-to-head with Mother was the wisest idea. I had learned a thing or two about diplomacy in the intervening years, no matter what anyone thought.

My hiss of frustration echoed over the crackling fire, and I shoved myself to my feet to pace. I wasn't going to challenge Mother outright for the throne; things were bad enough without adding that to the mix. We had to wait for her to come around to the idea of abdicating again.

But I wasn't going to get married either. I'd loved Portis too much, and even though we'd never gotten married, I couldn't just up and marry a total stranger. The very idea of it made me ill. I rubbed the heel of my hand over my heart.

Because that was the crux of the issue, I realized. I didn't want to forget Portis. I didn't want to marry someone else and have their baby like a gods-damned holy cow.

Even if I could.

The idea sprang into my head, awful and perfect all at once. I pressed a hand to my stomach, sinking to the ground with a silent gasping apology to a dead man for using his love as an excuse.

I didn't stay down long. One of my BodyGuards would notice the spike in my readings and come to investigate. It was better to move, better to be on the offensive. Grabbing my gold skirts in my hands, I scrambled to my feet and marched out the door.

"Let's go, boys. I need to speak with Mother."

Zin was already on his feet, had probably been on his way to check on me, but even he had trouble keeping up as I headed out of my rooms and up the hall to Mother's.

I dropped into a curtsy in front of the door Guards. "Princess Hailimi requesting an audience with Her Majesty."

There was a beat and then another as requests were issued and orders shot back over the *smati* comm lines.

"Granted, Your Highness. Please go in."

I nodded my thanks, sure that this was going to be the

subject of a hell of a lot of gossip in the thirty seconds it took me to get to the door of Mother's bedroom.

Bial stood just outside, a frown marring his handsome face. "Highness?"

"I need to speak to my mother about the wedding," I said. "How is she?"

Zin didn't quite suck in a breath, but I saw him stiffen. Bial raised an eyebrow, opened the door, and started to precede me through.

"Alone, please, Bial." I didn't have to force my awkward smile. "It's family business."

"Of course, Highness."

I was glad only my BodyGuards had access to my vitals so Bial couldn't see how hard my heart was hammering as I passed by him and pushed the door shut behind me.

"What is it, Hailimi?" Mother was still in her dressing gown, her skin paper thin in the morning light.

"Mama?" It was with cold deliberation that the little girl quaver wafted through the room. I was counting on Mother's instability to smooth the way for my lies.

Her haughty look melted and I felt doubly damned for the deception when she smiled. Swallowing back the guilt and my pride, I dropped to my knees at her feet. The tears that leaked out were real and my mother tilted her head to the side with a frown.

"Child, what is it?"

"Mama, I can't get married yet," I whispered, continuing in a rush when her face started to harden. "I can't, because I was already married—to Portis."

Mother blinked. "Oh, Hailimi, you didn't."

"I didn't know who he was!" I dropped my voice with a wince. "We were in love, Mama. I just—"

"You have been mourning. You went to temple. You offered prayers for your *sisters*." There was a dangerous flash of fire in Mother's black eyes and the cup in her hand rattled oddly as she set it down in its saucer. "All the while sullied with a marriage to a commoner!"

I scrambled to keep things on a sympathetic level. "I know. But I didn't think you'd want anyone to know so I had to play along. I was afraid it would embarrass the family." I wrapped both my hands around hers. "That's why I can't get married, Mama. Why I have to wait to have a child. You know it wouldn't—"

"Yes, I know." She pulled her hands out of my grasp, waving them in the air. The ring on her trembling finger winked and flashed in the sunlight. "Stupid child," she muttered. "The lighting of the sacred flame was permissible even with the mourning for your sisters, but if anyone found out you were mourning a husband—and a commoner at that." She rolled her eyes at the ceiling. "Shiva help the condemnation that would rain down on our heads."

My brief moment of sympathy was lost and I've never had to fight so hard not to punch someone in my whole life. Mother was relatively coherent this morning, but so deep in her role as empress that all she could see was how this would affect her rule. I wasn't even going to press her on just why she thought people would condemn me for something like that in this day and age.

I tried to tell myself that was fine, it was what I'd hoped for, and it didn't cut me to the bone. It didn't matter that Portis and I had never actually married—anyone who knew that was dead.

"Fine." Mother was lost in her own political world, unaware of my misery. "You may have your four months, but you are not to mention a word of this to anyone else. Do you understand me?"

"Yes, Mama." I folded my hands together and pressed them to my forehead. "Do I have your permission to involve myself at Court?" I asked formally.

"Yes, now go on so I can eat my breakfast in peace." She waved an irritable hand at me, so I got up without another word.

I curtsied low, then left the room, giving Bial a sharp nod on my way. I'd gotten what I wanted. Four months was the traditional mourning period. Hopefully by that time I could figure out what to do about this whole heir business. I'd gotten her approval to participate in Court—which I took to mean I could involve myself in anything I wanted.

And I'd fucking trade it all just to see Portis smiling at me again.

Halfway back to my rooms, the doubt that had been assailing me over Mother's dementia slammed into me with the same force as one of Johar's side thrusts. I spit curses into the air, grabbing for Zin when my knees gave out and I stumbled toward the wall.

"Highness!"

"I'm all right," I gasped, even though it was a lie. I wasn't all right. I'd never be all right again.

"Cas, find Dr. Satir." Zin didn't listen to me, scooping me up and striding down the hallway to my rooms.

"Zin, put me down."

My struggles almost earned me a broken nose, when Zin nearly dropped me on my face. He recovered enough to set me on my feet and I staggered for my bedroom, slamming the door when he tried to follow.

The awful thing I'd just witnessed replayed in front of my

eyes, overlaid on a memory. Mother's ring, flashing in the sun, the sparkle trembling in a distinctive rhythm. The way her cup had rattled in the saucer—once, twice, a third time.

"Well, this ended badly. I really thought we had something special." I raised my hands carefully, keeping them well away from my guns.

"Give me the money, Hao."

"You shoot her and I will peel the flesh off your body one centimeter at a time. After Portis is finished with you." Hao sounded pissed more than anything. I couldn't blame him. This piece of trash was messing with our already tight timetable.

The gun pointed at my right eye shook. Once, twice, a third time—the quick, rhythmic fluttering of an AVI-junkie.

"You're angel touched, Jones," I said, clicking my tongue. "How much longer do you have?"

"Shut up. Shut up!" His hand steadied, then repeated the distinctive tic that gave the drug its street name—Angel Wings.

Through the hazy memory, I heard Emmory just outside my door. "You left her alone?"

"She shut the door in my face," Zin replied.

"Next time kick it in."

I reached up and twisted the knob, opening the door before Emmory could do just that.

"Highness?"

I gestured at him to turn on his jamming device. "You'll be pleased to know Mother has agreed to a postponement of my duty to provide the empire with a daughter and has given me permission to involve myself at Court once more."

"We're alone," Zin said.

"She's got flutters." I got to my feet and pressed the back

of my free hand to my mouth. "Oh, holy—Emmory, Mother doesn't have dementia. She's addicted to AVI." The flutters appeared in long-term users, when rapid degeneration of the nerves set in and their bodies started failing.

"You saw it?"

A jerky nod was my only answer as terror crawled over my skin. She couldn't possibly be using intentionally. Someone had to have been dosing my mother with AVI for long enough that she was now in the end stages of addiction. Someone had to still be dosing her, or she'd be suffering from major withdrawal.

Amanita virosa indus. A fungus found on the planets in our home system similar to a poisonous strain found on Earth, but small doses only caused hallucinations rather than death.

Some enterprising soul had discovered that concentrating the mushroom concentrated the mind-altering effects of the drug. Mixing it with a counteragent removed the immediate deadly ramifications, but long-term exposure still resulted in death.

"Highness, sit down."

"I don't want to sit down. I want to kill someone. She's not a junkie, Emmory. This is my *mother*. The Empress of Indrana. Someone is dosing her. It's the only explanation." I grabbed on to my anger, using the heat to burn away my frozen fear.

I got the Look in reply then Emmory sighed and pulled a SColt 45 from under his jacket.

I had a heartbeat to panic and another to feel utterly foolish when Emmory flipped it around and handed me the gun.

"I saw the recording of the attack. You're right, Highness, you're safer armed. There're ammunition packs in the other room."

"That cost you a lot to admit, huh?" I took it. "I just said I wanted to kill someone, Emmory. Giving me a gun probably isn't the best of ideas."

"I second that."

Emmory shot Zin a look. "I trust you, Highness. Don't shoot anyone who's not trying to kill you, and for gods' sake, just kill them. Don't shoot pieces off them."

"Zheng Quen was fibbing, Emmy. I didn't shoot his toes off one at a time because he insulted me."

"True. I believe the reason for it was because he tried to kill you, ma'am."

I tucked my tongue into my cheek and dipped my head in acknowledgment. That actually wasn't the whole truth either. Quen had tried to kill Portis because I'd snaked a deal out from under him. We'd just left Po-Sin's employ, and I knew that without a reputation for violence, we'd be space junk before the year was out.

When I'd found out about the hit on Portis, I'd visited the man Quen had paid to kill him first, and then I paid Quen a visit.

Civilized people gasp and shake their heads at the story, but I don't regret it one bit. Gunrunning is as far from civilized as you can get—short of maybe the SpaceBoxing League. I could have killed Quen for what he'd tried to do, but live people spread your reputation around a hell of a lot faster. It bought us the space we needed to build our own business up without looking over our shoulders all the time.

After that incident, only the truly idiotic tried to cross us.

The gun Emmory had given me was a magnificent piece, matte black and compact enough I could hide it under a decent sari. I'd always liked the weight of the SColts but they were more appropriate for land use. Firing one on a spaceship could cause all kinds of problems, and not just for the person who got shot.

"You're being surprisingly sanguine about Mother." The weight of the gun in my hand calmed me down.

"The idea that someone would try to kill your empress-mother wasn't completely discarded," Emmory said.

"The fact that whoever's behind this actually managed to start with her is worrisome," Zin admitted with a grimace. "Ven was right to be paranoid."

"He'd heard some unsettling rumors, Highness," Emmory supplied before I could ask the question. "The kind of things a BodyGuard hates hearing. It worried him enough to send Ofa and Tefiz to meet with us."

"Speaking of BodyGuards, do we have to tell Bial?"

Emmory nodded his head. "I can't keep it from him. Dr. Satir will insist, and even if she didn't—"

"He could be part of the plot. How else could they have drugged her, Emmory?" I dragged a hand through my hair and hissed in frustration.

"If Dr. Satir didn't catch it on any of her scans, Bial might have missed it also," Emmory said. "It doesn't show up on normal tests. That's why it's such a popular drug. No one would think to check for something that common."

"Which is why they picked it. It's a perfect plan." Zin muttered a curse, winced when Emmory smacked him, and apologized. "This is getting worse by the minute. I don't like it."

"Right there with you," I said.

"Agreed," Emmory said at the same time.

The three of us shared a grim smile.

All it took was a simple test to prove me right. Dr. Satir's horrified look told me the answer before the words left her mouth.

"I don't understand, Your Highness, I didn't—"

"You didn't have a reason to look for it. Either of you."

Bial shook his head. "Very kind of you, Highness, but this is my job. I should have thought—" He broke off and rubbed a hand over his face. "How long has it been going on?"

"It's going to be impossible to pinpoint when she started ingesting it. I would need to know what kind of a dose she's been getting to even guess at a timeline."

"How bad is the damage?" I asked.

Translation: When is my mother going to die?

Dr. Satir paled. "Highness, as you noted, the shaking is a sign of nerve degeneration. Her liver is failing and so are her kidneys. The paranoia will only get worse."

"A Farian?" It was a stupid question to even voice. The last desperate gasp of a grieving daughter.

"You know they can't heal things like this," Emmory said.

He was right. Farians weren't magicians. Their powers encouraged the body's natural healing ability, speeding it up, nothing more. They couldn't reanimate dead tissue, repair dead nerves, or stop my mother's brain from slowly unraveling.

Bial cleared his throat. "Highness, we will need to convince your mother to abdicate the throne as soon as possible. We cannot risk having her—"

"You"—I whirled on Bial and the man actually backpedaled—"will not convince my mother to do anything! You are her BodyGuard. A task which you have failed at, I'll add.

"My mother is the Empress of Indrana, sick or not. I will speak to her and she will make the decision to abdicate the throne herself. I will not bully her like a child. Is that understood?"

"Yes, ma'am. I'm sorry." Bial bowed his head.

"Dr. Satir, come with me." I waved a hand at her as I headed for the door to Mother's bedroom.

"I take it you're done talking about me?" Mother was propped up in her massive bed, looking like a ghost against the mound of purplish pillows. Her hair was down, silver-black curls falling around her shoulders. "You look like someone's killed your dog."

"If I had one, that would cap things off nicely."

Mother laughed, but it quickly dissolved into coughing. I fumbled at her bedside table, pouring her a glass of water. Now that I was looking for it, I spotted the patterned flutter of her left hand with ease and it broke my heart into pieces.

"I swear sometimes it's like your father is talking out of your mouth, child. He was such a smart-ass."

"I'm sorry."

"Hush, Haili. Now, what's going on?"

"Majesty, you've been quite ill for some time now—"

"You're being poisoned, Mother." I shot Dr. Satir an apologetic look. We were lucky that Mother was coherent right now; I didn't want to run the risk of that changing with a long explanation.

Besides, I'd want this kind of news straight without a lot of dithering and I knew she would, too.

"We don't know how and we don't know how long," I continued. "We do know it's AVI."

"That awful drug the commoners poison themselves with every day?" Mother rolled her eyes. "Apparently my enemies have a sense of humor."

"Dr. Satir can tell you the specifics if you want. It's not good, Mother."

"Of course it isn't. I expect I will get worse?"

"Yes, ma'am," Dr. Satir whispered.

"Well then, I will meet with the Matriarch Council and announce my abdication. You will be there, Hail. I've just sent Tye a message to fill her in on what's going on. We will announce it immediately to quell any rumors. Tonight would be best. We'll plan for your coronation after Pratimas, though. I don't want to interfere with the holiday."

I exhaled a shaky breath and Mother smiled.

Then, just like a veil had been pulled over her face, her smile faded and she frowned at me.

"Haili, how many times have I told you and your sisters not to play dress-up in my clothes? You've made a mess of my closet and your father will be back any moment."

Oh, bugger me. My heart crashed into the floor.

"I'm sorry. I'll get it cleaned up."

"You do that. Quietly. I'm exhausted and I want to rest my eyes before your father gets home."

"Yes, ma'am." I backed out the door, nearly running into Tye in the process.

"The empress called me. Her message said she was going to abdicate the throne?"

I shook my head, unable to say anything without the tears coloring my voice. Thankfully Dr. Satir stepped in, explaining in a hushed voice what had just happened. Tye was equally on the ball. She had been with my mother for almost five years, and it seemed that little could shake her.

"Highness, the empress was supposed to sit in on a military briefing in half an hour. That will obviously be impossible."

"I'll do it."

Tye nodded sharply. "I will get together with Alba and figure out what to shuffle out of your schedule so you can meet with the Matriarch Council. I can have Admiral Hassan get you up to speed before the briefing starts."

"I've been following discussions somewhat, but I'd appreciate that." I glanced down at the relatively plain blue dress I'd talked Stasia into this morning and sighed. "I'm going to need to change. Please tell the admiral I'll meet her..." I fumbled. "Wherever we're supposed to be."

Tye didn't even crack a smile. "I'll send you the location, Your Highness."

"Thank you." I left Mother's rooms, my BodyGuards trailing behind me.

"Ma'am, you will want to breathe or you risk passing out," Emmory murmured. "Your heart rate is through the roof."

"I am panicking, Emmy. You'll just have to deal with whatever alarms are screaming in your head."

Not that anyone except my BodyGuards could have guessed my state of mind. My face didn't show the slightest evidence of my fear as Stasia helped me change. I was back out the door and striding across the palace to the conference rooms in under ten minutes, which had to be a record of some kind.

It was a good thing I didn't have a chance to think. That the little girl in me couldn't stop and mourn, wail over the loss of her mother. It was a good thing I was a gunrunner, trained not to show any fear.

If I stopped for a second, I was going to lose it.

"Your Highness." Admiral Hassan met me at the door. "Thank you for stepping in on such short notice. Chamberlain Tye informed me the empress is indisposed and asked if I would give you a quick briefing." She cracked a tiny smile and shrugged one slender shoulder. "Before the briefing as it were."

If the admiral was at all curious about my sudden appearance or my attire, she didn't show it. My dress was white, the three-quarter-length sleeves tight with no frills or lace to speak of, and my sari was the same blood-red one I'd worn to temple.

It was the sort of thing my mother would wear. The sort of thing an empress would wear.

"Today's meeting concerns some recent developments with the Saxons and our shared border. There have been some difficulties of late."

By difficulties, she meant the Saxons were chipping away at our border worlds while we sat by and did nothing about it. I didn't mention that and instead accepted the file the admiral sent me.

"I'm going to wander over here and read this," I said, waving to the corner of the room. "You can introduce everyone when we get the briefing started."

"Yes, ma'am."

"What do you think, Emmy?" I murmured as I skimmed over the file. "Should I announce the news and see what kind of reaction we get?"

"Unwise, ma'am. You still need approval from the matriarchs to take the throne."

"I'm her blood." Even as I protested, I knew he was right. It was a simple formality for the Matriarch Council to acknowledge my mother's abdication and approve of me as the empress, but that didn't mean that someone couldn't object.

Especially given that until I returned, Ganda had been dealing with them as though she would take the throne. I swallowed the curse. Tough luck for her. I wasn't leaving my people in Ganda's spoiled, selfish hands.

"They would need a concrete reason to deny you, Highness. The rules of succession are in your favor."

"I need to know what the atmosphere is before I go into that meeting. Alba?"

"Yes, ma'am?"

"Gather what you can. I won't need you while I'm here. There's a two-hour gap between this meeting and the one with the council. Luck hasn't been with me lately, but maybe we could figure out an angle of attack in that time. Maybe Ganda won't protest at all, if—"

I snorted back a laugh, drawing several looks from the military members filing into the room. I ignored them and sat down in my mother's seat.

If. Fires of Naraka, I was still so fucked.

"Go on, Alba, I'll see you after the meeting."

"Yes, ma'am."

I glanced quickly around the table so my *smati* could log the faces as people took their seats. The admirals in charge of 2nd and 3rd Fleets were only faces on holo-screens, their presence at the meeting beamed in from thousands of light-years away.

The other men and women around the table were dressed either in the black-on-black of the Imperial Guard or the dark blue of the Imperial Navy. Dressed in white, I blazed like a star amid the unrelenting backdrop of space.

"I have been informed that Her Majesty is indisposed and she asked if the heir would sit in on this meeting. Caspel, if you'll start off the introductions?"

The hawk-faced man in civilian dress to Hassan's right nodded sharply. "Director Caspel Ganej, Highness. Head of Galactic Imperial Security."

I nodded in reply and the introductions continued around the table.

"The Saxon Alliance has been pushing at the borders. Nothing overt enough to break truce, so long as their government keeps their peaceful-coexistence rhetoric pumping on the media lines," Hassan continued after the introductions were concluded. There was bitter laughter around the table. "They've 'convinced'"— there was no mistaking the sarcasm in the word—"three border worlds in the last two months to join the alliance."

"Why haven't we taken them back?" I could have bitten off my damn tongue when the question slid out.

Every single pair of eyes flipped in my direction—some filled with poorly concealed contempt, others with sympathetic agreement.

"Because, Your Highness," Admiral Shul, head of the 2nd Fleet, said slowly, speaking as if I were a child, "as long as the Sax claim to be sticking to the treaty, so must we. There's no obvious military involvement. The planets voted. At least according to the Saxons."

"Surely there are ways to get those planets back without overt military involvement on our part then?" I was already hip deep in it, so I figured I should just keep going.

"Don't you think we've discussed that already?" Shul replied, and the sharp bite of his voice over the speaker had several people at the table sucking in surprised breaths.

"Admiral Shul, you will modify your tone when speaking to the Crown Princess," Hassan snapped. "Highness, I realize you've..."

"Been out of the loop?" I supplied when she fumbled, and was relieved by the flash of humor in the admiral's brown eyes.

"If you wish, ma'am. I don't know if you've seen it yet, but the media lines have not been kind to us lately. With the economic problems in some of our outlying planets and the troubles here at home, one could make a case we've gotten a little too big for our own good. The whole galaxy pushed for the peace treaty with the Saxon Alliance, and it has held for longer than we could have hoped."

I remembered hearing the news of the peace treaty. Even as I'd tried to avoid information from the empire, the end to the seventeen-year war was enough to make the headlines across

213

the stars. We'd been in a little bar on some backwater planet, working hard at getting drunk.

"There's a sight I never thought I'd see," Portis said.

I turned my head toward the screen by the bar, blinking several times until the words shaped themselves into some semblance of order. "Peace treaty?"

"Yup, looks like those Earthies finally got their way. The Saxes and the Indys have signed a treaty." He grinned at me and lifted his drink in a salute. "Maybe we should expand our territory."

"No!" It came out sharp, but I was too drunk to care much about the look flashing over my Portis's face. "Those Saxon Alliance types get worked up about gunrunners. Besides, dumbass, they just signed a peace treaty. Not our market." I waved at the bartender for another shot and turned away from the screen before I could get a good look at the image of my sisters.

"Highness?"

"Sorry." I forced a smile out. "Please continue, Admiral."

"Caspel can probably tell us more," the admiral replied, looking at the hawk-faced man on my left. "What's the word on the ground?"

"Not good," he replied, rubbing a lean hand over the stubble of gray hair on his head. "We've lost contact with our assets on Primatoria IV. Could be dead, could be captured, could just not be able to answer their *smati*." There was a chuckle around the table at the dry humor.

"Reports from the Shiva System are unpleasant. It looks like the SA incited riots on the twin planets. It proved to be enough of a distraction for them to move troops in.

"What this means for us, Highness, is that as far as public opinion goes—those planets chose to leave the empire." He kept his brown eyes locked on me as he shrugged. "We could take them back by force, but—"

"There's no way for us to prove those planets didn't change allegiance willingly," I finished.

Caspel nodded. "Until we can, we are honor-bound to hold to the treaty or look the villain to the rest of the galaxy."

I nodded back, swallowing down the suggestion that we send in stealth teams of our own. A roomful of military minds probably wasn't the best place to suggest gunrunner tactics. I made a note in my *smati* to speak with the GIS officer later. Out of all the people present, he could be most receptive to my suggestions.

That is, if he wasn't part of the plot to kill me.

The conversation resumed around me, and I struggled to keep up with the myriad of names, dates, and systems flying through the air. By the time the meeting had ended, I had a file filled with information tucked away in my *smati* and a pounding headache.

16

"Caspel, will you hold back a moment?"

If he was startled, he hid it well. Caspel nodded and remained in his seat. No one else said a word to me as they filed from the room, though Admiral Hassan gave me a sharp nod and the briefest of smiles before she turned on her heel and headed for the door.

"What can I do for you, Highness?" The head of the GIS was the epitome of politeness and had a poker face that would be envied in most illegal gambling establishments on Resita Semora.

"What's the possibility of sending our own stealth teams in?"

"It's something ITS head General Vandi and I have discussed, Highness," Caspel replied. "I am trying to get a feel for the situation first."

"How many more planets do I lose before that happens?"

Caspel tilted his head and studied me. "As many as need to make certain your Highness doesn't lose the empire entire."

"Fair enough." I ran my tongue over my teeth and then smiled. "I'd like the names of the people responsible for the deaths of my sisters and my niece."

"I would give them to you, Highness, if I had them." His non-answer told me more than any names could have. "Your empress-mother had five men arrested for the transportation and sale of the ebolenza virus but we were never able to figure out how it made its way into the palace. Two of the men killed themselves in their cells, and the other three were executed before my people could finish questioning them.

"When Princess Cire and her daughter were killed, we were able to trace the explosives back to some of the more radical members of the *Upjas*. However, the two men and one woman whose names we obtained were killed in a shootout with royal BodyGuards the day you returned home. My contact with the *Upjas* was understandably edgy about the way things went down and hasn't been in touch since."

"A shootout? I heard they were executed."

"I suppose it depends on who you ask."

"Do you think it was the *Upjas*?" I didn't mention I had contacts of my own; it was just a matter of trying to get them to see me.

Caspel studied me for a silent moment before answering. "No, Highness. Not the main group anyway. Abraham Suda wants change, not bloodshed. But he doesn't have as tight a grip on the group as he once did, and there are factions who are a little more willing to see blood spilled to achieve their aims."

"Which are what?"

"The end of the matriarchy," Caspel said, flicking a glance at Emmory over my shoulder as he spoke. "I don't know if they're looking to put a man on the throne or dismantle the empire entirely, Highness."

"Do you think we'd be better with a man on the throne?"

"It will cause chaos we cannot afford. Whatever King Trace says in the public venue, his troops are moving. The Saxons have been preparing for this moment while we have been trapped by tradition and economic struggles. If Indrana goes down on a knee, Highness, we will lose the fight."

Besides Emmory, this was the bluntest response I'd gotten from someone since my return. Even Admiral Hassan had been vague in her replies.

"It's a risk to be so bold with me, Caspel."

He met my eyes unflinchingly. "I am the head of your intelligence service, ma'am. If I do not speak up, no one else will dare, and there is not much use for an intelligence service that does not share what it knows. Your sister appreciated the truth; I would hope you share that trait."

"A truthful spy. I confess that is a new one."

His grin was as quick and sharp as his bow. "Your spy, Highness. Indrana's spy."

"If you would send what information you have to Emmory, he and I will go over it. Perhaps a pair of fresh eyes will give us somewhere new to go with it. Given the number of times someone has attempted to kill me, it would seem that the perpetrators are still on the loose."

"Of course."

"Thank you, Caspel."

"A pleasure, Highness. Please call on me if you have need of anything." The smile transformed Caspel's face into something less severe.

I have stood up to murderers. Walked into Zheng-owned warehouses and back out again without even a scratch on me. I have fought my way through bars that even the law wouldn't set foot in just to have a drink. I have been shot, stabbed, blown up (or nearly so), had guns jammed under my chin and shoved in my eye.

None of that ever scared me as much as walking into those council chambers did.

The two hours flew by, barely giving us enough time to lay out all the possible objections and come up with compelling arguments against them. Thankfully, there were few realistic ones that Alba and Tye felt like the council might lay on the table.

I didn't know what I would have done without the help of the chamberlains or Zin. Despite his seaside upbringing, my Body-Guard had an impressive grasp of imperial politics and he came up with several objections we never would have considered.

It still took a hell of a pep talk to get myself through the door and an even sterner voice to keep me moving when I realized several of the matriarchs were already in the chambers.

Don't be a baby, Hail. You could take any one of them in a fight.

I'd have laughed out loud at that, except my eyes landed on Ganda at that exact moment. She was sitting in Mother's chair talking to Matriarch Saito. Her shocked face shook my mirth loose and I spied the quick narrowing of her eyes before she pasted a bright smile on her face.

"Hail! I was hoping your mother would allow you to join us. It's good to see you." She jumped up and extended her hands toward me.

Smiling back, I resisted the urge to break her fingers, instead squeezing her hands briefly and releasing her. "We have something important to discuss with the council today."

Fear flittered across Ganda's face, but I wasn't sure of the cause. It could have been my incredibly unsubtle use of the royal *we* or the fact that Tye was speaking quietly with Matriarch Desai.

Clara raised one gray eyebrow my direction but otherwise didn't react to the news Tye gave her.

I dipped my head at her and neatly slid into Mother's seat. I knew Ganda had been occupying it since Cire's death, and the look on her face as I took it back was priceless. Zin fell into parade rest behind my chair and I spotted the wary glances several of the other matriarchs aimed his way.

BodyGuards were not brought into the council chambers. While I was relatively confident about my ability to survive anything the women in the room threw at me, Emmory had insisted and I hadn't felt the need to argue with him.

Besides, I wanted Zin's eyes on the women in the room. He could look objectively at the matriarchs I'd grown up with.

"Ladies, take your seats," Clara said. "I am afraid I'm going to have to table our normal agenda in favor of something more important."

I leaned back. "Zin, be a dear and grab a chair for Ganda, will you? She seems to have lost her seat."

There was a moment of shuffling while Zin found a chair and put it right next to me. Once Ganda was settled, Clara continued.

"Her Imperial Majesty extends her apologies for her absence today and also for the imposition of allowing a BodyGuard into our session." She scanned the room. "Normally I would protest, but the decision is backed not only by the princess's *Ekam*, but the empress's as well. Given the recent dangers and in light of today's news, I have allowed it. Now would be the time to file a formal protest."

No one protested.

"You know no one is going to protest, Clara. Get on with it. You can't dangle a carrot like that and not expect us to start salivating." The elderly Matriarch Tobin grinned at me and thumped the floor with her cane. "What's the big news?"

"The empress is not suffering from Shakti dementia. She was poisoned," Clara replied.

The inhale was collective, except for Ganda, who was a half second late with her surprise. If I hadn't been listening for it, I would have missed it, and I couldn't be entirely sure my hatred wasn't making me hear things, which is the other reason I'd agreed to Zin's presence in the meeting.

"Chamberlain Tye has just passed Dr. Satir's report on to me. I will make it available to anyone here, but news of this is not to leave this room. Am I understood?"

There was a chorus of assent and I settled back in my chair, content to let Desai run the show for the moment even though several of the matriarchs shot looks my way that clearly expected an explanation from me.

"Her Majesty has also informed her chamberlain of her intent to abdicate the throne to her only surviving daughter as soon as she is approved and the coronation is complete. In light of her recent return and the current situation, I am sure the princess will not take offense to any legal objections that are raised during this meeting."

Oh, nicely handled, Clara. I kept my poker face on and did a quick sweep of the room. Now I'd be able to see the more obvious of my detractors, and hopefully more than a handful of allies.

"No objection." Matriarch Maxwell had been old before I ran away. Now she seemed practically ancient, but her family had always been crown loyalists. "She was proven the empress's blood at birth and proven the same when she returned."

It was a relief to have the eldest member of the council easily dismiss what could have been one of our biggest challenges—that I wasn't who I claimed to be. It didn't escape me that the one thing I'd been pissed at Emmory for in the beginning was now an important foundation for my rule.

Several other matriarchs murmured their agreement with Maxwell.

"Are you going to run again?"

Matriarch Gohil had passed away last year. Between my whirlwind briefing and the help of my *smati*, I identified the questioner as her eldest daughter, Alice. There hadn't been any malice in the question, but several women shifted uncomfortably as it danced along the edge of propriety. I met her cool, dark-eyed gaze. I liked the look of her.

"My reasons for leaving the first time were my own. I don't apologize for it. I've learned a lot in twenty years," I said. "Since I left home, I haven't run from anything—not a fight nor a duty. I'm here and here I'll remain until the Dark Mother calls me to temple." Every time I said the words, it felt more right, more like the thing I was supposed to do.

"No objection from the house of Gohil." Alice dipped her head slightly.

"Ganda has been running herself ragged for the sake of the empire since before the death of Princess Cire." Matriarch Khatri tugged on an auburn curl as she spoke. "She has done a great service to the Crown and shown an aptitude for leadership. I am not sure I see the wisdom in throwing her aside to put a gunrunner on the throne."

"Elsa, watch your tongue!" Matriarch Saito snapped. "Objections can be made without insulting the heir."

"What? It's not an insult if it's the truth. You've read the stories same as I have! She was a damn criminal from the minute she ran from the palace. Gods only know how many laws she's broken, how many people she's murdered!"

Things went predictably downhill after that.

"Zin, you will not say a word. I don't need you to defend my honor." I didn't have to look behind me to know my Body-Guard was watching the sniping in horror.

"They cannot insult you like this, Highness."

"Khatri is technically right. I was a gunrunner. She's deliberately insulting me to see what I'll do."

"Why aren't you telling them the truth of why you left?"

"Because I'm all right with this version for the moment. The chambers are protected space, and unless Clara decides she's out of line, we're keeping our mouths shut, understood?"

"Yes, ma'am."

I rested my elbows on the arms of my chair and steepled my fingers, trying not to smile as I watched the show. The older matriarchs were unwilling to engage in the behavior of the younger members, and I knew they were watching me even more than the women shouting at each other to see how I would react.

I had several very obvious supporters who were either genuine in their opinions or very good actresses. Those who supported Ganda seemed to be older, the matriarchs in the middle age range. Interestingly enough, they all came from houses that would stand to profit should Indrana go back to war.

I filed that tidbit of information away to discuss with Emmory later and glanced in Desai's direction. She answered my look with a raised eyebrow that said, *Do you want to stop this or shall I?*

People assume gunrunners conduct business with threats and snarls, waving weapons around and pummeling each other with fists.

There was some of that.

More often, though, it was detailed negotiations, promises, well-laid plans, and sly deals. The reminder that I'd done all this with people far more dangerous relaxed me, and I laid my hands on the table with a slow smile.

"Enough." I said the word with a forcefulness that cut through the din. "Ladies, this conversation, such as it is, is over. The empress has named me Heir Apparent, a right I already hold by proven blood. You are welcome to obtain some kind of legal proof to the contrary, but as of yet we've heard no real objection that would stand up against either tradition or the law. I wish you luck of it.

"I will, however, caution you. Further destabilizing the throne at a time when leadership is most needed is unwise. My mother is ill, my sisters are gone to temple, and our enemies are chipping away at our borders. There is no coincidence in this. Enemies of Indrana seek to divide us, and we will not sit by and watch our people suffer."

I rose and shook out my white skirts, smoothing the red sari draped over them, and smiled coldly. "We will announce Mother's abdication at the celebration this evening, and the throne expects your full support in public unless you choose to file a formal objection with Matriarch Desai."

To file a formal objection to my succession meant they not only had to come up with a solid legal defense, but also had to explain to their families why they'd broken from the decision of the empress on such a serious matter.

I'd effectively backed them into a corner, which could come back to bite me hard. Civilized people tend to panic when pushed, and they lash out with unpredictable results. I wasn't in the clear yet, and once they all settled down and read the report about the poisoning, I wouldn't be surprised to see an objection questioning Mother's competence.

Which was why we had to get her abdication signed before she lost it entirely. Right now we were going on the strength of Tye's impeccable reputation and Dr. Satir's witnessing my mother's lucidity.

Neither of which would stand up to a formal objection.

I didn't let that show as I strode from the room, Zin right behind me. Emmory was nowhere to be found.

"He headed back to your rooms, ma'am," Zin said at my sideways glance.

Cas and Jet fell into step ahead of me and at my side, and I hid my shaking hands in the folds of my skirts as we headed back to my rooms.

The raised voices hit me before we turned the last corner and I grabbed Cas by the arm to stop him.

"I have listened to your complaints, Nal."

"Have you? You haven't done anything about them. You continue to let your partner fulfill my role. You continue to ignore the fact that it is unseemly for the princess to be guarded by only men."

I arched an eyebrow at Zin, who shrugged in reply.

"I am choosing the heir's Guards based on their qualifications, not their gender. And I have been listening to your suggestions, Nal. But that doesn't mean that I have to take those suggestions." Emmory's voice was calm, but I could hear the heat bubbling under the surface. "You question me in front of the others. You have constantly thrown obstacles in my way as I try to keep the princess safe. It is no wonder that I have trusted Zin more. You have demonstrated to me that I *cannot* trust you, and if you continue this way, Nal, I will have you removed."

"You can't do that. The empress appointed me."

"I am the *Ekam*. I can and will do whatever is necessary

to keep the heir safe. Get on board with that, Nal, or get the hell out."

I moved the moment I heard the door slam, pasting an innocent smile on my face that I knew didn't fool Emmory for a second. Willimet and Rama looked uncomfortable. Both were staring at the floor and jumped when I greeted them.

"Highness." Emmory opened the door and gestured for me to precede him. I raised an eyebrow as I passed, but he was looking at Zin, who gave the minutest of shrugs.

There was a murmured conversation behind me, and when the door shut, I was alone with my Trackers.

"So that was an interesting conversation." I unwound my sari and tossed it over the arm of the rose-colored couch.

"With the matriarchs?"

I gave Emmory a look. "There was little 'conversation' there, actually. A lot of hand-wringing, accusations, insults of the veiled and not-so-veiled variety, and we ended with me telling them that if they didn't like me being their new empress, they could file a formal complaint. We'll see if anyone can come up with something that won't make them look like idiots. I was talking about that"—I waved a hand at the door—"little event with Nal."

"She was angry that I'd sent Zin into the matriarchs' meeting with you instead of letting her go."

"Sounded like a bit more than that. It's pretty obvious she doesn't like you being in charge, but is that Indranan conditioning or something else at work?"

Emmory shrugged. "I don't know, Highness. We can't afford to trust her. You've read her file. There aren't any obvious flags, but—"

"It makes you itchy," I finished. "I know."

I had read Nal's file, and it was so clean, it squeaked. Which, of course, made me nervous as all hell.

"I've already gotten a few comments from the matriarchs about having a male Guard in the chambers, and Alba has found several news stories where it's mentioned." I didn't add in the number of times it had been brought up on my Hansi. The younger generation using the service weren't particularly caught up in things like tradition, but there were some who seemed to be offended—on my behalf, of course—by the fact that my Guard teams were overwhelmingly male. "We have enough things on our plate, Emmory, without adding having to fight to keep you in your position. Let me know if she gets out of line again. I'll intervene."

17

haven't been this nervous since the first time I met Po-Sin," I murmured the thought to no one in particular, but it was Adail who responded.

"I'd think that would even make Emmory nervous, Highness."

"Auho!" I laughed. "I doubt it very much. He'd stand up to the whole Zhang family without blinking until they turned over their warehouse codes."

My green-eyed BodyGuard laughed, earning a glare from Nal. I grinned and moved from the window to the rose-colored couch. I was in a comfortable *salwar kameez* of gray silk decorated with silver embroidery and bells on the bottom hem. I wouldn't be able to sneak up on anyone with this outfit but I loved it nonetheless.

"Highness, your family is here," Nal said. Emmory's ass chewing appeared to have improved her attitude.

I stayed in my seat. Emmory and I had gone over the intricacies of this first meeting with my nephew and the tone I wanted to set right off the bat. If he was involved in the plot against the throne like Tefiz suspected, I wanted to know. Zin stood quietly in the corner and Emmory was in the surveillance room, where he could watch Laabh's every move unimpeded.

My nephew came through the door behind his wife. Leena Surakesh was tiny compared to her husband. Laabh, by constrast, was tall and blocky, dressed in a formal Naval uniform, and I could see the hint of Cire's loveliness in his handsome face. It was ruined by the dissatisfied expression smeared across his features, which he didn't hide behind a polite mask fast enough.

"Your Highness," Nal said. "Allow me to present Leena Surakesh and her husband, your nephew Laabh."

"Your Imperial Highness." The young couple both dropped their heads. Leena's pale yellow curls danced about her dark cheeks when she dipped a perfect curtsy. "It's a great honor."

"It's very nice to meet you." I waited a beat before waving a hand for them to rise and held the same hand out to Leena. There was genuine pleasure in her eyes, but my nephew's dark gaze flickered with poorly concealed anger. Anger at what, I couldn't begin to guess, so I gave him a smile and held my other hand out to him.

"I am sorry for the loss of your mother and your sister," I murmured.

"Your kindness is appreciated, Your Highness." His words were stiffer than his shoulders.

"Please sit down. Leena, I saw the news about your recent promotion at the accounting firm. Congratulations."

"Thank you, Your Highness."

"And Laabh, you recently graduated from the Academy."

"Yes, Your Highness," Laabh replied, straightening his shoulders under his dark blue uniform. "Just a few months ago. I was placed on the *Makara*."

"So you're following in your father's footsteps? I hear he left with 2nd Fleet for the Saxon border."

"Yes, Your Highness."

"How is Taran? It was very kind of you to take him in, Leena."

"He is holding up, Your Highness," she said. "And it was the right thing to do. He would have been all alone in the palace with his father constantly away and with the empress being ill..." She trailed off and the awkward silence filled in the gap left by her words.

"It is awful." I had to remind myself that everyone else still thought my mother was suffering from dementia. Forcing a smile, I gestured for Stasia to bring the drinks over. "I'm sorry it took me so long to see you. As you can imagine, things are slightly chaotic. I'd like to see Taran also when the time allows. I'll have my chamberlain contact you."

"Of course, Your Highness."

"Did you see him twitch when Leena mentioned my mother being ill?" I used our com link to talk to Emmory.

"I did, Highness. It's hard to say what it means though."

"Nothing good." Accepting a chai from Stasia, I returned my attention to my guests. "I appreciated your mother's support in the council meeting the other day, Leena."

"Of course, Highness. We are ever the throne's loyal subjects." She smiled softly. "Mother was quite irate about Matriarch Khatri's behavior."

Laabh fisted his right hand.

"To be honest," I said with a wink, "she didn't say anything that wasn't true. I was more surprised by Matriarch Prajapati's support of my cousin."

"According to my mother, you running away from home was Matriarch Prajapati's major complaint."

"I wonder if she'll change her mind when she finds out that I left home for a very different reason." I surveyed their confused faces over the rim of my mug. "Former GIS Director Britlen is giving an interview that should be going live any minute now about my hunt for the man who's responsible for my father's death. I suspect it'll clear up a lot of the objections the matriarchs have—most of them anyway."

"My mother never said a word about this," Laabh said, his eyes narrowed.

"She wouldn't have." I smiled and stood. "It was all kept very quiet."

"I suspect that will change more than a few minds on the council," Leena said as she rose. "Thank you for making time to see us, Highness. It was very kind of you."

"You're family, Leena, and I owe you for taking Taran in." I took her hand and squeezed it. "I'll see you again. Both of you."

"Highness." Laabh only hesitated a second before he took my hand, then he tried to release me but I tightened my grip.

"Take care of yourself, Laabh. Someone's after our family and there's not many of us left." I didn't smile as I said it and watched him swallow. "I have enough vengeance to deal out. I'd hate to have to add you to the list."

"Yes, ma'am."

"Good." I released him with a smile that almost split my face. The smile vanished as Nal and Adail followed my visitors out the door and I turned around to meet Zin's grim look. "He's up to his neck in this, isn't he?"

Zin nodded. "And you weren't very subtle there, Highness."

"I'm too mad for subtlety, and I want him to be terrified of what's going to happen when I find out he was directly involved in any of these deaths." I stopped and raised an eyebrow at him. "What?"

"You don't seem the slightest bit shocked he could do something that terrible, Highness."

"How did you stay so naïve, Tracker?" I hoped my smile softened the words. "Or is it just that I've spent most of my life in a world where a man would sell his whole family to pay off his gambling debts. I'm afraid there's very little left that would shock me. Money and power are shiny things; even the strong have trouble doing what's right when everything they've desired is laid out in front of them."

"Still, to push him might not be wise. Desperate people do desperate things. I'd rather they stick to whatever plan they have concerning you rather than some impulsive attempt to kill you that we might miss."

"I think we've blown their plan out of the water already, don't you?"

Zin shrugged, a half smile on his face as he studied the door. "Maybe, but it's early yet. If it were me—" He broke off when Emmory came into the room, but then continued. "If it were me, I'd have a decent backup plan or two. You've always been the wild card, Highness."

I snorted.

"I don't mean it that way. We're pretty sure they didn't know where you were until just recently, or they'd have tried to kill you a lot sooner than they did. But they would have had to take you out; leaving you alive wasn't an option."

"Memz joined my crew three months after an incident on Candless cost me my navigator. She rode with us for six years. If she'd been working for these people, wouldn't she have tried to kill me early?"

"Not necessarily. They could have got to her at Shanghai. That's a deal I'd want to do face-to-face."

I rubbed my hands over my face. We'd had five days of leave at Shanghai after closing the deal with the Chengs. More than enough time for someone to track her down and make the offer. I hated to say it, but it didn't surprise me at all that they'd gone after Memz, or that she'd agreed to it. My only consolation was that she'd never gotten to spend all those credits. "So how did they track me down?"

Zin glanced at Emmory and they shrugged in unison. "We would have followed the money, Highness."

I stood in the shadows, watching the colorful crowd below mingle in the cavernous ballroom in the north wing of the palace. They looked like butterflies dancing over a field of flowers. I snorted softly. Deadly butterflies dancing over a toxic field would be more appropriate.

The ballroom was reserved for special occasions, and the walls were covered with priceless tapestries. Golden statues were strewn about the room in an ostentatious reminder of my family's wealth, and vases older than the empire itself sat on pedestals protected by force shields.

Mother's coronation had been in the throne room, but the after-party had been here. My sister's wedding reception would have been in this room and the party to celebrate Atmikha's birth. Their funerals would have been in the temple.

Now I was about to be announced as the heir. Officially.

No objections had been lodged with Clara, and Mother had been lucid enough before the celebration not only to sign the declaration, but to record a brief message about her "illness" and what it meant for Indrana. I didn't know when my coronation would be but I was sure we'd try to do it as soon after the holiday as could be managed.

I'd told Alice Gohil the truth about not running, but it didn't mean I wasn't terrified of screwing all this up or, worse, for everything to go sideways while I was still in this limbo of being almost, but not quite, in charge.

The lives of billions were going to be in my hands.

That thought made me want to throw myself off the balcony. Surely the drop of thirteen meters and the impact on the pale gray marble below would kill me.

Except Emmory and Nal were right behind me. Knowing them, I'd be grabbed before I could get a leg over. I let go of the carved railing, dropping my hands to my sides.

They disappeared into my massive sleeves. The heavy white satin of my court dress was finished off with gold thread and little oil-slick pearls. The hanging sleeves dropped all the way to the ground, the wide openings showing off the golden silk wrapped around my arms.

I felt like a gods-damned mummy.

Stasia had done up my hair so that green curls spilled down my back and over one shoulder. There were enough gemstones in the crown buried among my curls to feed a large family for a month.

I was grateful for the slender reassurance of the knife tucked against my left forearm. Stasia had protested, but I wasn't going to be moved on the subject. Illegal or not, I wasn't going anywhere in the palace unarmed.

Just because I could kill someone with my bare hands didn't mean I liked how the odds shifted if they happened to have a gun.

After I promised not to draw it on any nobles unless they really tried to kill me, she'd relented and promised not to tell my *Ekam*.

"Ready, Highness?" Nal offered me a tentative smile. Her attitude had continued to improve, though her posture was still ridiculously formal.

"I suppose." I attempted to smile back, glanced over my shoulder at Emmory, and started forward down the wide stairs.

The swirling collection of people below us froze at the sound of the gong, and more than four thousand pairs of eyes turned our way.

"Ladies and gentlemen. Her Imperial Highness, Crown Princess Hailimi Mercedes Jaya Bristol!"

The crowd burst into applause and cheers—a predictable reaction, but I still jumped. Ostensibly they were there to celebrate my return and the holiday, but I knew better. Somewhere in this crowd were those who were plotting to overthrow the throne.

"Smile, Highness," Emmory whispered from behind me. "You look like you're about to shoot someone."

"If you'd let me have my gun with me, I would," I hissed back from between the clenched teeth of my fake smile. "Let's get this damn thing over with."

A nice thing about being royalty is you don't have to circulate at parties. Everyone else is expected to come to you. After I had presented myself to the empty throne and watched the shocked reactions of the crowd as the announcement of abdication was read, all that was left was for me to pick a spot and wait for people to approach me.

Everyone was all abuzz about Fenna's interview and the news about my involvement in catching my father's killers. Also the curious and more daring of the bunch asked me questions about gunrunning or Po-Sin. Those questions I avoided deftly or answered carefully.

I endured a number of not so subtle requests for assistance, poorly veiled insults, and insipid conversations, smiling politely and getting my own carefully worded stabs in when I could. When the flow of curious introductions trickled off, I was left standing across the room from Mother's empty chair, watching the intricate dance out on the floor.

There was at least food. I nibbled on an *idli* coated with spicy chutney from the plate Nal held as I attempted to catch up on the various factions at court. The subject, I figured, was safe enough to discuss in front of Nal.

"So the Surakesh are solidly on the side of the crown," Emmory murmured, gesturing unobtrusively at the woman with silver hair who sat at my eleven o'clock.

Leena's mother had been silent and watchful during the council meeting, agreeing with Matriarch Maxwell's position but not engaging in any of the debate.

"They always have been. Though I suspect it's as much a matter of self-preservation as anything. The matriarch had six daughters and"—I frowned and checked my *smati*—"four sons. The eldest daughter has four girls of her own—"

"Five now, Highness," Emmory murmured the correction. "Leena is second oldest of them." He gestured covertly and I followed the line of his gloved finger until I spotted my nephew.

"He doesn't look happy at all, does he? And he hasn't come to say hi." I cocked my head to the side and studied my nephew. "Interesting."

"I could have someone bring him over," Emmory replied.

I gave a minute shrug, watching the whirling dancers. The bright silken dresses and impressively cut jackets were a riot of colors on the dance floor.

Pace hadn't been old enough when I attended my first adult party, but Cire and I both got new dresses—silly, girlish things with too many ruffles. I remembered that my thirteen-year-old self had been delighted with it. Father danced with us, as did our uncles. Tefiz had even taken my hand and turned me in circles, all the while watching the crowd with those piercing blue eyes of hers.

I missed her. She'd been an older sister to me as much as a

BodyGuard. It was a relief that Mother hadn't sacked her out-right for my disappearance.

"Emmory..." I hesitated, suddenly unsure if I should even ask the question. "Did Tefiz—were she and Ofa angry with me?"

"No, Highness. They were worried."

"I'm relieved Mother didn't punish them," I murmured as tears pricked at my eyes. "Though I wish I'd had a chance to apologize to Ofa before she died."

"It was unnecessary, ma'am." Emmory's reply over our com link threw some steel into my backbone. *"They both spoke highly of you. So did Portis. I am glad to see their judgment wasn't clouded by their feelings for you."*

"Which is what you thought?"

"At first." His smile was fleeting. *"You've changed my mind."*

"Your Highness, if I may apologize for the interruption?"

I gave the stranger who'd approached a once-over. He was tall and wiry-thin with pale, almost white-blond hair and equally pale blue eyes. I'd heard the distinctive Saxon accent rasping in his voice, which explained why my BodyGuards had shifted uncomfortably.

"Ambassador Jaden Toropov, Your Highness." He executed an elegant bow that was an interesting counterpoint to his scarred hands.

"Ambassador."

Toropov smiled and extended a hand. "Might I interest you in a dance?"

"He didn't ask you, Emmory. You don't get to come with me," I said before he could protest. I put my hand in Toropov's with a smile of my own. "Of course, Ambassador."

People moved out of our way as we crossed the dance floor—a multicolored sea parting without question or even really conscious thought. I suppose it's another one of the perks of being royalty—people get the hell out of your way.

"I'm going to have to apologize to your *Ekam*."

"For testing to see if the gunrunner knew how to dance?"

Toropov blinked at me in surprise and then laughed. "I suppose so, Your Highness. Though I would have phrased it differently."

"That's why you're the ambassador." I let him spin me in a circle and gave him a bright smile as he cupped my waist with one long-fingered hand. "I'm pretty sure things haven't deteriorated quite that severely between our empires since this morning. Of course, ambassador or not, if you try to kill me, my BodyGuards will be the least of your worries."

He grinned at me, the expression transforming his austere face into something devilishly handsome. "So the rumors are true? Perhaps I should put some money down after all."

"There's a bet about me?"

I shouldn't have been surprised. Gambling was the national pastime. Bets about anything and everything were placed with frightening regularity. Sometimes the bets were just friendly wagers among a select group, but sometimes it was a publicly backed pool that attracted the attention of even the largest bookmakers.

I just hadn't had a chance to look into it.

"Several, Your Highness. I believe the popular one concerns the odds of your survival."

"That's dreary. What are the odds?" I whistled when Toropov told me. "Steep. You'd think people would have more faith."

"I don't know, Highness; the odds do seem stacked against you."

"I've had worse." I poked him in the chest. "Remind me to

tell you about the time I walked into a Zhang outpost and out again with four free boxes of their not-yet-released QLZ-57 handgun."

Toropov blinked at me, and then burst into laughter. It rang through the air, a sound as clean and bright as the bells on Temple Day. I choked back a giggle, then gave up and joined him, laughing until tears were rolling down my face.

"Four boxes?" he gasped.

"The guards helped me carry them out," I said breathlessly.

"That is a story I would love to hear," Toropov said as the song ended. "However, I'm afraid if I don't get you back to your BodyGuards, there's going to be blood spilt—probably mine." He took my hand and led me back across the dance floor. "I have been directed to convey His Majesty's greetings, Your Highness."

I swallowed back my laughter at the overly formulaic phrasing. "Tell King Trace I said hi, and message my chamberlain if you'd like to hear that story."

"I will, Highness. *Ekam*, my apologies for stealing your charge. I have brought her back in good condition."

Emmory didn't say a word to Toropov, who was unfazed by the nonresponse. He gave me another smile and a bow and left me alone with my BodyGuards.

"Well, that was interesting." I flagged down a passing servant and snagged a thin-stemmed wineglass off the golden tray.

Emmory caught my hand, passed three fingers over the top of the glass, and cocked his head to the side as he scanned the read-out from his sensors.

"Safe," he said, and let me go.

I picked at the *idli* still on the plate Nal was holding and popped one into my mouth. Wrinkling my nose at the too-sweet paste coating it, I spit it out in my hand and dumped it back on the plate. "Ugh." The dry bubbles of the shore-bred grapes helped cut through the sticky sweetness and I finished off my drink with a grimace.

"Did you know my odds of survival are 872 to 1 against? That's insulting. Emmory, are you insulted?"

"Extremely, Highness."

"I think—"

"Your pardon, Highness."

"Prime Minister." I offered my free hand. Phanin took it and bowed low.

"If I may have a moment of your time?"

"Sure, what's up?" I handed the glass off to a passing servant.

Annoyance flickered over his face at my casual reply and I resisted the urge to grin because Alba had been gently hammering away at my desire to behave like a gunrunner rather than a princess.

"Understand I'm in no way criticizing your behavior, ma'am, but you do realize that was the Saxon ambassador you just danced with?"

My amusement vanished. I straightened my shoulders. The shoes Stasia had forced on me had a decent heel and I was half a head taller than Phanin with them on.

"Do I look like an idiot, Prime Minister?"

He paled and bowed again. "Of course not, Your Highness. Of course not. Perhaps if I knew what your plan was, I could—"

"I don't have a plan. He asked me for a dance. I was being polite. Last I checked, we were not at war with the Saxons, Phanin. Have I missed something? Should I have shot the ambassador instead?"

Nal coughed behind me. Emmory was stone still.

"Highness, I realize you may not have caught up quite yet with the empire's affairs. I am merely trying to—"

"I was in a damn briefing not five hours ago and I am fully aware of what's going on in my empire, even though it has more affairs than a call girl from Holgan. Untwist your knickers, Phanin. The ambassador wished to pass on a greeting from his king and, I don't doubt, to be able to tell his peers he danced with the infamous gunrunner princess. Despite what you seem to believe, I can be trusted to not start an interstellar incident over a dance."

"Yes, ma'am."

"Go away." I waved a hand.

Phanin bowed again and scurried off.

"What in the fires of Naraka was that about?" I muttered.

"I don't know, Highness. Tensions are high right now."

"If they were that high, Toropov wouldn't be here." I grabbed another drink, hissing at Emmory when he insisted on performing yet another scan on it.

We fell into a somber silence. The odds were not in my favor, no matter what I'd said to Emmory and Toropov. This was going to be a hell of a fight. But since the options were death or the throne, I figured I didn't have anything to lose.

"Nal." I gestured at her and she leaned in. "I think we should put some money down on me." I tugged her closer and whispered an amount in her ear that made her mouth drop open in shock. "Go find the royal bookie and tell him to take care of it. If he wants to argue with you about it, tell him to come talk to me."

I smothered a laugh as Nal shared a look with Emmory and then vanished into the crowd. I sipped at my wine, watching the dancers with half-closed eyes.

"They're underestimating us, Emmory." I kept my voice low even though the music made it damn near impossible to eavesdrop.

"Thankfully, yes. I doubt their arrogance will last long. Especially if you keep showing people how smart you are."

"I'm not good at playing dumb, Emmy."

"Better that than dead. We need to have a conversation about your abilities."

I managed not to turn around and look at him, instead concentrating on the bubbles in my glass. They floated through the pale gold liquid, popping on the surface.

"What do you want me to tell you? That I could kill someone with the stem of this glass if I had to? That I can point out every single noble who's packing a weapon tonight despite the fact that it's illegal? I can even tell you which of them actually knows how to use it.

"I've got a knife in my left sleeve, four jeweled pins in my hair, and could probably beat someone to death with these monster shoes I'm wearing—though that's messy and exhausting, and I wouldn't want to do it in public."

"It's a good start," Emmory murmured back, the amusement in his voice wrapping around me like a security blanket, soothing my worry. "I knew all of it except for the glass. That hadn't occurred to me."

"That's because you're an honorable man. I'm only a princess by blood, Emmy—well, that and eighteen years of training which I can't seem to shake. But I was a gunrunner for longer and that sort of training has a steep learning curve."

"You don't say."

"You know, with all of us in one place like this, a thermo would take care of their problem in one shot."

"Highness, there are bomb detectors for a reason."

I shrugged. "The Chernovs figured out a way to break one down, smuggle in the separate pieces, and reassemble it in less than a minute. It's rather impressive."

"Your definition of *impressive* and mine do not quite line up, Highness."

I was right in the middle of another drink and my laughter turned into coughing as I sucked wine down my windpipe. "I'm all right," I gasped, swatting at Emmory with my free hand. "Just the wrong—"

My throat closed up, or more accurately my lungs just stopped working, and I realized that I wasn't okay. Someone's shocked gasp mixed with the shattering of glass as my nerveless fingers lost their grip on my wine and it plunged to the ground.

I dropped after it. I was desperately trying to convince any part of me to function, but I was paralyzed.

Emmory caught me before I shattered on the floor. "Hail?" He cupped my face. "Damn it! Nal!" He shouted something garbled before looking back at me. "Inhale for me," he murmured, pressing his hand above my mouth and nose. A pale yellow mist appeared and I tried to obey but my body wasn't having any of it.

As I passed out, I hoped that the panicked look on Emmory's face wasn't the last thing I'd see.

18

ighness, open your eyes for me."

Frowning, I forced my eyes open. I was back in my room. Emmory and a gray-haired doctor I recognized as Dr. Ganjen, who was Dr. Satir's backup, hovered over me. "What—" I choked on the word, cleared my dry throat, and tried again. "What in the hell is going on?"

"You were poisoned, Highness."

"How?" I pushed myself upright, waving off the doctor's anxious protests. "You checked everything that went into my damn mouth, Emmory. How did I get poisoned?"

"I don't know." His reply was an impolite snarl. "Sorry, ma'am."

"No, my fault, stupid question." I sighed and looked at the ceiling. The movement made me dizzy and I cursed, sliding back down to the bed.

"Please lay still, Highness. The poison is exacerbated by movement," Dr. Ganjen said.

"Where's Dr. Satir?"

"Family emergency," her colleague replied. "She had to leave the capital for a few days. Your *Ekam*'s quick reaction with the antidote saved your life." The older man patted me on the arm. "You'll want to take it easy for a day or two, Your Highness. There will be residual weakness from the neurotoxin. I'll have to do some scans to figure out what caused the reaction since your *Ekam* insists you didn't ingest any of the toxin directly."

"Pretty sure I didn't, though that *idli* tasted funny." I stuck my tongue out at Emmory and winked.

That dragged a chuckle out of him. It was frayed and ragged with stress, but the amusement was there.

"You're going to give me gray hair, ma'am."

"You don't have any hair."

"Princess, are you all right?" Nal's voice floated over Emmory's shoulder.

"Someone just tried to kill me, Nal. I am not 'all right' but I am alive."

"Nal was concerned for your safety, as we all were."

Confident that Nal couldn't see me, I arched a curious eyebrow at the edge in Emmory's voice. "Help me up, *Ekam*. I promise I won't dance around but I don't want to be lying here. It makes me feel worse."

He took my arm and helped me off the bed. Leaning against Emmory for support, I offered Nal a sarcastic smile. "See. I'm alive."

"You were poisoned, Highness. Right under your *Ekam*'s nose. I don't think—"

Trusting my legs to support me, I let go of Emmory and waved a dismissive hand at Nal. "You were there, too, Nal, and you heard the doctor. I am alive precisely because of Emmory," I snapped. "Doctor, thank you. Pass those results to us as soon as you have them."

The doctor bowed to me and left the room. Nal didn't go as quietly, her angry protests on her way out the door delivered in a voice too low for my ears to make out distinct words. Emmory replied with two snarled sentences that were equally incomprehensible. There was a moment of shocked silence, and then the door closed.

"Drink this, Highness." Stasia pressed a hot cup into my hands, but the heat of it didn't penetrate my icy fingers. "Do you want a fire?"

I wanted to burn the world down. I bit my tongue and tossed back the pepper-spiced liquor before the words could escape, unsure where my sudden anger had come from. The drink stole my breath, successfully keeping me from looking like a fool.

"I'll make a fire," Emmory said, taking the cup from my hand and passing it back to Stasia. She dipped into a curtsy and left us alone. He slid an arm around my back and, before I could protest, lifted me into the air, sliding his other arm under my knees.

"I can walk."

His lips curved into the briefest of smiles. Then he set me down on the couch near the fire and turned back to the bed for a blanket.

"So Zin was right about the desperation thing. I probably shouldn't have pushed Laabh, huh?"

"Highness, now is not the best time for this."

"When is? I was wrong and you were right and thank you for being on the ball so I didn't die." I leaned against the couch cushions, stifling a yawn as the drink hit me like a sledgehammer. "I really loved your brother. Did he love me back?"

Emmory knelt by the fire and piled logs as he spoke. "I knew my brother. He loved you, don't ever doubt that. He was there to keep you safe—"

I choked back the laugh, remembering some of the foolish escapades I'd been involved in over the years. "Portis apparently had a slightly different definition of the word *safe* than you."

Emmory gave me a smile that I thought was the first genuine one he'd shown since this whole thing started. "I know he left a lot out of his reports. He was there to keep you safe, but it was as much because of his feelings for you as his duty." He dusted off his hands and got to his feet. "I miss him, too. For so long I thought my little brother had betrayed our family, this empire, everything I believed in." Emmory's smile was quick, filled with a regret I'm sure was echoed in my eyes.

"Zin could tell you how I cursed Portis's name every night for that first year he was gone. Then the pain faded. My initial rage dulled to a bitter ache in my chest. I couldn't forget him, though, no matter how much I tried. I kept dreaming about him, would think of him at odd times. Part of me couldn't believe he'd really—" Emmory broke off and forced a smile. "Four months ago, Zin and I came home from a job and Tefiz was waiting for us. I didn't recognize her, but Zin did.

"She told us who she was and said that my brother had specifically suggested us to the heir. I couldn't figure out what she was talking about. Tired, dirty, and still stinking of gods know what, we went to meet your sister, Ven, and Ofa." Emmory's laugh sounded like he still couldn't quite believe it all. "I was so angry. Thank the gods for Zin, who kept me from saying something I'd regret when I saw Portis's face.

"Portis told us everything. Then Princess Cire told us the rest. The rising tension with the Saxons, the factions in the government who were too busy fighting with each other to notice the problems outside, the growing unrest of the people. Everything you've learned since you came home, Highness."

"And things have only gotten worse," I murmured.

"Somewhere in the middle of all that, I realized that little piece of me had been right all along. My brother wasn't a traitor. He hadn't been stripped of his service and banished, he'd just walked away from all of us to keep you safe," Emmory said. "That's how I knew he hadn't tried to kill you, Highness. He wouldn't have, because you were everything to him."

"He was everything to me, too," I murmured, holding my hand out. Emmory took it and I squeezed his fingers with a smile of my own.

"Whoever poisoned me fucked up." I changed the subject abruptly. "They are desperate. They're on some sort of time-table here. Otherwise they could just sit back until we got complacent and then strike. Eventually someone would get a lucky shot off. I'm not questioning your ability, that's just the odds, Emmory." I ignored the Look from him. "They tipped their hand. Now we have somewhere to really start looking because whatever they poisoned me with had to come from somewhere."

Emmory studied me for a long moment. "You would have made a good Tracker, ma'am."

I was saved from gaping foolishly at him by Zin, who appeared in the doorway.

"Highness, the prime minister has had Ambassador Toropov taken into custody."

"What? Why?"

"He's accused Toropov of poisoning you."

I sat up too fast and the room swirled around me. "Oh, bugger me. Emmory, did he just say what I thought he said?"

"He did, Highness."

I tossed back the blanket and got slowly to my feet, waving off both of them as I made my way toward the bed. "I've got it, Zin, I'm not an invalid. Go get Stasia. I want out of this damn dress. Call Clara and Phanin. I want the ambassador in my main room in five minutes or heads are going to roll. Emmory, you fetch him yourself if you have to."

"Yes, Highness." Zin obeyed.

Emmory, of course, did not.

I probably should have been grateful for it, since his disobedience kept me off the floor. "Damn it, Emmory."

"If I'd thought you could walk yourself, I would have left you alone. The doctor said the weakness would affect you for several days."

"If this damn dress didn't weigh three stone, I could. Don't pick me up, Emmory, it's embarrassing." I slung my arm around his neck. "Just help me over to the wardrobe."

I could barely walk, but Emmory—thankfully—was kind enough not to point it out and instead helped me across the room. I sank down onto a chair with a muttered curse.

"Ma'am, I'm sorry."

"It wasn't your fault."

"I'm not doing a very good job of keeping you safe."

"If you think for one second that I'm letting you abandon me here, *Ekam*, you're mistaken. I'm still alive and that means you're doing a good job. Sometimes you have to count your blessings where you can find them." I patted his arm. "Now stop wallowing and go rescue the ambassador before some idiot starts a war."

"Yes, ma'am."

My smile faded when Emmory left the room and I retreated into my thoughts, only murmuring a word or two to Stasia as she stripped the dress off me. I tugged on a pair of black pants and a tank top and tried to ignore the trembling in my limbs that wasn't all a residual reaction to the toxin.

I'd almost died.

It wasn't the first time. Hell, I couldn't even count the number of close calls we'd had out there in the years I was away from home. There were a handful of memorable ones—the bank job, the backwater ambush, staring down one of Po-Sin's rivals with a gun shoved up under my chin.

I shuddered a little at the memory. I still didn't know how I'd made it out of that one alive. That bastard had been fucking insane. The only reason I didn't have a hole the size of a planet in my head was because he'd liked the color of my hair.

It wasn't the almost dying part that was causing my hands to shake. It was the fact that Emmory had saved my life.

You can't fool yourself anymore, Hail.

I snarled at the voice in my head, burying my face in my hands, but it wasn't going away. I was in this and in it deep. I had fully put my trust in Emmory and Zin to handle things I wouldn't be able to almost without realizing it.

And to keep me alive.

At Stasia's insistence, I bundled up in a robe and let Emmory help me out into the main room. I was settled onto the rose-colored couch talking to Alba when Ambassador Toropov was brought in.

"Your Highness, a joy to see you safe."

"Ambassador." I held out a hand to him, smiling when he took it. "I apologize for the overzealous response from my people. We are all a little jumpy given the circumstances."

"Understandable, my dear. I take no offense. I hope you realize the Saxon Kingdom wants nothing more than peace with Indrana."

"Oh, of course."

Toropov was a consummate politician and didn't even bat an eyelash at my tone. Given all the recent tensions, I couldn't rule out that the Saxons could be behind this plot. The loss of Indrana's ruling family would throw the empire into a state of chaos that would make it even easier for the Saxons to swoop in and get back a lot of the territory they'd lost in the war.

I didn't think Toropov was so foolish as to have tried to poison me in full view of everyone; however, I also couldn't rule him out simply because of a gut feeling.

"Let's talk after the holiday. I'll have Alba get with your people?"

"That would be lovely, Highness. Thank you." Toropov bowed and left the room.

I waited a beat before raising a hand and signaling Zin to open the door again so the prime minister could come in.

"Highness, a blessing to see you well—"

"What in the fires of Naraka were you thinking?" I sliced a hand through the air before Phanin could finish. "Never mind that you acted without any orders whatsoever from the Crown. But you just yanked a *diplomat* into custody in the middle of a state function, Phanin. I couldn't have blamed his bodyguards for completely losing their shit. You're lucky we didn't have a shoot-out in the palace."

"You passed out after dancing with him, Highness."

"Actually, I passed out after talking to you," I countered and watched him swallow. "If we're using that logic, what's your defense?"

"Highness, surely you don't think—"

"You've overstepped your authority, Phanin. I realize Mother's been ill and others appear to have relied heavily on your advice."

He flinched a little at that and I stared at him impassively. From what Emmory had discovered, the only reason Phanin now enjoyed so much influence in the palace was because my sister had invited him into her confidence.

"There's been some fluidity in the chain of command around here, but in the future all decisions will go through either me or my mother. I will remind you only once that you are merely the prime minister and the amount of say you have in the politics of this empire is right about here." I held my hand down by the floor. "You are not a council member, nor a member of the royal family. Next time I catch you making decisions about matters of the empire without some kind of approval, I'm going to take you out back and shoot you myself. Is that understood?"

"Yes, Highness." He bowed. "My apologies, Highness."

"Get out of here." I tapped my fingers together, trying to get my foggy brain to cooperate.

"Highness, perhaps you should rest?"

"In a minute, Emmory. Alba, will you send a message to Admiral Hassan? Let her know I'd like to talk with her when it's convenient."

"It looks like she's back on the *Vajra*, Highness," Alba said. "I'll send her a message."

"Thank you."

"We can go over the rest of your schedule in the morning. I'll make adjustments as needed until the doctor clears you." Alba smiled. "Good night, ma'am. I'm glad you're all right."

"You and me both, Alba." I pushed to my feet, ignoring Emmory's frustrated sigh, but didn't try to move until Alba was out of the room.

I made it to the door of my bedroom and leaned heavily on the jamb with a few choice curse words.

"Highness."

"I have my pride, Emmy."

"Is it worth passing out for, ma'am?"

"It wouldn't be the first time." I shot him a look and gestured. "Come on, help a girl out, would you? I don't want to pass out, and you and I need to talk."

With a silence both concerned and frustrated, Emmory helped me to bed and then retreated back to the doorway.

I let him go.

"Do you think Toropov tried to kill me?" My stomach was twisted into edgy knots.

Or that could have been the poison.

"It would be an incredibly bold move, ma'am."

"More or less than stealing our border worlds?"

Emmory wiggled a hand, his shoulder shifting under the black material of his uniform in a half shrug. "The Saxons are on our list, Highness. Toropov is high-profile, but it doesn't remove him from suspicion."

"So you do have a list. Let me hear it." I raised a hand, stopping his protest. "People are trying to kill me. I tend to take that personally, so don't bother with the holy cowshit line of 'We'll handle it.' Give me the list."

19

The few people out at this hour hurried back and forth on the streets, bundled up against the early morning chill. Most likely, shopkeepers and others who benefited more from working through the monthlong break the rest of the capital took during the holiday. I wondered how much they worried about the possibility of renewed war or if they were consumed by their own lives.

"Highness, move away from the window." Emmory's tone made it clear it wasn't a request, so I moved because I was pretty sure otherwise he'd pick me up and do it himself.

Because I was still weak and shaky from the aftereffects of the toxin, I wasn't in much of a position to fight with him, even if I'd wanted to. Three attempts in two weeks made me nervous; I couldn't imagine how my *Ekam* felt.

"All they'd really need is a rocket launcher," I said, still unable to resist the tease. Matriarch Desai's house was well defended, but I could pick out at least three decent vantage points beyond the redbrick wall that lent themselves well to the weapon's range.

I got the Look in reply, though it was a bit more pained than normal and followed with, "I wish you would stop that."

"Humor helps the nerves," I murmured and settled down onto the cream-colored couch in Matriarch Desai's study.

"I would think that doing what your *Ekam* asks will help calm his nerves more, Your Highness," Clara said with a smile as she passed me a cup of chai.

"Emmory enjoys being nervous." I hid my grin behind the rim of my cup.

"Highness, Director Caspel and Admiral Hassan just pulled up." Emmory turned from the window. "Stay put."

"Little more than nervous," Clara said as Emmory left the room.

I shrugged a shoulder. "Given the circumstances, I find it hard to blame him." It had taken an hour of fast talking and agreement to two BodyGuard teams shadowing me inside the palace and no less than four outside it before Emmory had agreed to this meeting.

He'd also flat out told Nal to mind her own business and spend the day reviewing the Pratimas schedule when she'd asked where we were going.

"I appreciate your flexibility with this, *Ekam*," Caspel said as they came into the room. "At present it is challenging to figure out whom we can trust."

"It's understood, sir."

"Ah, Highness." Caspel's face creased into a smile. "Good morning."

"Morning, Admiral. You'll both forgive me if I don't get up," I said, extending my free hand to Caspel.

"Completely understandable. It's good to see you well." He squeezed my hand rather than brushing his lips over my knuckles.

"Ma'am." Hassan nodded her head at me.

"What was so important you had to give my *Ekam* gray hair by insisting I left the palace this morning?"

The smile that flickered over Caspel's face was drowned by the worry in his eyes. "We have two more visitors, Highness. I think once you hear what they have to say, you'll understand the need for as much secrecy as we could muster."

"They're at the back door now." Emmory's lack of surprise meant he must have known about Caspel's plans ahead of time, and when Kisah appeared at the door with Matriarch Gohil and General Saito, I knew why he'd been so agreeable. General Kaed Saito was the head of the Tracker Corps. She was tall and blond with distinctive Cheng features and her bow to me was as perfunctory as Alice's curtsy was elegant.

"Your Highness, welcome home."

I nodded at the greetings and sipped at my chai while beverages were prepared and everyone took a seat. My BodyGuards were spread out around the room, which was done up in rich brown leathers and pale cream. They all looked a little awkward among the finery. Emmory took up position just behind my left shoulder.

"To the empress. Long may she reign." Caspel's salute was without mockery, but he was looking at me and we were all too aware that my mother's reign was fast coming to an end.

"Early this morning, Lady Alice approached me," Caspel continued after the murmured declarations of loyalty had died down. "After last night's incident, she'd received a rather frantic message from Lady Zaran Khatri requesting a meeting. I'll let Lady Alice recount the details of that meeting."

"Her mother was quite vocal in her objections at the council meeting," I murmured with a raised eyebrow. "Leena mentioned that her mother was very unhappy about it."

"She has been Ganda's foremost supporter, which I found a bit odd. I didn't think they had much contact before Princess Cire's death. No formal objections were, of course, presented to me about you taking the throne, Highness." Clara frowned, then waved a hand at Alice. "Go on, dear. I'm curious to hear what she had to tell you."

Alice wrung her hands, a nervous gesture I found at odds with her calm demeanor in the council meeting. "Zaran is a loyal subject, Your Highness. She is young and rather sheltered. Her mother can be very overbearing and I think it led to Zaran looking for an escape."

"Stop making excuses for her decisions, Alice. Tell me what happened."

"Yes, sorry, Your Highness." She dipped her head at my rebuke and swallowed. "Zaran fell in love with a young man who is a member of the *Upjas*. She saw him just before Princess Cire was murdered and he confided in her that a violent offshoot of the group was claiming responsibility for the death of Princess Pace under the *Upjas'* name. He was afraid it was an effort to discredit the more levelheaded leaders and turn the rising tide of public support against their cause.

"It was no secret that the Crown Princess was sympathetic to the *Upjas'* message," she said.

I raised an eyebrow at Alice and she ducked her head slightly.

"She'd made several comments during interviews and council meetings, Highness. There were also more than a few arguments with the empress about her views."

"Did you agree with Cire?" I asked.

"Your pardon, Highness. I did not. I do not think men are capable of the kind of responsibilities your sister wished to place on them. Our ancestor-mothers took over when their men could not cope with the stresses of space travel. This method has worked for thousands of years, and I see no reason to change it now."

"Well, I like the honesty," I said. "Continue."

"Zaran says in the last few weeks there have been a lot of late-night visitors to her mother's house. Or that her mother has left the house in the dead of night with only a single Body-Guard. She gave me several names of people she recognized and I passed them on to Caspel. Last night, after you collapsed, Zaran came home with her mother, who claimed to be so upset by the incident she was going to bed. However, Zaran said her mother left the house shortly after and she followed her to a shop in the Back District."

The Back District was a dangerous place to be after dark, especially for a noble. I kept my surprised whistle from escaping and simply nodded at Alice to keep going.

"Matriarch Khatri met with your cousin Ganda, your nephew Laabh, and a man Zaran didn't recognize. Her *smati* wouldn't give her an identification either. All she could tell me was that he was about as tall as Laabh with broad shoulders. He wore a hooded jacket and his face was in shadow except for one brief moment in the light."

"We can see if we can pull a memory that's good enough to get a facial recognition print going. What did they talk about, Alice?" Caspel prompted.

"Ganda was upset with Laabh. Said he should have talked to her before they tried to poison you. She told him it was his fault for involving 'those *Upjas* bastards.' The hooded man interrupted their bickering with a reminder that his people had already set things in motion and time was running short. Ganda needed to move on to the next phase of her plans if this was going to work."

My muttered curse was echoed by several others, most notably Clara, and I grinned sharply in her direction. "I take it we have no clue what this next phase actually entails."

"Actually I have a suspicion, Highness," Caspel said. "Several news stations received anonymous reports overnight accusing

Princess Cire of being in a relationship with *Upjas* ringleader Abraham Suda before her death and insinuating that Atmikha was not Major Bristol's daughter."

This time my swearing was more violent and I pushed to my feet, intent on pacing the length of the study before my body reminded me that it wasn't going to cooperate. I fell back against the couch and snapped a hand up, stopping anyone from fussing over me. "I'm fine. What the fuck do they think smearing my sister's memory is going to prove, Caspel?"

"It's not just your sister, Highness. There are also several news stories about your exploits."

"Those have been running since I put my feet back on the ground here."

The GIS officer's smile was sympathetic. "Not like this. Are you familiar with the incident on Shotakan about five years ago?"

I froze. *Bugger me.*

"Caspel, I'd be very careful with the next words that come out of your mouth." It was the only thing Emmory had said so far, but it dropped the temperature in the room down into the freezing range.

"Easy," I murmured. "I'm pretty sure that he's not going to say I had anything to do with an explosion that resulted in the deaths of a hundred and fifty-three schoolchildren."

"Your employer did."

"Yeah, no." I ran my tongue over my teeth as I calculated the best way to tell this story without adding one more name onto the list of people who wanted me dead. I could handle my prissy cousin, dissatisfied nephew, and any other Indranan noble without blinking. Pissing Po-Sin off, however, was not something I wanted to do. "Po-Sin was embroiled in a territory war with an Irani up-and-comer named Roshanak. She turned several of his lieutenants, including a man named Jin, against him."

I rubbed a hand over the back of my neck and sighed. It'd been an ugly business, six weeks of hell where I'd very nearly ended up as pieces of human sashimi.

"Jin planted the bomb as an attempt to discredit Po-Sin. He implicated me in the bombing. Po-Sin pretended to believe him in order to draw Jin and any other conspirators into the light. I'll spare you all the details of how he did that and just what happened after. Suffice to say it was taken care of."

I'd delivered the boxes filled with pieces of Jin and Roshanak to the Shotakan military along with an exquisitely worded note from Po-Sin and reparations for the families whose loved ones had been injured or died. Then I'd been escorted off-planet and told never to return.

"I'll get with my people and see what kind of spin we can put on this. The good news is the story from Director Britlen has been running constantly since it aired. The fact that people now know you left home to find your father's killer works in our favor. You're pretty popular anyway. The populace feels like you're accessible, so keep that up.

"There's no possible way to do any kind of testing to prove the rumors about Atmikha, and I suspect we can quash them without too much trouble. She was too well loved by the people for this kind of smear campaign to do anything but anger the civilian population."

"I want Zaran in the palace within the hour. We'll make up some kind of excuse for getting her out of her mother's house," Clara said. "I want testimony about what she saw recorded and her visual of the unknown man downloaded so we can start searching for him. General?"

Saito nodded with a slight smile in Emmory's direction. "My

best team has been otherwise occupied, but I will find a team to put on this mysterious man as soon as you have a description for me, ma'am."

"Admiral." Inana Hassan looked up at me expectantly when I called. "Do you think that Major Bristol's decision to leave with Admiral Shul's fleet has anything to do with our current situation?"

Emmory and I had talked about this the night before. My sister's husband was on the list, as was my dear cousin. The Saxons were always on the list and I didn't think even a declaration from King Trace would convince me otherwise.

My *Ekam* hadn't seemed at all shocked when I suggested Prime Minister Phanin. His little shrug spoke volumes about his opinion of the man.

The problem was that Phanin's behavior was easily explained by Mother's sickness and the trust my sister had put in him. Someone had to run the empire and the fact that the Matriarch Council hadn't put the smackdown on him when he first stepped over the line said a lot. The man's background was totally clean.

"It's possible, ma'am," Hassan said carefully in answer to my question. "We don't have any proof that he's also involved."

"So who wants to talk about the elephant in the room? Why aren't Generals Vandi and Prajapati here?"

General Prajapati was head of the Army, while General Mila Vandi was head of ITS and an old friend of my father's.

"Someone authorized Phanin to use troops against the ambassador," Caspel said after a moment of silence descended on the room. "Regular Army troops, not BodyGuards. I don't have any hard evidence, Highness, but there have been rumors linking General Prajapati with Matriarch Khatri. And General Vandi's aide was on the list of names Zaran provided to Alice."

"We still don't know who's responsible for the leak in your

security. Only three people knew you were on that ship," General Saito said. "As much as Emmory assures me his brother wouldn't have—"

"It wasn't Portis who betrayed me," I cut her off. "You have my assurance on that, too, General. Someone got to my navigator at Shanghai. Offer her enough money and Memz would have strung up her own grandmother."

Saito dipped her head in acknowledgment. "No one knows General Vandi's position on the matter, so Caspel decided to be cautious."

"Someone probably should figure that out. If both the standing military branches are against us, we're going to be in trouble. I can't hold the palace with just my BodyGuards, General."

"I would hope it doesn't come to the point where you have to hold the palace, Highness," Clara said. "However, should it come to that, the matriarchs will provide the Throne with assistance."

"Assuming you won't be in need of defending yourselves." Saito's comment wasn't quite muttered and I bit my tongue.

"I suppose we'll deal with that as it comes, General." Clara smiled and rubbed her hands together. "I think we have pushed our luck as far as we dare today and I'm sure the princess needs to get back to her rooms and rest. Highness, I will message you if anything further comes up?"

"That would be fine." I nodded at the others as they stood, and I carefully got to my own feet. "Admiral Hassan?"

"Yes, Highness?"

"If you have some time free before Pratimas, I'd appreciate a full briefing on the present situation with the Saxons and our border worlds." I hid my smile at Hassan's curious eyebrow. "I have the minutes from the meetings I've missed, but making sense of them without some background is going to prove a little challenging. I'd like to be caught up before the coronation."

Pratimas was in six days, and the coronation would likely be after. Until that happened, I was in the rather awkward position of still not being empress. Mother could still overrule me, especially on matters of state, and with her sanity in question, we were going to find ourselves in deep shit if the Saxons decided to move on us in the middle of all this.

"Let me get with my aide, Highness? She can clear some time in my schedule."

"Send it to Alba. She'll be able to squeeze you in," I replied with a nod. "I've got a meeting with her later today anyway, and she knows my schedule better than I do." I caught the flicker of humor on the admiral's face before she controlled it.

"Yes, ma'am."

"Thank you, Admiral."

Hassan nodded sharply and left the room. Caspel had hung back by the door and pulled it closed again, leaving the three of us alone.

"Highness, I need to ask you something indelicate. Is there truth to the rumors about Princess Cire?"

"I'm not sure how I could know that, given how long I've been away from home."

The look he gave me wasn't a duplicate of Emmory's but it was close. I met it calmly.

"Tell you what, Director. I'll tell you what I know if you tell me why you smiled when I mentioned Shanghai."

Caspel's raised eyebrows spoke volumes, and I held in the smug smile at having been able to surprise the taciturn intelligence agent. "You're good, Highness. I had an agent in port. They mentioned you."

"You do realize this puts you in rather the same predicament as General Vandi?" I replied.

"I didn't put it all together until you were already home,

Highness. I could have killed you six times over since we met. Trust me, if I wanted you dead, it would have already happened."

"Not something you want to say in front of my *Ekam*, Caspel. And if you've bothered to read the extensive file you no doubt have on me, you know I'm a lot harder to kill than that."

"Fair enough. I have spilled my secret, Highness."

Hardly spilled, I thought with a mental snort. The man had barely acknowledged anything except what I'd already guessed for myself. Because of that I rolled my reply over in my head several times before I allowed the words to fly free.

"Twenty years ago, Abraham Suda was in love with my sister. Since I cannot read minds, I don't know if the affection was returned. And since I have been away, there is no possibility I can speak with any surety as to the rumors about Atmikha's paternal heritage."

"Spoken like a consummate politician, Highness. One would think you've been doing this for years."

"I have, Caspel. It just involved more guns."

He inclined his head and reopened the door. I followed him from Clara's house after a quick good-bye to my hostess and dozed in the aircar on the way back to the palace.

Back in my rooms, my thoughts were spinning all over and I stayed silent as Stasia helped me out of my gown and into bed.

Too many suspects. Several had been implicated today, but I still wondered about Bial and the *Upjas*.

My mother's *Ekam* was as difficult for me to read as Emmory, and I couldn't be at all certain that my opinion of the man hadn't been irreparably damaged by the fact that he'd let someone poison my mother and kill my sisters. I knew he didn't like me, but what I couldn't figure out was where the root of that hatred lay. It seemed excessive to be mad over the fact that I'd been a gunrunner.

I queued up my *smati* and called Fenna. "Good morning."

"Good morning, Highness. What can I do for you?"

"Is she there?"

"She's sleeping, Highness. Can I help you with something?"

"Tell me what you know about Bial."

Fenna arched a red eyebrow at me. "Could you be more specific?"

"I could if I knew what I was looking for." I muttered a curse under my breath and looked away. "I'm sorry, Fenna. It's been a long day already."

"You'll want to be careful pushing yourself too hard."

"Emmory already mothers me. Bial hates me, Fenna. Obviously he's not saying it out loud, but it's clear enough to me. What I don't know is why. He's spent an awful lot of time with Ganda, all of it in the course of his duties, and given how much she's been up Mother's skirts, it's understandable."

"And you need proof he's involved?"

"I need something." I threw my hands up in the air wishing I could pace. Unfortunately I'd probably end up flat on my face if I tried. "I can't bar the man from my mother without a good reason, and if he's involved, I don't want him near her, even if the damage is already done."

Fenna's eyes widened and she nodded sharply. "I'll send you what I have, Highness, later today. Don't argue with me. You need your rest."

I glared at her, but knew that she'd likely just call Emmory if I protested too much. So instead I nodded and disconnected the call.

Emmory shared my concern about Bial, and we'd all been proven right today about Ganda. I was having some trouble believing her capable of cooking up a scheme this complex, but I was also willing to admit my bias for her intelligence could be blinding my thinking.

The only ones Emmory and I couldn't agree on as suspects were the *Upjas*. He saw them as the enemy, but I couldn't separate my memories of my old friend, Taz, from the idea that someone had tried to kill me.

Not to mention Cire's involvement with the man in charge of the *Upjas*. I wouldn't admit it even to Caspel, but it wasn't a far stretch to assume that Atmikha wasn't Albin Bristol's daughter.

However, the very thought that Abraham Suda could have killed the woman he'd been so desperately in love with was anathema to me.

But just because I couldn't fathom him doing it didn't mean much—if anything at all. I'd seen too many versions of the same ugly betrayal all over the universe to fool myself into believing that love conquered all.

The only way to know for sure was to look Abraham in the eye and ask him. Of course, that meant I had to either convince Emmory to let me meet with traitors to the throne or dodge my BodyGuard.

I didn't like either option much, so I let the toxin-induced exhaustion drag me down into blackness.

The interview with INN two days later was all about damage control. The rumors about Cire had died out as quickly as we'd suspected they would, and only some of the fringe stations were still harping on them. Assaulting her memory had resulted in a lot of commentary on how crass it was to indulge in rumors against a dead woman and child.

The one about me was a little more exciting and one more brushstroke in this whole princess-gunrunner painting the press had been putting together since my arrival home.

I survived the interview, barely, and even managed to clear

up my part in the whole mess without actually saying anything that would have gotten Po-Sin or Hao pissed at me. The journalist from INN seemed sympathetic enough, but even if she wasn't, Emmory and Alba had final say on the piece before it was released to the public, so I wasn't too worried. I hadn't watched the footage yet, but I trusted Alba and Emmory hadn't let me make a total fool of myself on camera.

I staggered away from Emmory's punch, my head ringing and a stream of curses dropping from my mouth like B-5 cluster bombs.

"You need to watch that opening, ma'am."

I shook the stars out of my eyes and shot Emmory a narrow-eyed glare. It was the fifth time he'd tapped me in the head since we'd started. Not hard enough to do actual damage, but enough to ring my bell.

What had seemed like a good idea when he proposed it now looked like it was going to turn into a daily ass-kicking session. Normally, kicking ass wouldn't bother me, but in this case I was the recipient and Emmory was good at his job. I was good, too, but I had to grudgingly admit he was better than me.

"I am trying."

"Not hard enough," he replied.

The weakness of the toxins had worked itself out of my system after that first day. So yesterday, Emmory had brought me down into this small windowless room filled with workout equipment and weights just after dawn.

We'd started my training with a general workout, but today we'd moved on to more serious business.

Zin was perched on a stack of pads that stood against the far wall, coaching me and trading laughing insults with Emmory.

Cas and Jet were at the door, completing Team One. The traditional three-man team plus my *Ekam* were a normal escort inside the palace. Team Three was outside. True to his word, Emmory had broken with tradition and now two teams plus either himself or Nal followed me on palace grounds. It was quite the production when I had to go anywhere.

I didn't know what he was worried about. The man could beat me down and go on to defeat whatever enemies wanted me dead without breaking a sweat.

He wasn't sweating even though we'd been sparring for an hour. I, however, was soaked through; my black choli clung to my skin and even my pants were sticking in spots. Now that I was looking for it, I could see the similarities between Portis's and Emmory's fighting styles.

I shook out my arms and circled him. Before I could move, however, there was a commotion at the door. Mother and her cadre of Guards swept into the room, followed by Nal.

"Hailimi!"

"Oh, bugger me," I muttered, swiping sweat from my face. Bial was right on Mother's heels and his face was grim. She'd been bad the last few days, sliding into and out of lucidity with alarming unpredictability.

"Haili, what is going on here?" Mother demanded. She approached, holding up the heavy skirts of her blue dress as she padded over the workout room floor. I couldn't help but notice how pale the skin of her hands was against the dark fabric. I could see the veins beneath the paper-thin surface, a spiderweb of ice streaking down her fingers.

"I'm working out." My nerves seemed to have vanished entirely with the news of my ascension. Or maybe it was the attempted poisoning. I always had performed better when someone was trying to kill me.

"It's unseemly." Mother's eyes were bright, like twin points of light in her face, a sure sign she'd worked herself into another episode. I wondered how long she'd be able to hold together a tirade.

"You're a princess, not a tavern brawler. We won't have it."

"Mother—"

She cut me off, jamming a finger into my chest. "You're behaving like a hooligan. We won't have it in our house, Hailimi."

"I'll gladly move out, or off-planet, Your Majesty. Your choice."

I hadn't meant for it to sound snarky, but Mother's eyes narrowed. "Don't think we haven't heard about you threatening Prime Minister Phanin."

"I didn't threaten him. I put him in his place. Arresting the Saxon ambassador could have started a war." At least she hadn't found out about my meeting with Clara and the others; that really wouldn't have gone over well.

"He was just sending a message to them. If you'd been in any actual danger, your BodyGuard would have taken care of it. That's what he's here for. Not to teach you to fight like a street rat."

I gaped at her, trying to follow the tangle of sentences. "If I'd been in danger? Mother, someone tried to poison me. Let's get something straight here." I crossed my arms over my chest as I faced her down. Nothing I could say would go over well, but I wasn't going to stand there and let her treat me like a child. "I'm a grown woman and I'll be responsible for my own safety. I'm not sitting around getting fat and lazy when there's someone out there trying to kill me."

"Yes, precisely." I had enough time to frown at my mother's sudden agreement before she turned on Emmory. "*Ekam* Tresk, you are relieved of your duty."

"What?" Fear clogged my throat and I croaked the word out as the blood rushed to fill my ears with a roar.

20

ighness, it's best if you step away." Nal closed a hand on my upper arm and tried to pull me away from Emmory.

I snapped my right hand out, striking Nal in the throat, and she dropped like a rock tossed off a cliff.

"Highness, please calm down." Bial had his hands up, trying to placate me while staying out of arm's reach.

"Haili, do not make a scene. I have—"

"I will kill the next person who touches me." I didn't raise my voice at all, but the words cut through the din like a monomolecular blade.

Bial shut up. Mother blinked at me in shock. Nal gasped for breath on the ground like a fish. Zin swallowed back his protests and pressed his lips so tightly together they were a bloodless slash in his face. Cas and Jet had moved to my side and their hands were on their weapons.

Emmory hadn't said a word.

I folded my hands at my waist as everything fell into place around me with stunning clarity.

I was still only the heir and Mother's sanity seemed iffy at the moment, so I wasn't about to risk using the argument that she was willingly going to abdicate the throne. But when it came to my BodyGuards, the law was on my side. Mother couldn't remove my BodyGuards, not without proof that they were a threat to my life. There was no way I was letting anyone dictate who was keeping me safe.

I cleared my throat and set my shoulders. "Begging your pardon, Your Majesty. You cannot remove my *Ekam*. He has sworn an oath to me; only I can release him from it."

"He did no such thing."

"Ask Matriarch Desai, she witnessed it."

"I am the empress!"

"You are." I dipped into a reasonably competent curtsy given my lack of skirts. "However, the law dictates you can only remove the BodyGuards of the heir with my agreement or if you have proof the heir's life is in danger and the Guards are not able to counter the threat."

Mother smiled triumphantly. "Three attempts on your life would constitute a danger, Hailimi. As much as it pains me to admit it, I made a mistake. Three times your life has been in danger. It's clear this assignment is too much for this Tracker. We'll return him and his partner to their former positions and Nal will take over as your *Ekam*."

Swallowing back all the angry words I wanted to throw at her, I concentrated on the facts. "Three *unsuccessful* attempts, Mother," I replied calmly. "In two of those attempts *Ekam* Tresk was directly responsible for saving my life. You have no proof of incompetence and I will take this fight to the Matriarch Council if it is necessary."

The seconds ticked away as Mother and I stared at each other, silently battling it out. There was little question in my mind who was going to win. I was dead if she took Emmory away from me, so from my perspective, I didn't have anything to lose.

"What's it going to be?"

"Fine. If you're going to make an issue of it." She shoved past me, the force knocking me into Zin.

"Don't be a brat, Hailimi. We're sick to death of arguing with you. There will be no more of this foolishness under our roof. And you, BodyGuard Tresk, we've entrusted the welfare of the Crown to you." She glared at Emmory. "Don't disappoint us again."

"Never, Your Majesty," he murmured, dropping his head.

"Fix your damn hair, Hailimi." Mother snapped her fingers and I heard the sharp staccato of her footsteps as she marched back out of the room.

"Highness, are you all right?"

I didn't look up at Zin as he set me on my feet. My hands were shaking. Mother was well and truly gone. I couldn't do anything to save her, and her behavior was only going to get worse. All I could do was take on the burden she had shouldered for so many years.

"It's a responsibility, Haili, not a burden." Cire's voice rang in my head as one of the last conversations with my sister floated up from the depths of memory. *"I've been given the gift of this life. I can do something with it. Make life better for others. I'm not saying it's easy, duty never is, but it's a responsibility I'll take on gladly—the price of everything I've been given."*

"You always were so much better than me," I murmured, remembering our conversation.

"Pish," Cire had declared with a wave of her hand. *"You always sell yourself short. Stop playing the 'poor me' game, Haili. I know you could do this."*

She was right, as usual. I'd run from a lot of things in my life, but running from a fight wasn't my style at all.

"Nalmari." I stepped away from Zin and stared down at my

BodyGuard. "You told my mother Emmory couldn't protect me, knowing what's wrong with her and how she would react."

Defiant brown eyes met mine. "I was only looking out for your safety, Highness. This violation of tradition has put you in danger time and again."

"I am done with your attitude and your lack of cooperation with my *Ekam*. You are released from my service."

Nal gaped at me in shock. "Highness, your empress-mother appointed—"

"And I'm unappointing you. I am done. Get out of here before I borrow Emmory's gun and shoot you."

"Yes, Highness." Nal fled.

"If you're going to argue about this with me, too, I should warn you I'm not in the mood." I didn't bother waiting for the door to close fully before I spoke and stalked over to grab a towel.

"I'm honestly surprised you let her stay as long as you did, Highness."

I stopped drying my face and stared at him. "Are you kidding me? If you wanted her gone, why didn't you fire her?"

Emmory shrugged. "Your empress-mother appointed her. I suspect if I'd tried, we'd have had a much bigger fight on our hands. You have the right—as you just pointed out—to decide on your Guards."

"You could have just said something to me. I trust your judgment, Emmory."

He shifted uncomfortably. "Your Highness might not think that for long. I owe you another apology and a confession. Nal was on Pace's BodyGuard team and we have reason to believe she may have been the one responsible for the ebolenza."

A meteorite crashed into my chest and lodged itself there, burning me up from the inside.

Nal had been my little sister's BodyGuard. Nal had let her die. For all I knew, she could have been the one who slipped the ebolenza to her and then watched her choke to death on her own blood.

"But her files."

"I cleaned them before I gave them to you."

"You knew. You knew and you didn't tell me. Not only that but you *hid* it from me." I curled my hands into fists as fury closed its teeth in me and everything inside me froze.

"Highness."

I was moving before the plan was fully formed, but I knew I only had seconds. I grabbed Cas, shoving him into Emmory's path, bolting around them for the door. Jet hesitated, indecision costing him the precious seconds he needed to have a chance of stopping me.

Zin, however, had learned his lesson about my reaction time back on *Sophie*. He saw the look on my face, moved when I did, and caught me around the waist before I made it a full meter. I swung at him, my fist connecting with something solid. He released me with a grunt of pain.

"Highness, listen please. We can't go after Nal right now. There's no proof. Emmory kept her on in the hopes that we'd have the time to find it." Zin held his hands up. "Please."

I tossed my towel in one direction and came at him from the other. Moving with more grace than a man his size had a right to, Zin pivoted out of my way, and his blow to my kidney sent me to my knees.

I couldn't get enough air into my lungs. Zin followed me down, taking my face in his hands as I struggled for air past the pain.

"I'm sorry, ma'am. I'm sorry," he murmured. "I need you to

listen. I need you to put aside your anger for a minute and let me explain why we didn't tell you."

"No." I tried to grab his wrists, but I couldn't get my hands to obey my brain.

"Nal wasn't anywhere near her when Pace was infected with the ebolenza. She's got an alibi, and until we have proof otherwise, we can't move on her. She may have ties to whoever is behind all this, and we can't tip our hand. We decided not to tell you because we knew you'd react like this. You can't kill her. Not even your royal blood would protect you from what would look like cold-blooded murder."

Deep down I knew he was right, but I didn't want logic right now. I finally got my arms to cooperate and grabbed Zin's wrists.

He didn't let me go and instead pulled me in closer until his forehead was touching mine. "I swear to you with all that I hold sacred that we'll find out who's responsible for this. We'll make them pay. You need to trust me, to trust us, to handle this. You are going to be empress."

"She was my baby sister," I choked out. "I was supposed to keep her safe." Tears spilled out from behind the barrier I'd been desperately shoring up since I first heard the news about my sisters. Without the ice of my anger, the grief took hold and tore me apart.

"So were we," Zin replied, sorrow etched into his face. "We didn't and I'm more sorry for that than you'll ever know."

"I was supposed to keep them safe!" The dam broke at the same time my heart shattered all over again and I began to cry.

Zin still didn't release me. He pulled me to his chest, cradling my head against his shoulder as I wept out my broken heart.

"Zin."

"She's all right, Emmory. She just hasn't had a chance to really grieve. She needs this."

The material of Zin's uniform jacket was soft under my cheek. He rocked slightly, completely at ease with my tears, murmuring comfort to me until they died out.

Embarrassment set in shortly after. I untangled myself from Zin and landed on my ass. "Next time we fight, I'm bringing a gun."

"It wouldn't help, Highness. I'm sorry for hitting you."

"Stop apologizing. I'm still furious with you both." I rubbed at my back and shot him a rueful smile. "You're good. I underestimated you."

"Most people do. It's why Emmory keeps me around." He got to his feet and held out a hand.

"I need to clean up." I took his hand, wincing a little as I got to my feet. I snagged my towel from the floor and headed for the door, but Emmory dropped to a knee in front of me. Zin glanced at us and ushered the other BodyGuards out the door.

"I am sorry, Highness."

Studying my *Ekam*, I mulled over my replies before choosing the best option. "I've trusted you and thought you returned it. I'm not going to lie and say that doesn't hurt. Remember that next time I doubt you, it's a problem of your own creation. Get up. That makes me uncomfortable." I started walking again, figuring that would get him moving. "I'm still going to kill Nal."

"That's exactly why I didn't tell you," he said.

"He's dangerous," I said with a wave of my finger ahead of us at Zin as we started down the hallway.

Emmory's smile flickered. "You don't want to fight him, Highness."

"I just did and I got my ass kicked."

"You know what I mean, you've got that look."

"So I can't kill Nal right now," I said, restarting the conversation as soon as we were safely in my rooms. "Is there anything else I need to know?"

"Nal and her older sisters were all sponsored to either the Naval Academy or High Point by Matriarch Surakesh's youngest sister."

"And all of them are gone, lost to the war."

Emmory nodded sharply. "That's motive enough to hate your family, but it doesn't end there. Ganda spent a lot of time with Pace before she got sick. It would have been easy for her to get close with Nal."

"And to suggest her as my *Ekam* when she found out I was coming home." Hissing out my frustration, I stared up at the ceiling. "I'm going to kill my cousin, too, Emmory."

"I would advise against it, Highness."

"There've been an awful lot of accidents happening around here lately, especially to my family. It wouldn't be any more suspicious than the others."

Silence settled down around us, a cloak as heavy as the snow falling outside the window. Emmory conceded my point with a shrug of his shoulder and changed the subject.

"I doubt there'll be much fallout from this, though Bial may protest."

"Let him protest," I said with a shrug of my own. "I could take him if it came down to it."

The sound of surprised laughter was quickly—if poorly—camouflaged by a cough. I raised an eyebrow at Jet, who lowered his hand and gave me an innocent smile.

"Oh, I know it was you." I threw my towel at him. "I'm going to clean up. Clara sent me Zaran's full report, but I haven't had a chance to read it because I'm still working my way through the one Fenna sent me on Bial. Emmory, will you get me food? We can go over it while I eat."

An hour later I was clean, comfortable, and relaxing on the couch as I flipped through the report Fenna had sent me. I'd had Emmory put it up on the screen so we could all see.

"There's nothing here to suggest his involvement, Highness."

"I know." I made a face. "That's the problem. His behavior doesn't match his squeaky-clean file. He's from a good family, passed all the required loyalty tests. Even has a recommendation from General Saito. He was the first name on Ven's short list." I couldn't bring myself to replay the journal entry by Mother's former BodyGuard talking about how Bial was a "proud Indranan, fiercely loyal to the throne."

"Other than the first night, he hasn't been outwardly insulting toward you," Zin said.

"He doesn't like me; it's obvious every time I get near the man. I'm a good liar."

"Your pardon, Highness, but your readings go all over the place when you lie."

I shrugged. "It's not worth the effort it takes to hide it from you." I took a breath and looked right at Emmory. "I slept with Cas last night."

Emmory gave me the Look, clearly unimpressed.

"Not a blip." Zin blinked. "Not bad, Highness. I'm not sure what this proves. We know you're lying."

"Do you? No one was in my rooms last night and Cas wasn't on duty. Did you see him?"

Zin frowned and glanced at Emmory. "She's lying, right?"

Emmory didn't look away from me. "I actually can't tell. Your point, Highness?"

"I'm better at reading people than I am at lying. Bial's hiding something; he may as well scream it at me every time I come near him. Practically everyone is hiding something at one point or another, even you."

"I'm hiding things?"

I flipped him off. "I'm assuming it's normal shit and not that you're part of the plot to kill me. That may be a stupid move on my part."

"I've kept you alive so far, Highness."

"I know." I smiled. "My point is can we really discount Bial, or did my enemies do such a good job that they managed to get someone right next to my mother without showing their hand."

"The bigger question is why hasn't he just killed the empress? Why go to all the trouble of making her look crazy?" Zin asked.

"That's easy," Emmory replied, rubbing a hand over his head. "If you want to throw things into chaos, it's better to damage the foundation. If they'd just killed the empress, someone else would take her place."

"But if you make the people fear the monarchy first?" I finished his thought for him. "You get the empress to make a whole bunch of questionable decisions and suddenly people start questioning the government. Then when you kill them, people are a lot more open to a change in leadership."

"I'll keep digging on Bial, Highness," Emmory said as Stasia came in the room with my food.

I wiped the report from Fenna off the screen as I picked up my fork and brought up the report Matriarch Desai had sent over.

My fork clattered to the floor.

"Highness, what is it?"

I dragged in a breath and then another; tears were blurring the image on the screen. The face of the man Zaran had

279

seen with her mother. The face of the man I'd seen the day my father was killed.

"Highness." Emmory's voice was more insistent and I tore my eyes away from the screen.

"It's Wilson." Blinking the tears away, I faced my *Ekam*. "It's the man I was hunting. He killed my father. Killed my sisters. He strolled back onto my planet like he owns it!"

Rage clawed at my chest and I cast about for something to throw, but Emmory grabbed my arm and didn't back down even when I snarled at him.

"We don't know what his role is, Highness, or even who he is."

"Because he's a Shiva-damned ghost." I pulled out of Emmory's grasp and stalked to the window where Zin stood. "I don't even know why they let me go after him. Why they didn't send someone better."

"They sent the best Trackers, Highness," Zin murmured. "You're lucky you didn't vanish like they did."

"I'm not sure luck had anything to do with it." I tapped my fingers on the windowsill. "The fact that no one but Portis knew who I was out there probably had more to do with it than anything. I tracked the man I knew as Wilson as far as the edge of Solarian space, even met with a man who claimed to have intelligence on his network, but that information didn't pan out. The trail went cold after that."

Turning back around, I called Bial with my *smati* and projected the link onto the screen.

"Highness?"

"No one is to see my mother without my permission with the exception of Dr. Satir."

"Dr. Satir is still visiting family, Highness."

"Dr. Ganjen then. No one else, Bial."

"Highness, your cousin has breakfast with the empress daily."

"Then you can meet her tomorrow morning and inform her that I forbid it."

"I could call her now and tell her—"

"Did I fucking stutter?" It was petty payback for the earlier breakfast stunt of hers, but I figured Ganda would come see me when she found out and I didn't feel like dealing with her right now.

"No, ma'am. I'll see that it's done." Bial hung up without waiting for my dismissal and I arched an eyebrow at the blank screen thoughtfully.

"He was more cooperative than I expected. Do you think he's coming around?"

"Hard to say, Highness," Emmory replied. "What now?"

"I need to send a few messages. I want you to put someone on the security footage of the hallways and inform me if anyone gets in my mother's door besides the doctor."

21

Ganda was predictably angry the next morning. I could hear her coming down the hallway, though the closed door muffled whatever raging she was doing to something unintelligible.

I crossed my legs underneath me on the couch and picked up my mug. It was tempting to let her stand outside the door and shout for a bit, but I nodded at Emmory to open it instead.

"Do you want to explain to me why I can't get in to see Aunt Divya?" Ganda's cheeks were flushed and her carefully done hair was slightly disheveled. "We've been having breakfast for years. Now she's all alone and you're cutting off the one thing she enjoys—that she looks forward to every day? You've been gone, Hail. I'm doing the job you gave up to go running around the universe with some commoner."

That struck a nerve, but I was careful to keep a grip on my temper, even if it required that I bite my tongue. Ganda was too busy waving her hands in the air to notice.

"You have no right to keep me from her. None at all, and—don't you have anything to say?"

I took a sip of my chai, keeping my eyes on hers the whole

time. "My empress-mother is very ill. Dr. Satir thinks it's best not to stress her too much."

"Dr. Satir isn't here." Ganda licked her lips.

"She left the instructions before her departure." That was a bald-faced lie, but I was better at it than Ganda was. I set my cup down and stood, pleased that Ganda took a step back. "We are grateful for the kindness you've shown her over the years, but I'm home and I'm the heir and you will do as I say."

"You can't do this," Ganda hissed, her eyes narrowed.

I arched an eyebrow in reply, determined not to show my shock at her unbelievable boldness. "You know, I didn't miss you at all, Ganda. How surprising is that?"

"Likewise." This time she stood her ground when I advanced on her.

"Well, you can file a complaint with Mother. Though it's hard to say what kind of reaction you'll get."

"You would have done better to stay away, Hail." Ganda's girlish voice became suddenly menacing as she stepped forward and stabbed a finger into my breastbone. Zin's eyes widened at the enormous breech of protocol, but I just bared my teeth in a lazy smile and stopped Emmory with a surreptitious elbow in his stomach.

"You know, I was going to, but these two insisted I come home," I said. "And I'd keep your hands to yourself."

"Too bad for you. I'd suggest you find a way to do another disappearing act and go back to that pitiful life of yours before you lose it."

Did she really just threaten me? I blinked at Ganda, too stunned for a moment to register Emmory's hissed exhalation, then the point of her nail dug into my sternum again. I grabbed her finger, bending it back sharply until the bone cracked from the pressure.

Ganda let out a cry of pain and tears appeared in her eyes. I let her go and she staggered back toward the door. I could see her Guards hovering just outside, unwilling to cross mine to get to their charge.

"I've been out in the world, cousin. I know the value of wheat and lentils. That's more than you can say, having never worked a day in your life. You overstep your bounds. I'd suggest you find somewhere else to be and that you stay away from my mother." I waved a hand at her Guards. "I think Lady Ganda might need to see a Farian. It appears she's injured herself."

The woman nodded, not about to argue with me. Ganda shook off the hand she cupped around her elbow and stalked off, hiding her hand within the sleeve of her purple dress.

"That was worrisome," Emmory said.

I kept the smile pasted on my face and tried to shake the chill that Ganda's words had sent running down my spine. "Tell me about it. She always was an annoying bitch, but direct threats from her are something new. Usually she just liked to whisper and connive behind my back."

"I can't believe she threatened you." Admiral Hassan shook her head with a frown.

"Me either, but that just goes to show how much things have changed around here." I stopped in front of Bial and smiled at my mother's *Ekam*. "Good morning. How is she today?"

"Well, Highness." Bial exchanged a nod with Emmory that was just a shade frostier than the one he'd given me, and I made a mental note to ask him what the fallout had been from Nal's dismissal.

Admiral Hassan and I headed into the room. Mother was standing with Caspel, studying the projected worlds hovering above the massive table in the War Room.

"If we move the 107th and the 33rd from the Cerulean System, we could put them here and here." Planets lit up as Mother moved forces around with her fingertips.

"It leaves us awfully exposed on the backside." Caspel frowned. "Admiral Hassan, thoughts?"

"Good morning, Majesty." Hassan bowed and crossed the room. "It does leave us exposed, but the likelihood of the Solarian Conglomerate attempting anything is extremely small. However, I'd suggest moving the 81st from here to cover some of the gap left behind."

I circled around the other side of the table, staring up at all the planets as memories drifted through my head.

"You used to love coming in here with your father."

I bowed. "Good morning, Mother."

She smiled. It erased some of the exhaustion on her face. "I hear I have you to thank for me finally getting some peace and quiet in the mornings?"

I was so shocked, all I could do was blink at her and Mother snickered. Finally, I found my voice. "You're welcome? If you didn't want her around, why didn't you do something about it?"

"She's family, even if she does chatter like a schoolboy. And in all honesty, I was pretty out of it for a while."

"You seem much better."

"I'm still dying. Just a little more aware of it now. Dr. Ganjen is trying some experimental new treatment to counter the effects. It might kill me, but I figured since I was going out anyway, I may as well do one last thing worth noting." She fisted her hand when it started shaking and gave me a rueful smile. "Enough about my tragedy. What do you think?"

"Ma'am?"

Mother gestured at the table. "What do you think of all this? It's going to be your show, Haili. You may as well learn how to run it."

Forty-five planets spun around twenty-eight stars. Three of them by Admiral Hassan were red, the three that the Saxons had claimed. In the center of it all was the Ashvin System and home. Blinking designations hung in the air above the naval vessels and I continued my path around the table, studying them intently.

Two of the worlds the Saxons had claimed—Hanmas and Interia—orbited the same star, but the third was farther out and a reasonable distance away from both home and the border worlds. "Why did they take that one instead of this one?" I gestured at a reddish planet closer to me. "This would have made more sense."

"ITS training world, ma'am," Hassan replied. "There's no civilians."

"Ah, yeah, that probably would have been a little more obvious than they want at the moment." Clicking my tongue on my teeth, I stared at the pair of planets for so long that my vision blurred. I blinked and froze. "Bugger me."

"Highness?"

"Have you looked at this?"

Caspel arched an eyebrow and I grabbed Hassan by the shoulders and dragged her in front of me.

"Look past those worlds, Admiral, not at them." I sped up the time scale. The planets moved along their paths, opening up a corridor that led straight to home, and I heard Caspel's quiet curse behind me as it sank in. "I'm only paranoid because people are trying to kill me, but there's an awful lot of empty space leading right up to Pashati in the next few months."

"They would never," Mother said, shaking her head. "To strike at us here, to strike so deep into the empire, would take a force greater than they have."

"Plus they'd be cut off from supplies, support, everything

once they got past Canafey. We'd grind them up from the front and the back," Hassan agreed, though her brows were knitted together as she contemplated the possibilities.

"I take it you don't agree either?"

Caspel wore a deep frown, but he, too, shook his head. "It's risky. Bold, though, and King Trace is known for that. I need more intel before I'm willing to accept it."

"Speaking of Canafey, can we pull the 44th from there and send them back to support the ITS troops on New Vesa?"

"I wouldn't, Mother," I said. "Even with the *Vajrayana* Initiative docks there, they wouldn't be able to get them up and running fast enough if the Saxons hit us." I wasn't going to say it out loud, but I didn't know why she was suggesting it when I'd just shown her that taking any troops away from Canafey was a very bad decision.

"I can take into advisement your concerns, Hail; however, I'd caution you to not jump to conclusions on this, and remember that we've been following what the Saxons are doing for quite a bit longer than you have." Her smile took some of the sting out of her words. "Admiral, send me an action plan by the end of the day for approval."

"Yes, Majesty."

Mother squeezed my forearm with a second smile. "I'm going to go lie down for a bit."

I smiled back and watched her as she carefully walked to the door, then turned back to look at the map again.

"Highness, whatever your empress-mother says, I will keep an eye on this. If I come across more information, we can perhaps change her mind."

"Thank you, Caspel. Let's hope we have time for that." My gut was screaming at me, and after all these years, I'd learned to listen to it.

The GIS director bowed and left the room.

"Admiral, I'm having dinner tonight with Leena Surakesh and my nephew. If you're free, would you care to join us?"

"Of course, Highness."

"Good." I laughed. "To be honest, I'm not entirely sure I trust myself not to grab him by the throat and shake him until he confesses."

"Understandable, ma'am."

"I'll see you this evening then."

She took the hint and left me alone to stare at the map and wonder just what in the fires of Naraka Trace was up to. I was tempted to just call him up and ask, but I was pretty sure it wouldn't go over well.

As uneasy as I'd been earlier, it multiplied itself tenfold by the time my aircar pulled up outside Shivan's later that evening. Convincing Emmory that having dinner with a man we were pretty sure was trying to kill me had taken some doing.

"I realize the security risks here. Believe me when I say I'm not being reckless. I need to look Laabh in the eye again now that I know for sure. See what he's made of, and maybe if I drop a few hints, we can shake him up enough that he'll fold. Shivan's is one of the few restaurants in the city the media can't get into, and frankly I'd rather no one overhear this conversation we're about to have."

"I realize that, Highness." Emmory gave me the Look.

"Hey, I haven't killed Nal, have I? I think you can trust me not to kill my nephew."

"I'm still getting out of the car first," Emmory said, stopping me with a hand when I moved forward. "Jet, you're with me." The big man nodded and followed Emmory from the car.

Shivan's was an exclusive restaurant buried in the heart of the capital's warehouse district. The building was a narrow, three-story structure covered with unassuming gray brick and surrounded by warehouses that bustled with activity day and night.

I stayed in the aircar with Zin and Cas, not arguing with Emmory about the need to check out the restaurant. Our enemies had been given plenty of warning if they wanted to try something, and I didn't want anyone hurt because of me.

Several moments later, Cas tilted his head to the side and said, "We can go." The door to the aircar slid open and Zin stepped out as a roar of sound hit us again and the bright snap of digital camera lights filled the air.

Oh, bugger me. The media.

Taking Zin's offered hand, I plastered a smile on my face and lifted my heavy skirts as I stepped from the car. The multihued fabric looked like the ocean after a storm, shimmering with color and light in the entire spectrum of blue.

"Your Highness, what can you tell us about the accusations you were involved in the killing of children?"

"Princess! Is it true you were a hitman for Po-Sin?"

I didn't know any of the people shouting questions at me. The media events at the palace were more controlled, with carefully selected members of the press allowed in for an audience. My interview with INN had been the third carefully orchestrated one since my return.

I turned toward the crowd of reporters and released my skirts to give them a wave.

"Dinner at home might have been easier," Zin whispered out of the corner of his mouth.

"I know," I muttered back. But this was safer, as weird as it sounded.

"Princess Hailimi, do you have any response to these accusations?"

I looked at the young man who'd shouted the question. "You've seen my interview with INN. I hope that answered all your questions about the incident. If not, feel free to put in a request with my chamberlain about another interview. I will reiterate that the accusations are false, though I think you've all figured that out for yourselves. The venerable Po-Sin is not the sort of man who handles dishonorable employees well."

Nervous laughter answered my reply.

"Your Highness, why are you having dinner with your nephew and the admiral?"

My reply slipped out before I could stop it. "Because I'm hungry."

Laughter echoed up from the cluster of media personnel and I tossed the crowd a wink. "Not now," I said in response to the deluge of questions. "I really am hungry. Hang around and I'll answer a few questions after dinner." Grabbing for my skirts again, I headed up the short stairs toward the orange double doors of Shivan's.

Emmory had come back out of the restaurant and was scowling at the crowd. "Hang around?" he said shortly.

I grinned at him. "They're harmless."

"The media?" He snorted with another sweeping glance. "Maybe. But I'm not worried about them. All they can damage is your reputation."

"I think we're far past that concern, Emmory."

He spared me a look. "Inside, Highness."

I resisted the urge to give him a salute because I knew the cameras would pick it up immediately.

"There's the admiral. You did realize this whole dinner is probably going to tip off our enemies, Highness?"

"I'm counting on it," I replied. I wanted to wait for Admiral Hassan, but instead I let Emmory direct me into the restaurant. Adail, Jet, and Salham stood just inside the door. They fell into step behind us.

The doors shut, closing the jarring roar of the media outside, and I sighed a little as the soothing sounds of the restaurant wrapped around me. Quiet music floated in the background, slipping among conversations without drowning them out.

The interior of Shivan's was quite different from its outside skin. The entryway opened up into the wide reception area, and beyond was the first floor dining area. The interior of the building had been hollowed out, and a tower of a glass elevator stretched up through open air toward the ceiling. The second and third floors were sectioned off into private rooms ringing the exterior of the building.

Orchids and other exotic plants dangled from the balconies, spilled from carefully stacked displays, and filled the air with subtle scents intended to enhance rather than compete with the food.

"Fasé." I smiled at the Farian and the other two members of Captain Gill's squad as we came through the doorway. "It's good to see you again."

"Likewise, Your Highness."

"Do you have plans for the holiday?" Farians tended to assimilate into the cultures they were living in, somehow seamlessly blending their own beliefs into Indranan holidays and celebrations.

"No, ma'am. We're on duty."

A rotund little man bustled through the crowd toward us.

"Your Imperial Highness, you do me a great honor." Avan Shivan bowed low, popping up before he overbalanced and landed face-first on the polished wood floor. His round face was dominated by a pleasant smile, and he held out both hands, palms up.

"So formal," I teased, taking them without hesitation. I

ignored Emmory's pained noise of protest, and leaned down to press my cheek to Avan's. "It is very good to see you again, old friend. You haven't changed at all."

Shivan's was a haven for the rich and powerful. Not only was the food excellent, but Avan's grandfather had fought for—and won—an injunction keeping the media from being allowed on the property. That ruling had instantly made his restaurant the preferred place for people who wanted more than the usual privacy, for whatever reason.

Avan kept up the tradition of his grandfather and father—great food, and a little peace for those whose lives were constantly in the spotlight.

He'd also taken in one restless royal princess. I'd spent a large chunk of the year before and the months after my father's death hiding in the kitchens of Shivan's.

Avan smiled even wider, a feat I wasn't sure was possible without damaging his face. "I'm afraid I can't say the same about you, Princess," he teased, pulling away with a quick apologetic glance at my BodyGuards. "You've made quite the transformation since I saw you last."

"Evidence of my misspent youth."

Avan barked a laugh that sounded very much like a pure Earth sea lion. "So I've heard. Please, come this way. I have a room ready for you on the third floor." He waved a hand over his shoulder, heading not for the glass elevator that dominated the center of the building, but for the stairs. "Your *Ekam* requested we avoid the elevator."

"Of course he did," I murmured.

"If your Highness would rather—"

"No, Avan," I replied with a wave of my hand. "I've upset my BodyGuards enough tonight. Let's not push our luck. Two flights of stairs won't kill me."

We wound through the crowd, diners rising to greet me as we passed. I spotted Alice in the corner having dinner with her father and gave her a brief smile. We'd set her up in the main room to see if there would be any buzz about my dinner plans.

Nal and Willimet stood at attention in the hallway outside our room. "Lady Surakesh and her husband are already here," Nal said. "I showed them in. Kisah and Rama are in the room."

"Thank you." I spotted the admiral and her aide approaching from the other direction. "Oh sure, she gets to take the elevator."

Admiral Hassan's brown eyes widened in shock at my comment and Zin's muffled laughter. Emmory didn't even bat an eyelash as he replied, "No one has tried to kill her lately, Highness."

"No one's tried to kill me for several days now either," I muttered. "Though, Admiral, you'll probably want to sleep a little lighter. If you stay at my side for much longer, they might decide you're a target."

"I always sleep lightly, Your Highness." Admiral Hassan bowed, her short black hair shifting with the movement. "You remember my aide? Commander Hamprasade."

"Admiral," I replied with a nod of my own. "Commander."

The woman at Hassan's side bowed to me with a murmured "Highness."

"Avan, it's good to see you again," Hassan said to the proprietor, who beamed at her. I stepped behind Avan so he could say his hellos, heading through the dark green door Nal held open.

The room within was small but well lit, with walls covered in rich green fabric. A table for five was the centerpiece of the room, its dark wood surface gleaming under the lights.

"Your Highness." Leena dropped into a perfect curtsy, her silver-blue dress looking like a pool of liquid mercury. Laabh was dressed in uniform and his perfunctory bow wasn't fast enough to hide the surprised confusion when he'd spotted Admiral Hassan.

"Leena. So good to see you again." I took her hands and urged her to her feet, kissing her cheeks. She was the puzzle. Either up to her neck in the whole plot or totally innocent, and I hadn't figured out yet which it was.

"You, too, Highness. I am very relieved you are feeling better." Her face was open, dark eyes filled with hesitant delight.

"You and me both," I quipped and her surprised blink seemed genuine. "This is Admiral Hassan and her aide." I passed Leena off to the admiral and turned to my nephew. "Laabh."

His smile was brief and filled with nervousness. "Your Highness."

"I think in private we can be a little less formal. Have you met Admiral Hassan yet?"

"No, ma'am. It's a pleasure."

"Highness." Emmory handed me a glass of wine and I took it with a smile. After the poisoning debacle, the only way to get my *Ekam* to agree to this meeting was to allow him to set the rules for food. Everything I got to eat tonight had been checked and rechecked, analyzed together and alone, until Emmory was certain it was clean.

The report from Dr. Ganjen had been both enlightening and disturbing. An innocuous substance in my drink—in all the drinks at the party, in fact—had reacted with another that the doctor thought had been introduced through contact absorption. What we couldn't pinpoint was if that had been from what I was wearing or the long list of people I'd come in contact with that day. Given how fast my reaction had been, I was sure it had to have been something—or someone—I'd touched in the moments right before I collapsed. That narrowed the suspects somewhat, but the only thing I knew for sure was that Emmory's quick response was the reason I was still alive.

I smiled at Zin when he pulled my chair out for me, and I settled into my seat, letting the bustle of the BodyGuards and Avan's silently efficient staff flow around me.

Admiral Hassan and Commander Hamprasade took the seats on the left side, leaving the ones for the right for Leena and my nephew, and a few moments later quiet descended as Avan bowed his way out of the room.

Emmory and Cas took up positions on the inside of the door, their hands tucked behind their backs and masks of disinterest plastered over their faces. Zin and Jet were on the far side of the room, and the rest of my BodyGuards were outside.

I closed my fingers around the delicate stem of my wineglass and lifted it slightly. "My empress-mother, long may she reign," I said, impressed that I managed to keep the irony out of my voice.

The others echoed the toast and we started in on the spread of appetizers Avan had provided. I easily slid into casual conversation with the commander, who, it turned out, was from the same coastal town of Tible where Emmory and Zin had grown up.

I grabbed for an asparagus spear wrapped with cheese and meat and bit the end off. A happy sigh escaped me, and I saw Admiral Hassan smother a smile, but I was too blissed out by the smooth Earth Havarti to care. I took a sip of my wine. The deep rose vintage was from Shallot with the same dry finish that characterized all the wines of the arid planet. It complemented the food perfectly.

We continued the pleasant, if useless, conversation through dinner. As the last of the plates were cleared and Avan vanished with a promise of coffee and dessert when I rang for it, a silence descended on the room.

"It's a terrible business, all this," I said, leaning back in my chair. "Nice to know I still have family left and people I can count on."

Laabh's hand tightened almost imperceptibly on his glass. Leena didn't flinch at all; instead she smiled. "Times have been rough. It is our great hope to see Indrana strong again, Highness."

"She will be. We're closing the net on those responsible. It won't be long now."

There'd been a lot of discussion as to just how I should phrase the sentences I was going to poke my nephew with. It needed to be vague enough not to startle Leena, but direct enough to make him nervous. I kept my eyes on him as I said it and felt a little thrill of vindictive joy when he looked away first.

"I thought the *Upjas* responsible were already executed," he said, his voice strained.

"Some *Upjas* were executed," Hassan interjected. "However, we are still looking into things."

"Cleaning up some loose ends, so to speak." I hoped my easy smile didn't look forced.

"It's an awful business," Leena said with a shake of her head. "Taran spent so much time with the empress before his mother died. The empress made time in her schedule specifically to see him. He would bring her the *lokum* she loves so much. I'm sure he would love to see you also."

"I would like that very much." I smiled, surprised that I felt no bitterness at all that Mother went to such lengths to spend so much time with her grandson when it seemed like she'd never had time for us. Bribery with the sticky candy probably helped convince her. "All this will be over soon. Once things have settled down, I'll let you know when he can visit."

"Speaking of, we really should get home before his bedtime." Laabh rose and I debated for a moment staying in my seat to drive home the rudeness of his behavior, but judging by the look his wife gave him, he'd get an earful on the way home.

Instead I got to my feet and said my good-byes.

"That was fucking awkward," I muttered to Admiral Hassan as the door closed behind the pair.

"Tell me about it." Hassan swallowed and added, "Ma'am."

"What's your opinion on Leena?"

"I doubt she's involved. We should be able to tell here shortly, though. Some of General Saito's women are following them. If Laabh drops his wife off at home and goes back out, we can be pretty sure she's not involved."

"I hope so. I like her." It would be bad enough that she'd lose her husband and the disgrace that was likely to follow. From what I could tell, she'd been very kind to Taran and I hated to repay that kind of loyalty with the death of her husband.

"Highness, we're leaving. Now."

I blinked at Emmory. "What? Why? I haven't had dessert yet."

"They just found Dr. Satir's body in her home." Emmory had both of us moving before he finished the sentence and Admiral Hassan's gasp of surprise echoed my own.

"How—"

"She's been dead since the night of the celebration, Highness."

"Does that necessitate us rushing out of here?"

"I'm not taking any chances. Move, please." Emmory propelled me out the door and my other Guards formed up around us as we hustled for the stairs.

"My car is at the back door, *Ekam*." Hassan didn't flinch from the look that Emmory gave her when we hit the landing.

"You need to trust me. We have no idea if they've planned all this. Your charge could be dead the minute you walk out the front."

"Or dead the minute I let her go with you," he replied.

"Emmory." Zin's quiet voice cut through the chaos. "Out the front. I'll go."

The grip on my arm loosened as Emmory passed me wordlessly off to Zin with only the briefest of glances at his partner. Cas and Jet handed off their weapons to Commander Hamprasade and the admiral. I held a hand out for the gun that Zin was already passing my way and he allowed a smile to flicker.

"I'll watch your back." My heart was pounding in my throat as I said it and Zin nodded. Half a second later we burst through Shivan's kitchens. Zin was in front with me right behind. I could feel Admiral Hassan's hand on my back as we made a mad dash through the startled employees and emerged out the back door.

I was shoved into the back of the aircar. The others piled in after me and we took off at a speed that threatened to ruin the meal I'd just eaten.

Coming off the adrenaline rush left me with a wicked headache. I took the cup of chai from Stasia with a grateful smile and looked over at Emmory. "Okay, we're safe again. Now tell me what the hell is going on?"

"Dr. Satir is dead, Highness. Presumably from an overdose of AVI."

I raised an eyebrow at him. "That's a lot of AVI."

"A contact of mine with the police messaged me the scene photos and the doctor's alleged suicide note."

"Emmory, she never would have—"

"Desperation, remember?" he replied, pushing away from

the windowsill to pace the room. "Time of death is the evening of the celebration. Dr. Satir must have known something. Maybe she was going to talk. Whoever is trying to kill you had to take her out of the picture also."

My cup rattled on the table when I set it down and got to my feet. I ignored Admiral Hassan's curious look and hooked my hands behind my neck as I wandered to the windowsill Emmory had just vacated.

"What did she know?" I voiced the question even though I didn't expect an answer from anyone in the room. "We need to find out, Emmory. Are they—" I broke off, the grief slamming into me, and pressed a hand to my mouth as I tried to hold it back. "Are they going to download her *smati*?"

He nodded. "My contact promised me a copy. Once we're done sifting through the information, I'll let you know what we find."

"If anything," I murmured. It was likely that most of the files would be corrupted given how long she'd been dead. I should have pressed about her absence, but it hadn't crossed my mind that something could be wrong.

"We're already reasonably sure your cousin and nephew are behind this, Highness," Admiral Hassan said.

"We're missing something. I can feel it." Shaking my head, I tapped myself in the stomach. "Right here. I don't deny Ganda and Laabh are up to their necks in this whole thing, but they couldn't have pulled this all off on their own." I looked at Emmory with a frown. "Wait, you said alleged suicide note?"

"She confessed to poisoning the empress."

"Holy cowshit," I countered.

Hassan attempted to cover up her laughter, failed miserably, and settled for a reproving look that I met with a grim smile.

"If Dr. Satir had wanted to take out the royal family, she could have done it a lot sooner than the last six months."

"She had the access, ma'am, and timing is everything. We already suspect the recent tensions with the Saxons are part of this plot. It makes sense that they'd have to wait to put certain parts of their plan in motion until the right moment."

"You said alleged."

Emmory shrugged one shoulder. "Only because I don't think she killed herself, Highness. I'm not discounting the possibility that she was involved."

"She loved my mother, Emmory. I don't believe it."

He looked at Hassan and then back at me. "With respect, ma'am, you'll believe your nephew is responsible for the deaths of his sister and mother without any proof? Why? Because he's a man?"

Emmory's comment dropped on the room like an LCT into a combat zone, leaving a stunned silence in its wake. Hassan half rose out of her chair, gaping at my *Ekam* in appalled shock.

"Ouch," I said, waving Hassan back down into her seat. "Point taken, Emmory. And even though that was a rhetorical question, I'll give you an answer. I've seen the depths people will go to when they think power is in their grasp. I've seen the lengths they'll go to get it and keep it and it's always worse when it's someone who doesn't have the power to begin with. So yes, to a certain extent I'm able to believe that Laabh is more likely to do this because he's a man, but—bugger me."

Several ideas collided at once in my head and I turned on a heel.

"Ma'am?"

I held up a hand at Emmory, snapping my fingers. "Hang on, I need to think." The thoughts crystallized as I paced. "Oh, bugger me. What do we know about this whole thing so far?

One, my cousin managed to insinuate herself rather quickly into position to become heir when Cire was killed. It would have stood to reason; she's not my mother's issue, but she's the eldest daughter of the eldest son of my grandmother. She'd still be in line for the throne after the rest of us were dead."

I walked a circuit from the window to the fireplace and back, throwing up fingers as I rattled off points. "Two, somehow the people behind this whole mess managed to convince a radical sect of the *Upjas* to join forces with them. How do you do that if you're still going to put a woman on the throne?"

Hassan frowned.

"I suspect Ganda wouldn't be on the throne for long, Highness," Emmory said. "If it were me, I'd tell the radicals that Laabh would rule."

"While telling Ganda she's the one who's going to be in charge just to get her support?" I shrugged. "It would make sense. Who had the initial idea, though? My cousin?"

"And then Laabh decided to double-cross her."

"What happened to him to make him so heartless?" I rubbed my hands over my face with a sigh.

"Sometimes people are born that way, Highness."

We fell into an uneasy silence for several moments.

"Number three, you prove the empress incompetent." Hassan got to her feet and started pacing also. "Which would be enough to sway certain members of the military to your side when the princesses are suddenly removed from the picture?"

"It would have been perfect if they'd managed to kill me, too."

"It's close enough even with you alive." Hassan dragged a hand through her hair. "Your pardon, Highness, but your past has apparently still been enough to convince members of the military to support Ganda in this foolishness."

"True enough," I said after a moment. "I wonder if they will continue to support Ganda when they realize she's killed three members of my family to get to this point."

"They might," Emmory said thoughtfully. "If they're supporting Laabh instead of Ganda. Remember that his father left with Admiral Shul the same day you returned home, Highness."

"This is a Shiva-damned viper's nest." I rubbed both hands over my face. "And they're on some kind of timetable that I'd bet a good chunk of ravga has to do with that corridor we saw this afternoon on the map, Admiral."

"I already sent the empress my report, Highness. She approved it and orders went out. I can message the commander at Canafey and let them know to be on the lookout, but that's about all I can do."

"Do it," I said. "It might be enough. I need to know what else they're planning and when it's supposed to go down."

"Hit the weak link and the chain will shatter." Zin, who'd been quiet up to this point, shifted away from his spot near the door. "We can find out, Highness. I just don't know if it will be in time."

"We'll deal with it if it happens. Go."

"No protests about coming with me?"

I stuck my tongue out at the tease. "I have plenty to deal with here and this is your job. Who are you going after?"

Zin shook his head with a slight smile. "Sorry, Highness. It's better if you don't know."

"Zin, I can't leave her." Emmory's voice was low and edged with regret.

"I know. I'm a decent enough Tracker on my own, Emmory. I think I can manage."

"Admiral, why don't I see you to the door while these two hash it out," I said with a grin and headed across the room. I'd seen the way her jaw had tightened at Zin's remarks and pinned her down with a curious look when we reached the door.

"I'm not questioning your judgment, ma'am, but can you trust them?"

"With my life, with the empire. I know their methods might seem a little mercenary. Dark Mother, I know *my* methods probably seem that way." I laughed briefly and then sobered. "We're not up against people who are willing to play by the rules, Admiral. They've killed my sisters, my niece, and my mother—your empress—and too many other innocent people. They're pushing this empire to the brink of a war you and I both know we can't win. If that means I must take the slightly less civilized road to protect the people of my empire, I will do it. If you have a problem with it—"

"I don't, ma'am." She dipped her head. "I understand the necessity."

"Good. I'd like you to take Zaran back to your ship with you. I'll feel better if our sole witness to my cousin's treachery is somewhere with very few access points."

Of course, if they really wanted to remove her, all they'd have to do is blow up the admiral's ship. I could tell by the look in Hassan's eyes she'd thought of it, too, but neither of us wanted to say it out loud.

"Yes, ma'am. I'll see you after Pratimas."

I nodded in reply and closed the door behind her. When I turned, Emmory and Zin were standing silently, their foreheads pressed together and their eyes closed. "Did you two finish your argument?"

Emmory gave me the Look. Zin grinned. "We've got five

days until Pratimas, Highness," he said. "I probably won't see you until then, so try to keep your head down and stay out of trouble?"

"Likewise," I replied, my cheeky salute ruined by the unexpected yawn. "Good night, gentlemen."

"Good night, Highness. Sleep well."

22

M a'am?" I nodded at the steward and she poured more chai into my mug with a deft hand. Mother shook her head, pressing a hand to her stomach with a sigh.

"I'm stuffed, Hana. Tell Olizi that was his best meal yet."

"I will, ma'am. He'll be pleased to hear it." She bowed and left the room.

Mother and I sat in silence. We were alone in the room—even our *Ekams* were outside the door—but the silence wasn't awkward.

It was three days since Zin had taken off. Three days filled with a ridiculous schedule of meetings, more meetings, and Pratimas rituals. For once in my life I enjoyed the rituals—mostly because they gave me respite from the meetings. The one today had involved touring several carefully selected private homes to light lamps and trade gifts with the owners. Neither Emmory nor Bial had allowed Mother or I to eat any of the carefully prepared treats the men of the house had presented to us until Mother snappishly reminded them she was dying anyway. In an almost comical scene both BodyGuards scanned each treat, then Mother ate part of it and handed the rest to me with a nod and a smile.

I hadn't spent so much time with Mother since before she'd been crowned. It was bittersweet and I found myself blinking back tears at the oddest moments. The experimental treatment Dr. Ganjen was trying appeared to be working. Over the last few days Mother had been more alert, more stable, and even more like the pre-empress mother I remembered.

I knew it wasn't going to last, so I was trying to stay with her as much as possible. The first day had been stiff and strange as we navigated between the past and the present, trying each in our own way to find some common ground—and failing with laughable results. That, I think, was what broke the tension between us.

Mother's yawn interrupted the silence. I finished my drink and stood. "I should go, let you get your rest."

She reached a hand out and I took it. "Sometimes I think it's easier you've changed so much. You looked so much like your father I'm not sure I could have stood it." Her smile was sad. "Good night, Haili."

"Night, Mother." I kissed her cheek and headed for the door.

Alba met me at my rooms. "I'm sorry, ma'am. I know it's late, but can I trouble you?"

"Sure. What is it?" I stood back as my Guards swept my apartments and then followed Alba into the room.

"I've been screening your incoming mail for you, for junk mostly. I am passing on anything that looks legitimate."

"You don't have to apologize, Alba, it's your job to look at my mail. What's going on?"

"At first I dismissed it, but you've gotten fifty or so in the last week."

"Fifty or so what?"

"Of the same e-mail. There were a few early on, but lately there've been more and more." Alba shifted, clearly uncomfortable, and I couldn't stop the laughter.

"Shiva's bones, woman, what it's it? Naked pictures? I can't imagine death threats would bother you so, I'm sure I get a dozen a day."

"No, ma'am, nothing of the sort. It's just weird."

"Well, let me see it then. Throw it up on the screen, though I'm sure Emmory's already in the loop on this?" Alba nodded and sent the offending message to the screen on the far wall. I took one look and laughed out loud. "Bugger me; Hao, you ass."

It was just white text on a black background that said: *V sorry about P. You owe me 100 credits.*

"You know who it's from?" Emmory was shooting for casual and missed it by a meter and a half.

"Yeah." I shrugged. "When did the first one come in?"

"About a week ago, Highness."

"It's Hao. He must have been on a news fast or something. That took him longer than I figured it would. I'll have to think of a reply."

"Highness, you cannot send one hundred credits to a known associate of Po-Sin's."

"I don't owe him one hundred credits, Emmy." I paused. "At least I think I don't, maybe I do—either way." I waved a hand in the air. "It's just Hao letting me know it's him. He's not looking to collect. He always liked it when I owed him money because he could bring it up as often as possible."

"Should I message back a reply, ma'am?" Alba asked.

"Tomorrow. I need to think of what to say and I have to be up ridiculously early in the morning. Night."

The next morning found me up before the sun, dressed in a horrible petal-pink sari that clashed with my hair. It was traditional, so I hadn't complained—out loud anyway—and my mutterings were quickly followed with an apologetic prayer.

Normally I wasn't one for paranoid superstitions, but we could use all the help we could get in surviving this mess. Both literally and figuratively.

So I knelt in the flickering light of the temple dressed in that awful pink sari with the statue of Ganesh looming over me. He was massive, our dancing god with one foot raised in the air and his four arms spread wide. His ears were stained with red, and a great stripe coated the length of his trunk. Garlands of flowers in red and yellow were draped around his neck and lay in great piles around his foot along with the piles of offerings brought by devotees.

The temple was still except for Father Westinkar's quiet chanting. The sweet smell of the treat offerings—*modak* and *laddus*—mingled with the spice of burning incense.

The great elephant-headed god looked down at me with an expression I always felt was a mixture of amusement and pity, and I found myself wondering if He remembered that time Cire and I stole his sweets.

"I don't think we should be doing this."

"Hush," I hissed, tugging Cire back down by my side. "The priests will hear you if you don't shut up."

Together we crouched, hidden in the broad leaves of the midget palms that ringed the reddish columns of the temple belonging to Lord Ganesh. We found some relief from the oppressive heat of late Bhadrapad in places like this around the palace grounds. The dying summer sun did what Mother couldn't—it made us too tired and lazy to attempt to outwit our BodyGuards and venture out into the city.

Instead, we confined our mischief to the palace grounds and today, on the last day of Ganesh Chaturthi—the ten-day festival—I'd promised Pace modak.

She'd been sick with fever for most of the festival and Mother was being mean. I knew a few of the sticky sweet treats wouldn't harm my little sister, but the physician said no so Mother said no. Not even Father had been moved by my pleas.

So I was taking matters into my own hands.

"We can't steal from a god, Haili!"

"Be quiet." I felt a little pang of guilt as I brandished my fist at my sister and she subsided with tears in her eyes. "Sorry, Cire. Really. But Ganesh isn't going to begrudge a few sweets. They're not for us. They're for Pace. He loves Pace, and if you do, too, then you'll quit your bitching and help me."

Cire's lip quivered. "I do love Pace," she whispered in a voice thick with tears, and I knew I'd gone too far. I wrapped my arm around her. Cire was the oldest, the heir, but sometimes I wondered if my kindhearted sister would survive as empress.

"I know you do," I whispered back. "You keep watch; whistle twice if you see anyone. I'm going in."

"*Om Gam Ganapataye Namaha,*" Father Westinkar chanted, jerking me back to the present. He pressed his thumb to my forehead and left a smear of precious red sandalwood paste there before bowing low. "*Om Gam* Salutations to the Lord of Hosts."

I echoed the chant, folding my hands together and bowing until my forehead touched the cool temple floor. I was suffering from the early morning hours so I focused on the *puja* instead of the sun crawling up over the horizon on my left.

It was a ritual we'd repeated every morning for the last several days. A plea to the One who trampled obstacles under his broad feet. A lead-in to the holiday, a wish for Him to guard the light and keep us all safe.

For all my bitterness about the gods, there was a special place in my heart for Ganesh. I'd never told Cire, but when

I scrambled up on the base of Ganesh's statue to steal those *modak* for Pace, I'd left the bracelet our father had given me at the start of the celebration and whispered a quick, reverent prayer to the god to make my sister better. I'd told my father I'd lost it and he'd looked at me with disappointment, but it was worth it when Pace recovered that very evening.

"Highness?" Emmory's voice was worried, and I realized why when a hand to my face came away wet. "Are you all right?"

"I was just remembering something." I squeezed his forearm. "Give me a moment, would you?" He nodded and moved off to stand with Jet, two silent shadows against the reddish column less than ten paces from me.

Ganesh's temple on the palace grounds was a small one, meant more for private ceremonies like ours. I'd always preferred it to the gigantic temple on the far side of the capital, which was filled with too much noise and confusion. But even here I apparently wasn't safe. Cas was on the other side of the temple and the members of Team Three stood at parade rest along the far wall.

Sinking to my knees again, I reached a hand out and rested it on the god's foot. The flowers tickling my arm were forgotten when I made contact with the statue. A tingle of electricity shot through me and I closed my eyes, dropping my head and pressing my free hand to my heart.

"I haven't been the most faithful, Father," I whispered in the Old Tongue. "My travels took me far from home and I'm afraid I've forgotten how to pray. But I haven't forgotten what you did for Pace, and I won't—not ever. I don't know if I can do this, but I do know there's no one else.

"I need help, Father. Clear the obstacles from my path. Help me save my empire, my people." I knew a request of that magnitude required an equally great sacrifice, and I dragged in a deep breath. "I don't have anything I can offer you but my freedom. Do this for me and I swear I'll do my duty for as long as you require of me. I swear I will be faithful to you for the rest of my days."

It was a hell of an open-ended vow, dangerous enough to make to a person, but to a god it was a promise of endless devotion.

My heart tore itself open as I sacrificed myself for my people the same way my ancestors had so many thousands of years ago when they volunteered to go out into the blackness of space.

"What the fuck are you doing, Hail?" I muttered the question even as I unwound the leather band from my wrist and took off Pace's heavy silver ring, leaving them both amid the piles of flowers. Wiping my face with the heels of my hands, I rose to my feet, gave the god a final bow, and headed out of the temple with my shadows following me.

Alba met us outside the temple and I answered her bow with a smile. We were halfway back to my rooms when the ping of an incoming call sounded. "Emmory, it's Admiral Hassan," I said, holding up a hand and stopping to answer the call.

"Admiral," I greeted Inana when she appeared on the screen I threw onto the nearest blank wall.

"Highness, I've got Caspel on the line also," she said. The screen split and the hawk-faced head of GIS appeared in the second panel. I added Emmory to the link with a thought.

"Your Highness, I have bad news."

The knots in my stomach that had been slowly loosening themselves snapped taut. "What?"

"I've just received reports from our assets on the ground in Canafey. Less than ten minutes ago Saxon Shock troops hit the governors' palaces on Major and Minor. Governor Phillus is dead. Governor Ashwari has been taken prisoner. I've got an operative trying to get her out, but I can't give you any promises."

"The shipyards?"

"They're intact, ma'am. The lockdown order went out from Governor Phillus's office; that's all I know at the moment. So the ships in the yard—all forty-seven of them—are pieces of floating rubble as far as the Saxons are concerned. Unless they can get the lock codes from Governor Ashwari." Caspel's expression was so cold it froze my skin. "If she's still alive, ma'am, they'll get them one way or another."

"You get her out of there, Caspel." I'd seen what Saxon Shock troops could do to their prisoners and I'd be damned if I'd leave any of my people in their hands. "Alive. Do you hear me?"

"We're working on it, Highness. I've got one of my best trying to get in there now."

I barely smothered the curse threatening to crawl up my throat. The man knew his job and so did whoever he'd just sent in to rescue the governor. My railing at him wasn't going to help matters.

"It's the day before Pratimas, Caspel. They know what this holy day means, how could they—"

"It's not how could they, Highness. It's that they did. They know we're vulnerable right now. Governments in transition always are. I wanted to move your coronation up, solidify your rule. This delay makes things wickedly unstable, but—"

"What? No one told me that."

"Your empress-mother disagreed and no more was said on the matter." Caspel glanced away from the camera. "We're landing. I'll be at the palace in five minutes, Highness."

I didn't bother to ask how the head of Galactic Imperial Security knew I was in the palace and instead nodded sharply. "I'll meet you in the War Room."

312

"I'll join you on-screen," Admiral Hassan said. "It would take me too long to get to the surface. I've already commed the other members of the Raksha. They'll meet you in the War Room."

"We're on our way." I waited until the com was off before I blistered the air with curses. "Alba, where's Toropov? I want an explanation from him and I want it immediately." Rubbing my hands over my face, I started down the hallway again at a speed that forced my chamberlain to run to keep up with me.

"I'm messaging his aide now, ma'am. I also sent a note to Leena about your meeting with Taran."

"Bugger me," I muttered. I'd forgotten about my lunch plans. "Make sure it gets rescheduled, Alba. After Pratimas probably. That is, if we don't end up at war again."

Mother and Bial met us at the door to the War Room, with Caspel showing up just a heartbeat later.

"Highness," Bial said with a short nod.

"Your Majesty." Caspel bowed. "I didn't think you'd want to bother with this."

"I am still empress. Sick or not. Next time you try to tell my *Ekam* not to trouble me, I'll have you cut into pieces and fed to my cats."

I raised an eyebrow, but Caspel didn't look the slightest bit abashed. He shrugged a shoulder. "You know as well as I do, Your Majesty, that emergencies are taxing. I thought calling you into a crisis of this magnitude would only complicate matters and it was better left to the heir."

"Don't try to drag me into this," I said before Mother could reply. "Let's get a move on here."

The other three members of the Raksha arrived only minutes later. The Raksha was the military council of Indrana, consisting of the heads of the armed forces, the Tracker Corps, and the BodyGuard Corps.

"Your Royal Highness, we haven't met. I'm Esha Suvish." The commander-general of the BodyGuard Corps was a no-nonsense-looking woman with a shaved head and piercing dark eyes. She nodded briskly at Emmory and Bial after shaking my hand.

Mila Vandi, the head of the Imperial Tactical Squads, was the only woman I'd had a lot of contact with before my flight. My father's old friend extended her hand with a smile, bowing at the same time.

"Your Highness, it's a pleasure to see you again."

"You're the first person I think who's actually meant that, General." I shook her hand, feeling more than a little guilty that I didn't trust her.

"Have you met Generals Saito and Prajapati?" Mila gestured at the two women next to her.

"Yes. They were at the briefing I was at the other day. Generals."

"Good to see you again, Highness." General Saito bowed.

"A pleasure, Highness." I didn't know Prajapati at all, but the tiny dark-haired general couldn't quite meet my eyes every time we'd been in the same room together, putting one more mark in the case against her.

"Admiral Hassan is joining us on-screen. Ambassador Yen has been notified, but obviously with message times what they are, it'll be tomorrow most likely before we hear from her. If you'll all have a seat." I leaned on the table, wishing briefly I wasn't dressed in such a gods-awful color. Thankfully no one had said a word about it. Admiral Hassan nodded and cleared her throat. "As you all know, Saxon Shock troops hot dropped into the capital of Canafey Major at 0300 hours local time. The governor's palace security was overwhelmed. Governor Phillus issued the lockout order for the forty-seven ships of the *Vajrayana* Initiative in dock before he took his own life.

"Canafey Minor suffered a simultaneous assault, and Governor Ashwari was taken alive. Caspel tells me he has an operative on the ground and they are attempting to retrieve her."

No one stated the obvious. If Caspel's agent couldn't get the governor out, he would need to kill her and dispose of her head so the Saxons couldn't access the lock codes.

"How many ships do they have in the area?" Mother asked.

"Unknown, ma'am. Admiral Shul and the 2nd Fleet are two systems away. I could have him move and be at Canafey the day after tomorrow, but we have no idea what he'd be wading into."

"A slaughter most likely," I murmured, not mentioning out loud that we probably couldn't trust Shul, and heads nodded around the table.

"I shouldn't have moved that battle group. I'm sorry, Hail, you were right," Mother said.

"I wish I hadn't been." I knew there wasn't anything I could do to lessen the guilt my mother was feeling. "General, do you have contact with the troops on the ground at Canafey?"

According to my *smati*, there was a large contingent of Army personnel on Major and a smaller outpost on Minor. All told, we were looking at close to half a million soldiers.

Trapped on the ground with enemy forces. *Bugger me.*

"We've gotten running commentary; that's about it," General Prajapati replied with a shake of her head. "There have been pitched battles in both capitals and probably throughout most major townships."

"If you can get in touch with your people on the ground, you tell them to keep fighting. Protect the civilians. We haven't forgotten about them. They have the right to keep themselves safe by any means necessary."

"Yes, ma'am."

"Highness—"

I held up a hand, cutting Caspel off before he could get started. "We can't go toe to toe with the Saxons," I said. "Everyone is thinking it, but no one will say it out loud."

"We got hurt badly in the war," Hassan said cautiously. "Then came the treaty talks, the Conglomerate's interference, and your empress-mother's failing health. The naval budget has been slashed for the last five years running by the Ancillary Council. I was lucky to keep the *Vajrayana* Initiative on the table."

"I know." It didn't escape me that this was the second time she hadn't disagreed with me outright over this, but it just made me feel sick to my stomach rather than vindicated. We were in trouble, serious trouble, if I couldn't convince the Saxons to back off.

Which was the reason for the *Vajrayana* Initiative in the first place. These state-of-the-art ships would help narrow the imbalance with the Saxon Alliance. But now they were all locked down in dock above an enemy-controlled planet.

"We've got three ships that were out on maneuvers. I sent them messages to bug for home as fast as they could. Hopefully they did."

"Your Majesty, Ambassador Toropov is here," Emmory said quietly from behind me.

"Hail, you go. I don't want to speak to the man."

"Highness." Caspel's quiet voice broke into the uneasy silence that dropped as I got to my feet. "You will not be able to declare war. Until the coronation, the empress is still the only one who can do that."

"I have no intention of declaring war. Despite whatever rumors you all might have heard, I have excellent control of my temper. I care about our dockworkers, our military members on those ships and the ground, and our citizens. Our priority, ladies and gentlemen, is to keep them safe. Right now that means we use diplomacy until there is no other choice."

Emmory opened the door. Cas and Jet were on the other side, eyeing the ambassador and his men warily. I slipped between them, ignoring Emmory's hissed protest and gestured for him to close the door.

"The Saxon Kingdom wants nothing more than peace with Indrana, isn't that what you said, Ambassador?"

Toropov paused, mid-bow, and glanced up at me. "I expected a call from your mother."

"She is indisposed, Ambassador, and as the heir, I have been tasked to handle such things."

"Until your coronation, you are still under her authority."

"So everyone keeps telling me. And yet the shit is conveniently hitting the fan before that can happen. Now tell me, Ambassador, did I mishear you when you said the Saxons only wanted peace?"

"I spoke truly, your Highness."

"So why are there Saxon Shock troops on my sovereign soil?" Keeping my voice level and low was a challenge, but I managed it.

The ambassador straightened, his pale eyes still on mine, and he lied straight to my face, "I have heard of no such troop movements, Your Highness. All our ST battalions are accounted for."

My hand flexed at my hip, looking for a weapon that was no longer there. Toropov saw it, and so did his guards. All three of them froze, though the ambassador didn't look nearly as worried as his men.

I smiled coldly. "Be grateful, Ambassador. Today you got the princess instead of the gunrunner. My people are dying and *someone* is responsible. I suggest you call your king and find out just what in the fires of Naraka he thinks he's doing attacking my people right before a holy day. Because next time it might be the gunrunner you're staring down.

"As of right now, I've authorized my troops on the ground to return fire in the protection of themselves or civilians. Since it's not *Saxon* troops they'll be shooting at, I'm sure you don't have a problem with that decision. I would love to resolve this as peacefully as possible, Ambassador, but I will not allow my people to suffer for the sake of diplomatic dithering."

"Your Highness." Toropov's bow was a lot stiffer this time around. "I will beg your leave and consult with my king. Though I warn you, expecting the story to change will result in disappointment. The Saxon Kingdom signed a treaty; we would never violate that without expressly informing you of our intent first."

"So good to hear." I dipped my head. "I look forward to hearing Trace's side of this." I watched Toropov and his guards move off down the hallway before I turned and went back in the War Room.

The conversation cut off when I walked back through the door and I raised an eyebrow with an amused smile. "I don't think Ambassador Toropov will be inviting me to dinner anytime soon."

I recounted the conversation, leaned a hip on the table, and looked at Caspel. "He was lying to me. I just don't know which part, if any, was true."

He shook his head. "It would be hard for me to say for sure without having seen his face. I've gotten confirmation from my agents on the ground about the Shock troops, Highness. But I would hazard a guess that any decisions made were not passed on to the ambassador. Plausible deniability goes a long way."

"Makes sense." I nodded.

Now that the adrenaline rush was fading, the indecision struck hard and fast, paralyzing me like the venom of a Viperidae. I was ridiculously unsuited for this. I wasn't fooling anyone. Any suggestions I had about this would probably be met with the same derision I'd faced at the military briefing.

Words dried up in my mouth. I lost a piece of my nerve, and watched it skitter over the floor, where it curled into the corner and died.

Bugger me, I couldn't do this.

"Liar." Portis wasn't bothered by my glare, meeting it with a cheeky grin as he smoothed down the lapel of my jacket.

"I can't do this, Portis." I hated the panic in my voice, but the thought of walking through those doors was now more than I could stand. "I'm not diplomatic enough. I'm a gunrunner. This is important. I'll screw it up. I'll ruin everything. I'll—"

"Cress, hey, look at me." His smile faded and he took my face in both his hands. "Hao wouldn't have suggested you for this, and Po-Sin damn sure wouldn't have agreed to it if they hadn't thought you could handle it. I know you." His hands tightened briefly for emphasis. "And you can do this."

"Highness?"

I blinked, realized that everyone was staring at me, and cleared my throat. "Sorry." Forcing a smile, I sat down and said with a confidence I didn't feel, "Let's get a game plan together, people. I want every possible scenario discussed."

23

Four hours later I left the War Room, my head swimming with facts and possibilities, rumors and fears, plans and potential outcomes.

"I need a drink," I muttered to Emmory as we headed down the hallway.

"You need some food, Highness. Alba had lunch sent to your rooms."

"Can I have a drink with lunch?"

He didn't crack a smile and waited until we passed a group of young nobles—all of whom stopped their excited chatter about the news long enough to bow and curtsy to me—before he answered. "You don't have to play the uncouth gunrunner with me, Highness."

"Who's playing?" I asked, and picked up my pace. I was desperate to get out of this hideous sari. "I *am* an uncouth gunrunner."

"I would prefer not to remind them of that."

"Yes, it would upset their delicate sensibilities."

Now he did smile and it was amused. "I am thinking more of the fact that I'd rather not remind them how dangerous you are. The events of the other day notwithstanding, several enterprising reporters have already discovered that many of the rumors about you are not rumors at all. I don't want our enemies figuring that out for themselves before we have a chance to show them."

"You're getting bloodthirsty, *Ekam*," I said, pausing outside my door as we ran through the security check. Amazing how something could become so routine in so little time. Willimet stayed at my side with Emmory as the other two went through the door.

"It's a necessity, Highness. My job is to keep you safe. I can't do that when there're people out there trying to kill you."

"They die or I die, huh?"

"No, Highness. They die. There is no *or*."

I didn't know how to respond to his deadly quiet certainty, so I swallowed and headed into my rooms.

"Highness." Zin nodded at me as I came through the door. "Welcome back. We missed you."

"Your lunch is ready," he said.

"I want to get out of this first." I pointed a finger at him. "Then I want your report."

Zin bowed.

I stopped short in the doorway to my bedroom. "What in the fires—" I swallowed the curse back as Stasia straightened and stared at me in shock.

"Ma'am?" The flowers trembled in her hand, steadied. "You don't like it? Zin said you'd—"

Spinning back around, I jabbed a finger in Zin's direction. "You did this?"

He looked as shocked as Stasia. "Emmory mentioned that you'd—yes, ma'am. If you don't like it, we'll take it out."

I shook my head, tears clogging the words in my throat, and

turned away again. Striding into my room, I dropped down in front of the statue of Ganesh that now rested on the dark wooden table in the corner.

It was gorgeous. Perfect. Exactly what I would have picked out for myself. My hand shook as I reached it out and touched His lifted foot.

Emmory and Zin had done this. Like Portis, they understood me—the real me—and I couldn't even blame it on the extensive file they'd compiled on me as Trackers. They just got me. Emmory must have heard my vow to Ganesh and passed the information on to Zin before he came back to the palace.

Tears slid down my face, but I didn't even care as the last piece of my broken heart slipped into place with the quiet snick of an unlocked door. The statue did exactly what I needed, cutting through the bands of tension and anxiety wrapped around me with effortless speed.

My Trackers had turned into my touchstones in such a short time. Zin would never question me like Emmory did, but I was starting to suspect he'd keep me sane even in the darker days.

In just a few short weeks I trusted these men as much as I had trusted Portis after years of being together. I couldn't explain it, didn't even want to question it and risk the whole thing crumbling around me. It wasn't logical, it was just life.

The sounds of Stasia quietly shooing everyone out of my room filtered through the ringing in my head.

"Ma'am?" The smell of chai preceded her words, sweet spice and steam chasing away the memory before I could fully recall it.

I took the cup with a smile. "They did good."

"They did, ma'am. Should I tell them?"

"If you would, please. Tell Emmory I'll be out to eat in a moment, too, or he'll fuss."

As soon as the door closed, I bowed low before the altar, whispering a chant I knew by heart. I kissed my fingertips and patted Ganesh's foot before I rose and started unwinding the mile-long pink atrocity I'd been suffering in since daybreak.

I didn't bother to call Stasia back into the room, dressing myself in a pair of black pants and a plain white shirt. The fabric settled around me, a far better fit than the sari I'd just discarded.

"Alba, what's the likelihood of a huge outcry if we had the coronation tonight?" I asked the question as I came back into the main room.

I was a little surprised my chamberlain considered my suggestion instead of dismissing it outright. She cocked her head to the side, her eyes focused on the window to my right and her lips pursed. I'd come to recognize it as a sign that she was running through options, so I took the opportunity to grab some food.

"Highness."

I took the glass of Alcarix whiskey from Emmory with a grin. He gave me the Look and leaned a hip on the table. I cheerfully ignored him, flopping down into my chair and grabbing a fork.

"I just don't think it's doable, Highness," Alba finally said. "Technically, all we really need is for someone to put the crown on your head and the matriarchs to swear their allegiance. But the logistics of that and the subsequent rumors that would accompany such a rush job…" She trailed off with a tiny shrug.

We were in limbo here, vulnerable as long as Mother was still on the throne in her unstable mental state. Worse, I didn't have a huge power base and I couldn't afford to start off my reign under any suggestions of impropriety.

Knowing exactly what she meant didn't make it any easier.

If the Saxons decided to really start something in the next forty hours—

"Alba, what happens if the Saxons declare war on us? Officially, I mean?"

Bless my chamberlain, but she didn't even blink. Even in this short amount of time she'd started to figure out how my brain worked and could follow along without missing the beat.

"We'd be at war, Highness. The Articles of Conflict would be in effect."

The articles called for zero confusion in the chain of command during times of war. One such provision dealt directly with the scenario we were facing here: that if the current empress was in the process of abdicating the throne, the heir would automatically assume control. No coronation, no fuss, no approval from the Matriarch Council.

"Good." Sipping at my drink, I waved the other hand in the air. "We won't worry about it then."

Maybe it was arrogance on my part, but I already knew I had the backing of a chunk of the military and of most of the Matriarch Council anyway. They would do what was necessary until my coronation to keep the empire safe, and if not, I had a legal excuse to put my ass on the throne without all the pomp and circumstance.

"Yes, ma'am. If that's all?"

I stretched my legs out and nodded at Alba. "It is. You go on. I know you have a lot still to do for tomorrow."

"I'll see you in the morning." She bowed and left the room.

"Emmory?"

He spotted my gesture, answering it with a nod. "We're clear, Highness."

"What did you find out?" I asked Zin. "Quick and dirty version."

His grin was bright and Emmory actually elbowed him, dragging a laugh from me. I cleared my throat and gave them both a look.

"I followed Laabh around for a bit. He's got a group of friends, some of whom are interesting company for a member of the royal family. Then I had a long conversation with the youngest grandson of Ganda's number-one fan on the council, Matriarch Khatri."

"Did you now?" I murmured, digging into my food.

"He's going to spend the next few days in a Tracker holding facility. Technically it's not illegal detention, Highness. He did confess to plotting against the throne." Zin continued when I nodded. "About a year ago young Hebin fell in with a bad crowd, radical members of the *Upjas* who weren't happy with the alliances Abraham Suda was making."

"You mean my sister."

"Hebin didn't say as much, but I suspect that's what it was. Laabh and several others in their social circle used to throw parties and sneak out to attend these clandestine meetings. Anyway, he and Laabh were approached by a man shortly after one of the gatherings. Laabh and the man hit it off and regularly went out to dinner. Hebin occasionally tagged along. One night about ten months ago, the man—Hebin didn't know his name—asked for an introduction to his grandmother."

I raised an eyebrow. "Let me guess. This is our mystery man."

"I'm assuming so. The alternative is that there's yet another person involved here, someone else we don't know about." Zin shrugged. "I'd just as soon that not be the case. Hebin managed to arrange a meeting. He doesn't know what was discussed, only that both Laabh and Ganda were there. After that, he said it seemed like Ganda was hanging around his grandmother's house more often.

"About five months ago he stopped going to the underground meetings, said that the tone had taken a decidedly ominous turn and that Laabh had started acting weird."

"Define *weird*."

"Being more and more outspoken about how his sister had no right to rule. More aggressive in the meetings with the *Upjas*. He was always properly polite when at the matriarch's house and around Ganda, but Hebin said his behavior with other women was decidedly improper."

"Interesting." I got to my feet and leaned against the mantel, staring down into the fire. "There's more, I gather?"

"A lot, but that's the quick version. I'll write up a report for you."

"Do you think that they're really dealing with a radical sect of the *Upjas*?" That was the catch here, and it was difficult for me to be clearheaded about the whole mess. I wanted to believe that Abraham Suda hadn't sold my sister out for some promise of change that was going to jeopardize the stability of the empire itself.

"I think so, Highness, but there's no way to know for sure."

There was, but Emmory wasn't going to like it. "Emmory, would you do a favor for me?" Tossing back the rest of my drink bolstered my courage some, and I plowed forward with all the grace of a Carsian mastodon. "I want you to go get Abraham Suda. Tell him I want to talk, see if he'll come with you; but if he won't, then drag his ass out of whatever hole he's hiding in."

"You want me to try to track down the leader of the *Upjas* the day before Pratimas? Highness, the Saxons practically declared war on us a few hours ago. You're going to be out in the open the majority of the day tomorrow and someone is still trying to kill you. Do I really need to remind you how dangerous the next forty hours are going to be?"

"No, but I apparently need to remind you that I'm not an idiot." I set my glass down and went back to eating, but the food tasted like ash and I tossed my fork onto the plate. "I didn't say track him down, Emmy. I said get him. I'm pretty sure you figured out where he was the day after we got settled in here."

"You have a high estimation of my skills, Highness." Emmory had his poker face on.

"You still think they're trying to kill me," I countered and got up to refill my glass, poking a finger at Zin on my way by. "And your partner here isn't as good at the blank-face thing as you are. I'm not going to let this go, Emmory, and lying to my face will only force me to do this on my own. Besides I don't want to wait until tomorrow, I want to talk to him now. I need an answer. I need to know if he's trying to kill me or not."

"Highness—"

"No, listen, Emmory. I need to talk to Abraham. I need to see his face." The whiskey burned on the way down and I turned to my BodyGuard. "It's the only way I'll know if he's still in love with my sister or if he's responsible for her death."

You'd have thought I'd pulled out my gun and shot Emmory the way he was gaping at me.

Zin cleared his throat. "Highness, I don't know if you've thought this all the way through. We can find him, but it's unlikely that he'll come with us willingly, especially into the palace. If we have to drag him back, it means the *Upjas* will be fighting us the whole way."

I had thought it through, actually, which meant I felt like ten shades of bastard for what came out of my mouth next. "I know, Zin. That's why you're going with Emmory and why you'll stay there."

If Emmory could kill with just that Look of his, I'd have

died on the spot. Ice-cold fingers dug into the back of my neck, shooting a tremor down my spine.

"Let's go, Emmory." Zin's movement startled us both. "Don't take this the wrong way, Highness, but you two will stand there all night if I let you. Exchanging me for Abraham will prove we don't want to harm him."

"And Taz will make sure no harm comes to you," I said with a nod. "Believe me, Zin, if I thought there were any other way—"

"There's not. It's damn brilliant and he knows it." Zin jerked his head in Emmory's direction.

"Take the exit in my closet." I was surprised my knees held as I headed for my bedroom and keyed the hidden door open with shaking fingers. "You can get in this way if I let you in. Everyone will think you're still with me."

Zin smiled and nodded once at me before he ducked into the opening. Emmory didn't say a word and he froze when I grabbed his arm.

"We need to know, Emmory. I promise they won't hurt him."

"You can't know that," he replied and slipped into the darkness without saying good-bye.

I am no good at waiting. Working with Hao taught me patience of a sort, and I could plan out my moves with what others must have assumed was some bottomless well of calm. Once I had my plan, however, it was no holds barred.

The hour Emmory and Zin were gone was an eternity. I paced my bedroom and drank whiskey because there wasn't anything else to do until I heard a tapping on the door in my closet. Grabbing my SColt, I held it loosely in my right hand while I unlocked the door with my left.

"You asked me here, Hail, why the gun?" The years had been

kind to the man my older sister had loved. Abraham's blue eyes were like pools of water in his dark-skinned face—a handsome face that gave no hint of the steel resolve within his soul.

I still didn't understand how Cire had walked away from Ab to do her duty. How he had let her marry another man. So gods-damned noble—the both of them—it made my teeth hurt.

"Someone's trying to kill me. I think I'm entitled." I rolled my eyes at him and shoved the gun into my waistband so I could help him and then Emmory to their feet. My *Ekam* no longer vibrated with anger so I dared a little smile in his direction.

It wasn't returned.

"Okay, let's get this done. If you're gone too long, your people might get twitchy, and if anything happens to Zin, I'll have to kill you. Believe me, it'll be nicer than letting him do it." I pointed my thumb at Emmory.

"Same old Hail, making threats you can't back up."

"I think I'd surprise you, Ab."

"You don't need to worry about your man, Taz is watching him. The only reason they'd kill him is if I don't come back."

"Come have a seat." I headed over to the fireplace and settled into my chair.

"Even your mother can't match your sheer arrogance. Sending your BodyGuards waltzing into my headquarters, asking me to come see you like we're old friends? You're lucky no one got killed." He shook his head.

"You mean we're not friends? I was kind of hoping we were, Ab. I've been hearing that some radical offshoot of your group is up to their necks in murder, or am I wrong and you're the one responsible for killing my sisters?"

Ab froze halfway into his seat. The look of abject grief that flashed across his face was quickly eaten by fury as he let gravity take over and drop him the rest of the way down. It told me more clearly than his next words that the answer to my question was no.

"You always were a coldhearted bitch, Hail. Never cried a tear over your father's death. I should kill you for even asking me that question. You *know* what Cire meant to me."

Emmory snarled and I gave a tiny shake of my head. "That's deserved, but I'd watch your tongue from here on out, Ab."

He ignored the warning. "No, I didn't kill your sisters. Neither did I order them killed, and I promise you no one in my organization was responsible for their deaths. Christoph thought I was selling out by agreeing to work with Cire. He split off from the group, and took a bunch of idiots who were more interested in blowing things up than actually making life better for the people of Indrana. I don't know if he was responsible, but it wouldn't surprise me. Happy?"

"No. It doesn't bring them back, but I'm satisfied you're telling me the truth." I crossed my legs and folded my hands over my knee.

"Well, I'm relieved. Your good opinion has always meant so much to me. You could give two spits about this empire, Hail. You said as much before you ran away. Why are you back pretending like you give a damn?"

Surging forward, I grabbed Ab by the throat before he or Emmory could react and jerked him out of his chair so he was on his knees in front of me.

"Does this feel like me pretending?" I hissed in his ear, tightening my grip until he choked. "This empire is my business, and I left for a reason. *My family* is my business, no matter how many gods-damned years have gone by and how far away I was. They may have had to drag me back but I'm here now and gods help you all. I get that you loved Cire, but she was *my* blood. You question me on how much I loved her again and I will kill you and burn the *Upjas* to the ground. Is that clear?"

He nodded once and I shoved him back into his chair. Seething rage rolled around in my gut, begging for blood, and I fought to get it under control while Ab struggled to catch his breath.

I managed to drag in a breath of my own, ironically feeling just as desperate for air as Ab probably was. When I didn't feel like my heart was going to explode in my chest, I spoke again.

"What about me? I saw Taz in the crowd just before someone took a potshot at me, and a servant claiming to work for you tried to shank me my first day back."

"What happened to you, Hail?" Ab whispered, rubbing at his throat.

"I left home. I grew up. You don't want to know the details. Trust me. Now answer my question."

"We didn't," Ab said, still rubbing at his throat as he got back to his feet and sat down again. "I told Taz to stay away from you. He listens as well as you always did."

"You'll have to tell him I said hi. Someone poisoned Mother with AVI."

"Excuse me?"

"And that answers that question," I murmured, shooting Ab a sad smile. "She's got flutters. Probably has had them for a while. Dr. Ganjen has her on some experimental drug and it's made her more lucid, but she doesn't have much longer."

His sharp inhale jabbed at the wall I'd constructed to keep all the pain inside, and it shook a little. I looked at my hands, struggling to steady the wall before it all came crumbling down. I'd always liked Abraham. He'd treated me like a bratty little sister rather than a princess.

"I'm sorry, Hail. So sorry."

That simple apology meant the world. I mustered up a smile and met his eyes. "We don't know when it started, but it's likely that whoever is responsible somehow got to her first. Cire sent Emmory to find me, Ab. I think she knew something was wrong before Pace died. I didn't want to come back, even after I found out what had happened."

"But you did."

"Emmory didn't give me much choice." I laughed and the edges of it caught in my throat on the way out, ripping me open. "We'll probably have to thank him properly when this is all over for saving the empire.

"I'm going to be empress," I continued after a deep breath, and looked up at Ab. "I'm sure you heard Mother has already abdicated. The matriarchs—most of them anyway—have agreed to my ascension to the throne. The official coronation will be the day after tomorrow. We'll release the news about the AVI after that, so if you'd keep it to yourself until then, I'd appreciate it."

Ab nodded. "I can do that. What else do you want from me?"

Initially, all I'd wanted was to confirm that Ab hadn't killed my family and that he wasn't trying to kill me. But now that I was staring him in the face, it occurred to me that maybe we had a chance to achieve the things Cire had wanted for our people.

"I want you to come see me again—officially—after my coronation. I'll offer pardons for the *Upjas* where I can and we'll start working on building the future."

Ab studied me for a long moment before he finally nodded. "Deal, Your Highness."

I stood, offering him my hand, and he took it with an amused smile.

"I think I underestimated you."

"Most people do. Thank you, Ab, for everything."

He nodded once more and squeezed my hand. Then he followed Emmory back to my closet and ducked into the tunnel.

"Get some rest, Highness. Zin and I will come back into the palace via another route. You don't need to wait for us."

Normally it would be amusing how easily my *Ekam* could dismiss me, but right now it just raked over my raw and bleeding heart like salt-coated fingers. His face was emotionless. His eyes were as icy as the frost-laced windows.

All I could do was drop my chin in acknowledgment and then close the hatch behind him. Sliding down the wall, I buried my face in my knees and wept.

I'd betrayed his trust by sending Zin deliberately into danger. This hadn't been about protecting me, not really, though I could make some argument to that end. It'd been about information gathering and gaining allies and I'd used my Body-Guards like pawns.

If it had been just Emmory, I had a feeling he wouldn't have cared. But I put Zin in danger, and I wasn't sure Emmory would ever forgive me for that.

24

Pratimas morning dawned clear and cold. I woke up early and watched the lights from my bedroom window as they flickered to life outward from the palace. I couldn't take any joy from the ritual of hope. The events of the night before had surged up to smother me the instant I opened my eyes. I'd made contact with the *Upjas*, possibly even secured their support, but at what cost?

I shouldn't even care so much about the opinions of a man I barely knew, but I did. I valued Emmory's counsel and his respect; and he was my last link to Portis. That I might have lost those precious things cut me to the bone. Emmory was the first man to earn such trust from me since Portis. Not even Po-Sin or Hao had gotten under my skin like my *Ekam* had managed.

"Oh, bugger me," I muttered, blinking back the tears as I slid from the bed. Starting the day off with swollen eyes wasn't particularly appealing to me, especially since I'd be on camera from the moment we left the palace.

Stasia was nowhere to be seen, so I headed for the bathroom. By the time I'd showered and composed myself, evidence of her presence was on the table by the window. A steaming cup of blue chai and a plate of breakfast made my stomach sit up and take notice.

I belted the heavy white robe and passed the table, sinking to my knees in front of the colorful statue of Ganesh. I lit a stick of incense and settled back on my heels. As the sweet smoke wafted through the air, indecision struck and I stared at my hands until my eyes crossed.

Was I supposed to talk out loud? To just sit here? I had been telling the truth when I said I'd forgotten how to pray. It seemed wrong to ask for something every single time I sat down, but I was pretty sure Ganesh didn't need a litany of my day either.

"I don't know what the fuck I'm doing," I hissed.

Portis would have laughed at me. The thought made me giggle. "I miss you, you jerk. You'd be laughing so hard at me that you'd be crying right now."

I rubbed at my face and looked up at the statue. "I'm sorry I'm messing this all up, Father. I hope you can bear with me here. I promise I'll get it figured out sooner or later."

I offered up an uncertain genuflection and got to my feet. I'd just settled into a chair and grabbed for my mug of chai when there was a knock at the door.

"Come in."

Jet stuck his head in. "Morning, Highness."

"Morning."

He bowed low. "*Anand.* May your light be stronger than the darkness."

"To you also. How's your wife doing?" I saw the surprised look on his face turn into delight.

"Well, Highness. Both she and my daughter are doing well. I'll tell Reva you asked about her."

"Do that." I smiled and sipped my chai. "I'd love to see them both after the holiday."

"Reva would love that, ma'am. Thank you. *Ekam* Tresk asked me to let you know the security briefing is starting in a few minutes."

"Right." Rising, I snagged a piece of bread. "Let's go."

"Ma'am..." Jet paused, looking distinctly uncomfortable. "You should probably..."

I laughed. "Oh, change the clothes, huh? Emmory will fuss."

"He will, Highness."

Grinning at Jet, I shooed him out of the room. "I'll be right out," I said, closing the door. I shoved the bread into my mouth to free up my hands. Throwing the robe onto the bed, I crossed to the wardrobe and snagged a few pieces. I jerked them on and shouldered the door open as I scooped my wet hair up into a knot at the base of my neck.

"Better?" I twirled in a circle, delighted when Jet actually chuckled.

"It will keep the *Ekam*'s blood pressure even, Highness."

"Let it never be said I'm not concerned about *that*." I didn't know where my newfound good cheer had come from, but I was determined to hold on to it for as long as I could.

The BodyGuard rooms were next door to my quarters. The main room had bunks along the far wall for the Guards on duty and a smaller kitchen tucked into the corner. There were two doors off to my left—one led to the bath facilities and the other was the command center. There was a third door that joined the rooms with my waiting room, making the whole section a self-contained compound in the event of an emergency.

I really hoped it never came to that.

The Guards scattered around the room scrambled to attention when Jet and I walked through that door. "Sit back down,"

I said, waving a hand at them. "Finish your breakfast. Kisah, how are you this morning? Is your son feeling better?" I smiled at the well-built blonde with short hair and a wide smile.

"Very well, Your Highness, and yes. He's back up and moving again. May your light be stronger than the darkness."

"And yours also." I folded my hands together and bowed as I exchanged the Pratimas greeting with the other Guards. I was still working my way through what seemed like an endless amount of information about all the people who'd been assigned to my detail, but I at least had the names of the four primary teams memorized.

"Would you like tea, Highness?" Willimet, the other female Guard, was smaller with flawless dark skin.

"Thank you, no. I actually have chai in my room. I'll just go get—" As I turned for the door to retrieve my drink, Cas came through with the pale gray cup in his hand. "Thank you, Cas."

"Of course, Highness."

"Did you tell your grandmother thank you for me? Her embroidery work is lovely."

"I did, Highness." He smiled. "You should have seen her preen over it. All the ladies in her circle will be green with envy."

I settled into a chair out of the way and sipped at my chai while I watched the rest of the BodyGuards trickle in. I chatted with them all—Adail's younger brother was just entering primary school, Rama's younger sister had just been accepted to the Naval Academy on their open-enrollment program. The members of Team Four—Salham, Calumn, and Erik—were all much younger than their counterparts and answered my questions in soft voices with nervous smiles. It was amusing to note that their comrades didn't warn the latecomers of my presence, leading to several embarrassing incidents and more than a few good-natured laughs at their expense.

Emmory wasn't one of them. My *Ekam* spotted me the second he walked through the door.

"Highness," he said with a nod of his head.

It could have been my hopeful imagination, but it seemed like his voice was less frigid than last night. There was a moment of awkward silence, and then Emmory cleared his throat. "All right, people, let's get this done. We're expected for the Pratimas ritual at the temple in two hours."

I had promised to keep my mouth shut during the briefing, and as it turned out, that wasn't a hard promise to keep. I found myself fascinated by the way Emmory ran the proceedings.

I suspected things were a little restrained because of my presence, but only a little. There was some laughter and a few snarky comments that reminded me of my crew when we'd plan our next job.

Emmory allowed it—to a point—but he was also very accomplished at keeping the Guards focused and on task.

"He's very good at this." I subvocalized the comment to Zin over our dedicated comm channel rather than risk the chance of someone overhearing me.

Zin was leaning against the wall. He looked down at me and smiled briefly before returning his attention to the diagram on the wall. *"More so than he'd admit, Highness."*

"Is he still mad at me?" It was ridiculous how much that sounded like a little girl wondering if she was still in trouble. Thankfully, Zin didn't tease me about it.

"No, ma'am. I had a talk with him."

"Oh really?"

Zin's smile was fleeting. *"You sacrificed a lot for us, ma'am. It's only fair to return the favor. It wasn't that he was mad about your idea of using me for a hostage, so much as it was—"* He fumbled suddenly for words and I had to keep myself from raising an eyebrow at him.

"Cold? Not his idea? What?"

"Dangerous. I know you think Emmory is invincible, ma'am, but the same rules don't apply with Tracker pairs. If something happens to either one of us, you know the other will probably lose it, right? We've been together for a very long time. Emmory was worried, but not for me or himself. He was worried about leaving you unprotected. He swore an oath, and that means more to him than our safety—or our lives."

I knew it and the very thought of losing either of them made me sick to my stomach. *"Whatever Portis told you, I did take care of myself pretty well for twenty years."*

"Of course you did." There was laughter in Zin's voice. *"I don't particularly feel like dying anytime soon, but it is an occupational hazard, Highness. Emmory just—he doesn't like losing."*

"Join the club."

"I am glad to be along for the ride; it's proving to be pretty damn exciting."

"Trust you to say that." I had to swallow back my own laughter so it didn't spill into the air. *"I bet you jump out of tall things just for fun."*

"Only if they're also moving fast, Highness."

My snort of laughter was little more than an exhalation before I stifled it. Emmory heard me anyway and gave us a curious eyebrow before returning his attention back to Willimet's report about the security inside the temple.

The meeting lasted a little over half an hour. When it was done, I headed back to my rooms so Stasia could poke and fuss and prepare me for the day.

An hour later I emerged from my bedroom dressed in a

brilliant emerald sari a shade darker than my hair and weighted down with enough gold to pay for *Sophie*'s fuel for a year.

"Are you ready, Highness?" Emmory asked.

"Not yet," Stasia answered before I could. "She needs her coat." She shook out the same silver-fur-trimmed one I'd worn down to the beach and held it out to me.

"Stasia, we'll be inside most of the—" I swallowed down my protest at her fierce look, wondering just when my maid had turned into such a terror, and obediently turned around to put it on.

Zin was grinning at me and I couldn't stop myself from sticking my tongue out at him. That dragged a burst of laughter out of Emmory, who tried to cover it up with a cough.

The public ceremony was a blur of light, color, noise, and chanting. Colored sparklers flared even with the sun high in the sky, and people greeted each other with kisses on cheeks and holiday blessings spilling from their lips.

The unease that had plagued the empire had disappeared in the flood of celebration washing through the capital. Today, the grief over my sisters' deaths faded. Today, the concern over the Saxons' recent attacks was put aside.

Pratimas was, quite simply, the release we all needed to shake off the miasma of the dark year. The triumph of the light over the dark, the end of all the things that had plagued us. I knew all this hope was being pinned on me, but for once it didn't scare me.

"*Anand*, Highness." The young woman bowed low, her bracelets jingling.

"May your light be stronger than the darkness." I pressed my hand to her dark hair.

She glanced at Emmory as she rose. "Highness, may I?"

Emmory nodded so I pressed my cheek to the girl's and smiled for her picture. She thanked me again and moved on with her friends, all of them giggling with delight.

"Highness." The young man who followed had solemn brown eyes and a threadbare coat. He held out an unlit sparkler. "For you, Light of Indrana. I hope your reign brings us the peace and equality we have so long awaited."

I let Emmory take the sparkler; our agreement about how best to handle the potential dangers had been discussed in the aircar on the way over. "Thank you for your faith in me." I took the young man's hand in mine. "What is your name?"

"Mika, Highness."

He couldn't have been more than fifteen, still a baby in a society that so clearly discarded his worth without a second thought. I forced a smile out past the sadness, squeezing his hands as I did. "Your family?"

"Just my father and I, Highness. We work at the Hollster Docks. He does traffic control and I clean the building."

Hollster was a Solarian company, one of the newer non-Indranan space docks on Pashati. "Do they pay you well?"

"Well enough, Highness." His smile was shy. "My father was laid off from the Naidu shipyard when my mother fell ill because of the time he missed from work. We were lucky they were willing to hire both of us."

I nodded, feeling the anger coil up in my gut. "I'm glad of it. Please tell your father to have a blessed Pratimas."

"I will, Highness, and you also."

I smiled, moving on through the crowd. *"Alba,"* I subvocalized over our com link. *"Please make a note somewhere to look into the fair employment practices of the major shipyards."*

"Yes, Highness."

Families were entitled to spend time with ill loved ones

without losing their jobs. The FEA—Fair Employment Act—had carried over from the early days of the colonization.

My good mood dampened by the conversation, I continued through the celebration. Even convincing Emmory to let me light the sparkler Mika had given me and spin it around to the delight of several nearby children. The shadowlike attachment of Emmory or Zin—who appeared to have temporarily filled Nal's absent spot—didn't waver until we were back in the family's private temple. Only then did either of them relax and, along with the rest of my teams, faded back along the walls as I knelt next to my mother at Lakshimi's altar.

Mother was dressed in a deep purple sari. Normally a color that would have suited her, now it seemed to make her skin ashy, and the circles under her eyes took on the bluish cast of bruises.

I'd never felt much of a connection with the Goddess Lakshimi. I'd always felt too awkward around her beauty and grace. Even after Father's explanation of how she was the eighteen-armed warrior who killed the demon Mahishasura, I couldn't seem to transfer my affections from the Dark Mother to this lighter one.

"Are you feeling all right, Mother?" I wasn't even sure I'd actually said the words until she responded.

"You mean other than dying from the poison running through my veins? Oh, I'm fine." Her lips curled into a smile that was surprisingly not bitter. "Are you ready for the coronation?"

"No." I couldn't even say why the terror wrapped around my throat when she said that. This was where things had been headed all along. This was exactly why Emmory dragged me back here, why Cire had told him to bring me home.

"Don't fuss, Haili. You knew this was where things were

going." Mother echoed the words in my own head with uncanny accuracy. "I know this wasn't how you wanted it, but then I didn't really want to lose my husband, my daughters, and my granddaughter. You're included in that, by the way. I let you go because I thought it was what your Father would have wanted and I could see that what I wanted was killing you.

"I'd always hoped I would have a chance before the end to tell you that I loved you, even if I wasn't always the best at showing it. I got more than that. Our time together over the last week has meant the world to me." Her smile was fleeting. "Funny how staring your own mortality in the face makes one sentimental."

"This isn't the end." I was shocked by the tears in my voice.

"For me it is. For you, it's just the beginning. You will be empress."

I didn't know what to say to that, so I stared back up at the candles, trying to ignore the tears tracking down my face. "It's not fair. I'm going to lose you, too."

"That's life, Haili. I'm sorry. Sorry to leave you with this mess. Sorry that I couldn't figure out how to let you live your life a little sooner. Sorry that I couldn't keep your sisters safe." She gave my hand a squeeze. "I'm exhausted, Hail. I'm going on back to my rooms. I'll see you in the morning."

Leaning heavily on my shoulder, she pushed herself to her feet, then transferred her weight to Bial and shuffled from the temple.

I stayed on my knees and stared at the flickering candles until my vision blurred.

"Highness?"

Turning to look at Emmory, I blinked my now dry eyes until they cooperated and refocused. He was crouched at my side, the only evidence of his worried frown hidden away in his dark-brown-and-silver eyes. "I'm all right," I said, reaching out and squeezing his forearm. "We're running late, aren't we?"

"Just a little, Highness." Alba melted out of the shadows to answer my question. "You need to be at the Garuda Square to see the children's dance troupe in about fifteen minutes."

"We'd better get moving then." I pushed to my feet and took my coat from Cas.

We took an aircar and made it to the square with just enough time to get settled for the performance.

I'd loved the square as a child, even though our visits were rare, and the older I got, the more I was expected to behave, rather than splash through the colored waters rolling in tiny waves around the base of the massive fountain.

Garuda Square was named for that fountain topped with a white marble statue of Krishna riding on the back of an eagle, but other statues of imperial heroes decorated the kilometer-sized area. Right now the fountain was dry for the winter but still popular with the children milling around its base.

They sang and danced, their bright costumes standing out against the gray sky and their voices tumbling through the chill air. A pair of older girls performed an intricate dance routine, their saris swirling as they spun across the stage in a mock battle. One was dressed all in black, the other in shimmering white. They fought and spun and sang until the dark one dropped exhausted to the floor. The girl in white posed in heroic triumph over the top of her vanquished foe, beaming with pride. The performance ended and I rose with the rest of the crowd, clapping my hands for the beaming children onstage.

"There's a sweetshop on the far side of the square. I want to pop in after we're done here," I whispered to Emmory.

"I'd rather you not."

"Come on, I want to see if Mr. Haversham is still there. *Dhatt*, Emmy, it's not like some member of this shadowy group is going to be in a candy shop just waiting for me to come in so they can kill me."

"It's not outside the realm of possibility," he replied without looking away from the crowds. Through the whole conversation he kept scanning left to right, his augmented eyes tracking more things than I could hope to follow on a good day.

"I realize I pay you to be paranoid, but really—" I broke off when the message rang through my head, locking my knees to keep from falling to the ground. I knew the others who were linked into the palace network received it at the same time because their faces reflected the same shock and sorrow in mine.

"The empress is dead. Long live the empress."

"No." My denial was useless, a wasted breath lost in the collective inhale of the men and women around me.

"Majesty, please sit down." Emmory, of course, recovered before everyone else and didn't seem at all hesitant with the sudden change in my title.

"What happened? Emmory, what happened, she was just—" I pressed my gloved hand to my mouth to keep the insane babbling from spilling out into the air.

"I have an incoming message from Bial," he said. "It appears your empress-mother suffered a stroke shortly after returning to her rooms. Dr. Ganjen was summoned and was present at the time of death. Bial wishes to know if you would like him to send out an official notification."

"No, I'll do it. We need to get back to the palace." I wrapped my arms around my waist at the news, knowing full well I couldn't lose it in front of everyone. This was the moment I had known was coming all along.

Those closest to us in the crowd were throwing curious glances our way, but no one except my BodyGuards and Alba had been near enough to hear the news. The kids were still clustered around the stage, laughing and chattering with their parents and each other.

That's the future, Hail, the voice in my head reminded me firmly. *That's who you need to keep it together for.* I got it now, this need to present a face like stone to reassure everyone else around you that things were going to be okay. Even Hao had done it from time to time when things were really bad, and I had to admit it was better than people seeing me cry.

A gentle tug on my fingers dragged my attention away from the scene, and I looked down into a pair of wide dark eyes in a tear-streaked face. My heart skipped a beat, and I looked around for the girl's mother before the oddness of her appearance broke through my surprise.

Emmory moved to shoo the girl off. "Majesty, we should—"

I waved him off and dropped into a crouch. The little girl was dressed in a frilly pink concoction that looked as brand-new as her shiny black shoes. But her brown hair was tangled, her hands were dirty, and she wasn't wearing a coat.

"Are you lost, sweetie?" I didn't have much experience with kids, and in truth I wasn't sure how I felt about them. But she looked upset, so I reached out to push her tangled hair from her face. She flinched, jerking away from me but not releasing the fingers of my other hand.

"They said to come find you. Said Alim would be okay if I did."

I frowned. "Who said? What's your name, sweetie?"

"Ramani," she replied, scrubbing at her eyes with her free hand. "The men over there said." She waved behind her. "I was supposed to come find the lady with the green hair and stay with you until it's over. Alim will be safe if I do what they say."

Emmory was still talking with Zin and I reached up to touch his hand. "Emmory, this little girl's lost her parents." As I stood back up, her words slapped me in the face.

Until it's over.

"Bomb!" Emmory and Jet shouted it at the same time the warning bells in my own *smati* went off.

I realized in horror that my *smati*'s *Bomb in Proximity* warning was flashing directly over Ramani.

Everything slowed and a strange roar filled my ears. Emmory grabbed me, spinning me around, dragging me away from Ramani. I heard the girl's frantic screams, saw Zin grab for Alba as the other BodyGuards converged on us.

It was Jet who saved me. Jet who lunged forward and snagged Ramani around the waist, lifting her into the air. He barreled through the crowd, away from me. I could see Ramani's mouth opening in a screaming protest as she reached for me over his shoulder.

My self-preservation instincts were apparently on vacation, because I fought against Emmory's iron grip. I was no match for him and Cas, who was surprisingly strong for his wiry build.

"Cas! Shield!" Emmory ordered as they muscled me the other direction toward the dubious safety of the nearest statue.

We didn't make it. The explosion scarred the winter sky with light as the concussion wave picked us all up and threw us like rag dolls.

25

crashed into the ground and then was crushed by what felt like falling rock. Something—probably a rib or two—cracked with a spike of pain. The lack of sound was eerie, until the ringing filled my head—loud and painful. The rock rolled off me and I realized it was Emmory. I gasped, flopping around like a fish out of water on the pavement as I tried to get my body to cooperate and failed.

"Hail!" His panicked shout was muffled, coming through the haze of pain and chaos surrounding me. He slid his hands over me, concern plastered across his face as he searched for injuries. "Dark Mother of all, talk to me. How much of this blood is yours?"

I could taste the copper on my tongue and swiped a hand under my nose. It came away red.

I opened and closed my mouth, my lungs refusing to drag air inward, and the panic must have shown in my eyes because Emmory swore—something he'd yet to do in front of me.

I'd have to remember that. Though getting myself nearly blown up every time I wanted to make him swear and call me by name didn't seem like that great of an idea.

"Up, Majesty, I need you to get up." Emmory glanced over his shoulder, then returned his dark gaze to me. "We have to move." He hauled me to my feet, and practically plastered himself to my back, one hand on my neck to keep my head low. Cas was on my other side, his gun out and his young face stone hard.

"This is *Ekam* Tresk. Confirmed Charlie Level emergency at Garuda Square. Suicide bomber. At least four BodyGuards dead. I need a check-in from all BodyGuards now."

"I'm okay," I finally managed to gasp as I got some air into my lungs. "I'm not hurt."

Which was essentially true. I *hurt* and I probably had a cracked rib. But beyond that and a few cuts and some bruises that were going to make me not want to move tomorrow, I was fine. Jet was—

"Jet." I struggled to turn in Emmory's grip. "Oh Gods, Emmory. He—"

"I saw," he said grimly. "Don't look, Majesty. You don't need to see."

"That poor little girl. Where's Alba? Where's Zin?" I was babbling as we stumbled along, the panic rising in my throat and threatening to choke me. The screams of the wounded started to filter past my clogged ears.

"Right here, Majesty." Like a ghost, Zin melted out of the smoke, supporting my chamberlain.

"Let me see," I said, reaching out for the hand pressed to her temple.

"I'm all right, Your Majesty. Just a cut. We can deal with it once you're safe." She mustered up a smile. "How bad are you hurt?"

"My nose already stopped bleeding. Everything else is incidental."

Zin clamped a hand down on Emmory's shoulder, and Emmory reached up, their fingers brushing.

I thought I'd lost you.

You didn't.

It was all said without any words at all. I turned my head, feeling like I'd intruded on a sacred moment.

"We need to get moving. I want to get to the aircar." Emmory spotted Rama crumpled against a lamppost. He grabbed the dark-haired young man and hauled him up. "Focus for me, Rama."

"I'm all right, sir. I just clipped my head. Where is everyone else?"

"Jet and all of Team Four are dead." Emmory's response was clinically cold, and I found myself struggling to remember the names of the men who'd just given their lives for me. I'd just spoken to them a few hours ago.

"I'm getting responses—Pezan was injured in the blast, Adail is with him. Willimet hasn't checked in yet. Tanish and Jul were on the perimeter and are circling around to meet us at the aircar." Emmory was already on the move, hustling me down the street as he filled the others in. "I've notified the other teams of the situation."

"There's Adail—" Rama's announcement broke off and my concussion-stomped brain was so foggy it took me a full second to comprehend why. He crumpled in a heap, the blood spreading out in a crimson pool on the gray sidewalk.

Adail opened fire again.

"Get down!" Zin pushed me toward the building. We slammed into the doorway, falling through the door when the lock gave. My already bruised body protested the additional abuse, and the air left my lungs for the second time in less than an hour.

He slid off me with a muttered curse. "You okay?"

"No," I wheezed, lying there a minute struggling for breath. "Never mind bombs and shooters, you two are going to crush me to death."

"Sorry."

The breathy pain in that single word slapped at me. I rolled over and scrambled onto my knees, pressing my hands to the wound in Zin's side. "No. I've lost too many today, I'm not losing you, too. Do you hear me, Starzin? I'm not losing you!"

"Watch the door," Emmory snapped the order to the others, dropping to a knee at Zin's side.

"Where's Adail?" I snarled. The older green-eyed Guard had always been kind to me; his sudden betrayal sent my brain spinning.

"Dead." Grabbing a sari off a toppled mannequin, Emmory tore a strip off. "Sit up, Zin. I've got ITS incoming to the landing site, but we've got bigger problems."

"Other than me being shot?" Zin's laugh was cut short by coughing and he spat blood onto the floor. "Shit, that must have nicked my lung. I'm getting some warnings here, Emmory."

"I know, just hold on. ITS says we've got troop movements. There're reports of firefights in the palace. I think our traitors are making their move." He swore again, sheer anger racing over his face. "I didn't think they'd move this fast. I didn't think they'd dare to do this on Pratimas."

"None of us did," I said. "Let it go and focus, Emmy." I tore strips from the sari as fast as Emmory could pack them against Zin's wound and bandage him up. Once that was done, I wiggled out of my coat and unwound my own sari with Alba's help, piling the jewelry Stasia had draped on me that morning on top of the green fabric.

"I'll keep it for you, Majesty. I'm going to stay here and try to help with the wounded. No one will bother going after me."

"Alba—"

"It's better this way. I don't want your BodyGuards to have to worry about me. Their focus should be on you."

I embraced her. "Stay safe, please."

"You, too, Your Majesty. We need you." She smiled. "I know you don't think it sometimes, but we need you. You will carry us through this dark."

Pulling my SColt from the holster at the small of my back, I shrugged into a long jacket taken from another downed mannequin and crouched at Zin's side. Emmory was funneling updates to my *smati* as fast as he got them and the news drove frozen claws into my chest.

I wasn't badly hurt because Team Four had put themselves between me and the blast and brought up their kinetic shields to cover us. They'd paid for it with their lives and the blast had still been bad enough to knock us around like dolls.

Things were too scattered and confused for a clear picture, but what I was piecing together was that at the same time as the explosion there'd been an assault on the palace from a force of unknown strength and origin.

"I've got troops assaulting the palace gates, Saxon uniforms."

"Security for all the matriarchs reports their residences on lockdown."

"I need some backup over here!"

The ground shook beneath us.

"Holy Mother, ITS headquarters just disintegrated!"

I turned off the audio when the incoming ping rang in my ear. "Admiral."

"Thank Vishnu, you're all right. You dropped off the grid and I thought—" Admiral Hassan didn't even try to hide her relief. "Majesty, where are you?"

"Can't tell you. A shop in Garuda Square." I looked around,

catching Emmory's eye and mouthing the admiral's name. He nodded once and held up four fingers then jerked his head toward the door before he went back to binding Zin's wound. "Someone tried to blow me up. And it sounds like ITS HQ just went up in flames."

Hassan's little gasp was as clear as the gunfire that suddenly echoed outside. "Majesty, we don't have much intel, but I'll send you what we've gathered so far. All Navy ships are holding at present."

"Are there any Saxon ships incoming?"

"No, ma'am."

"Well, that's something at least. Pass the word, Admiral, we've got a coup in progress. Unsure if foreign or domestic. If anyone approaches the planet and won't stand down in my name, you blow them into dust, is that understood?"

"Yes, ma'am."

A second broadcast tone sounded in my ear and it took me a moment to realize this one was coming over the planet-wide system, not just the palace *smati* link.

"Citizens of Indrana." Ganda somehow looked both regal and girlish, facing the camera with only a hint of tears still staining her cheeks. "It is with great sadness that I must announce to you not only the death of our beloved empress, but of her heir.

"One of them was stolen from us by fate, the other—my dear cousin—was murdered this very afternoon in an explosion set by Saxon spies. This act of war will not go unanswered!"

"Oh, bugger me," I swore, getting to my feet. "Emmory, why does everyone think I'm dead?"

"I cut your *smati* off from the network, Majesty," he replied. "It seemed safer."

The shoes I was wearing were crap for running and I cursed

myself for letting Stasia talk me out of my boots. "Admiral, are you still there?" I didn't even bother listening to the rest of Ganda's speech.

"Yes, Majesty."

"Coordinate with Caspel and General Saito, tell them that I'm still kicking but to keep it quiet for right now. I don't think this is actually the Saxons but I could be wrong. If I'm not, then Ganda is trying to take my throne and start a war all at the same time. Funnel the information back to me. Find Toropov, too, make sure he's safe. We're going to be on the run for the aircar. I won't be able to talk until we're back in the palace, but I'll see what you send me.

"And Admiral, if General Vandi is still alive, find out if she's loyal to me. I don't care if it's a breach of protocol—you ask her directly. I need to know if I can count on more than just one gods-damned ITS squad."

"Yes, ma'am. Gods be with you."

"With you also," I replied and cut the connection. "Alba, I want you to stay here until we're long gone. No one will make the connection if they don't see you with us."

"Yes, ma'am." Her smile was forced and I hugged her again. "I'll see you soon."

"Tanish reported Willimet met up with him and Jul," Emmory said to me as he helped Zin to his feet. "Her com got taken out by Adail. He apparently finished off Pezan and tried to kill her, too. I'm having them backtrack and meet us here." He tossed me the location over our link.

I slid under Zin's arm. "This one didn't try to do something stupidly noble like staying and bleeding to death, did he?"

Humor fought free of the concern on Emmory's face. "Only momentarily, Majesty. I'm down to protecting you in the middle of a coup with only two healthy BodyGuards until we can get to the others. Sergeant Terass is going to meet up with us at the aircar.

"I know it won't do any good to ask you to keep your head down," he said. "So please just try to stay alive for me?"

I winked at him and wiggled my gun at the door. "Let's get moving, *Ekam*, before Ganda plants her ass on my throne." There were a thousand things jockeying for prominence in my head, but I let my training take over as we hit the open air and my focus sharpened on the world around us.

We came around the corner and Emmory jerked his gun up when a uniformed police officer sprinted toward us. "*Ekam* Tresk, Officer. I will drop you if you don't back off."

The woman skidded to a halt. "Sir, yes sir." She blinked at me. "Is that the princess? But they just said she was—"

"Not dead," I said with a grim smile. "And not a princess anymore. What's your name?"

"Officer Hajuman, Your Majesty. Iza Hajuman." The young woman kept her hands away from her weapons as she dropped to a knee and bowed her head. "I am your loyal subject. My life for you, Shining Star of Indrana."

I arched an eyebrow at her earnest devotion. "Let's hope it doesn't come to that." I looked past Zin to Emmory. "What do you say, Emmy? Right now we can use all the guns we find."

My BodyGuard nodded. "Iza, get up and take point. You kill anyone who won't drop their weapons at first challenge. Understood?"

"Perfectly, sir."

We kept moving. I didn't have a clue where Emmory was headed, but I trusted him. Cas was on my other side, blue eyes scanning the deserted landscape around us. "Sir, I've got ITS on the landing pad. They say everything is secure. Captain Gill wants to know if she should send troops out to meet us?" Blood coated his neck and my throat constricted when he turned away from me to scan the scene. His back was cut up from flying debris. Emmory's order about the shield had come too late to keep him from being injured.

Emmory shook his head. "We're almost there. Tell her to hold. Do we have a sitrep on the palace?"

"Nothing yet, sir. It's chaos over there."

Tanish melted out of a side street so fast it even startled Emmory.

"Shiva, man. I almost shot you," he muttered, lowering his gun.

"Sorry, sir. Jul and Willi scouted out an approach to the landing pad. Everything looks good. We didn't contact ITS, though. I wasn't sure what the situation was."

"Good job." Emmory patted the younger Guard. "The ITS is Captain Gill's squad; we're safe." He turned around and looked at Zin, who gave a sharp nod.

We sprinted down the sidewalk, across the landing pad to meet the ITS shuttle. Troops had fanned out, weapons at the ready, and they hustled me into the relative safety of the shuttle's interior.

The shuttle lurched, taking off before I made it to a seat. Zin stumbled, throwing me into Emmory. I felt my *Ekam* wince as he tried to steady us. "You're hurt, too," I whispered, swallowing past the lump in my throat when the realization hit me.

"I'll be fine."

His black coat was charred on one side and he was as spattered with gore as I was. He was bleeding from several cuts and holding his left arm tight to his side—the side he'd used to shield me.

"No, you won't. Where's Sergeant Terass?" I demanded.

"I'm right behind you, Majesty." Fasé's lilting voice drifted into the air over my left shoulder. "If you'll sit down, I'll take a look at you."

"I'm fine." I lowered Zin into a seat. "Look at Zin, then Emmory, and then Cas." All my BodyGuards were injured, but those three were the worst of the lot.

"Look at her first," Emmory replied.

I snarled a curse at him and grabbed him by his uninjured arm. "Sit. Down."

Emmory stared at me for a long heartbeat, but finally sat. Fasé, however, wasn't quite so cooperative.

"Majesty, I really should insist, your ribs—"

"It's just cuts and bruises. I'm *fine*," I lied, knowing full well that Emmory knew the truth. "I swear to the Dark Mother the next person that argues with me is going to get my fist in their face, is that understood? Heal them. That's an order, Sergeant."

Fasé swallowed, glancing at Emmory. Thankfully, he gave her a little nod and she put her hands over Zin's. Silence descended and I realized I was holding my breath. I exhaled when Zin did, some of the tight lines of telling pain easing out of his face.

"May you feel better," Fasé whispered, touching her forehead to Zin's. The motion left a smudge of soot and blood on her pale skin. "Your Majesty?"

"Do the others first."

"Majesty." This time it was Zin, not Emmory. "Please sit down. At least let her check you. We need to be sure you aren't seriously injured."

I already knew I wasn't and Emmory did, too, but he wasn't speaking up. Muttering a vicious curse under my breath, I sat and held a hand out to Fasé. "All right. Get on with it."

Her fingers were cool as she wrapped them around my wrist. "I meant what I said about not healing me. You need to save your strength for them."

I closed my eyes, resting my head against the back of the seat. I felt vulnerable just lying here. I wanted to be up doing something. It was a bad idea to close my eyes. The minute my lashes fell, I saw Ramani's face, Jet's back, and then the explosion. "Oh, bugger me." I shoved away from Fasé, stumbling for the facilities and barely making it before emptying the contents of my stomach into the toilet.

"Majesty?"

"Fasé, if you don't go take care of the others, I'm going to be very upset with you." I didn't even look up from the toilet when I said it.

"Easy, Majesty."

"Don't you tell me to be easy, Starzin," I snapped, struggling to keep my voice low. "Someone just tried to blow me up. Someone just killed my mother." I stood up, steadying myself against the wall. "Emmory got toasted, you got shot— the others—and Jet—all these people dying for me. What's the fucking point? I'm nothing more than a gunrunner."

Zin caught me when I sagged forward. The door closed behind him, shutting us in the tiny bathroom. "You've got a minute, Your Majesty. Then you have to pull yourself together." His words were shocking—flat and cold. All I could do was stare at him in astonishment. "Those are friends out there, but you don't want them to see you like this. They need to see their empress. They need to see—"

"Stone." I shoved away from him as far as the space would allow. "You want me to be a gods-damned statue."

"I want you to be the empress! Those people need you to be that leader."

"No." I shook my head so hard stars flashed in my eyes. "I saw what that did to my mother, Zin. I won't do it. I won't pretend like I'm not grieving for my people or the fact that Jet's wife will have to raise their daughter alone. That I'm not dreading having to talk to Rama and Salham's parents and tell them how their sons died. That I don't feel like total shit because I can't remember the names of the other three BodyGuards who put themselves between that bomb and me and paid for it with their lives! I won't pretend that a little girl"—I jabbed a finger into his chest with such force I was surprised it didn't sink knuckle deep—"didn't die right in front of me today."

"I'm not asking you to pretend. I'm asking you to do something with it rather than wallow in it. You don't understand how much your people love you. Look." He held his hand up, using his *smati* to project the images onto the bathroom wall with the tech in his fingers. News articles about my return, comments on the Hansi network, more beaming selfies that I only half remembered taking.

"Being loved doesn't make me a good empress, Zin. I don't know what I'm doing."

"Cowshit," he replied. The curse so at odds with his normally polite demeanor that I blinked at him in shock. "You're smarter than you give yourself credit for. We're on the brink of war. The gunrunner I retrieved knows what she's doing and right now we need her."

"Make up your gods-damned mind," I hissed at him. "Gunrunner or empress, Zin."

He shook his head slowly and smiled. "This isn't an either-or proposition, Majesty. You are a gunrunner. You are the empress."

Which meant I got to decide, I realized. I was the Empress of Indrana. I got to decide how I behaved and no one could tell me otherwise. "Let me out of here."

"Of course, Majesty." Zin reached behind him and opened the door, stepping out of my way with his head lowered.

"Emmory, find us a safe place to get into the palace. Don't argue with me about it, just do it. I know you'd rather take me to some damn safe house but that's not the way this is going to work." I whirled in a tight circle, meeting the eyes of everyone on the shuttle.

"Listen up, all of you. I've lost some very good people today and I will probably lose more before the day is done. Innocent lives were sacrificed by people who value power more than decency. Those are not the people who control the fate of Indrana. I do. You do.

"I don't know what's going on out there, but it doesn't matter if the enemy is my cousin or the Saxons. I'm not going to cower in a hole while they try to destroy everything we have built here. You won't get stone-faced cowshit from me, you won't get some prim and proper royal line. Get used to this now. Everyone wanted me back, well, now they're going to have to deal with having a former gunrunner as an empress. Is that understood?"

Their murmured "Yes, ma'am" was somewhat stunned.

Emmory, however, didn't seem at all shocked. "I got in touch with security at the landing pad, Majesty," he said. "We'll land and get you in as fast as we can. You're right, I don't like it, but I do think that we're better off dealing with this now as swiftly as we can."

There was just the barest flicker of emotion in his eyes. A tangled dance of relief, pride, and amusement that winked out of existence before it was even fully formed and tipped me off to just what Zin had been after.

"We're coming up on the landing pad now, Your Majesty," Zin said, putting a hand on my arm. "If you'll find a seat."

I snapped my mouth shut, crossed back to Emmory, and dropped into a seat next to him. There was a flurry of activity around me as the members of Captain Gill's team and my remaining BodyGuards prepared for the landing.

"You two are going to keep me on my toes," I said over our *smati* link.

"Zin said what he thought would help, ma'am. You were teetering on the edge. The shock is understandable." He gave a little shrug, not looking at me as he checked and double-checked his guns. *"Anger clears the mind, puts things in focus."*

"And going into the palace?" I pulled out my own gun, letting my restless hands do their work.

"I don't like it, any of it. But we need to be in there. I couldn't suggest it outright. As your Ekam, *my duty is to keep you as far away from danger as possible, not drag you right into a trap."*

"So what's the plan? Hopefully it doesn't involve one of us getting shot, because we've done that already today." I grabbed Emmory by the forearm and squeezed until he looked at me. *"I'm serious. Don't die, Emmy. I'm not saying ever, I know what your job is. I know what you're prepared to do for me and this empire. But just today, please, don't die. Promise me."*

"Emmory, we're—"

I snapped my free hand up, cutting Zin off. "Promise me," I repeated out loud.

Emmory blinked and, after what seemed like an eternity, nodded at me. "I promise, Majesty. And no, the plan is not to get shot."

Zin shook something dark at me. Clothes, I realized, or more accurately an ITS uniform. "From the pilot," he said with a grin. "Sergeant Hoff is living every soldier's nightmare of going to war in his underwear so we can hide you in plain sight."

My laughter startled everyone in the shuttle, while Emmory groaned and covered his face with a hand. "Could you take this seriously?" he asked Zin, who shrugged.

"Just another day as BodyGuard to the Gunrunner Empress. You're going to want to get dressed, Majesty. We're on the clock."

I grabbed the uniform from him and hustled into the bathroom again, stripping out of what remained of my outfit and wriggling into the flat black pants and jacket. When I came out, Fasé handed me a helmet. There were dark bruised circles under her eyes and her hands were shaking a bit.

"You're exhausted," I said. "You should stay with the shuttle."

"No, ma'am. I need to stick close to you. Just in case."

I forced myself not to argue and not to run back into the bathroom to be sick again. *Get used to it.* The voice in my head sounded like Portis and it was sympathetic. *You're the most important person in their world right now. They'll give up everything, even their lives, for you.*

I twisted my hair up into a knot, put on the helmet, and keyed into the com system. The display lit up, making the shield in front of my eyes as transparent as glass from my side.

From the outside it was just one of a dozen blank helmets. No one would know who I was.

Emmory tapped me on the helmet. "No heroics, ma'am." His voice was clear on the com.

"Back at you," I replied. "Let's go get my throne." It felt right to say it after days of fighting the idea. I was the Empress of Indrana. "May the gods save us all."

Everyone echoed me and we sprinted from the shuttle.

My breathing and heart rate shot up through the atmosphere. Adrenaline is a funny thing. After all these years, all this separation from our birthplace, from Earth, our biology hasn't changed all that much. The moment we were all clear of the ramp, Sergeant Hoff pulled back off the landing pad and bugged out for a rendezvous point known only to Emmory and myself.

We were now stranded at the palace, but at least we'd still be able to get off-planet if it became necessary.

I really hoped it didn't become necessary.

I stayed low, Zin at my front and Fasé at my back, a pretty impressive M2220 in my hands. I was surprised Emmory let me have such a cannon without any kind of hesitation.

Getting into the palace proved easier than I'd suspected, but it made perfect sense if Bial was trying to trap us. We slipped in through a service door used for deliveries without seeing a soul and followed Emmory down the hallway.

We approached an intersection, Emmory slowing cautiously. He whispered something to Iza I couldn't make out. Emmory gestured for us to stay put, and they proceeded around the corner.

The silence that followed carried a tension with it that felt like someone had turned up the gravity on us.

"Majesty, will you join us?" Emmory called for me just before I thought my head was going to implode.

I shoved my visor up and shared a curious glance with Zin. "Well?"

"I don't know, Majesty. I'll go first."

No one had said anything about leaving weapons behind, so I kept a hold of the M2220 and followed Zin around the corner. What we saw brought us both to a standstill.

Bial and half a dozen BodyGuards were on their knees with their hands behind their heads. Emmory stood off to the side, talking with a pale-skinned man with icy eyes.

"Well, this is a surprise," I said, drawing everyone's eyes to me. I locked eyes with Bial. "And yet not, disappointingly. Emmory, can you tell me what's going on?"

"He was conspiring against the throne, Majesty. Some of the other Guards disagreed and disarmed him before we got here."

"I wish I could say I was shocked. Damn it, Bial, for a moment there I was starting to trust you."

"I did what was best for Indrana," Bial said. His jaw was set and there wasn't a trace of remorse on his face. "Ganda should be empress."

"Is that so?" It took everything I had not to take the gun off my shoulder and blow him to pieces.

"You're a criminal! What authority would we have if we just looked the other way for you? How could you enforce any laws when you've broken most of them yourself? How could we trust you to keep us safe when you've probably sold weapons to the very people who are looking to tear this empire apart?"

"I never sold guns to the Saxons," I snarled, advancing on him until Zin brought me up short.

"A convenient sense of honor, Your Majesty." Bial spit my title at me. "A gunrunner on the throne of Indrana would reduce the empire to laughingstocks of the universe."

"Don't you dare talk to me about honor!" It was a good thing Zin had stopped me. I was too far away to kick the man in the face. "If you hadn't wanted me to come home, you sorry bastard, you shouldn't have helped Ganda and Laabh kill my sisters! You shouldn't have let someone poison my mother! I would have happily stayed away and let Cire have the throne.

"She would have been twice the empress I could ever be. You killed them and I had to come home. This is your fucking fault in the first place, you bastard. You were supposed to keep them safe!"

All the color drained out of Bial's face. "What? I didn't kill them. I didn't have anything to do with that. It was the *Upjas*. I swear, Majesty, I don't know what you're talking about."

"Liar." The rejection was automatic, but the misery in his blue eyes drove a wedge of doubt into my fury. "How else did you think they were going to clear the path for Ganda?"

"Clear the path?" There was real confusion in Bial's voice now. "Majesty, I don't know what you're talking about. I wasn't involved in anything until you arrived. All I have been trying to do is talk your mother into naming Ganda as the heir. I don't—"

"Shut up." I popped the M2220 off my shoulder at Zin. He was surprised enough that, instead of letting it fall and stopping me, he bobbled the gun. I pulled the Hessian45 we'd retrieved from Rama's corpse from my belt and advanced on Bial.

Emmory caught my wrist and jerked my hand to the side. The blast I'd been meaning to put between Bial's eyes instead drove into the cement between him and the man next to him. Bial didn't even twitch. The other guy dove to the side with a panicked shout.

"He's got information we need, Majesty," Emmory said. "Plus, we need him mobile at the moment."

"What for?"

"To get into the throne room. Indula here says they weren't going to kill us. They were just supposed to stop us and give you the choice of abdicating or being taken to your cousin."

"So why aren't we in custody, *Ekam*?"

"Apparently, the idea of taking you off the throne didn't sit right with some of the Guards."

"I've seen the video of you taking out that assassin, Majesty. I've heard the stories about your exploits." The man Emmory had been speaking of gave me a quick nod, lowering his pale eyes to the floor for a moment. "It looks like we're headed into another war with the Saxons, and I'd rather have someone on the throne who knows what they're doing." Indula shrugged a shoulder. "Plus you're the heir, there's no denying that. If we were that chaotic mess they call a democracy in the Solarian Conglomerate, our opinions would matter on the subject, but they don't."

"She's a gunrunner!" Bial protested.

I kicked him in the stomach, not hard enough to damage anything but just enough to knock the air out of his lungs. "You wouldn't let me shoot him," I said when Emmory gave me the Look. "So you decided to side with the gunrunner rather than my royal cousin?" That was aimed at Indula.

Indula shrugged. "My mother worked in a bar, Majesty. My father was a mechanic. Bial's mistake, and your cousin's, I guess, was thinking those of us in the Guard care about someone's breeding. We're all common folk, though. Most of the nobility go into the Navy. We don't care where you come from, we care what you do now."

"I like you," I said, pointing a finger at him and he gave me a surprisingly boyish grin.

"I'm glad to hear it, Majesty."

A similar conversation with Jet echoed up in my memory, carrying with it a wash of pain that brought tears to my eyes and I struggled to get back under control. "All right." I took a step away from Bial and stuck my gun back in my belt. "What's the plan, Emmory?"

26

The plan made me realize just how much information about my gunrunning life my *Ekam* had managed to access. It was damn close to a replica of a job we'd pulled early in my career with Hao on Banosh IX.

We left the Guards who'd sided with Bial tied up and stashed in a storage room. Emmory had executed his controversial ability to shut down their *smatis* just after arriving so there was nothing for the men to do other than sit in the dark and wait for our return.

Bial was not as lucky. We gave him an empty gun and I glued myself to his side.

"Here's how this is going to work," I hissed as we headed down the hallway. "You're going to pretend like you've captured Emmory and the others. You're going to take them in front of my traitor of a cousin. You're going to keep your mouth shut about me or I'll put a hole through your chest."

"Majesty, I—"

"If you try to tell me once more that you weren't involved in this, I'll ruin Emmory's plan by drilling you here and now. So shut your mouth." I jabbed him with my gun and snapped my helmet closed. My ribs were killing me, but I shook off the pain and focused.

I didn't want to believe him, but his insistence was odd for a man who clearly disliked me and didn't want me on the throne. There was nothing for him to lose by admitting he'd killed— or been responsible for the deaths of—my sisters and mother.

So why wouldn't he?

I shoved the conundrum into the back of my head as we crossed out of the hallway and through one of the side entrances of the throne room.

Not being the first person through the door gave me more of a chance to get my bearings, though I'm sure my BodyGuards were just as quickly absorbing all the information about the terrain that they could. It said a lot about the "Saxon" attackers that Ganda was sitting on the throne. No BodyGuard with a milliliter of sense would have allowed their charge to be so exposed in the middle of a crisis like this.

Unless that charge was me.

I choked back the laughter at that thought and gave Bial a subtle prod in the back as we moved into the room.

Nal was, unsurprisingly, standing next to my cousin. No big shock there, even if it did make my hand twitch with a desperate desire to shoot her.

"There aren't very many Guards," I subvocalized to Zin over our *smati* link. *"And it's a mishmash of her own personal guards, Mother's BodyGuards, and what looks like some Army personnel. Either Ganda has enough support that she isn't worried about a counterattack or she's an overconfident idiot."*

I wanted to go with option B, but I knew I couldn't let my feelings cloud my judgment.

"Remember she thinks we're on her side, too, Majesty."

"*Ekam* Bial. Given that my poor aunt is dead, I am sorry that your services will no longer be needed." Ganda's tone went off in my head like a great bell.

"Brace yourselves—"

I'd no sooner gotten the words out than Ganda smiled nastily. "As you can see, I've chosen a new *Ekam* for myself." She waved a hand. "Kill them."

Firefights don't happen in slow motion. They're messy, chaotic things filled with noise, pain, and blood. I had eyes only for my cousin and brought my gun up.

Bial moved faster than I could, knocking my gun out of the way and tackling me with such force that we went sliding across the marble floor. We slammed into a column on the far side hard enough to knock the air from my lungs and send my helmet spinning into the corner.

"You bastard!" I kicked at him, flopping around like a beached dolphin for a few stunned seconds until I got my feet under me. "Bial?" He wasn't moving and my heart twisted unexpectedly when I spied the streak of blood that tracked our path across the floor.

Had he just saved me?

I was reaching to check his pulse when the boot kicked me in the face. Pain burst behind my eyes as I spun through the air and landed in a heap a meter away.

"Your Majesty." The mocking voice as hard as diamond plating and colder than space cut through the air, through my confusion. I looked up to see Nal approaching me.

We were in the back of the throne room, shielded from the firefight by the columns. The sounds of shouting muted by the marble.

"You're like a fucking sewer rat, nearly gods-damned impossible to kill." She didn't have a gun. I didn't know why but I was grateful for it. I let her kick me again, trying to steel myself

369

against the pain, but there's little you can do to prepare yourself for more broken ribs.

I'd pushed off when Nal's foot connected, lessening some of the impact, but it still lifted me off the ground and I rolled onto my back gasping in agony.

A spike of black pearls I'd missed came loose from my hair and dropped to the ground by my ear. I closed my hand over it as Nal locked a hand in my hair and dragged me upright.

"We had everything set up and you had to go and ruin it by refusing to cooperate."

"Ganda should have told you that's how I am." It is surprisingly easy to drive something small and thin through human skin, but harder to get it through the tendon and bone. I aimed for Nal's knee and she howled with pain as the hairpin sliced through flesh and broke off in her knee joint.

"Bitch!"

She backhanded me. I used the momentum to roll away and up onto my feet. Pain made me dizzy, but I wasn't about to show it. "I'm not going to pretend to be shocked over your treachery or my cousin's. I just want to know why."

Fury transformed Nal's face into something unpleasant. "And you think I'll tell you just because you ask?"

"I'm actually hoping you'll let me beat it out of you." Then with a grin and a wink I said, "Come get some."

I could see the rage crowd out the good sense. Nal rushed in like an AVIer high on the pure stuff.

I hit her, following the uppercut to her mouth with a kick to the chest that drove her back into the wall. I got in two more good shots before Nal reacted, catching my wrist and spinning me to the side. I twisted my wrist out of her grasp and avoided the worst of the side thrust she aimed my way. Stars exploded in my vision and I bit the inside of my cheek to keep from gasping out loud.

"Your family's arrogance is sickening," Nal spit. "Your mother gave up in the war against the Saxons just because she lost her precious husband. I lost my sisters because of your mother's weakness!

"She threw away the might of our empire because of a man. And your stupid sister was no better, involving herself with the *Upjas*, promising them the same rights as the rest of us as if they were somehow equal to us. When we're finished here, the rest of the universe will think that the Saxons killed you. We'll be at war and the people will welcome Ganda's rule. We'll crush the Saxons and restore the glory of the old days to the empire."

"Did I miss something? The Saxons will roll over the fucking top of us if we try to go to war with them."

"What do you know, gunrunner?" Nal scoffed. "The Saxon Kingdom isn't as strong as you—or they—might think. General Prajapati has plans; starting with the news that the Saxons were responsible for the death of your entire family."

There was shouting in the background, and the sounds of more gunfire, but I didn't take my eyes off Nal. I trusted that my BodyGuards were handling the threat. This was my fight.

"Did you kill Pace?"

Nal's smile was vicious. "It's amazing the things you can do as an *Ekam*. The trust they give you. It was pitifully easy to infect one of her favorite Guards the same time I was scheduled to be away for a week. We wouldn't have even bothered with the sniveling brat except they'd have put her on the throne after Cire and her spawn were dead and Ganda felt it was best to start with the unimportant people."

White-hot fury poured into me and I gave Nal a look that would have sent even the most hardened gunrunner in the universe screaming for cover. She was too stupid to realize what it meant. Nal wasn't as good as Emmory, or me for that matter, but my ribs were hurting me and the pain slowed me down. She blocked my first punch and threw out a sweep I easily avoided, but my timing was off and she followed up with a strike that clipped my eyebrow as I pivoted out of the way.

More stars exploded behind my left eye, but I didn't slow.

Stepping into her, I slammed my elbow into the side of her head and brought it back once again with equal force. She staggered backward, stunned, and I moved with her. I jammed my palm up into her ribs, ducked under her swing, and swept her leg out from under her.

The blood dripping into my left eye blinded me, and I didn't see Nal's hand snake out and wrap around my forearm. She jerked me to the ground. I landed on my knees, straddling her waist, and twisted my arm out of her grip.

Nal whipped her arms up to protect her head from my elbow strikes, rolling to her side in an attempt to get away from me.

It was a mistake.

I let her roll underneath me, sliding the other direction so I was behind her. I snaked my arm around her throat, my elbow up under her chin, and locked my other arm behind her head as I slid across her back. Wrapping my legs around her waist, and ignoring the screaming pain in my ribs, I cranked back, cutting off her air.

Nal fought, but couldn't free herself. She went limp in my arms when she passed out. I released her, and slumped backward with a groan.

"Majesty!" It was Cas, not Emmory, who rushed to me. He shoved Nal to the side. "Are you hurt?"

I lay there for a moment, staring at the ceiling and concentrating on my breathing until I was sure I wasn't going to pass out.

"Yes. Bugger me. I'm going to sleep for a week. Help me up," I groaned, holding a hand up to Cas.

"Sergeant Terass is headed over, Majesty, just hang on."

"I can stand on my own, Cas. Get her tied up." I poked at Nal's unconscious form with my foot. What I really wanted was to take Cas's sidearm from him and put a hole through the woman's head, but the bitter realization that she was worth more to us alive kept me from doing it.

"Majesty?" Emmory's voice echoed over my *smati* just as Zin and Fasé arrived, weapons in hand and concern splashed over their faces.

"I'm fine, and you'll be pleased to know I was a grown-up and didn't kill Nal." I waved a hand at Zin and touched my temple to let him know I was talking as I mouthed "Emmory" at him.

"It's clear out here," Emmory replied. *"Your cousin is in custody."*

"Great, I want to talk to her." I turned a little too fast and would have slid to the floor if Zin hadn't caught me.

"Easy, Majesty. Let's have Fasé take a look at you first."

"I'm fine. She just got in a few lucky shots is all. Plus Bial—" The spot where he'd been lying was empty and I muttered a curse.

"You are not fine," Zin hissed in my ear. "Your ribs are even worse now and you've been beat to shit. Let Fasé heal you or I'm going to hold you down while she does it."

I swallowed back the automatic challenge that rose in my throat. I couldn't breathe with my ribs like this, my head was pounding, and at this point it was more foolish pride than good sense to limp around half-conscious. Nodding sharply, I held out my hand to Fasé.

Relief was immediate and made me light-headed enough that Zin had to tighten his grip to keep me on my feet. In turn I locked my hands around Fasé's wrists when her eyes rolled back in her head, and I lowered her to the floor. "Cas, stay with her."

"Yes, ma'am."

I reached back and patted Zin's shoulder to get him to let me go. As I turned, he dropped to a knee and lowered his head.

"My apologies, Your Majesty. That was forward."

I leaned in. "Nothing's changed except my title," I whispered in his ear, suddenly understanding the weight that had settled on Mother's shoulders that instant in the corridor when she'd made the same promise to me.

Everything had changed, whether I wanted it to or not.

"Up, Zin." I dragged him to his feet. "I trust you to know when challenging me is appropriate and when it isn't." I grinned. "And that your feelings won't be hurt if I step on you when you forget. Come on, we shouldn't keep my cousin waiting."

I slipped between the columns and scanned the room, taking in the row of prisoners lined up against the wall facedown against the marble. The dead still lay where they'd fallen, and even though I didn't recognize any of the bodies, I wasn't naïve enough to believe we'd made it through unscathed.

But I spied Iza and Willimet guarding the doors and Indula gave me a nod as I crossed the line of jagged black obsidian. Some of my people had survived to die another day.

Ganda was on her knees at the base of the dais, her face tearstained. The shock when she spotted me spread faster than a palace rumor, and I felt a small tug of satisfaction curl my lip.

"You're alive!"

"Poor Ganda, you need to keep up." I spread my hands wide. "You didn't think this through. You really should have killed me first. Leaving me to the end..." I *tsked* and shook my head. "Obviously that wasn't a wise decision." In two steps I closed the gap between us and grabbed her by the hair, dragging her away from the throne. "This throne will never be yours and you would have been a pale, pale substitute for my sister." I threw her to the floor. She landed on all fours, crying out as the obsidian shards pierced one of her hands. Blood flowed, staining the white marble.

"Ganda Naidu. For betraying the people of Indrana, you will die. For your part in the conspiracy to murder my sisters and my empress-mother, you will die. If I could, I would just kill you now. But don't think this is a weakness on my part. I want you to know…" I dropped to a knee beside her and jerked her head up so her eyes met mine. "That death here would have been a mercy compared to what you will face in the days to come. Because I will know every detail of your plans and every conspirator involved in this treachery before death finds you."

Great tears appeared in Ganda's blue eyes and her sobbing followed me when I climbed the steps to the throne. I eyed the golden monstrosity with distaste for just a second, then sank down onto the thick cushion embroidered with gold thread and crossed one leg over the other.

"Emmory, broadcast?"

"Yes, Majesty."

I sat up straighter when my *Ekam* turned his dark eyes toward me and started counting down from three with his fingers. At one, I knew my smoke- and bloodstained face was being shown throughout not only the palace but the whole empire.

"Citizens of Indrana, heed our words. Our empress-mother is gone to temple on this most holy of days. As you can see, we have not followed her despite the most recent of attempts. Traitors to the throne detonated a bomb that claimed the lives of too many innocent Indranans today. These same conspirators now assault this palace and the homes of your matriarchs.

"Those who thought to support my cousin and others in their attempt to take the crown, we call upon you to lay down your arms and surrender! This is your only chance for mercy. Surrender and be subject to the laws that govern our empire.

"Loyal citizens, we have not had long to get to know one another. However, I am my mother's daughter, and I will not desert this empire in its time of need. I am your empress until the Dark Mother calls me home. I swear this to you all on our most holy of days. May the light of Indrana be stronger than the darkness."

I touched my hands to my heart, lips, and head, never taking my eyes off Emmory.

He nodded at me. "You're off broadcast, Majesty."

"Contact Admiral Hassan. Tell her the insurgents have one chance to surrender their arms and remit themselves into custody. If they won't..." I stopped and exhaled. "Kill them."

"Yes, ma'am. I heard from Kisah: Your rooms are secure and Stasia is safe."

I cut off the sob with a hand over my mouth. The rush of relief was so strong, it made me shake. "I'm glad to hear it. Find Alba, please."

"I'll send someone to retrieve her. Admiral Hassan says ITS is on the way. Still no word from General Vandi. I'd like to get you back to your rooms, Majesty."

Pushing out of my throne was harder than I'd expected. Even though Fasé had healed me, the adrenaline had left me and I found my knees only slightly cooperative.

"Sir, we've got incoming."

"They're loyal, Will, let them in," he replied.

"If they're loyal, Emmy, why are you standing in front of me?"

"I don't trust to luck?" He smiled over his shoulder.

"Given the circumstances, I'll humor you. I want Captain Gill to take Ganda and Nal into custody. I'd rather the pair of them not end up mysteriously dead before we have a chance to get some information."

Emmory didn't look away from the troops filing into the

throne room but I saw him smile. "I had the same thought myself, ma'am."

"Nal incriminated General Prajapati. Find her and Matriarch Khatri."

"Yes, ma'am."

"Cas is with Nal." Zin approached us. "I already had him touch base with the captain to get someone over to help Fasé. And a medical team for her." He waved a hand in Ganda's direction.

"Good. Go round up the others. Tell Iza to stay here with Captain Gill's team for the moment. As soon as I get done running a background check, though, I suspect she'll be changing careers."

Zin nodded, holstered his gun, and took off.

"Tresk!"

Emmory stiffened and then all the tension drained out of his shoulders. A pair of unfamiliar Trackers crossed the marble floor. The man was light-skinned, shorter than Emmory but with shoulders almost a meter across. The pale blond woman at his side was tiny by comparison, but the muscles in her arms and shoulders said she could take care of herself just fine.

They stopped on the far side of the obsidian line and dropped to a knee, both of them dipping their heads with a murmured "Your Imperial Majesty."

"Friends of yours?" I asked.

"Yes, Majesty. Allow me to introduce Trackers Peche and Winston." Emmory gestured at the pair.

"Up."

"Your loyal servants, Your Majesty. I am Raj Peche." The man's voice was like a bell. "This is my partner, Tu Winston."

"Majesty." Tu had navy blue eyes and a dimple in her left cheek.

"Tanish said it had been quiet at the empress's quarters for a while, but clear the hallway for us, would you?" Emmory watched them go and handed me his Hessian45. "Give them a moment and we'll follow, ma'am."

"I think Bial saved my life, Emmory," I said, staring across the throne room at the smear of blood still decorating the marble. "At first I'd thought he was trying to keep me from killing Ganda, but someone took a shot at me that hit him."

"It certainly seemed that way." He shrugged.

"He's a puzzle. I want you to find him."

"That may be more difficult than you think, Majesty. He's one of us."

"One of—he's a Tracker? Bugger all, why didn't you tell me this earlier?"

Emmory shrugged again and tilted his head toward the door. "We can move now. He's not officially a Tracker. Not trained anyway, but he was tested and paired. His sister died in an accident less than a month after the pairing."

I snapped my mouth shut to keep from blurting something profane.

"Bial was in the accident also. The coma the doctors put him in probably kept him from losing it. His scores were nearly as good as mine, Majesty. He's got the talent for it."

"So we have an expert-level Tracker with BodyGuard training who wants me dead on the loose?" I stopped outside my rooms and exchanged a quick nod with the Trackers waiting there.

"I'm not entirely sure he wants you dead, Majesty. I saw the whole thing. If he'd wanted you dead, he could have achieved that by not throwing himself in front of Nal's shot."

"Point." After Emmory popped the door, Raj and Tu slipped inside and I followed them. "I want to talk to him, though. Put your best on him. Whatever it takes."

"I could find him." He shrugged.

"But that means leaving me alone." I grinned over my shoulder at him as I crossed the room to Stasia.

My maid dropped into a deep curtsy. I snorted at her and scooped her into a tight hug. "I'm so glad you're safe," I murmured.

"Likewise, Majesty. I am sorry about your empress-mother."

Her quiet condolence lit a fire of panic in my gut. I was going to mess this up. Trip over my own feet and my sharp tongue so much until I started a damn war, or mortally offend everyone until I was all alone.

Please, you idiot. The drill sergeant voice in my head snapped at me in aggravation. *Mother's tongue was sharper than yours and she didn't alienate everyone. You survived the initiation into Po-Sin's gang at the age of nineteen, Hail. You commanded a crew of mercurial misfits and are a gods-damned legend in the gunrunning world. I think you can handle this if you stop whimpering for a few minutes and just follow your gut.*

"Right."

Okay, I hadn't meant to say that out loud. My BodyGuards all stopped their rapid-fire discussion to look at me. I forced out a smile and let Stasia go.

"I want Bial," I said. "And this damned mystery man. Find them, Emmory."

"Yes, Majesty."

"Alba, I'm glad to see you unharmed." I smiled at my chamberlain when she came into the room, but it was brief and crowded out by the grief that settled around me. "Where's my mother?"

"The empress-mother's body is still in her quarters. Bial locked them. I believe now that your *Ekam* has access, he can unlock them."

"Emmory?"

"Yes, Majesty?"

"I want to see my mother."

27

Not only had Bial gone to the trouble of protecting Mother's maids, but he'd instructed them to prepare her body for the funeral. The mystery about my mother's *Ekam* deepened. If he'd been involved in her death, it made no sense for him to be so concerned about her body.

It looked like she was asleep, dressed in a pristine white dress and a purple sari with her hands folded neatly on her stomach.

"Majesty."

I flinched, startled by the sound of Emmory's voice, and blinked up at him. "I never told her. I meant to, but it just never came up. She didn't know why I left home. She didn't know I was trying to—" I gave up and rubbed my hand over my stinging eyes.

"It doesn't matter, Majesty. We don't get to say everything that needs saying before the end. She knew you loved her. You have to let that be enough."

I grabbed his hand and pulled him down to the floor. "Thank you."

"Majesty?"

"For bringing me home," I said. "Thank you for giving me

the time with her. Sometimes I still"—I laughed—"think that this might be a huge mistake for the empire because I'm pretty sure I'm going to screw it all up. But I owe you for this."

"You don't owe me anything, Majesty. I was just doing my duty."

"I couldn't do it without you. How long have I been sitting here?" The sudden pain of movement answered my question before he could and I didn't fuss when Emmory helped me to my feet.

"A while, ma'am."

The time stamp on my *smati* confirmed his words. I'd been sitting there for over an hour.

"Bugger me." I leaned on him, abruptly aware of the weight of the crown still on my head and the fact that I hadn't eaten anything since early in the morning. Coupled with the massive adrenaline crash, I wasn't entirely sure that I could make it back to my rooms without falling on my face.

"Breathe." Emmory held his hand up in front of my face, the tips of his gloved fingers brushing against my cheek. "There's food in your rooms."

I raised an eyebrow at him, but inhaled. My head cleared and my legs no longer felt as limp as oct-noodles. "Emmy, did you just drug me?"

"Temporary fix, Majesty. I am assuming you don't want to be carried back to your rooms."

"Good call." I straightened and cracked my neck. "Right." Confident I wasn't going to fall over, I let go of Emmory and cleared my throat. "You said food?"

"Waiting for you in your rooms."

I didn't look back at my mother's body again as I left the room. I'd see it at the funeral, and anyway it didn't matter. She was gone.

My family was gone.

Emmory's hand on my elbow stopped the tangle of emotions before they could well up and strangle me. It kept me from losing it when Mother's head maid stopped and bowed before me.

"Your Majesty."

I'd never much cared for Subra; she had been constantly on my case to behave as a proper princess when I was younger. But she'd taken care of my mother so faithfully right up until the end.

"Thank you," I said, holding out a hand.

She took it, the grief clear in her blue eyes. "It was an honor, Majesty. You will need maids."

"I know." I smiled at Subra as I laid my other hand over hers. "And we both know that trying to corral me would drive you crazy within the hour. You were always very good to my mother. I won't forget that. Please, go grieve. When this is all over, we'll talk about your retirement. I promise that you and all of Mother's maids will be well taken care of."

"Of course, Majesty. Thank you."

Surrounded by BodyGuards, I made my way back to the rooms.

Collapsing onto the couch, I took the offered plate from Kisah. "Thank you."

"Of course, Majesty."

I wasn't sure I was ever going to get used to people calling me that, but I tried to roll with it. I wasn't going to get her or anyone else to just call me Hail, not without almost getting myself blown up again.

"Majesty, Ambassador Toropov would like to see you," Alba said.

"All right. Send him in." I made an effort to sit up, and even though it was a useless gesture, I tugged my stained shirt into some semblance of order.

Cas came through the doorway first. "Highness—" He

broke off, crimson stains appearing on his cheeks. Clearing his throat, he tried again. "Your Majesty, my apologies." His new rank as second-in-command gleamed on his low collar. I was privately surprised that Emmory had chosen Cas to replace Nal instead of Zin and made a note to ask him about it later.

"Forgiven. The promotion suits you, Cas."

"Thank you, Your Majesty."

"Your Majesty, it's a relief to see you well." Ambassador Toropov didn't look at all like he'd just spent the last several hours holding off an assault on his living quarters and I felt a little uncomfortable in my disheveled state.

"You also, Ambassador. Have a seat. Are you hungry? Would you like something to drink?"

"A drink would be appropriate at this point, I think." He nodded once and sat across from me. "If I may, Your Majesty, it has been an interesting few weeks since your return. I am an old man. I'm not sure my heart can take all the excitement."

I laughed and picked my plate up again. "I suspect you've caused your share of excitement in your time, Ambassador."

"True enough." He took the glass Stasia handed him with a nod of thanks. "I have heard rumors that some of the insurgents were dressed as members of my kingdom's military?"

"I heard the same rumors. I have yet to see any actual proof of it. Though it's not outside the realm of possibility that those responsible for all of this decided to play on the tensions between our nations."

"Well said," Toropov murmured, sipping at his drink. "It would also explain the supposed attacks by Saxon military on your territories."

Thankfully I had just taken a bite of *ajazut*—a local lamb-like creature—and couldn't say the first thing that came to my mind. Instead I gave Toropov a smile and a tiny shrug.

I set my plate aside and swallowed as I stood. "Well, I am glad you're unhurt. I'm sure someone is taking care of cleanup around your quarters. If you need anything else, please don't hesitate to let Alba know."

Ever the consummate politician, Toropov took his cue and rose. "Your concern is appreciated, Your Majesty, and I am much relieved to see you well. We will talk again soon. I will, of course, inform King Trace. I suspect he will contact you tomorrow."

"I look forward to it."

The incoming ping of a call sounded as soon as the door had closed behind Toropov. I sat back down to answer it.

"Admiral."

Admiral Hassan smiled. "Your Majesty. Cleanup is almost complete. We've got the insurgents who surrendered in custody. We'll see what, if anything, we can get out of them about this plot."

"Probably nothing," I replied, shrugging. "If whoever is behind this is the least bit capable, they wouldn't have shared their plans with the grunts on the street."

"True. We can always hope, though."

"Any news on General Vandi?"

"None, ma'am." Hassan's look was grim. "No one can raise her *smati*. It looks like the blast that took down HQ may have killed her. Admiral Shul just reported that Major Bristol stole a shuttle with a handful of ITS troops and fled the battle group. According to Shul, your brother-in-law was headed for Canafey Major."

Bugger me. I swallowed down the curse. "I just had Toropov in here trying to convince me that the attack on Canafey was part of this whole plot. Was he right?"

Hassan shook her head. "We've had too much physical proof to believe anyone but the Saxons are responsible for that attack,

Majesty. Scattered sightings like the ones here on home world are easier to discount, but they've taken two whole systems. We can't turn a blind eye to this."

"I know we can't." I hissed out a breath and shoved a hand into my hair.

Hassan's expression was grim. "We can't not respond, Majesty. They've backed us into a corner. And now with Major Bristol bolting—"

"Do you believe Shul?" I said abruptly. "Or do you think he's lying?"

She froze and the silence in the room was absolute. It took effort, but I kept from cursing out loud at my faux pas.

"Ma'am," Hassan said carefully. "I do not currently have any reason to disbelieve the admiral."

I suspected that if she had proof, this conversation would be a bit different.

"I do think it's best that we send someone to verify the news, Your Majesty," she continued. "Unfortunately, by the time they get there—"

"We'll already know one way or the other, and if Shul is against us, we'll have sent someone to their death." I finished the sentence for her, and Hassan winced imperceptibly at my bluntness.

"Yes, Your Majesty."

"I'm going to mull this over, Admiral. Keep an eye on Shul but don't do anything until we have another chat."

"Yes, ma'am."

I nodded and disconnected the call.

"I don't know what the Saxons are up to." I tapped my fingers on my knee. "King Trace and I knew each other when I was young. We got on well together. The last time I saw him was when King Geri visited Mother the year before the war broke out. I suspect it was a last-ditch attempt to stop the growing tension. Obviously, it didn't work," I said to no one in particular.

"The king was killed in a battle shortly after your father died, Majesty," Emmory said. "King Trace was only seventeen when he took the throne."

"He fought Mother to a standstill." I wandered over to the windows and cracked one open. The winter sky swept over the water like a painter's fantasy in blue. "That says something."

"He is a master strategist, ma'am." Emmory didn't move from his spot when I passed him. "And very good at the political game. He knows the rules."

"True, but I've never much cared for playing by the rules. Emmory?"

"Yes, ma'am?"

"If the Saxons were involved in this plot, there's a chance Trace didn't know about it. They are a constitutional monarchy after all. Who knows what Parliament has been deciding behind his back?"

Blowing out the breath I'd been holding, I tried to push my jumbled mass of thoughts aside. "I suppose we'll burn that bridge when we come to it," I said with a humorless laugh.

Emmory didn't answer. Instead, he crossed the room in several quick strides, and I frowned at his back. The reason for his abrupt movement became clear when he opened the door.

Captain Gill entered, and when she stepped to the side, two ITS officers were revealed.

My heart sank at the grim looks on everyone's faces as General Vandi, her uniform stained with blood and covered in dust, lowered herself to a knee.

"Majesty, it is my understanding you thought me disloyal. Allow me to offer my apologies for my failure to keep you safe and to—"

"Shiva's bones, woman!" I interrupted her. Hope sprang out of the ashes. "Why aren't you in a hospital?"

"My mother is a stubborn woman, Your Majesty," the young man at her side said with a ghost of a smile. "When Director Ganej's people finally dug us out and spoke with her? Well, the general wanted to see you immediately."

"Captain Gill."

"Yes, ma'am?"

"Sergeant Terass is indisposed. Is there another Farian on the grounds?"

"I'll see, ma'am."

"In the meantime, Emmory, find Dr. Ganjen." I crossed to Mila and urged her to her feet. "Stasia, get some water."

"Majesty, I'll ruin your couch."

"Fuck the couch," I said and watched her eyebrows shoot upward. "Where are you hurt?"

"Everywhere, ma'am, but nowhere seriously. I don't know how we survived. My son—" She looked at the young man hovering uncertainly next to her. "Majesty, this is my son, Lieutenant Yara Vandi." Mila took the glass Stasia gave her with a smile.

"Majesty." He snapped a perfect salute.

"Lieutenant. At ease and sit down. Are you injured?"

"No, ma'am. I'd come into the general's office to tell her of the explosion in Garuda Square. I thought you were dead. Alarms started going off. Mom's—the general's—secretary ran in shouting we were under attack. I shoved the general under her massive desk and then the building came down around us." He swallowed. "I don't know how long I was out. Our *smatis* were fried from some kind of disrupter, ma'am. When I came to, the general was still unconscious."

"I woke up shortly after," General Vandi said. "We were

trapped for maybe an hour before the rescuers found us. Took almost as long to get us out. Caspel had some men looking for me; they filled me in and brought me to the palace." She shook her head. "I'm sorry, ma'am. Sorry I gave you cause to doubt my loyalty and sorry I didn't see the rot sooner. I suspect some of my inner circle were involved."

"Your apology is accepted, as unnecessary as it is." I reached out and squeezed her hand. "We'll talk more when you're feeling better."

"Yes, ma'am." Mila got slowly to her feet, her son immediately supporting her with an arm around her waist.

The room spun around me and I had to lock my knees as whatever drug Emmory had used on me ran its course. My readings must have dropped because my *Ekam* was at my side, one arm unobtrusively holding me upright.

He shared a look with Alba, who began to herd everyone out of the room. Stasia appeared on my other side, and between the pair of them I shuffled for my room.

"Sleep well, Majesty." Emmory lowered me to the bed. I mumbled something that was unintelligible and slumped over, letting the blackness take me.

I slept hard but still woke up before sunrise and stumbled out into the main room wrapped in a robe against the chill. It was empty and silent. I padded over to the fireplace in the dim light and moments later had a decent fire going.

"You could have had someone do that for you, Majesty."

I shot Emmory a glare. "It'd be a pity for me to survive everything only to die from a heart attack because my *Ekam* snuck up on me."

"I think you'll survive."

"You might not. Damn it, Emmy, have you slept at all? You

look awful." I grabbed him by the arm and dragged him to the couch. The fact that he didn't resist said it all.

"An hour, I think." He rubbed a hand over his face. "We got conflicting stories from Ganda and Laabh—they were playing each other. It's fitting in a way. Nal's story aligned with Ganda's; I think she was a handy tool and little else."

"I'll make sure she knows that before she dies."

"I'm sure you will."

"Those three repeatedly tried to kill me, Emmy. That in itself isn't much of a shock." I shrugged, nonchalance seeming a better reaction than wincing at how easily he'd accepted my declaration. "What pisses me off is that the last time they used a little girl to get to me and killed my people in the process. I'll stand for a lot, but that crosses a line. Sixty-four people died in that explosion, hundreds more were wounded. We lost twice that at the ITS headquarters. They deserve justice."

"They almost got you, Majesty. Jet—" Emmory broke off and grimaced. "I've got readings on the bomb. He sent them to me before it exploded. It coalesced in that little girl less than ten seconds before it went off."

"Ramani."

"Majesty?"

"Her name was Ramani," I murmured. "She was—wait. What? It coalesced *in* her?"

"We had no warning until just before it went off." Emmory nodded sharply. "If we'd been trapped in a building, the explosion would have been magnified, or if Jet had been a few seconds slower, we wouldn't be having this conversation. I've got Kisah and Tanish working on a way to detect the bomb components before they fuse together inside the person."

"They put the bomb *inside* that little girl." Shock and horror waged a war inside my chest, reducing my heart to ashes.

I didn't know why this was so much more awful than the idea of a bomb strapped to her but something about it shut down the tender, forgiving parts of me.

"Majesty."

"I am going to kill them myself."

Emmory caught me by the arm before I could get up. "First, Majesty, you're still in your robe. Secondly, you've already forbidden a trial for them. The public will support you on that because they're still in shock. You won't get away with it for everyone who's involved in this."

"There will be no trials! There will only be those guilty of this massacre. I have every right to bring judgment down on their treacherous heads."

He met my venomous tone with calm silence, staring at me until I felt like I was about four years old.

"They killed a *little girl*, Emmory," I whispered.

"They killed my men," he countered. "They killed and injured a lot more people than just Jet and Ramani. Don't mistake my calm for apathy, Majesty. I want this rot cut out and destroyed as much as you do, but I've already told you we're dealing with powerful people. There's your mystery man to think of. We're not so lucky as to have Ganda and Laabh be the ones actually behind this. We have to be careful, doubly so because you're trying to cement your position."

Emmory put his hand on mine. The warmth of it sank past my horrific chill. "The empress thinks ten steps ahead, not just one or two. You damn sure can't afford to make any snap judgments here. These aren't gunrunners with nothing to lose. They're powerful people who'll stop at nothing to keep their power and to get more."

"What do we do?" I asked.

"We wait. He won't hide in the shadows forever. We'll find

him, I promise you. And we'll make them all pay for what they've done."

I exhaled, turning my hand up to squeeze his once, and then nodded. He'd promised me revenge, what seemed like so long ago in the temple as I mourned my sisters. Soon I would have it, at least partially. The satisfaction echoed in my hollow chest.

"Zin's compiling all the data now. He'll have a clearer idea in a few hours," Emmory said, trying unsuccessfully to stifle a yawn.

"You have time to rest then."

"Majesty, I should—"

I put a hand on his chest and leaned down. "Learn to obey orders. I promise I won't toss them around frivolously."

A crooked smile surfaced. "There is nothing frivolous about you, Majesty. I should go back to my quarters."

"You won't sleep there and we both know it. Just close your eyes, Emmory. I'll be in the other room if you need me."

"I think that's my line." His words were slurred, and before I'd hit the doorway of my bedroom, my *Ekam*'s breaths had evened out into sleep.

I distracted myself for close to two hours until the jitters won out and I messaged Zin. *"What have you got?"*

"Good morning, Majesty. Did you sleep well?" He looked better than Emmory had, but not by much.

"Well enough, I can catch up later. What have you got for me?"

"It'd be easier to show you. I'll come over."

"No, you'll wake Emmory. I'll come to you."

He raised an eyebrow at me. "You won't get out the door without waking him up."

"How much would you like to bet?" I wasn't expecting him to agree and the number Zin named had me grinning. "I've rubbed off on you, Starzin."

"Maybe a little, ma'am. I'll see you and Emmory in a minute."

I stuck my tongue out at him before I cut the connection and tossed my robe onto the bed. I took a deep breath and released it as I carefully opened the door to my room. The lights were still dim and Emmory's breathing steady as I took slow, rolling steps across the room.

The door to the hallway was the problem, electronic and heavy; all I could do was tap my fingers to the panel and slip through the moment it opened. I reached a hand out.

"Majesty, what are you doing?"

"Paying your husband a lot of money." I slapped the panel and crossed the hallway into the Guard quarters, shooting Zin a dirty look on my way through the door.

"I told you, Majesty."

"How much did she bet you?" Emmory asked, rubbing his face as he followed me through the door.

"Three thousand."

Emmory stopped, whistled, and couldn't quite conceal his grin. "She did make it to the main door. And her readings were steady the whole time."

"What woke you up?"

He shrugged. "Instinct. Sorry, Majesty, it's the truth."

I made a face and grabbed a chair, spinning it around so I could lean my forearms on the back. "Let's get down to business. I want to know how someone like my cousin nearly brought my empire crashing down."

"We questioned everyone in custody," Zin said without preamble. "Nal and General Prajapati seemed to know the least—Nal because she's little more than hired muscle and the general because she was operating under the assumption that Ganda would serve us better in a war with the Saxons than you would.

If anything, she's a weak link in the chain, Majesty. She didn't come on board the plot until after you came home."

"Did you bring Elsa in?"

Emmory shook his head. "With apologies, Majesty, but we were unable to find Matriarch Khatri. General Saito has released a Tracker team; I doubt it'll take them long to find her."

I waved a hand. Khatri was the least of my worries at the moment. "Go on, Zin."

"Obviously Laabh and Ganda were our main focus yesterday. Their stories intersect occasionally, but it's where they don't match that things get really interesting. According to Ganda, our mystery man approached her a year ago with this plan to put her on the throne. She met with Laabh, who incidentally claims the mystery man made contact with him separately around the same time about accepting Ganda's offer."

"They both identified him from the image we got from Zaran, Majesty." Emmory hissed a little in frustration. "Ganda said he called himself Kama. But Laabh said his name was Wilson. I'm running searches on both."

"Wilson was also the name he used when I was tracking him. They're probably both fake." I shrugged a shoulder. "He hasn't stayed alive this long by being stupid, and giving either of them his real name would have been very dumb."

"Laabh was their connection to the radical *Upjas*. He befriended Christoph, encouraged his rage, and provided him with his mother's schedule so that they could plant the bomb. We suspect it was the same type they attempted to use on you."

"But they didn't have the same in with me and couldn't get a good handle on my schedule?"

Emmory nodded.

"Plus we were lucky, ma'am," Zin said. "That's the plain truth of it. According to Laabh, Wilson had a plan that would put him on the throne, not Ganda. He played them off each other and yet somehow got them to work together, Majesty. They never even questioned it.

"Ganda's job was to insinuate herself into the empress's inner circle. A job made easier by your empress-mother's illness."

"How did they manage that?"

"Laabh, Majesty." Zin swallowed and looked down at his hands. "Sort of. He laced the *lokum* his brother was bringing on his visits."

"And because it was Taran bringing the candy, no one ever checked it?" Rubbing the bridge of my nose between thumb and forefinger, I swore. "I owe you an apology for your obsessiveness, Emmy."

"It's my job, ma'am," he replied without a hint of a smile. "I think Ven was starting to get suspicious; that's when they killed him."

"So my nephew used his little brother to addict Mother to AVI. He used the *Upjas* to kill his mother and his sister. Nal said she killed Pace by infecting one of her other Guards with ebolenza. I'm the only one left, but no one knows where I am."

Zin nodded grimly. "Our best guess is that Wilson found the man who did your mod and was tracking you himself. He paid off Memz in Shanghai to kill you."

"Everyone from the royal family is dead or incapacitated. Ganda takes over. It's a perfect plan." I leaned back in the chair. "What happened?"

Emmory's laughter was loud in the stillness. "You ruined it, Majesty."

28

ruined their plans by surviving?" I laughed myself, shaking my head as I did. "They'd have had better luck if they'd just blown up *Sophie*. Memz never could beat me at anything."

"I'm glad Wilson didn't take the time to figure that out," Emmory said. "It threw things into serious chaos when you came home. I suspect that's part of why the attempts on your life since your return have seemed desperate and disjointed. They've had to scramble to reconfigure plans that were set more than a year ago. Ganda was supposed to poison your empress-mother further against you, but didn't count on you cutting off her access or on you working so hard to repair your relationship. She got Nal appointed as your BodyGuard, but we all saw how well that worked out.

"Matriarch Khatri's job was to try to discredit you, but again, she misjudged your appeal with both the general population and with the other matriarchs. Even your history wasn't as much of a black mark as they'd thought. When you owned it, that only weakened their position further, and when the news about what you'd done to track down your father's killers broke, that was the final blow for any campaign to discredit you."

"It pushed them to put a bomb in a little girl." My amusement fled and I stared at the ceiling until I was able to push Ramani's face from my mind. "How does Bial factor into all this? And are the Saxons working with Wilson or is this just convenient timing on their part?"

Zin held his hands up. "The Saxon involvement is going to take us longer to suss out, Majesty. My gut says they might have been pushed into making their move on Canafey and the other border worlds without actually realizing the purpose behind it.

"And as far as I can tell, Bial wasn't involved. The man has an impeccable past, no gambling debts, no indiscretions, nothing that they'd have been able to use against him to get close to the empress. Don't forget he was on Ven's short list. Everything was legitimate in terms of his appointment."

"So he was telling the truth? He just hated that I was going to be empress?" I threw my hands in the air. "If that was the case, why did he save my life yesterday?"

"When we find him, I'll be sure to ask, Majesty. Good morning, Alba."

"Good morning, Your Majesty." My chamberlain smiled and gave a little curtsy then nodded to Emmory and Zin.

"You're still hurt." I spun out of the chair the moment I saw the shadowed bruising at her temple but Alba waved me off. "Why are you still hurt?"

"It's a trifle, Majesty, and already healing. Stasia patched it up last night. The Farians were busy with far more important matters to see to than my head. I'll be fine."

"Your head is my head, Alba. If you're not better by this evening, I'll march you to Fasé myself."

"Yes, ma'am."

"Told you she'd say that," Stasia said as she came in the room with a steaming cup in her hands. "Good morning, Majesty."

"Bless you, Stasia." I took the chai and settled back into my chair. "Why are you looking at me like that, Emmory?"

"No reason, Majesty."

I stared at him a moment longer, then gave up and drank my chai as BodyGuards began to trickle into the room. The sounds of the day starting swirled around me, mixing with the pinging of my *smati* as Alba sent me the messages she was reviewing. Most were condolences from governors and foreign heads of state, including a note from King Trace that said, *Sorry about your mother. Let me know when it's a good time to talk.*

"Interesting."

"I thought so, Majesty," Alba agreed. "Do you want me to reply?"

"No, let me think on it. Put it in the file for later."

"Majesty, Matriarch Desai has been cleared through the checkpoint and is here to see you." Emmory rose from his seat and moved toward the door. "Would you like to move back to your rooms?"

"She can come in here," I replied with a shrug. "Morning, Clara."

"Your Majesty." Matriarch Desai dropped into a deep curtsy. "We are so very relieved you are well. Please accept the sympathy of my house at the loss of your empress-mother."

"Mother would have laughed at you, you know." I smiled softly and tapped my mug on the edge of the chair. "Get up, Clara, and accept my sympathies at the loss of one of your oldest friends." I held a hand out and she took it.

"Thank you, Majesty." Clara smiled. "We need to discuss the details of your coronation."

"Clara, of the six million things I have to deal with today, that's at the bottom of the list. I am the empress, the coronation is window dressing."

"Majesty, it's an important tradition—"

"That we will do later, Clara. Right now I have traitors to hunt down, executions to set, funerals to attend, and a war to avoid." I held a hand up before she could respond. "Here's what I am willing to do: You may plan the coronation, and if there's time tomorrow evening, we'll do it. Deal?"

"Yes, Majesty." She nodded sharply and dipped a curtsy. "With your permission, then, I'll leave you to get your day started."

Later that day, Stasia strolled at my side through the ornate gardens at the center of the palace. It was almost noon, and the gigantic atrium was filled with the heavy scents of blooming flowers and greenery. Water splashed and hammered down over the wide bronze waterfall fountain set in the middle of the room, and the calls of several exotic species of birds imported from all over the empire echoed off the wide glass ceiling.

I'd always loved the atrium, especially in the depths of winter. A storm had hit about an hour ago, and snow swirled above us, battering at the glass with the whim of the wind. But inside it was warm—almost unpleasantly so—and I trailed my hand through the pale orange blossoms on the trellis bush. They danced with the disturbance, releasing their spicy vanilla perfume.

I was dressed in a cream dress almost the same color as Stasia's skin with wide, belled sleeves. My crimson mourning sari streaked across the surface of the fabric like a jagged wound. It seemed like a petty, useless gesture.

Jet deserved better.

My heart twisted at the sight of the two women I had come here to see, with their heads bent over a wiggling bundle. Jet's family. I didn't know what to say. What did you say? What could you possibly say to ease the pain?

Some noise alerted them to our presence, and the younger of the two raised her dark head. Emotions flashed too quickly through her pale blue eyes for me to read and then she was dropping into a bow, still holding her baby.

"Your Imperial Majesty."

"Up, up, please." I crossed the space between us with my hands held out.

Reva Gaiden was about as tall as her husband had been, putting her just above my shoulder. Her hair was a wild mass of dark curls and her face—though lovely—showed the strain of grief. "Majesty, this is my sister, Joi."

"Thank you both for seeing me," I said, feeling awkward as I squeezed one of her hands. The older woman took my other hand with a slight smile.

"Of course, Majesty. Jet—" Reva stopped and swallowed. "He always spoke so highly of you. He'd said you wanted to see Abha. Would you like to hold her?"

A thousand panicked thoughts whipped through me, but I nodded and gingerly took the tiny bundle from her mother. She was surprisingly heavy, only slightly more than the weight of the M2220 I'd carried into the palace.

She was so tiny and perfect, her eyes a startling blue and her hair as dark and curly as her mother's. I could see the echoes of Jet's features in her little face and had to bite back the tears.

"She looks like her father," Reva said, as if she'd read my mind.

"She will want for nothing." I looked up at Reva, saw the confusion in her face.

"Yes, ma'am. Your *Ekam* explained Jet's benefits to us when he escorted us into the palace."

"Beyond that, Reva. Those benefits are for you. What's for Abha comes directly from me. Whatever she needs, whatever she wants to do with her life, I will take care of it. It is not enough to repay what Jet did for me, but—" I lost the words and shrugged helplessly.

Reva's composure cracked, tears filled her eyes, and she turned into her sister's embrace.

"Thank you, Majesty," Joi said, her voice filled with soft island lilt. "May the gods bless you." She smiled sadly.

Abha wiggled and made a pitiful little noise. I froze and the panic must have shown on my face because Joi's sadness transformed into amusement that she struggled just as quickly to hide from me. Reva turned, tears still streaking her face, and took her baby back with a soft smile.

"She's just hungry, Majesty."

"I have to go." I stumbled over my words like an awkward teen. "I will see you at the memorial?"

"Yes, Majesty. Thank you."

I nodded and strode away from the women before they could see my tears.

"Majesty?" Cas was at my side, frowning at me. If it had been Emmory, I would have slipped my arm through his, but I had a feeling my baby-faced *Dve* wouldn't quite know how to react if I took such a familiarity with him.

"It seems like such a useless gesture."

He glanced back over his shoulder at Reva. "It doesn't ease the pain, ma'am, but at least she won't have to worry. I was only fifteen when my father died in a mining accident."

"I'm sorry."

He shrugged a shoulder. "It's an old hurt, ma'am. He was there that morning to see me off to school and wasn't there when I came home. My mother had to take a second job to make ends meet because the death bennies weren't even a fraction of what he'd been making and she refused to let me quit school to get a job. Said I deserved a life away from the mines."

"What did you want to do?"

"This, ma'am." He seemed surprised by my question. "All I ever wanted was to become a BodyGuard. Same with Jet, you know. He loved this job, and I don't mean any offense, but he loved you, too. I'll miss him every day from here on out, but I don't doubt for a second he'd do it again even knowing the cost."

It was too much. I dropped down onto a bench with my arms wrapped around my head and wept.

"It's all right, Majesty." Zin rubbed my back. "It's all right."

"I'm sorry, ma'am. I didn't mean to make you cry." Cas hovered helplessly at my side.

"Sit down." I put an arm around his shoulders when he obeyed, and I hugged him. "It's all right, and thank you."

An inexplicable wave of relief washed over me. The grief was still there, true, but something about Cas's words released the iron bands digging into my heart. I wasn't alone. I would have preferred it to be more like the crew on *Sophie*, where we were all more or less equal, but this would do. I had Emmory and Zin and the rest of the BodyGuards. I had Stasia and Alba, Admiral Hassan and some of the matriarchs. I had Leena and Taran.

It wasn't all blood family, but it was good enough for me.

thought this would be appropriate, ma'am."

I nodded in approval at the black uniform that was laid out on my bed. Matriarch Desai had planned the coronation, and true to my word—and some none too gentle nudging from Emmory—I'd agreed to show up the next day.

"Very much so, Stasia. Thank you. Make a note," I said as I wiggled into the pants she handed me. The long-sleeved shirt slid over my skin like water and I smoothed it out before I sat down so she could fix my hair. "As much as the idea of being fussed over pains me, we're probably going to have to get a few more maids." I shot her a sideways glare when she snickered. "You're in charge there, Stasia. I want you to pick out a few of the younger girls from my mother's set who can handle themselves."

"I'm assuming that means what I think it does, ma'am?"

"Yes." I smiled at her. "I suspect Emmory would like to give you a few names also and he'll definitely want to vet them."

It would also give Emmory one less thing to worry about.

Stasia twisted my hair up into a trio of knots at the base of my neck, the severity of the style not softened by the few braids she left out to frame my face. She painted a swatch of black across my eyes, then the same red-gold onto my mouth I'd donned when I first got to the palace.

Had it really been three weeks? It seemed like yesterday. It seemed like a lifetime ago.

"Here, Majesty." Stasia handed me a shoulder holster. I shrugged into it and slid the gun she handed me next into place.

I knelt at the altar, but the chant that hissed between my lips wasn't one for Ganesh. Rather it was to the Dark Mother, a plea for vengeance, for justice. I'd learned the chant in the days after my father's death, clinging to it with the obsession of a teenage girl, and now it rose up out of me without any thought at all.

As I listed off the names of the dead, I was all too aware that for every one I mentioned, there were ten more whose names I didn't know. People—my people—who were innocent bystanders like Ramani, caught up in a vicious political game.

"I will not stand for it any longer. This will stop," I swore after I finished with the names of the dead. I rose to my feet, pulled open the door to my room, and crossed the threshold into the waiting area.

I passed by Cas and Zin with a nod. The whole of Team Five stood by the door, their hands nervously hovering by their weapons. All my BodyGuards were already dressed in mourning black, red slashes of paint arching across their cheeks.

"Are we ready, Emmory?" I asked.

He nodded.

"Let's get on with this," I said, heading for the door. The remainder of my BodyGuards fell into step around me, and we strode in silence down the hallway. When we reached the steel door, Emmory pushed it open and held aside the pristine white tapestry so I could pass through.

The throne room was packed. The throne empty, silent. Only the crown sitting on the cushion.

The eyes of the assembled nobles locked on me, and the silence of breathless anticipation built as I crossed over the line of jagged black obsidian and dropped to one knee before the throne. I lowered my head, blinking back tears that threatened to spill over and fall to the white marble floor.

The empress can't let people see her cry. I remembered Father saying that to me once when I asked why Mother didn't cry anymore. Now I knew why, and just what it had cost her to keep that stone expression in place.

I stood and the entire assembly went down on a knee, bowing their heads to me when I turned. Looking out at the sea of faces, I suddenly felt very alone. Then I spotted Zin, who raised his head for just a second and smiled at me.

My panic vanished and I folded my hands. "Like my mother before me, I do not suffer fools gladly. There will be no second chances for those who think to undermine my power, or the power of the empire." I looked out over the crowd, saw the uneasy shifting as people threw glances back and forth.

"This has been a dark time for the empire. These horrible events have tarnished the face of Indrana and brought us to the brink of war. I am here to take the throne that is rightfully mine. Those responsible for the unrest and division in our empire will be punished." Utter silence echoed back at me.

Zin marched a limping Nal to the front of the crowd, stopping on the far side of the jagged obsidian line. Behind them Kisah practically carried Ganda, dropping her next to Nal with an impassive look on her face. Finally Cas dragged Laabh in. My nephew was disheveled and dirty and had an impressive black eye.

I won't lie. I struggled with the urge to pull my gun free and splatter their brains all over the marble.

"BodyGuard. Cousin. Nephew." I came down the dais as I spoke. "Conspirators. Traitors. Murderers."

The silence in the room was absolute.

"Lady Ganda, so good of you to join us." I crossed the line of jagged rock and bent down. "I didn't want you to miss seeing me crowned." I whispered the words in her ear and watched the hatred flash across her face.

"For waging war against the state, treason, and regicide, you three are sentenced to death."

That caused a ruckus.

I let the noise swell, watching calmly as the exclamations and protests flew through the air. After counting to ten, I looked at Emmory.

"Silence!" His amplified voice sliced easily through the din.

"Understand these traitors are proclaimed guilty from their own mouths! There will be no trials, no courts for them. There will only be the justice of the throne for the royal blood that has been spilt and justice of the empire for the blood of its citizens. We have other names, other conspirators who can consider themselves lucky that we will turn them over to the courts. But these three..." I gestured at my feet. "These three are *mine*.

"Ganda Naidu, you are hereby stripped of your titles and any inheritance you may have received," I continued. "Nalmari Zaafir Windhausen, you are no longer considered a Body-Guard and your name will be blotted from the lists, forever forgotten for your treachery. And you, my dear nephew whose name I will never again utter, you, too, will be erased. It will be as if you had never existed, not even as a warning to those who would think to sink to such defiled depths as you have. I will wipe you from the fabric of the universe, and I can think of no better punishment for one who thought himself worthy to wear this crown."

The room stayed dead silent for several heartbeats, almost as if the assembled crowd couldn't believe what they were seeing.

"May the gods turn their merciful faces away from you." I turned my back on them and went back up the steps, kneeling in front of Father Westinkar.

He held up the crown for the assembled to see. "Hailimi Mercedes Jaya Bristol, recognized Heir Apparent of the Indranan Empire. Receive the crown that the gods in all their glory decreed you were destined to wear." He placed the crown on my head and the weight of it seemed to sink into my bones, anchoring me to the floor.

Get up, Hailimi. The empress kneels to no one. Mother's voice rang in my memory and I fought back the cloying panic rising in my throat.

Somehow I made it to my feet without dislodging the crown and turned to face the assembled crowd as Father Westinkar's voice rose up to the buttressed ceiling of the chamber.

"Her Imperial Majesty, Empress Hailimi Mercedes Jaya Bristol. Long may she reign!"

Look out for the sequel to

Behind the Throne...

Coming Winter 2016

ACKNOWLEDGMENTS

I have the best support system a person could ask for and I'm terrified I'm going to forget names, so I'll say it now—if I don't remember you here I still love you and thanks for everything.

To my husband, Don, for your unwavering love and support throughout the years, for your position as chief science advisor of the house, and for the numerous grammatical arguments (that you usually win). I love you, forever and always. To my son, Benjamin, for your excitement and for buckling down at school so I didn't have to worry about you. To my parents, for my life and love of reading and always being there no matter what. To my sisters—blood and heart—for being absolutely fabulous. To my brothers—blood and heart—for being rock solid.

To my critique partner and amazing friend, C. J. Redwine—you know there's too much to write here. Thank you for everything. To my critique partner and shisuta, Lisa DiDio—your brutal honesty and the magical way you get my writing has made all the difference. This book wouldn't exist without you. To my critique partner and logic checker, Ana Ramsey—thanks for always asking the tough questions. To my mentor and friend Yasmine Galenorn—thank you for all the years of support and love.

To my agent, Andrew Zack, for all your patience as we went through draft after draft and for seeing the value of the story I was trying to tell and all your work to make this happen. I couldn't have done any better than to convince you to represent me. To Susan Barnes, Jenni Hill, Lindsey Hall, Anne Clarke, and everyone else at Orbit Books who've worked to make this book amazing, thanks for your faith and your enthusiasm.

To all those who read early drafts and provided me with valuable feedback, there's too many names and I know I'll forget some but I wanted to especially mention Beena, Wendy, and the Jennifers for your important and delightful commentary in the early days. To all my other friends who have so enthusiastically supported me over the years. I am very lucky to have you in my life. I love you all.

And finally to you. Yes, you reading this right now. Thanks for letting me tell you this story.

extras

orbit

meet the author

Photo Credit: Donald Branum

K. B. WAGERS has a bachelor's degree in Russian studies, and her nonfiction writing has earned her two Air Force Space Command Media Contest awards. A native of Colorado, she lives at the base of the Rocky Mountains with her husband and son. In between books, she can be found playing in the mud, running on trails, dancing to music, and scribbling on spare bits of paper.

interview

When did you first start writing?

I've been writing my whole life. Started getting serious about writing novels my junior year of high school and actively attempted to get published since about 1995. If anything I'm the poster child for sticking with something if you want it bad enough.

Where did the idea for Behind the Throne *come from?*

Laying on my couch around Christmastime staring at my tree. My ornament collection is pretty eclectic, and includes a lot of tatted snowflakes and shapes from my great-grandmother, my grandmother, and my mother. A diamond-shaped design caught my eye and next thing I knew the opening pages of the story unfolded in my head. The design is tattooed on Emmory's cheek (and on my arm) and that scene has remained virtually unchanged through all the edits we've done to the book over the years.

Did you have to do any research in preparation for writing **Behind the Throne***?*

Nope. I do my research on the fly as I'm writing. I just let the story tell itself and go back with whatever details are needed afterward.

There was a wide-ranging cast in **Behind the Throne.** *Who is your favorite character?*

laughs This is like asking a mother who her favorite child is. But since you're forcing me to choose I'm going to have to say Emmory. His silent presence, excellent sarcasm, and unwavering loyalty often make me wish I'd written this book in third person so that I could share more of him with the reader than just what we see through Hail's eyes.

What is one piece of information that you know about the story or characters that you loved but couldn't fit into the book?

There's quite a bit actually that I couldn't fit anywhere because it happened outside of Hail's eye/earshot and therefore just didn't work in the format I'd set up for the story. Some of my favorites though are pieces between Emmory and Zin that I wrote early on in order to get a feel for their motivations.

Lastly, we have to ask: If you could be friends with any superhero, who would it be?

Captain Steve Rogers is my hero. If I could have the ability to hang with him and Agent Carter I'd be a happy woman.

introducing

If you enjoyed
BEHIND THE THRONE,
look out for the sequel!

AFTER THE CROWN

Coming in Winter 2016

by K. B. Wagers

1

The execution site was an unremarkable building in the government sector across town. The room went quiet, the rolling murmuring on the air vanished when I walked in with my BodyGuards around me. My teams were still in disarray a week out from the coup attempt that had taken the lives of too many of my Guards, so Emmory and Cas were at my sides with Zin, Willimet, and Kisah behind us.

I was dressed in a black, military-style uniform—no sari, no mourning powder streaked across my face in a deliberate statement about the traitors whose deaths I'd come to witness. My cousin Ganda and my nephew Laabh.

"Your Majesty."

Everyone in the room either dropped into a curtsy or bowed low.

"Everyone up, please." I moved across the room, exchanging greetings with the judge, the lawyers, and the police.

"Majesty." Prime Minister Phanin executed his perfect bow and held a palm out to me in greeting. "We are glad to see you well."

"You also. I was relieved to hear you weren't injured in the chaos."

Phanin waved a long-fingered hand in the air. "I was in my offices when the incident occurred. Thankfully we went into lockdown and I don't think I was at all on their list of targets given how unimportant my position is."

I didn't have a good reply for that. Technically he was the head of the General Assembly, but the political body was more for show than anything. Phanin had no real power in the governing of Indrana. He was there to placate the masses.

That wasn't something I was going to say out loud.

"Your Majesty." Two naval officers approached, saving me from the awkward situation. Phanin murmured his good-bye and stepped away.

"Commander Timu Stravinski." The commander was a man with graying hair at his temples and clear gray eyes. He saluted.

"Commander."

The young woman with him was barely eighteen; her eyes were dark blue and her blond hair twisted up into a smart knot off the collar of her naval uniform.

I knew who she was before she said her name. A cousin. A member of my family—same as the woman I was about to kill.

"First Lieutenant Jaya Naidu, ma'am." She saluted me.

"Lieutenant." Ganda's little sister wasn't the spitting image of her treacherous sibling, but I could see the resemblance and I felt Emmory brace for a scene.

"I volunteered to witness, Your Majesty. To spare my parents further pain. They have removed the traitor's name from the family tree. I am not here for sympathy or to ease her passing. I'm only here to see justice done." Jaya bowed sharply. "My family is loyal to you, Majesty."

"Of course. Thank you," I murmured the reply because I couldn't think of a thing to say. Lieutenant Naidu nodded again and left me alone.

There was no one here for Laabh except his lawyer, who bowed low in front of me. My nephew's father was gone, fled to the Saxons. His mother and sister dead from a bomb he helped radicals plant. His marriage family had already washed their hands of him, lest the displeasure of the throne splash back on them. There was no one left for quiet denunciations and murmured declarations of loyalty.

I spotted Leena when she slipped in through the door, already dressed in widow's white. There were circles under my niece-in-law's eyes and she gripped her sari so tightly that her knuckles stood out in stark relief against her skin. What had been a social coup for her was now a nightmare.

Murmuring my apology to Laabh's lawyer, I crossed to the door and pulled Leena into a hug before she curtsied. She froze, startled, and then clung for a moment.

"I left Taran at home," she said as she stepped away. "I didn't think it was appropriate. He doesn't understand what's happening."

"That was a wise choice. Leena, he's still my family. Whatever his brother was responsible for having him do, we don't hold Taran accountable."

419

We'd retrieved some of the data off Dr. Satir's *smati* and it had corroborated Laabh's story that the AVI had been slipped to Mother in the weekly gift of *lokum* Taran brought her. I had to contend with the idea that Dr. Satir might have known about the drug, though that secret died with her. There were no records of the treat being scanned when it was brought and my suspicions over Mother's still-missing *Ekam* were high.

"Please don't take him, Majesty. I've come to care for Taran."

"I have no plans for that, Leena. I received your mother's petition and I'm in agreement with it. Taran will stay with you."

Leena's eyes strayed over my shoulder toward the chamber on the far side of the room. "I loved my husband once. I'd thought he could be so much more."

"That's not a crime," I replied, watching as the bailiff escorted Laabh and Ganda in. "You've never seen anyone die, have you?"

"No, I—no, Majesty."

I took her gently by the shoulders. "There's no shame in looking away. This way is quieter than most, but you're still watching someone's life vanish right in front of you. It changes a person to witness it."

"You've seen it."

I felt the smile flicker to life at the corner of my mouth. "More times than a person should." I let her go and looked at Willimet. "If she needs to get out of here, go with her."

"Yes, ma'am."

"Your Imperial Majesty and the others in attendance." The judge was a tall, slender woman named Sita Claremont. She addressed the small crowd as the technicians strapped Ganda and Laabh onto the tables. "We're here today to see justice done in the matter of the Empire of Indrana versus Ganda Rhonwen Naidu and Laabh Albin Bristol Surakesh."

Laabh was calm, his dark eyes still burning with fanatical hatred when they met mine. Ganda was less calm, her eyes darting around the room and her breath coming high and fast in her chest as the table was tilted slightly up.

Judge Claremont turned to look at the prisoners behind the glass. "You have both been found guilty, through evidence and your own confessions, of waging war against the state, direct participation in regicide, attempted regicide, and treason. Your right to trial was dismissed at the empress's pleasure. It is the empress's wish that on this day you take your last breaths and let the Dark Mother have her justice over you."

Ganda flinched. Laabh remained perfectly still.

"Your Imperial Majesty, is there any mercy in you for these two traitors?"

I'd known the judge's question was coming. The palace had been inundated with calls and messages about the execution. I'd read most of them, and answered several of the calls personally. The Amnesty Galactic one had been the most interesting.

In the end, I couldn't let much of it influence my decision. We had written confessions from each of them about their involvement in the deaths, and no matter my personal feelings on the matter that was enough to condemn them.

Plus I knew better than to leave a live enemy behind me. I'd learned that lesson the hard way from Po-Sin, the gunrunning gang leader and my former employer.

"There is not."

"Very well." Judge Claremont nodded. "Do the condemned have anything to say?"

"I did what I had to for the good of the empire." Ganda's voice didn't ring with the same conviction as my mother's *Ekam* when he'd claimed the same thing. "The empress turned us belly-up to the Saxons and drove this empire into the ground. Now you'll all allow that trash upon the throne. A criminal, a self-admitted gunrunner! She's not worthy of your respect or your loyalty!"

I kept my face blank as she railed. I wasn't ashamed of the things I'd done after I left.

"If you didn't want me to come back, Ganda, you shouldn't have killed my sisters. Cire should have been empress, or her daughter, or even Pace. All of them would have been a better choice than I am. It's your conspiracy, your treachery that put me here."

"No." Ganda shook her head, tears rolling down her face, but she didn't have any argument to make that would have swayed anyone's sympathy.

Laabh lifted his chin, the haughty look unable to fully hide the fear in his eyes. "You will all regret this," he said. "We see farther than you can imagine, and our plans are far more glorious than this piddling empire. You won't live through the next spin of the planet around the sun, you gunrunning whore."

There were gasps of outrage in the room. I crossed my arms over my chest and met Laabh's glare with a cold smile. "You won't live to see them fail," I replied.

Whatever he shouted in reply was cut off by Judge Claremont's quick gesture. The comm system was deactivated and the two technicians in the room donned their helmets as the tables were lowered once more.

Nitrogen asphyxiation had been the preferred method of execution in the empire for thousands of years. It was a quick and painless method, but as I'd pointed out to Leena, it was still taking another human life.

The lights on the wall of the chamber flashed, and at Judge Claremont's nod the technicians threw the switch. The air circulators in the chamber filled it with pure nitrogen as they sucked the oxygen out.

Laabh was unconscious in under a minute with Ganda quickly following suit as the oxygen in their lungs and then their blood was replaced with nitrogen. The hypoxia that followed would cause brain death in a matter of moments.

I'd seen messier deaths and been directly involved in more than a few of them myself. This wasn't even the first time I'd stood on the other side of a glass window and watched people die, but there was undoubtedly something cold about these quick and silent deaths. It felt weird, clinical, and made me uneasy.

I watched their chests rise and fall, breaths growing shallower as the heartbeats on the monitors above the tables slowed. Laabh convulsed, and Leena's choked sob echoed through the room.

"Take her outside, Will," I murmured without looking away from the people dying in front of me.

The shrill tone of the flatline filled the air only moments after Willimet ushered Leena out the door, as first Laabh's and then Ganda's hearts gave out. The masked techs moved around the tables, efficiently checking their patients and passing the information along to Judge Claremont.

"Heart death confirmed," she announced. "Brain death to follow in approximately ninety seconds."

The flatline tone had been turned off with the confirmation so we all stood in silence again as we waited for the final words from the techs. The one at Laabh's side turned and nodded once, but I didn't release the breath I was holding until Ganda's tech nodded also.

"Brain death confirmed. Execution sentence carried out at 2253 Capital Standard Time. Let the record reflect that justice has been served."